SS-GB

Len Deighton was born in 1929. He worked as a railway clerk before doing his National Service in the RAF as a photographer attached to the Special Investigation Branch.

After his discharge in 1949, he went to art school – first to the St Martin's School of Art, and then to the Royal College of Art on a scholarship. His mother was a professional cook and he grew up with an interest in cookery – a subject he was later to make his own in an animated strip for the *Observer* and in two cookery books. He worked for a while as an illustrator in New York and as art director of an advertising agency in London.

Deciding it was time to settle down, Deighton moved to the Dordogne where he started work on his first book, *The IPCRESS File*. Published in 1962, the book was an immediate success.

Since then his work has gone from strength to strength, varying from espionage novels to war, general fiction and non-fiction. The BBC made *Bomber* into a day-long radio drama in 'real time'. Deighton's history of World War Two, *Blood, Tears and Folly*, was published to wide acclaim – Jack Higgins called it 'an absolute landmark'.

As Max Hastings observed, Deighton captured a time and a mood – 'To those of us who were in our twenties in the 1960s, his books seemed the coolest, funkiest, most sophisticated things we'd ever read' – and his books have now deservedly become classics.

By Len Deighton

LEN DEIGHTON

SS-GB

HARPER

Harper
An imprint of HarperCollins*Publishers*
77–85 Fulham Palace Road,
Hammersmith, London W6 8JB

www.harpercollins.co.uk

This paperback edition 2009
1

Previously published in paperback by Triad Grafton 1980
Reprinted twelve times

First published in Great Britain by
Jonathan Cape Ltd 1978

Copyright © Pluriform Publishing Company BV 1978
Introduction copyright © Pluriform Publishing Company BV 2009

The verse from 'The White Cliffs of Dover' is reproduced by permission of EMI
Publishers Ltd 138–140 Charing Cross Road, London WC2H 0LD. © 1941 by
Shapiro Bernstein & Co., Inc., sub-published by B. Feldman & Co. Ltd

Len Deighton asserts the moral right to
be identified as the author of this work

A catalogue record for this book is
available from the British Library

ISBN 978-0-00-785182-9

Set in Sabon
Printed and bound in Great Britain by
Clays Ltd, St Ives plc

Mixed Sources
Product group from well-managed
forests and other controlled sources
www.fsc.org Cert no. SW-COC-1806
© 1996 Forest Stewardship Council

FSC is a non-profit international organisation established to promote the
responsible management of the world's forests. Products carrying the FSC
label are independently certified to assure consumers that they come
from forests that are managed to meet the social, economic and
ecological needs of present and future generations.

Find out more about HarperCollins and the environment at
www.harpercollins.co.uk/green

Introduction

'*My book,* Inside the Third Reich, *never reached the top of the New York best seller list,*' Albert Speer told me. '*It was* Everything You Always Wanted to Know About Sex but were afraid to ask *that always remained at number one.*'

I am still not sure if he was joking. Hitler's onetime Minister of Armaments had a sharp sense of humour, especially about the men with whom he had been in Spandau prison; he always referred to Field Marshal Milch as 'Milk'. And when writers get together sales talk is not unusual.

But Albert Speer was not the catalyst for *SS-GB*. It began over a late-night drink with Ray Hawkey, the writer and designer, and Tony Colwell, my editor at Jonathan Cape. '*No one knows what might have happened had we lost the Battle of Britain,*' said Tony with a sigh as we finished sorting through photos to illustrate my book, *Fighter: The True Story of the Battle of Britain.*

'*I wouldn't go as far as that,*' I told him. '*A great deal of the planning for the German occupation has been found and published.*'

I had read some of that material and, after this conversation, I sought out the official German publications and began wondering if Britain under German rule would make a book. It would have to be what was then called an 'alternative world' book and that was outside all my writing experience. On the other hand, research for *Fighter* and *Funeral in Berlin*, and particularly *Bomber*, had brought me into contact with many Germans, mostly men who had fought in the war.

I work very slowly so I don't embark on a story until I am confident that I will be able to get the material for it and live with it for many months, perhaps years. The plot problems seemed insurmountable. Would I create a hero in the German occupation army? I wouldn't want a Nazi as a hero. If I told the story through the eyes of a British civilian how would such a person have enough information to make the plot work? A notable member of the resistance would qualify as a hero but such heroes would all be dead, or fugitives.

This story had to be told from the centre of power. The police would be the people who connected the conquerors with the conquered but that sort of compromise role was not attractive to me. I went round and round on this until I thought of a Scotland Yard detective as hero. A man who solved crimes and hunted only real criminals could have contacts at the top and yet still be acceptable as a central character. I would frame it like a conventional murder mystery, with corpse at the start and solution at the end.

I like big charts and diagrams. They serve as a guide and reminder while a book is being written. Using the German data I drew a chain of command showing the connections between the civilians and the puppet government, black-marketeers and quislings, and the occupying power with its security forces and bitterly competitive army and Waffen SS elements. My old friend, and fellow writer, Ted Allbeury had spent the immediate post-war period in occupied Germany as what the locals called 'the head of the British Gestapo'. Ted's experience was very valuable indeed and I used his experience and anecdotes to the full.

For the London scenes, I used only places that I had known in the war, so in that respect there is an autobiographical element in the story. I remembered London in wartime: the dimly lit streets, gas lights that hissed and spluttered, tin baths in front of the fire, rationing that made food a constant subject of thought and conversation, and bombed homes that spewed their intimate household contents into the streets.

The Scotland Yard building had to be the stage upon which my story was played but the police were no longer using it. It had become an office building for members of parliament and was strictly guarded. The Metropolitan Police were very cooperative about letting me use their fascinating library and their archives too. I spent many days studying wartime crimes and looking at pictures of Scotland Yard detectives in the natty suits that were mandatory at that time. But the police had no authority over the building they had vacated.

By a wonderful piece of luck I found an elderly ex-policeman who knew the building from cellar to attic. I recorded hours of his descriptions but I still could not get into it until a friend named Freddy Warren devised a method by which I could explore every nook and cranny of the building. Freddy's authority as an official of the Whip's office was to allot the offices to the politicians. He took me on a guided tour. With him I went everywhere; opening doors, interrupting conferences, awakening sleepers and declining liquid refreshment. No one was going to risk upsetting Freddy. I remain indebted to him and I hope that this record of the Scotland Yard building, as once it was, justifies the trouble he took on my behalf.

When writing begins I have found it beneficial to step away from phones and friends and any social commitments. Together with my wife Ysabele and two small children and a trunk filled with research material, I went to Tuscany. Al Alvarez the writer and broadcaster lent us his wonderful mountainside house near Barga. It was winter and, no matter about the pictures in the brochures, winter in northern Italy is cold and wet. I searched everywhere to buy an electric typewriter and failed to find one. All I could find was a tiny lightweight portable Olivetti. It was secondhand and past its prime. After the joys of an electric machine, pounding the mechanical keyboard took a lot of getting used to. My fingers swelled up like *salsiccia Toscana*. But rural Italy worked its magic. Our elderly 'next door' neighbours adopted us. Signora Ida and her husband Silvio lavished our children with love, made pizzas for us in their outdoor oven and showed us the secret of making ravioli. We will never forget those two wonderful people. They made my time in Tuscany writing *SS-GB* one of the happiest times of my happy life.

Len Deighton, 2009

'In England they're filled with curiosity and keep asking, "Why doesn't he come?" Be calm. Be calm. He's coming! He's coming!'

Adolf Hitler, 4 September 1940,
at a rally of nurses and social workers in Berlin.

Berlin, den 18.2.41

Der Oberste Befehlshaber der Wehrmacht

A.O.S.15,1° Nr. *220* /41 g. Kdos. Chefs.   **10 Ausfertigungen**

                                                 Ausfertigung

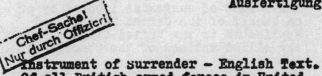

Chef-Sache!
Nur durch Offizier!

Instrument of Surrender – English Text.
Of all British armed forces in United
Kingdom of Great Britain and Northern
Ireland including all islands.

1. The British Command agrees to the
   surrender of all British armed forces
   in the United Kingdom and Northern
   Ireland including all islands and
   including military elements overseas.
   This also applies to units of the
   Royal Navy in all parts of the world,
   at port and on the high seas.

2. All hostilities on land, sea and in
   the air by British forces are to cease
   at 0800 hrs Greenwich Mean Time on
   19 February 1941.

3. The British Command to carry out at
   once, without argument or comment, all
   further orders that will be issued by
   the German Command on any subject.

4. Disobedience of orders, or failure to
   comply with them, will be regarded as
   a breach of these surrender terms and
   will be dealt with by the German
   Command in accordance with the laws
   and usages of war.

5. This instrument of surrender is
   independent of, without prejudice to,
   and will be superseded by any general
   instrument of surrender imposed by or
   on behalf of the German Command and
   applicable to the United Kingdom and
   the Allied nations of the Commonwealth.

6. This instrument of surrender is written
   in German and English. The German
   version is the authentic text.

7. The decision of the German Command will
   be final if any doubt or dispute arises
   as to the meaning or interpretation
   of the surrender terms.

Chapter One

'Himmler's got the king locked up in the Tower of London,' said Harry Woods. 'But now the German Generals say the army should guard him.'

The other man busied himself with the papers on his desk and made no comment. He thumped the rubber stamp into the pad and then on to the docket, 'Scotland Yard. 14 Nov. 1941'. It was incredible that the war had started only two years ago. Now it was over; the fighting finished, the cause lost. There was so much paperwork that two shoe boxes were being used for the overflow; Dolcis shoes, size six, patent leather pumps, high heels, narrow fitting. Detective Superintendent Douglas Archer knew only one woman who would buy such shoes: his secretary.

'Well, that's what people are saying,' added Harry Woods, the elderly Sergeant who was the other half of the 'murder team'.

Douglas Archer initialled the docket and tossed it into the tray. Then he looked across the room and nodded. It was a miserable office, its green and cream painted walls darkened by age and the small windows heavily leaded and smeared by sooty rain, so that the electric light had to be on all day.

'Never do it on your own doorstep,' advised Harry now that it was too late for advice. Anyone other than Harry, anyone less bold, less loquacious, less well-meaning would have stopped at that. But Harry disregarded the fixed smile on his senior partner's face. 'Do it

1

with that blonde, upstairs in Registry. Or that big-titted German bird in Waffen-SS liaison – she puts it about they say – but your own secretary . . .' Harry Woods pulled a face.

'You spend too much time listening to what people say,' said Douglas Archer calmly. 'That's your trouble, Harry.'

Harry Woods met the disapproving stare without faltering. 'A copper can never spend too much time listening to what other people say, Super. And if you faced reality, you'd know. You may be a bloody wonderful detective, but you're a shocking bad judge of character – and that's *your* trouble.'

There weren't many Detective Sergeants who would dare speak to Douglas Archer like that but these two men had known each other ever since 1920, when Harry Woods was a handsome young Police Constable with a Military Medal ribbon on his chest, and a beat littered with the broken hearts of pretty young housemaids and the hot meat pies of doting cooks. While Douglas Archer was a nine-year-old child proud to be seen talking to him.

When Douglas Archer became a green young Sub-Divisional Inspector, straight from the Hendon Police College, with no more experience of police work than comes from dodging the Proctors in the back streets of Oxford, it was Harry Woods who had befriended him. And that was at a time when such privileged graduates were given a hard time by police rank and file.

Harry knew everything a policeman had to know and more. He knew when each night-watchman brewed tea, and was never far from a warm boiler house when it rained. Harry Woods knew which large piles of rubbish would have money under them, never taking more than a third of it, lest the shopkeeper found some other way to pay the street-cleaners for their extra work. But that was a long time ago, before the generosity of the publicans and barmen of London's West End had provided Harry with his ruddy face and expanded his waistline. And before Douglas Archer's persistence got him into CID and then to Scotland Yard's Murder Squad.

'C Division have got a juicy one,' said Harry Woods. 'Everyone else is busy. Shall I get the murder bag ready?'

Douglas knew that his Sergeant expected him to respond in surprise, and he raised an eyebrow. 'How the devil do you know about it?'

'A flat in Shepherd Market, crammed with whisky, coffee, tea and so on, and Luftwaffe petrol coupons lying around on the table. The victim is a well-dressed man, probably a black-marketeer.'

'You think so?'

Harry smiled. 'Remember that black-market gang who killed the warehouse manager in Fulham . . . they were forging Luftwaffe petrol coupons. This could be the same mob.'

'Harry. Are you going to tell me where all this information comes from, or are you going to solve the crime without getting out of your seat?'

'The Station Sergeant at Savile Row is an old drinking pal. He just phoned me. A neighbour found the body and told the police.'

'There's no hurry,' said Douglas Archer. 'We'll move slowly.'

Harry bit his lip. In his opinion Detective Superintendent Douglas Archer never did otherwise. Harry Woods was a policeman of the old school, scornful of paperwork, filing systems and microscopes. He liked to be talking, drinking, interrogating and making arrests.

Douglas Archer was a tall, thin, thirty-year-old. He

was one of a new generation of detectives, who'd rejected the black jacket, pin-stripe trousers, roll-brim hat and stiff collar that was almost a uniform for the Murder Squad. Douglas favoured dark shirts and the sort of wide-brimmed hat he'd seen on George Raft in a Hollywood gangster film. In keeping with this, he'd taken to smoking small black cheroots as often as his tobacco ration permitted. He tried to light this one for the third time; the tobacco was of poor quality and it did not burn well. He looked for more matches and Harry threw a box across to him.

Douglas was a Londoner – with the quick wit, and sophisticated self-interest for which Londoners are renowned – but like many who grow up in a fatherless household, he was introspective and remote. The soft voice and Oxford accent would have better suited some more cloistered part of the legal profession but he'd never regretted becoming a policeman. It was largely due to Harry, he realized that now. For the lonely little rich boy, in the big house on the square, Harry Woods, without knowing it, became a surrogate father.

'And suppose the Luftwaffe petrol coupons are not forgeries; suppose they are real,' said Douglas. 'Then you can bet German personnel are involved, and the case will end up with the Feldgericht der Luftwaffe, Lincoln's Inn. Waste of time our getting involved.'

'This is murder,' said Harry. 'A few petrol coupons can't change that.'

'Don't try to re-write the laws, Harry, there's enough work enforcing the ones we've got. Any crimes involving Luftwaffe personnel, in even the smallest way, are tried by Luftwaffe courts.'

'Not if we got over there right away,' said Harry, running his hand back over hair that refused to be

4

smoothed down. 'Not if we wrung a confession out of one of them, sent copies to Geheime Feldpolizei and Kommandantur, and gave them a conviction on a plate. Oherwise these German buggers just quash these cases for lack of evidence, or post the guilty ones off to some soft job in another country.'

For Harry the fighting would never end. His generation, who'd fought and won in the filth of Flanders, would never come to terms with defeat. But Douglas Archer had not been a soldier. As long as the Germans let him get on with the job of catching murderers, he'd do his work as he'd always done it. He wished he could get Harry to see it his way.

'I'd appreciate it, Harry, if you'd not allow your personal opinions to intrude into the preferred terminology.' Douglas tapped the SIPO Digest, 'And I'm far from convinced that they *are* soft on German personnel. Five executions last month; one of them a Panzer Division Major, with Knight's Cross, who did nothing worse than arrive an hour late to check a military vehicle compound.' He tossed the information sheets across to his partner's desk.

'You read all that stuff, don't you?'

'And if you had more sense, Harry, you'd read it too. Then you'd know that General Kellerman now has his CID briefings on Tuesday morning at eleven o'clock, which is just ten minutes from now.'

'Because the old bastard drinks too much at lunchtime. By the time he reels back from the SS Officers' Club in the afternoon he can't remember a word of English except, "tomorrow, tomorrow!"'

Harry Woods noted·with satisfaction the way that Douglas Archer glanced round the empty chairs and desks, just in case anyone had overheard this pronouncement. 'Whatever the truth of that may be,' said Douglas cautiously, 'the fact remains that he'll want his briefing. And solving a murder that we've not yet been invited to investigate will not be thought sufficient excuse for my not being upstairs on time.' Douglas got to his feet and collected together the documents that the General might want to see.

'I'd tell him to go to hell,' said Harry. 'I'd tell him the job comes first.'

Douglas Archer nipped out his cheroot carefully, so as to preserve the unsmoked part of it, then put it into the top drawer of his desk, together with a magnifying glass, tickets for a police concert he'd not attended, and a broken fountain pen. 'Kellerman's not so bad,' said Douglas. 'He's kept the Metropolitan Force more or less intact. Have you forgotten all the talk of putting German Assistant Commissioners upstairs? Kellerman opposed that.'

'Too much competition,' muttered Harry, 'and Kellerman doesn't like competition.'

Douglas put his report, and the rest of the papers, into his brief-case and strapped it up. 'In the unlikely event that West End Central ask for us, have the murder bag ready and order a car. Tell them to keep the photographer there until I tell him to go and to keep the Divisional Surgeon there, as well as the pathologist.'

'The doctor won't like that,' said Harry.

'Thanks for telling me that, Harry. Send the doctor a packet of wait-about tablets with my compliments, and remind him you are phoning from Whitehall 1212, Headquarters of Kriminalpolizei, Ordnungspolizei, Sicherheitsdienst and Gestapo. Any complaints about waiting can be sent here in writing.'

'Keep your shirt on,' said Harry defensively.

The phone rang; the calm impersonal voice of General Kellerman's personal assistant said, 'Superintendent Archer? The General presents his compliments and asks if this would be a convenient time for you to give him the CID briefing.'

'Immediately, Major,' said Douglas, and replaced the phone.

'Jawohl, Herr Major. Kiss your arse, Herr Major,' said Harry.

'Oh for God's sake, Harry. I have to deal with these people at first hand; you don't.'

'I still call it arse-licking.'

'And how much arse-licking do you think it needed to get your brother exempted from that deportation order!' Douglas had been determined never to tell Harry about that, and now he was angry with himself.

'Because of the medical report from his doctor,' said Harry but even as he was saying it he realized that most of the technicians sent to German factories probably got something like that from a sympathetic physician.

'That helped,' said Douglas lamely.

'I never realized, Doug,' said Harry but by that time Douglas was hurrying up to the first floor. The Germans were sticklers for punctuality.

Chapter Two

General – or, more accurately in SS parlance, Gruppenführer – Fritz Kellerman was a genial-looking man in his
late fifties. He was of medium height but his enthusiasm
for good food and drink provided a rubicund complexion
and a slight plumpness which, together with his habit of
standing with both hands in his pockets, could deceive
the casual onlooker into thinking Kellerman was short
and fat, and so he was often described. His staff called
him 'Vater' but if his manner was fatherly it was not
benign enough to earn him the more common nickname
of 'Vati' (Daddy). His thick thatch of white hair had
beguiled more than one young officer into accepting his
invitation for an early morning canter through the park.
But few of them went for the second time. And only the
greenest of his men would agree to a friendly game of
chess, for Kellerman had once been the junior chess
champion of Bavaria. 'Luck seems to be with me today,'
he'd tell them as they became trapped into a humiliating
defeat.

Before the German victory, Douglas had seldom visited
this office on the first floor. It was the turret room used
hitherto only by the Commissioner. But now he was often
here talking to Kellerman, whose police powers extended
over the whole occupied country. And Douglas – together
with certain other officers – had been granted the special
privilege of entering the Commissioner's room by the
private door, instead of going through the clerk's office.
Before the Germans came, this was something permitted

only to Assistant Commissioners. General Kellerman said it was part of das Führerprinzip; Harry Woods said it was bullshit.

The Commissioner's office was more or less unchanged from the old days. The massive mahogany desk was placed in the corner. The chair behind it stood in the tiny circular turret that provided light from all sides, and a wonderful view of the river. There was a big marble mantelpiece and on it an ornate clock that struck the hour and half-hour. A fire blazed in the bow-fronted grate between polished brass fire-irons and a scuttle of coal. The only apparent change was the shoal of fish that swam across the far wall, in glass-fronted cases, stuffed, and labelled with Fritz Kellerman's name, and a place and date, lettered in gold.

There were two men in army uniform there when Douglas entered the room. He hesitated. 'Come in, Superintendent. Come in!' called Kellerman.

The two strangers looked at Douglas and then exchanged affirmative nods. This Englishman was exactly right for them. Not only was he reputed to be one of the finest detectives in the Murder Squad but he was young and athletic looking, with the sort of pale bony face that Germans thought was aristocratic. He was 'Germanic', a perfect example of 'the new European'. And he even spoke excellent German.

One of the men picked up a notebook from Kellerman's desk. 'Just one more, General Kellerman,' he said. The other man seemed to produce a Leica out of nowhere and knelt down to look through its viewfinder. 'You and the Superintendent, looking together at some notes or a map . . . you know the sort of thing.'

On the cuffs of their field-grey uniforms the men wore 'Propaganda-Kompanie' armbands.

9

'We'd better do as they say, Superintendent,' said Kellerman. 'These fellows are from *Signal* magazine. They've come all the way from Berlin just to talk to us.'

Awkwardly Douglas went round to the far side of the desk. He posed self-consciously, prodding at a copy of the *Angler's Times*. Douglas felt foolish but Kellerman took it all in his stride.

'Superintendent Archer,' said the PK journalist in heavily accented English, 'is it true that, here at Scotland Yard, the men call General Kellerman "Father"?'

Douglas hesitated, pretending to be holding still for the photo in order to gain time. 'Can't you see how your question embarrasses the Superintendent?' said Kellerman. 'And speak German, the Superintendent speaks the language as well as I do.'

'It's true then?' said the journalist, pressing for an answer from Douglas. The camera shutter clicked. The photographer checked the settings on his camera and then took two more pictures in rapid succession.

'Of *course* it's true,' said Kellerman. 'You think I'm a liar? Or do you think I'm the sort of police chief who doesn't know what goes on in my own headquarters?'

The journalist stiffened and the photographer lowered his camera.

'It's quite true,' said Douglas.

'And now, gentlemen, I must get some work done,' said Kellerman. He shooed them out, like an old lady finding hens in her bedroom. 'Sorry about that,' Kellerman explained to Douglas after they'd gone. 'They said they would need only five minutes, but they hang on and hang on. It's all part of their job to exploit opportunities, I suppose.' He went back to his desk and sat down. 'Tell me what's been happening, my boy.'

Douglas read his report, with asides and explanations

where needed. Kellerman's prime concern was to justify money spent, and Douglas always wrote his reports so that they summarized the resources of the department and showed the cost in Occupation Marks.

When the formalities were over, Kellerman opened the humidor. With black-market cigarettes at five Occupation Marks each, one of Kellerman's Monte Cristo No 2s had become a considerable accolade. Kellerman selected two cigars with great care. Like Douglas, he preferred the flavour of the ones with green or yellow spots on the outer leaf. He went through a ceremony of cutting them and removing loose strands of tobacco. As usual Kellerman wore one of his smooth tweed suits, complete with waistcoat and gold chain for his pocket watch. Typically he had not worn his SS uniform even for this visit by the photographer. And Kellerman, like so many of the senior SS men of his generation, preferred army rank titles to the cumbersome SS nomenclature.

'Still no word of your wife?' asked Kellerman. He came round the desk and gave Douglas the cigar.

'I think we have to assume that she was killed,' said Douglas. 'She often went to our neighbour's house during the air attacks, and the street fighting completely demolished it.'

'Don't give up hope,' said Kellerman. Was that a reference to his affair with the secretary, Douglas wondered. 'Your son is well?'

'He was in the shelter that day. Yes, he's thriving.'

Kellerman leaned over to light the cigar. Douglas was not yet used to the way that the German officers put Cologne on their faces after shaving and the perfume surprised him. He inhaled; the cigar lit. Douglas would have preferred to take the cigar away with him but the General always lit them. Douglas thought perhaps it was a way of preventing the recipient selling it instead of smoking it. Or was it simply that Kellerman believed that, in England, no gentleman could offer a colleague a chance to put an unsmoked cigar in his pocket.

'And no other problems, Superintendent?' Kellerman passed behind Douglas, and touched the seated man's shoulder lightly, as if in reassurance. Douglas wondered if his General knew that his internal mail had that morning included a letter from his secretary, saying she was pregnant and demanding twenty thousand O-Marks. The pound sterling, she pointed out, in case Douglas didn't know, was not the sort of currency abortionists accepted. Douglas was permitted a proportion of his wages in O-Marks. So far Douglas had not discovered how the letter got to him. Had she sent it to one of her girl-friends in Registry, or actually come into the building herself?

'No problems that I need bother the General with,' said Douglas.

Kellerman smiled. Douglas's anxiety had led him to address the General in that curious third-person form that some of the more obsequious Germans used.

'You knew this room in the old days?' said Kellerman.

Before the war it had been the Commissioner's procedure to leave the door wide open when the room was unoccupied, so that messengers could pass in and out. Soon after being assigned to Scotland Yard, Douglas had found an excuse for coming into the empty room and studying it with the kind of awe that comes from a schoolboy diet of detective fiction. 'I seldom came here when it was the Commissioner's room.'

'These are difficult times,' said Kellerman, as if apologizing for the way in which Douglas's visits were now more frequent. Kellerman leaned forward to tap a centimetre of ash into a white china model of Tower Bridge that some enterprising manufacturer had redesigned to incorporate swastika flags and 'Waffenstillstand. London. 1940' in red and black Gothic lettering. 'Until now,' said Kellerman choosing his words with care, 'the police force has not been asked to do any political task.'

'We have always been completely apolitical.'

'Now that's not quite true,' said Kellerman gently. 'In Germany we call a spade a spade, and the political police are called political police. Here you call your political police the Special Branch, because you English are not so direct in these matters.'

'Yes, sir.'

'But there will come a time when I can no longer resist the pressure from Berlin to bring us into line with the German police system.'

'We English don't take quickly to new ideas you know, sir.'

'Don't play games with me, Superintendent,' said Kellerman without changing the affable tone of voice or the smile. 'You know what I'm talking about.'

'I'm not sure I do, sir.'

'Neither of us wants political advisers in this building, Superintendent. Inevitably the outcome would be that your police force is used against British Resistance groups, uncaptured soldiers, political fugitives, Jews, gypsies and other undesirable elements.' Kellerman said it in a way that conveyed the idea that he didn't consider these elements nearly so undesirable as his superiors in Berlin thought them.

'It would split the police service right down the middle,' said Douglas.

Kellerman didn't answer. He reached for a teleprinter message on his desk and read it, as if to remind himself of the contents. 'A senior officer of the Sicherheitsdienst

13

is on his way here now,' said Kellerman. 'I'm assigning you to work with him.'

'His duties will be political?' asked Douglas. The SD was the SS intelligence service. Douglas did not welcome this sinister development.

'I don't know why he's coming,' said Kellerman cheerfully. 'He is on the personal staff of the Reichsführer-SS and will remain directly responsible to Berlin for whatever he has to do.' Kellerman inhaled on his cigar and then let the smoke drift from his nostrils. He let his Superintendent dwell upon the facts and realize that the new man presented a danger to the status quo for both of them. 'Standartenführer Huth,' said Kellerman finally, 'that's this new chap's name.' His use of the SS rank was enough to emphasize that Huth was an outsider. Kellerman raised his hand. 'Under the direct orders of Berlin, so that gives him a special . . .' he hesitated and then let the hand fall, '. . . influence.'

'I understand, sir,' said Douglas.

'Then perhaps, my dear chap, you'd do everything you can to prevent the indiscretions – more particularly the verbal indiscretions – of your mentor downstairs from embarrassing us all.'

'Detective Sergeant Woods?'

'Ah, what a quick mind you have, Superintendent,' said Kellerman.

Chapter Three

Some said there had not been even one clear week of sunshine since the cease-fire. It was easy to believe. Today the air was damp, and the colourless sun only just visible through the grey clouds, like an empty plate on a dirty tablecloth.

And yet even a born and bred Londoner, such as Douglas Archer, could walk down Curzon Street, and with eyes half-closed, see little or no change from the previous year. The Soldatenkino sign outside the Curzon cinema was small and discreet, and only if you tried to enter the Mirabelle restaurant did a top-hatted doorman whisper that it was now used exclusively by Staff Officers from Air Fleet 8 Headquarters, across the road in the old Ministry of Education offices. And if your eyes remained half-closed you missed the signs that said 'Jewish Undertaking' and effectively kept all but the boldest customers out. And in September of that year 1941, Douglas Archer, in common with most of his compatriots was keeping his eyes half-closed.

The scene of the murder to which, as Detective Sergeant Harry Woods had predicted, they were called, was Shepherd Market. This little maze of narrow streets and alleys housed a mixture of working-class Londoners, Italian shopkeepers and wealthy visitors, who found in these tortuous ways, and creaking old buildings, some measure of the London they'd read of in Dickens, while being conveniently close to the smart shops and restaurants.

The house was typical of the neighbourhood. There were uniformed police there already, arguing with two reporters. The ground floor was a poky antique shop not much wider than a man could stretch both arms. Above it were rooms of doll's-house dimensions, with a twisting staircase so narrow that it provided an ever-present risk of sweeping from its walls the framed coaching prints that decorated them. Only with difficulty did Harry get the heavy murder bag to the top floor where the body was.

The police doctor was there, seated on a chintz-covered couch, a British army overcoat buttoned up tight to the neck, and hands in his pockets. He was a young man, in his middle twenties, but already Douglas saw in his eyes that terrible resignation with which so many British seemed to have met final defeat.

On the floor in front of him there was the dead man. He was about thirty-five years old, a pale-faced man with a balding head. Passing him in the street one might have guessed him to be a rather successful academic – the sort of absent-minded professor portrayed in comedy films.

As well as blood, there was a large smudge of brown powder spilled on his waistcoat. Douglas touched it with a fingertip but even before he raised it to his nose, he recognized the heavy aroma of snuff. There were traces of it under the dead man's fingernails. Snuff was growing more popular as the price of cigarettes went up, and it was still unrationed.

Douglas found the snuff tin in a waistcoat pocket. The force of the bullets had knocked the lid off. There was a half-smoked cigar there too, the band still on it, a Romeo y Julieta worth a small fortune nowadays; no wonder he'd preserved the unsmoked half of it.

Douglas looked at the fine quality cloth and hand stitching of the dead man's suit. For such expensive, made to measure garments they fitted very loosely, as if the man, suddenly committed to a rigorous diet, had lost many pounds of weight. Sudden weight loss was also suggested by the drawn and wrinkled face. Douglas fingered the bald patches on the man's head.

'*Alopecia areata*,' said the doctor. 'It's common enough.'

Douglas looked into the mouth. The dead man had had enough money to pay for good dental care. Gold shone in his mouth but there was blood there too.

'There's blood in his mouth.'

'Probably hit his face as he fell.'

Douglas didn't think so but he didn't argue. He noted the tiny ulcers on the man's face and blood spots under the skin. He pushed back the shirt sleeve far enough to see the red inflamed arm.

'Where do you find such sunshine at this time of the year?' the doctor said.

Douglas didn't answer. He drew a small sketch of the way that the body had fallen backwards into the tiny bedroom, and guessed that he'd been in the doorway when the bullets hit him. He touched the blood on the body to see if it was tacky, and then placed a palm on the chest. He could feel no warmth at all. His experience told him that this man had been dead for six hours or more. The doctor watched Douglas but made no comment. Douglas got to his feet and looked round the room. It was a tiny place, over-decorated with fancy wallpapers, Picasso reproductions and table lights made from Chianti bottles.

There was a walnut escritoire, with its front open as if it might have been rifled. An old-fashioned brass lamp had been adjusted to bring the light close upon the green leather writing top but its bulb had been taken out and

17

left in one of the pigeon-holes, together with some cheap writing paper and envelopes.

There were no books, no photos and nothing personal of any kind. It was like some very superior sort of hotel room. In the tiny open fireplace there was a basket of logs. The grate was overflowing with ashes of paper.

'Pathologist here yet?' Douglas asked. He fitted the light bulb into the brass lamp. Then he switched it on for long enough to see that the bulb was still in working order and switched it off again. He went to the fireplace and put his hand into the ash. It was not warm but there was no surviving scrap of paper to reveal what had been burned there. It was a long job to burn so much paper. Douglas used his handkerchief to wipe his hands.

'Not yet,' said the doctor in a dull voice. Douglas guessed that he resented being ordered to wait.

'What do you make of it, doc?'

'You get any spare cigarettes, working with the SIPO?'

Douglas produced the gold cigarette case that was his one and only precious possession. The doctor took the cigarette and nodded his thanks while examining it carefully. Its paper was marked with the double red bands that identified Wehrmacht rations. The doctor put it in his mouth, brought a lighter from his pocket and lit it, all without changing his expression or his position, sprawled on the couch with legs extended.

A uniformed Police Sergeant had watched all this while waiting on the tiny landing outside the door. Now he put his head into the room and said, 'Pardon me, sir. A message from the pathologist. He won't be here until this afternoon.'

Harry Woods was unpacking the murder bag. Douglas could not resist glancing at him. Harry nodded. Now he realized that to keep the Police Surgeon here was a good idea. The pathologists were always late these days. 'So what do you make of it, doctor?' said Douglas.

They both looked down at the body. Douglas touched the dead man's shoes; the feet were always the last to stiffen.

'The photographers have finished until the pathologist comes,' said Harry. Douglas unbuttoned the dead man's shirt to reveal huge black bruises surrounding two holes upon which there was a crust of dried blood.

'What do I make of it?' said the doctor. 'Gunshot wound in chest caused death. First bullet into the heart, second one into the top of the lung. Death more or less instantaneous. Can I go now?'

'I won't keep you longer than absolutely necessary,' said Douglas without any note of apology in his voice. From his position crouched down with the body, he looked back to where the killer must have been. At the wall, far under the chair he saw a glint of metal. Douglas went over and reached for it. It was a small construction of alloy, with a leather rim. He put it into his waistcoat pocket. 'So it was the first bullet that entered the heart, doctor, not the second one?'

The doctor still had not moved from his fixed posture on the couch but now he twisted his feet until his toes touched together. 'There would have been more frothy blood if a bullet had hit the lung first while the heart was pumping.'

'Really,' said Douglas.

'He might have been falling by the time the second shot came. That would account for it going wide.'

'I see.'

'I saw enough gunshot wounds last year to become a minor expert,' said the doctor without smiling. 'Nine millimetre pistol. That's the sort of bullets you'll find

19

when you dig into the plaster behind that bloody awful Regency stripe wallpaper. Someone who knew him did it. I'd look for a lefthanded ex-soldier who came here often and had his own key to get in.'

'Good work, doctor.' Harry Woods looked up from where he was going through the dead man's pockets. He recognized the note of sarcasm.

'You know my methods, Watson,' said the doctor.

'Dead man wearing an overcoat; you conclude he came in the door to find the killer waiting. You guess the two men faced each other squarely with the killer in the chair by the fireplace, and from the path of the wound you guess the gun was in the killer's left hand.'

'Damned good cigarettes these Germans give you,' said the doctor, holding it in the air and looking at the smoke.

'And an ex-soldier because he pierced the heart with the first shot.' The doctor inhaled and nodded. 'Have you noticed that all three of us are still wearing overcoats?' said Douglas. 'It's bloody cold in here and the gas meter is empty and the supply disconnected. And not many soldiers are expert shots, doc, and not one in a million is an expert with a pistol, and by your evidence a German pistol at that. And you think the killer had a key because you can't see any signs of the door being forced. But my Sergeant could get through that door using a strip of celluloid faster than you could open it with a key, and more quietly too.'

'Oh,' said the doctor.

'Now, what about a time of death?' said Douglas.

All doctors hate to estimate the time of death and this doctor made sure the policemen knew that. He shrugged. 'I can think of a number and double it.'

'Think of a number, doc,' said Douglas, 'but don't double it.'

The doctor still lolling on the couch pinched out his cigarette and put the stub away in a dented tobacco tin. 'I took the temperature when I arrived. The normal calculation is that a body cools one-and-a-half degrees Fahrenheit per hour.'

'I'd heard a rumour to that effect,' said Douglas.

The doctor gave him a mirthless grin as he put the tin in his overcoat pocket, and watched his feet as he made the toes touch together again. 'Could have been between six and seven this morning.'

Douglas looked at the uniformed Sergeant. 'Who reported it?'

'The downstairs neighbour brings a bottle of milk up here each morning. He found the door open. No smell of cordite or anything,' added the Sergeant.

The doctor chortled. When it turned into a cough he thumped his chest. 'No smell of cordite,' he repeated. 'I'll remember that one, that's rather rich.'

'You don't know much about coppers, doc,' said Douglas. 'Specially when you take into account that you are a Police Surgeon. The uniformed Sergeant here, an officer I've never met before, is politely hinting to me that he thinks the time of death was earlier. Much earlier, doc.' Douglas went over to the elaborately painted corner cupboard and opened it to reveal an impressive display of drink. He picked up a bottle of whisky and noted without surprise that most of the labels said 'Specially bottled for the Wehrmacht'. Douglas replaced the bottles and closed the cupboard. 'Have you ever heard of post-mortem lividity, doctor?' he said.

'Death might have been earlier,' admitted the doctor. He was sitting upright now and his voice was soft. He, too, had noticed the coloration that comes from settling of the blood.

21

'But not before midnight.'

'No, not before midnight,' agreed the doctor.

'In other words death took place during curfew?'

'Very likely.'

'Very likely?' said Douglas caustically.

'*Definitely* during curfew,' admitted the doctor.

'What kind of a game are you playing, doc?' said Douglas. He didn't look at the doctor. He went to the fireplace and examined the huge pile of charred paper that was stuffed into the tiny grate. The highly polished brass poker was browned with smoke marks. Someone had used it to make sure that every last piece of paper was consumed by the flames. Again Douglas put his hand into the feathery layers of ash; there must have been a huge pile of foolscap and it was quite cold. 'Contents of his pockets, Harry?'

'Identity card, eight pounds, three shillings and ten-pence, a bunch of keys, penknife, expensive fountain-pen; handkerchief, no laundry marks, and a railway ticket monthly return half; London to Bringle Sands.'

'Is that all?'

Harry knew that his partner would ask for the identity card and he passed it across unrequested. Harry said, 'Travelling light, this one.'

'Or his pockets were rifled,' said the doctor, not moving from his position on the sofa.

Harry met Douglas's eyes and there was a trace of a smile. 'Or his pockets were rifled,' said Douglas to Harry.

'That's right,' said Harry.

Douglas opened the identity card. It was written there that the holder was a thirty-two-year-old accountant with an address in Kingston, Surrey. 'Kingston,' said Douglas.

'Yes,' said Harry. They both knew that, ever since the Kingston Records Office had been destroyed in the

22

fighting, this was a favourite address for forgers of identity documents. Douglas put the card in his pocket, and repeated his question. 'What sort of game are you playing, doctor?' He looked at the doctor and waited for an answer. 'Why are you trying to mislead me about the time of death?'

'Well it was silly of me. But if people are coming and going after midnight the neighbours are supposed to report them to the Feldgendarmerie.'

'And how do you know that they didn't report it?'

The doctor raised his hands and smiled. 'I just guessed,' he said.

'You guessed.' Douglas nodded. 'Is that because all *your* neighbours ignore the curfew?' said Douglas. 'What other regulations do they regularly flout?'

'Jesus!' said the doctor. 'You people are worse than the bloody Germans. I'd rather talk to the Gestapo than talk to bastards like you – at least they won't twist everything I say.'

'It's not in my power to deny you a chance to talk to the Gestapo,' said Douglas, 'but just to satisfy my own vulgar curiosity, doctor, is your opinion about benign interrogation techniques practised by that department based upon first-hand experience or hearsay?'

'All right, all right,' said the doctor. 'Let's say three A.M.'

'That's much better,' said Douglas. 'Now you examine the body properly so that I don't have to wait here for the pathologist before getting started and I'll forget all about that other nonsense . . . but leave anything out, doc, and I'll run you along to Scotland Yard and put you through the mangle. Right?'

'All right,' said the doctor.

'There's a lady downstairs,' said the uniformed police

23

Sergeant. 'She's come to collect something from the antique shop. I've told the Constable to ask her to wait for you.'

'Good man,' said Douglas. He left the doctor looking at the body while Harry Woods was going through the drawers of the escritoire.

The antique shop was one of the hundreds that had sprung up since the bombing and the flight of refugees from Kent and Surrey during the weeks of bitter fighting there. With the German Mark pegged artificially high, the German occupiers were sending antiques home by the train-load. The dealers were doing well out of it, but one didn't need lessons in economics to see the way that wealth was draining out of the country.

There were some fine pieces of furniture in the shop. Douglas wondered how many had been lawfully purchased and how many looted from empty homes. Obviously the owner of the antique shop stored his antiques by putting them in the tiny apartments upstairs, and justified high rents by having them there.

The visitor was sitting on an elegant Windsor chair. She was very beautiful: large forehead, high cheekbones and a wide face with a perfect mouth that smiled easily. She was tall, with long legs and slim arms.

'Now maybe someone will give me a straight answer.' She had a soft American voice, and she reached into a large leather handbag and found a US passport, which she brandished at him.

Douglas nodded. For a moment he was spellbound. She was the most desirable woman he'd ever seen. 'What can I do for you, Madam?'

'Miss,' she said. 'In my country a lady doesn't like being mistaken for a Madam.' She seemed amused at his

24

discomfiture. She smiled in that relaxed way that marks the very rich and the very beautiful.

'What can I do for you, Miss?'

She was dressed in a tailored two-piece of pink wool. Its severe and practical cut made it unmistakably American. It would have been striking anywhere, but in this war-begrimed city, among so many dressed in ill-fitting uniforms or clothes adapted from uniforms, it singled her out as a prosperous visitor. Over her shoulder she carried a new Rolleiflex camera. The Germans sold them tax-free to servicemen and to anyone who paid in US dollars.

'My name is Barbara Barga. I write a column that is syndicated into forty-two US newspapers and magazines. The press attaché of the German Embassy in Washington offered me a ticket on the Lufthansa inaugural New York to London flight last month. I said yes, and here I am.'

'Welcome to London,' said Douglas dryly. It was shrewd of her to mention the inaugural flight on the Focke-Wulf airliner. Göring and Goebbels were both on that flight; it was one of the most publicized events of the year. A journalist would have to be very important indeed to have got a seat.

'Now tell me what's going on here?' she said with a smile. Douglas Archer had not met many Americans, and he'd certainly never met one to compare with this girl. When she smiled, her face wrinkled in a way that Douglas found very beguiling. In spite of himself, he smiled back. 'Don't get me wrong,' she said. 'I get on well with cops, but I didn't expect to find so many of them here in Peter's shop today.'

'Peter?'

'Peter Thomas,' she said. 'Come on now, mister detective, it says Peter Thomas on the door – Peter Thomas – Antiques – right?'

'You know Mr Thomas?' said Douglas.

'Is he in trouble?'

'This will go faster if you just answer my questions, Miss.'

She smiled. 'Who said I wanted to go faster . . . OK. I know him – '

'Could you give me a brief description?'

'Thirty-eight, maybe younger, pale, thin on top, big-build, six feet tall, small Ronald Colman moustache, deep voice, good suits.'

Douglas nodded. It was enough to identify the dead man. 'Could you tell me your relationship with Mr Thomas?'

'Just business – now what about letting me in on who you are, buddy?'

'Yes, I'm sorry,' said Douglas. He felt he was handling this rather badly. The girl smiled at his discomfort. 'I'm the Detective Superintendent in charge of the investigation. Mr Thomas was found here this morning: dead.'

'Not suicide? Peter wasn't the type.'

'He was shot.'

'Foul play,' said the girl. 'Isn't that what you British call it?'

'What was your business with him?'

'He was helping me with a piece I'm writing about Americans who stayed here right through the fighting. I met him when I came in to ask the price of some furniture. He knew everybody – including a lot of London-based foreigners.'

'Really.'

'Peter was a clever man. He'd root out anything anybody wanted, as long as there was a margin in it for him.' She looked at the collection of silver and ivory objects on a shelf above the cash register. 'I called this morning to collect some film. I ran out of it yesterday, and Peter said he'd be able to get me a roll. It might have been in his pocket.'

'There was no film found on the body.'

'Well, it doesn't matter. I'll get some somewhere.'

She was standing near him now and he smelled her perfume. He fantasized about embracing her and – as if guessing this – she looked at him and smiled. 'Where can I reach you, Miss Barga?'

'The Dorchester until the end of this week. Then I move into a friend's apartment.'

'So the Dorchester is open again?'

'Just a few rooms at the back. It's going to be a long time rebuilding the park side.'

'Make sure you leave a forwarding address,' said Douglas although he knew that she'd be registered as an alien, and registered with the Kommandantur Press Bureau.

She seemed in no hurry to depart. 'Peter could get you anything: from a chunk of the Elgin marbles, complete with a letter from the man who dug it out of the Museum wreckage, to an army discharge, category 1a – Aryan, skilled worker, no curfew or travel restrictions – Peter was a hustler, Superintendent. Guys like that get into trouble. Don't expect anyone to weep for him.'

'You've been most helpful, Miss Barga.' She was going out through the door when Douglas spoke again. 'By the way,' he said, 'do you know if he had been to some hot climate recently?'

She turned. 'Why?'

'Sunburned arms,' said Douglas. 'As if he'd gone to sleep in the hot sunshine.'

'I only met him a couple of weeks back,' said Barbara Barga. 'But he might have been using a sun-lamp.'

27

'That would account for it,' said Douglas doubtfully.

Upstairs Harry Woods had been talking to Thomas's only neighbour. He had identified the body and offered the information that Thomas had been a far from ideal neighbour. 'There was a Luftwaffe Feldwebel . . . big man with spectacles – I'm not sure what the ranks are – but he was from that Quartermaster's depot in Maryle-bone Road. He used to bring all kinds of stuff: tinned food, tobacco and medical stuff too. I think they were selling drugs – always having parties, and you should have seen some of the girls who came here; painted faces and smelling of drink. Sometimes they knocked at my door in mistake – horrible people. I don't like speaking ill of the dead mind you, but they were a horrible crowd he was in with.'

'Do you know if Mr Thomas had a sun-lamp?' Douglas asked.

'I don't know what he *didn't* have, Superintendent! A regular Aladdin's cave you'll find when you dig into those cupboards. And don't forget the attic.'

'No, I won't, thank you.'

When the man had gone, Douglas took from his pocket the metal object he'd found under the chair. It was made from curved pieces of lightweight alloy, and yet it was clumsy and heavy for its size. It was unpainted and its edge covered with a strip of light-brown leather. It was pierced by a quarter-inch hole, in line with which a screw-threaded nut had been welded. The whole thing was strengthened by a section of tube. From the shape, size and hasty workmanship Douglas guessed it was a part of one of the hundreds of false limbs provided to casualties of the recent fighting. If it was part of a false right arm the doctor might have made a remarkably accurate guess and Douglas could start looking for a left-hand ex-service sharpshooter.

Douglas put the metal construction back into his pocket as Harry came in. 'You let the doctor go?' said Douglas.

'You rode him a bit hard, Doug.'

'What else did he say?'

'Three A.M. I think we should try to find this Luftwaffe Feldwebel.'

'Did the doctor say anything about those sunburns on the arms?'

'Sun-ray lamp,' said Harry.

'Did the doctor say that?'

'No, I'm saying it. The doctor hummed and hawed, you know what they are like.'

Douglas said, 'So the neighbour says he was a black-marketeer and the American girl tells us the same thing.'

'It all fits together, doesn't it?'

'It fits together so well that it stinks.'

Harry said nothing.

'Did you find a sun-ray lamp?'

'No, but there's still the attic.'

'Very well, Harry, have a look in the attic. Then go over to the Feldgendarmerie and get permission to talk to the Feldwebel.'

'How do you mean it stinks?' said Harry.

'The downstairs neighbour tells me everything about this damned Feldwebel short of giving me his name and number. Then this American girl turns up and asks me if I found a roll of film on the body. She tells me that this man Peter Thomas was going to get a roll of film for her last night . . . ugh! A girl like that would bring a gross of films with her. When she wanted more, she'd get films from a news agency, or from the American Embassy. Failing that, the German Press Bureau would give her as

29

much as she asked for; you know what the propaganda officials will do for American newspaper people. She doesn't have to get involved with the black market.'

'Perhaps she *wanted* to get involved with the black market. Perhaps she is trying to make contact with the Resistance, in order to write a newspaper story.'

'That's just what I was thinking, Harry.'

'What else is wrong?'

'I took his keys downstairs. None of them fits any of the locks; not the street door or this door. The small keys look like the ones they use on filing cabinets and the bronze one is probably for a safe. There are no filing cabinets here, and if there is a safe, it's uncommonly well hidden.'

'Anything else?' said Harry.

'If he lives here, why buy a return ticket when he left Bringle Sands yesterday morning? And if he lives here, where are his shirts, his underclothes and his suits?'

'He left them at Bringle Sands.'

'And he intended to go to bed here, and then get up and use the same shirt and underclothes, you mean? Look at the body, Harry. This was a man very fussy about his clean linen.'

'You don't think he lived here?'

'I don't think *anyone* lived here. This place was just used as somewhere to meet.'

'Business you mean – or lovers?'

'You're forgetting what Resistance people call "safe houses", Harry. It might have been a place where they met, hid or stored things. And we can't overlook the way he was wearing his overcoat.'

'You told the doctor it was cold.'

'The doctor was trying to irritate me and he succeeded. That doesn't mean he was wrong about someone sitting

30

here waiting for Thomas to arrive. And it doesn't explain him keeping his hat on.'

'I never know what you're really thinking,' said Harry.

'Watch your tongue when you are over at the Feldgendarmerie, Harry.'

'What do you think I am – stupid?'

'Romantic,' said Douglas. 'Not stupid – romantic.'

'You think he got those burns from a sun-lamp?' said Harry.

'I never heard of anyone going to sleep under a sun-lamp,' said Douglas, 'but there has to be a first time for everything. And try to think why someone has taken the light bulb out of that adjustable desk light. There was nothing wrong with the bulb.'

Chapter Four

The beer seemed to get weaker every day and anyone who believed those stories about the fighting having destroyed the hop fields had never tasted the export brands that were selling in German soldiers' canteens. In spite of its limitations Douglas bought a second pint and smothered the tasteless cheese sandwich with mustard before eating it. There were several other Murder Squad officers in the 'Red Lion' in Derby Gate. It was Scotland Yard's own pub, more crimes had been solved in this bar than in all the offices, path labs and record offices put together, or so some of the regulars claimed, after a few drinks.

A newspaper boy came in selling the *Evening Standard*. Douglas bought a copy and turned to the Stop Press on the back page.

MAN FOUND DEAD IN WEST END LUXURY FLAT

Shepherd Market in Mayfair was visited by Scotland Yard officers today when the body of a man was discovered by a neighbour bringing the morning pint of milk. The dead man's name has not yet been released by the police. It is believed that he was an antique dealer and a well-known expert in pearls. Scotland Yard are treating the death as murder, and the investigation is headed by 'Archer of the Yard' who solved the grisly 'Sex-fiend murders' last summer.

Douglas saw the hand of Harry Woods in that; he knew Douglas hated being called 'Archer of the Yard' and Douglas guessed that Harry had spoken over the phone and said the dead man was an 'expert in girls' before incredulously denying it on the read-back.

It was raining as Douglas left the 'Red Lion'. As he looked across the road, at the oncoming traffic, he saw Sylvia, his secretary. She'd obviously been waiting for him. Douglas let a couple of buses pass and then hurried across the road. He waited again for two staff cars flying C-in-C pennants. They hit the ruts left by bomb damage and sprayed water over him. Douglas cursed but that only made it rain harder.

'Darling,' said Sylvia. There was not much passion in the word but then with Sylvia there never had been. Douglas put an arm round her and she held her cold face up to be kissed.

'I've been worried all morning. The letter said you were going away.'

'You must forgive me, darling,' said Sylvia. 'I've despised myself ever since sending the damned letter. Say you forgive me.'

'You're pregnant?'

'I'm not absolutely sure.'

'Damn it, Sylvia – you sent the letter and said . . .'

'Don't shout in the street, darling.' She held a hand up to his mouth. The hand was very cold. 'Perhaps I shouldn't have come here?'

'After three days I had to report your absence. The tea lady asked where you were. It was impossible to cover for you.'

'I didn't want you to take any risks, darling.'

'I phoned your aunt in Streatham but she said she'd not seen you for months.'

'Yes, I must go and see her.'

'Will you listen to what I'm saying, Sylvia.'

'Let go of my arm, you're hurting me. I *am* listening.'

33

'You're not listening properly.'

'I'm listening the same as I always listen to you.'

'You've still got your SIPO pass.'

'What pass?'

'Your Scotland Yard pass – have you been drinking or something?'

'Of course I haven't been drinking. Well, what about it? You think I'm going to go down Petticoat Lane and sell the bloody pass to the highest bidder. Who the hell wants to go into that hideous building unless they are paid for it?'

'Let's walk,' said Douglas. 'Don't you know that Whitehall has regular Gendarmerie patrols?'

'What are you talking about?' She smiled. 'Give me a proper kiss. Aren't you glad to see me?'

He kissed her hurriedly. 'Of course I am. We'll walk up towards Trafalgar Square, all right?'

'Suits me.'

They walked up Whitehall, past the armed sentries who stood immobile outside the newly occupied offices. They were almost as far as the Whitehall Theatre when they saw the soldiers doing the spot-check. Parked across the roadway there were three Bedford lorries, newly painted with German Army Group L (London District) HQ markings: a crude Tower Bridge surmounting a Gothic L. The soldiers were in battle-smocks with machine pistols slung on their shoulders. They moved quickly, expanding the spiked barrier – designed to pierce tyres – so that only one lane of traffic could pass through in each direction. The check-point command car was parked against the foot of Charles the First's statue. The Germans learned quickly thought Douglas, for that was the place the Metropolitan Police always used for central

34

London crowd-control work. More soldiers made a barrier behind them.

Sylvia showed no sign of apprehension but she suggested that it would be quicker if they turned off at Whitehall Place and went towards the Embankment. 'No,' said Douglas. 'They always block the side roads first!'

'I'll show my pass,' said Sylvia.

'Have you gone completely out of your mind?' said Douglas. 'The Scotland Yard building houses the SD and the Gestapo and all the rest of it. You might not think much of it, but the Germans think that pass is just about the most valuable piece of paper any foreigner can be given. You've stayed away without reporting illness, and you've kept your pass. If you read the German regulations that you signed, you'd find that that's the same as theft, Sylvia. By now, your name and pass number will be on the Gestapo wanted list. Every patrol from Land's End to John O'Groats will be looking for it.'

'What shall I do?' Even now there was no real anxiety in her voice.

'Stay calm. They have plain-clothes men watching for anyone acting suspiciously.'

They were stopping everything and everyone; staff cars, double-decker buses, even an ambulance was held up while the Patrol Commander examined the papers of the driver and the sick man. The soldiers ignored the rain which made their helmets shiny and darkened their battle-smocks, but the civilians huddled under the protection of the Whitehall Theatre entrance. There was a revue showing there, 'Vienna Comes to London', with undressed girls hiding between white violins.

Douglas grabbed Sylvia's arm and before she could object he brought out a pair of handcuffs and slammed

35

them on her wrist with enough violence to hurt. 'What are you bloody well doing!' shouted Sylvia but by that time he was dragging her forward past the waiting people. There were a few muttered complaints as Douglas elbowed them even more roughly. 'Patrol Commander!' he shouted imperiously. 'Patrol Commander!'

'What do you want?' said a pimply young Feldwebel wearing the metal breastplate that was the mark of military police on duty. He was not wearing a battle-smock and Douglas guessed he was a section leader. He waved his SIPO pass in the air, and spoke in rapid German. 'Wachtmeister! I'm taking this girl for questioning. Here's my pass.'

'Her papers?' said the youth impassively.

'Says she's lost them.'

He didn't react except to take the pass from Douglas and examine it carefully before looking at his face and his photo to compare them.

'Come along, come along,' said Douglas on the principle that no military policeman is able to distinguish between politeness and guilt. 'I've not got all day.'

'You've hurt my bloody wrist,' said Sylvia. 'Look at that, you bastard.' The Feldwebel glared at him and then at the girl. 'Next!' he bellowed.

'Come on,' said Douglas and hurried through the barrier dragging Sylvia after him. They picked their way through the traffic that was waiting for the check-point. They were both very wet and neither spoke as a luxury bus came through Admiralty Arch and into Trafalgar Square. Its windows were crowded with the faces of young soldiers. Softly from inside there came the amplified voice of the tour guide speaking schoolboy German. The young men grinned at his pronunciation. One boy waved at Sylvia.

A few wet pigeons shuffled out of the way as they walked across the empty rainswept square. 'Do you realize what you said, just now?' said Sylvia. She was still rubbing her wrist where the skin had been grazed.

It was just like a woman, thought Douglas, to start some oblique conversation about something already forgotten.

'One of the most important pieces of paper that the Germans issue to *foreigners*; that's what you said just now.'

'Give over, Sylvia,' said Douglas. He looked back to be sure they were out of sight of the patrol, then he unlocked the handcuff and released her arm.

'That's what we are as far as you're concerned – *foreigners*! The Germans are the ones with a right to be here; we're the intruders who have to bow and bloody scrape.'

'Give over, Sylvia,' said Douglas. He hated to hear women swearing like that, although, working in a police force, he should by now have got used to it.

'Get your hands off me, you bloody Gestapo bastard.' She pushed him away with the flat of her hand. 'I've got friends who *don't* go in fear and trembling of the Huns. You wouldn't understand anything about that, would you. No! You're too busy doing their dirty work for them.'

'You must have been talking to Harry Woods,' said Douglas in a vain attempt to turn the argument into a joke.

'You're pathetic,' said Sylvia. 'Do you know that? You're pathetic!'

She was pretty, but with the rain making rats' tails of her hair, her lipstick smudged, and the ill-fitting raincoat that had always been too short for her, Douglas suddenly saw her as he'd never seen her before. And he saw her, too, as she'd be in ten years hence; a tight-lipped virago with a loud voice and quick temper. He realized that he'd never make a go of it with Sylvia. But when her parents were killed by bombs, just a few days before Douglas lost his wife, it was natural that they sought in each other some desperate solace that came disguised as love.

What Douglas had once seen as the attractive over-confidence of youth, now looked more like unyielding selfishness. He wondered if there was another man, a much younger one perhaps, but decided against asking her, knowing that she would say yes just to annoy him. 'We're both pathetic, Sylvia,' he said, 'and that's the truth of it.'

They were standing near one of the Landseer lions, shining as black as polished ebony in the driving rain. They were virtually alone there, for now even the most stalwart of German servicemen had put away their tax-free cameras and taken shelter. Sylvia stood with one hand in her pocket, and the other pushing her wet hair off her forehead. She smiled but there was no merriment there, not even a touch of kindness or compassion. 'Don't be sarcastic about Harry Woods,' she said bitterly. 'He's the only friend you've got left. Do you realize that?'

'Leave Harry out of it,' said Douglas.

'You realize he's one of us, don't you?'

'What?'

'The Resistance, you fool.' The expression on Douglas's face was enough to make her laugh. A woman, pushing a pram laden with a sack of coal, half turned to look at them before hurrying on.

'Harry?'

'Harry Woods, assistant to Archer of the Yard, protégé of the Gestapo, scourge of any who dare blow raspberries at the conqueror, and yet, yea, verily, I say unto you, this man dare fight the bloody Hun.' She walked to the fountain and looked at her reflection in the shallow waters.

'You *have* been drinking.'

'Only the heady potion of freedom.'

'Don't take an overdose,' said Douglas. It was almost comical to see her in this sort of mood. Perhaps it was a reaction to the fear she'd felt at the spot-check.

'Just look after our friend Harry,' she called shrilly, 'and give him this, with all my love.'

The hand emerged from her pocket holding the SIPO pass. Before Douglas could stop her, she lifted her arm and threw it as far as she could into the water of the fountain. The rain pounded the stone paving so heavily that the water rebounded to make a grey cornfield of water-spray. She walked quickly through it, towards the steps that led to the National Gallery.

Under the rain-spotted water it was only just possible to see the red-bordered pass as it sank to the bottom amongst the tourists' coins, Agfa boxes and ice-cream wrappers. Left there, it might well be spotted by some high-ranking official, who would make life hell for the whole department. Douglas stood looking at it for a moment or two but he was already so wet that it would make little difference to go into the water up to his knees.

Chapter Five

When Douglas got back to his office that afternoon, he had barely enough time to clean himself up, and put on dry shoes, before there was a message from the first floor. General Kellerman wanted a word with Douglas, if that was convenient. It was convenient. Douglas hurried upstairs.

'Ah, Superintendent Archer, so good of you to come,' said Kellerman as if Archer was some sort of visiting dignitary. 'I seem to have such a busy day today.' Kellerman's senior staff officer passed his chief a teleprinter sheet. Kellerman looked at it briefly and said, 'This chap from Berlin, Standartenführer Huth . . . you remember?'

'I remember everything you said, sir.'

'Splendid. Well, the Standartenführer has been given a priority seat on the afternoon Berlin–Croydon flight. He'll be arriving about five I should think. I wonder if you would go there and meet him?'

'Yes, sir, but I wonder . . .' Douglas couldn't think of a good way to suggest that an SS-Standartenführer from Himmler's Central Security Office would consider a welcome from one English Detective Superintendent less than his rank and position merited.

'The Standartenführer has requested that you meet him,' said Kellerman.

'Me personally?' said Douglas.

'His task is of an investigative nature,' said Kellerman. 'I thought it appropriate that I assign to him my best detective.' He smiled. In fact Huth had asked for Archer by name. Kellerman had energetically opposed the order that put Douglas Archer under the command of the new man, but the intervention of Himmler himself had ended the matter.

'Thank you, sir,' said Douglas.

Kellerman reached into the pocket of his tweed waist-coat and looked at his gold pocket watch. 'I'll start right away,' said Douglas, recognizing his cue.

'Would you?' said Kellerman. 'Well, see my personal assistant so that you know all the arrangements we've made to receive the Standartenführer.'

Lufthansa had three Berlin–London flights daily, and these were additional to the less comfortable and less prestigious military flights. Standartenführer Dr Oskar Huth had been given one of the fifteen seats on the flight which left Berlin at lunch-time.

Douglas waited in the unheated terminal building and watched a Luftwaffe band preparing for the arrival of the daily flight from New York. The Germans had the only land-planes capable of such a long-range, non-stop service and the Propaganda Ministry was making full use of it.

The rain had continued well into the afternoon but now on the horizon there was a break in the low clouds. The Berlin plane circled, while the pilot decided whether to land. After the third circuit the big three-engined Junkers roared low over the airport building, and then came round for a perfect landing on the wet tarmac. Its hand-polished metal flashed as it taxied back to the terminal building.

Douglas half expected that any man who had his doctorate included with his rank on teleprinter messages might have retained a trace of the bedside manner. But Huth was a doctor of law, and a hard-nosed SS officer if

Douglas had ever seen one. And by that time Douglas had seen many.

Unlike Kellerman, the new man was wearing his uniform, and gave no sign of preferring plain clothes. It was not the black SS uniform. That nowadays was worn only by the Allgemeine SS – mostly middle-aged country yokels who donned uniform just for village booze-ups at week-ends. Dr Huth's uniform was silver-grey, with high boots and riding breeches. On his cuff there was the RFSS cuffband worn only by Himmler's personal staff.

Douglas looked him up and down. There was something of the dress-maker's dummy about this tall, thin man, in spite of the state of his uniform which was carefully pressed and cleaned but unmistakably old. He was about thirty-five years old, a powerful, muscular figure with an energy in his stride and demeanour that belied the hooded eyes that made him seem half-asleep. Under his arm he carried a short silver-topped stick, and in his hand a large brief-case. He didn't go to the door marked for customs and immigration, he rapped the counter-top with his stick, until a uniformed Lufthansa official opened the gate for him to go into the reception hall.

'Archer?'

'Yes, sir.' The officer shook his hand perfunctorily, as if his briefing had said that all Englishmen expect it.

'What are we waiting for?' said Huth.

'Your staff . . . your baggage . . .'

'Shot-guns, golf-clubs and fishing tackle, you mean? I've no time for that sort of nonsense,' said Huth. 'Have you got a car here?'

'The Rolls,' said Douglas, pointing to where, seen through the doors of the terminal, there stood the highly

42

polished car with uniformed SS driver and Kellerman's official pennants.

'Kellerman let you have the Rolls-Royce, did he?' said Huth as they got into it. 'What is he using this afternoon, the coronation coach?' Huth's English accent was perfect, with the sort of polish that comes only from multi-lingual parents, or a multi-lingual mistress. And yet, for all Huth's smooth polish, there was no mistaking the hard ambition that shone beneath it.

Huth's father was a professor of modern languages. The family had lived in Schleswig-Holstein until, after the first war, the new frontier had made their home a part of Denmark. Then they had moved to Berlin, where Oskar Huth had studied law before going on to complete his studies at Oxford, where Douglas Archer had gone a few years later. In spite of the disparity in their ages, Douglas Archer and Huth were able to find memories and acquaintances in common. And Douglas's mother had, as a young woman, been an English governess in Berlin; Douglas knew it from her stories of that time.

'What are you working on at present?' Huth asked very casually as he looked out of the window. The car slowed for the traffic at Norwood. A long line of people waited in the rain for the bread ration to arrive. Douglas half expected Huth to comment on them but he leaned forward with balled fist, and used his signet ring to rap against the glass of the driver's compartment. 'Use the siren, you fool,' he said. 'Do you think I've got all day!'

'Double death in Kentish Town Tuesday. They fell on the electrified rail of the Underground railway. I treated it as murder at first, but then decided it was a suicide pact; the man was an escapee from the camp for British POWs at Brighton.' Douglas scratched his cheek. 'A shooting in a night-club in Leicester Square on Saturday

43

night. A machine-pistol was used, about one hundred and fifty rounds; no shortage of bullets it seems. All the signs of a gang killing. The proprietor says the takings were about six thousand pounds – if you allow for what he's probably falsifying on his tax returns, it's probably double that – in used notes: O-Marks mostly. Manager and cashier both dead, three customers injured and one still in hospital.'

'What about the Peter Thomas murder?' said Huth, still looking out of the window at the drab, rainswept streets.

'That was only this morning,' said Douglas, surprised that Huth was so up to date on what was happening.

Huth nodded.

'So far we've found no one who heard the pistol shot but the doctor thinks death occurred about three A.M. The dead man carried papers saying he was Peter Thomas but the papers are probably forgeries. Criminal records have nothing listed under that name. Fingerprints are working on it but it will take a long time before they finish. He had a railway ticket from Bringle Sands. That's a small coastal holiday-resort in Devon.'

Douglas looked at Huth who was still staring out of the window. 'I know exactly where Bringle Sands is located,' said Huth. Douglas was surprised. He'd not known where it was himself until consulting an atlas.

'Go on,' said Huth without looking at him.

'There were military stores in the apartment . . . not much. Typical black-market items: cigarettes, drink, petrol coupons. We have a written statement from the neighbour who insists that a Luftwaffe Feldwebel was there frequently. He gave a description so my Sergeant went to see the Feldgendarmerie this afternoon. I will

44

wait now to see if they want to take over the investigation, or whether I continue.'

'What about the murder?'

'It has all the signs of a killer who let himself in, waited for the victim to arrive home . . .'

'But you don't think so?'

Douglas shrugged. There was no way to tell this SS officer of the problems such investigations brought. The penalties for even slight breaches of the regulations were now so severe that ordinarily law-abiding men and women would give false evidence. Douglas Archer understood this, and, in common with all the rest of the police in Britain, he turned a blind eye to many less serious offences. 'Probably a black-market murder,' said Douglas, although his instinct told him that there was more to it.

Huth turned and smiled. 'I think I'm beginning to understand the way you work, Superintendent,' he said. 'Probably a black-market killing, you say. And Saturday's was a gang killing. Tuesday's was a suicide pact. Is this the way you work at Scotland Yard? You have these convenient pigeon-holes that are a cunning way of classifying cases that would otherwise be put together in a gigantic file marked "unsolvable". Is that it?'

'I didn't use that word, Standartenführer, you did. In my opinion, such cases are perfectly straightforward, except that Wehrmacht personnel are involved. In such cases my hands are tied.'

'Very plausible,' said Huth.

Douglas waited, and when he added nothing more said, 'Would you please elaborate on that, sir?'

'You don't for one moment think it's a "black-market killing",' said Huth contemptuously. 'Because a man like you knows every damned crook in London. If you thought this was anything to do with the black-market you'd have searched out every important black-marketeer in London and told them to hand over the culprit within a couple of hours, or find themselves doing ten years' preventive detention. Can you tell me why you didn't?'

'No,' said Douglas.

'What do you mean, no?'

'I can't tell you, because I don't know why I didn't do that. All the evidence is as I told you . . . but there's more to it, I think.'

Huth stared at Douglas and tipped his peaked cap back on his head with the tip of his thumb. He was a handsome man but his face was colourless, his grey drill uniform, and its black and silver SS collar patches, little different from the pale complexion resulting from a life spent in ill-lit offices. Douglas found no way to discover what was going on inside this man's head, and yet he had the uncomfortable feeling that Huth could see right through him. But Douglas did not avert his eyes. After what seemed an interminable time, Huth said, 'So what are you doing about it?'

'If the Feldgendarmerie identify the Feldwebel mentioned in the neighbour's written statement, it will be up to the Feldgericht der Luftwaffe to decide . . .'

Huth waved his hand disdainfully. 'A teleprinter message from Berlin instructed the Luftwaffe to pass all papers back to you.'

Douglas found this truly astonishing. The Wehrmacht jealously guarded the right to handle their own investigations. The SD – the intelligence service of the SS – had achieved the seemingly impossible when it extended its investigative powers to include not only the SS, but also the SA and the Nazi Party. But even they never attempted to bring charges against a member of the armed forces.

There was only one level at which the Luftwaffe could be ordered to pass an investigation over to the SIPO – and that was the supreme controller of civil power and supreme commander of the armed forces, Adolf Hitler.

Douglas's imagination raced ahead, to wonder if the crime might have been committed by some high-ranking Nazi, or a relative, associate or mistress of such a person. 'Is there a theory about who the killer might be?'

'You find the killer, that's all,' said Huth.

'But why this particular crime?' persisted Douglas.

'Because it's there,' said Huth wearily. 'That should be enough for an Englishman surely.'

Douglas's mind was filled with fears and objections. He didn't want any part of this very important investigation, with a sinister SS officer looking over his shoulder all the time. But this was obviously not the moment to voice his objections. A little watery sunlight dribbled through the clouds and lit the shiny streets. The driver used the distinctive police siren and sped past the high walls of the Oval cricket ground.

Douglas said, 'I will collect you at seven-thirty for the reception in your honour at the Savoy Hotel. But, on the way to your accommodation, in Brook Street, Mayfair, General Kellerman thought you might like to see Buckingham Palace and the Houses of Parliament.'

'General Kellerman is a peasant,' said Huth affably in German.

'And does that mean you *would* like to drive past Buckingham Palace or not?'

'It means, my dear Superintendent, that I have not the slightest intention of spending the evening watching a roomful of army officers, and their over-dressed women, guzzling champagne, and, between mouthfuls of smoked salmon, telling me the best place to buy Staffordshire china.' He continued to speak German, using the word 'fressen', normally used to describe the eating habits of livestock.

'Take me to my office,' said Huth. 'And get the best damned pathologist available to look at Peter Thomas tonight. I want to be there for the post-mortem.' He saw the bewilderment on Douglas's face. 'You'll soon get used to the way I work.'

A man can get used to yellow fever, thought Douglas, but many of them die in the attempt. 'So I'll cancel the reception?'

'And deprive Kellerman and his friends of their party? What sort of fellow are you, Superintendent, a kill-joy?'

He gave a soft laugh. Then he rapped the glass partition again and shouted 'Scotland Yard!' to the driver.

Chapter Six

And so, at the very time when General Kellerman, HSSPf (Senior SS and Police Leader) Great Britain, was playing host to some of the senior officials in London, their guest of honour was in a mortuary behind Baker Street wearing a white, butcher's apron and watching Peter Thomas's corpse being slashed open by Sir John Shields, the pathologist.

It was a grim little building, set back from Paddington Street by enough space for the hearses and ambulances to unload behind the oak doors that make the entrance so innocuous to passers-by. The interior of the mortuary building had received so many coats of dark green and brown paint that the brickwork was now smooth and shiny, like its stone stairs and polished wooden floor. The low-power light-bulbs provided only small puddles of dull yellow light, except where a green-shaded brass lamp had been pulled down close to Peter Thomas's pale dead belly.

There were nine people present: Huth, Sir John Shields and his assistant, Douglas Archer, a man from the coroner's office, a clerk, two mortuary workers in rubber aprons and waterproof boots, and a fussy little German police Major who had also flown in from Hamburg that day. He took notes, and continually asked for translations of bits of Shields's impassive commentary. There were too many people round the slab, and Douglas readily conceded his place in the front row. He had no taste for these gory excursions, and even with his eyes averted, the sounds of the knife and hacksaw and the gurgling liquids made him want to retch. 'Haemorrhage, haemorrhage, haemorrhage!' said Shields, indicating with the knife. They peered closely at the dead man's insides. 'I don't like the look of his liver,' said Shields, grabbing it, cutting it free and holding it nearer to the light. 'What do you think, doctor?' His voice echoed in the dark mortuary.

Shields's assistant prodded the liver, and looked at it through a magnifying glass for a long time. Shields bent down to sniff at the corpse.

'Explain to me,' said Huth impatiently.

'Diseased,' said the doctor. 'Most interesting. I've never seen one quite like it. I wonder how the fellow kept going.'

The little German police Major was scribbling in his notebook. Then he, too, wanted to look at the liver through a magnifying glass. 'How near to death was he due to failure of the liver?' he asked in German and waited while his query was translated by Huth.

'I'd not like to answer that,' said Sir John. 'A man can go the devil of a time with a bad liver – you should see the chaps at my club!' He laughed.

'This is not a joke,' said Huth. 'Was the man sick?'

'He certainly was,' said Sir John.

'To death?'

'I wouldn't have given him more than a couple of months, would you, doctor?'

Sir John's assistant demonstrated agreement by means of a noisy intake of breath, and a slight shake of the head.

Huth put his arm round the shoulder of the Major and steered him away, out of earshot, where they stood and whispered together. Sir John clearly thought this a breach of good manners and he did nothing to hide his annoyance.

When Huth returned to the slab he told Sir John that he would want all the internal organs packed and ready to be flown to Berlin on the next day's flight from Croydon.

'Then there is nothing to keep me here,' said Sir John Shields.

'Don't be offended, Sir John,' said Huth with a smooth charm that Douglas had not seen him use before. 'We've no one in Berlin with your knowledge and experience. I'm hoping very much that you and your colleague will continue with the post-mortem so that we can have a report by tomorrow morning.'

Sir John took a deep breath, and came to his full height, as Douglas had seen him do so often in the law courts just before crushing some over-confident counsel. 'There can be no question of my attempting any further examination of this body without the facilities of a hospital laboratory, fully equipped and fully staffed.'

Huth nodded but said nothing.

Sir John continued. 'Even then, it would be a long job. All the London hospitals are over-worked to a point of near exhaustion, and that for reasons that I will not embarrass you, or your army colleague, by elaborating.'

Huth nodded gravely. 'Of course not. And that's why I have arranged for the SS Hospital, at Hyde Park Corner, to have their laboratory entirely at your disposal. I have two cars and an ambulance here, a telephone line has been kept clear for you and you have only to ask for any extra personnel and materials.'

Sir John looked at Huth for a long time before answering. 'I would like to believe, Brigadier, that this extraordinary display of German military resource is a compliment

51

to me. However, I suspect it is more accurately a measure of your concern with this particular death. I'd therefore appreciate it if you'd be a little more forthcoming about its circumstances – and what you know already.'

'Standartenführer,' said Huth, 'Standartenführer, not Brigadier. All I can tell you, Sir John, is that I dislike mysteries even more than you do, and that especially applies to mysterious death.'

'Epidemic?' said Sir John. 'Contagious disease? Virus? Plague? Pestilence?' His voice rose a fraction. 'You mean you've seen something like this before?'

'Some of my staff have seen something like this before,' admitted Huth. 'As for plague and pestilence, we're dealing with something that could prove so deadly that not even the Black Death would compare with the consequences – at least, that's what my experts tell me.'

Chapter Seven

It was after midnight before Huth and Douglas Archer got back to Scotland Yard. For the first time Huth was persuaded to go to the office that had been prepared for him on the mezzanine floor. It was a magnificent room, with a view across the Thames to County Hall. Endless trouble had been taken to get the room exactly right, and General Kellerman had inspected it twice that afternoon, showing great concern that the rose-wood desk was polished, the cut-glass light-fitting washed and the carpet cleaned and brushed. There was a new Telefunken TV set ready for the BBC's resumed service that was promised for Christmas. Under it, a panelled cabinet contained Waterford cut glass and a selection of drinks. 'He's sure to like it, isn't he?' Kellerman had asked in that hoarse whisper that Harry Woods could imitate to perfection.

'Anyone would, sir,' said Kellerman's senior staff officer, whom Kellerman liked to call his 'chief of staff'.

'A very nice place,' said Huth sarcastically. 'A very nice place to hide me away so I don't interfere with the workings of the department. Even my phone goes through Kellerman's switchboard, I notice.'

'Is it the location you don't like?' said Douglas.

'Just get rid of all this furniture and junk,' said Huth. 'It looks more like a Victorian brothel than an office. Does Kellerman think I'm going to sit here getting drunk until the TV begins?'

'There is a cable TV connection,' said Douglas. 'It can

53

be used to carry police information; photos of wanted persons and so on.'

'I'll get you a job in the bloody Propaganda Ministry,' said Huth. 'How would you like that?'

'Perhaps I could have time to think about it,' said Douglas, pretending to take it seriously.

'Just get this furniture out of here. I want metal filing-cases, with good locks on them, and a metal desk with locks on the drawers, and a proper desk light, not that damned contraption. You'll be sitting in the adjoining office, so you might as well get whatever you want in there too. Get phones: four direct lines and have your extensions changed to up here. In the corridor I want a table and chair so that my sentry won't have to stand all the while – and where the hell is the sentry?'

'Sentry, sir?'

'Don't stand there repeating everything I say,' said Huth. 'The Peter Thomas murder investigation is part of an operation we have code-named "Apocalypse". No information of any sort – in fact nothing at all – goes outside this room without my written permission, or that of the Reichsführer-SS, Heinrich Himmler. Is that clear?'

'Unforgettably so,' said Douglas, desperately trying to fathom what could be behind it.

Huth smiled. 'In case the unforgettable quality lessens, there will be an armed SS sentry outside in the corridor for twenty-four hours of every day.' Huth looked at his wristwatch. 'He should be on duty now, damn him. Get on the phone to the SS guard commander at Cannon Row. Tell him to send the sentry and half-a-dozen men to clear this furniture out.'

'I doubt if there will be workmen available at this time of night,' said Douglas.

Huth tipped his head back and looked from under his

heavy-lidded eyes. Soon Douglas learned that this was a danger sign. 'Are you making another of your jokes? Or is this some new kind of provocation?'

Douglas shrugged. 'I'll phone.'

'I'll be in the number three conference room with Major Steiger. Tell the SS officer I want all this furniture out of here before I get back. And I want the new furniture installed.'

'Where do I get metal desks?' said Douglas.

Huth turned away as if the question was hardly worth answering. 'Use your initiative, Superintendent. Go along this corridor and, when you see the sort of thing you need, take it.'

'But there will be a terrible row in the morning,' said Douglas. 'They'll all be here moving it back again.'

'And they will find an armed SS sentry preventing them taking anything out of this room on the orders of the Reichsführer-SS. And that includes metal furniture.'

'Very good, sir.'

'In my brief-case you'll find a cardboard tube containing a small painting by Piero della Francesca. Get it framed and hang it on the wall to hide some of this ghastly wallpaper.'

'A real painting by Piero della Francesca?' said Douglas who'd heard amazing stories of the artifacts plundered during the fighting in Poland, France and the Low Countries.

'In a policeman's office, Superintendent Archer? That would hardly be appropriate would it?' He went out without waiting for an answer.

Douglas phoned the SS guard commander, and passed on Huth's message with the friendly rider that Standarten-führer Huth was in a great hurry.

The guard commander's response was one of consternation. Kellerman's briefing about the arrival of the new man was obviously taken seriously by the security force.

Douglas stepped across to the window and looked down at the Embankment. The curfew ensured that few civilians were on the street – Members of Parliament, and shift workers in essential industries and services, were among the exceptions – and the street and bridge were empty except for parked lines of official vehicles and an armed patrol who visited the floodlit perimeters of all the government buildings.

A motor-cycle and side-car combination stopped at the check-point where Victoria Embankment met Westminster Bridge. There was a brief inspection of papers before it roared away into the dark night of the far side of the river. From across the road there came the loud chime of Big Ben. Douglas Archer yawned and wondered how people like Huth seemed to manage without sleep.

He opened Huth's brief-case to get the Francesca reproduction for framing, but before he had time to unroll it he saw, inside the pocket of the case, a brown manila envelope sealed with red wax and bearing the unmistakable heraldic imprint of RSHA – the Central Security Department of the Reich, and holy of holies of Heinrich Himmler and all he commanded. The envelope had already been opened along the side and a folded paper was visible.

Douglas could not repress his curiosity. He pulled out a large sheet of paper and unfolded it to find a complex diagram, as big as the blotter on the desk. It was drawn in black indelible ink upon hand-made paper that was as heavy as parchment. Even Douglas Archer's fluent German did not equip him to comprehend fully the handwriting of the German script, but he recognized some of the symbols.

There was a reversed equilateral triangle, inscribed within a double circle. The triangle contained two words, written to form a cross – Elohim and Tzabaoth. Douglas Archer's successful investigation of a series of Black Magic murders in 1939 enabled him to recognize this as a 'pentacle' representing 'the god of armies, the equilibrium of natural forces, and the harmony of numbers'.

A second pentacle was a human head with three faces, crowned with a tiara and issuing from a vessel filled with water. There were other water signs too. Handwritten alongside it was 'Joliot-Curie laboratory – Collège de France, Paris'. And close against another water sign was written 'Norsk Hydro Company, Rjukan, Central Norway'.

Heaped earth, spades and a diamond pierced by a magic sword 'Deo Duce, comite ferro' was an emblem of the Great Arcanum representing, according to the chart, 'the omnipotence of the adept' and here the runic double lightning of the SS was lettered, and followed by 'RSHA Berlin'.

The third symbol was the spiral marked 'Transformatio' which became a spinning toy top with 'Clarendon Laboratory, Oxford, England' written there, and the words 'Formatio' and 'Reformatio' arranged over 'Transformatio' to make a triangle. Below it 'German army reactor in England' was written against a spinning device. In another hand, 'Peter Thomas' appeared here in pencil, as if added hurriedly at the last moment.

Douglas straightened as he heard the sound of German boots on the mosaic stone of the corridor. He folded the diagram too quickly to be sure that it showed no sign of

57

being tampered with. Then he tucked the envelope away into the red-lined pocket of the case and closed it.

There was a knock at the door. 'Come in,' said Douglas as he unrolled the Francesca reproduction.

'One sentry and six men for duty,' reported the SS officer.

'Standartenführer Huth wants this furniture removed,' explained Douglas. 'Replace it with metal furniture from offices on this corridor.'

The SS officer showed no surprise at the order. Douglas had the feeling that this farmer's son from Hesse – as Douglas accurately guessed him to be – would have obeyed an order to jump out of the window. The officer took off his jacket to work with his six brawny lads while their armed comrade stood on duty in the corridor.

The job was almost finished by the time Harry Woods arrived at 2 A.M. He'd been at the reception at the Savoy. Douglas noticed, with some apprehension, that Harry was slightly drunk.

'Talk about a new broom sweeping clean,' said Harry as he watched furniture being moved. 'I haven't seen this kind of activity since that night when the invasion started.'

'Do you know where we can get this picture framed?' Douglas asked him.

Harry Woods held the edge of the picture and looked at it. It was 'The Flagellation'. Douglas knew the painting – a fine colonnaded piazza, flooded with overhead sunlight from a blue sky. In the background Christ is scourged. Three magnificently attired men – Count of Urbino and his two advisers – turn their backs upon the scene and converse calmly together. In real life, the advisers depicted in the painting were suspected of complicity in the murder of the Count. For centuries art experts have argued about the hidden meaning of the picture. Douglas found it appropriate as a decoration for the office of this hard-eyed emissary from the Byzantine court of the Reichsführer-SS.

'Funny bugger, isn't he?' said Harry, looking at the painting.

'We'd better learn to live with him,' said Douglas.

'He's down in number three conference room,' said Harry, 'talking to that squeaky-voiced little police Major that he took along to the mortuary. Who is he?'

'I've no idea,' said Douglas.

'They're talking together as if the world was about to come to an end.' Harry brought out his cigarettes and offered them to Douglas, who shook his head. It was no longer done to accept a friend's tobacco ration. 'What's it all about, chief?' said Harry. 'You understand all this double-talk. What's it all about?'

'I thought you might be able to tell me, Harry. I saw Sylvia today. She told me that you have a finger in everything that's going on in town.'

If Harry guessed what Sylvia actually said, he gave no sign of it, but he didn't seem surprised that Sylvia had turned up at Scotland Yard. Douglas wondered if she'd seen Harry too.

'I'll tell you one thing,' said Harry. 'That little Major is nothing to do with pathology or medicine or anything like that. I'd like to know why he was at the mortuary. Do you think this bloke Huth let him come along just for a laugh?'

'You'll soon find out that our new Standartenführer is not that keen on laughs,' said Douglas.

'There are some bloody peculiar people about, you know that. I mean, letting that little wireless mechanic come along there was wrong. And I'd tell Huth that straight, and to his face. I'd tell him it was all bloody

59

wrong. You think I wouldn't but I'd tell him.' Harry swayed slightly and steadied himself by gripping the desk.

'Wireless mechanic?'

'Hah!' said Harry with the arch smugness of the slightly drunk. 'I saw his file. He's got a police uniform but that's just for show. I phoned Lufthansa, and got his number from the flight manifest, then I went upstairs and looked up his record.'

'You got his file?'

'Just his card. Say you work for the Gestapo and you can get any bloody thing. Do you know that, Douglas?'

'You *don't* work for the Gestapo,' Douglas pointed out.

Harry waved his hand in front of his face as if trying to remove a speck from a dirty windscreen. 'Wireless mechanic, it said, a doctor of wireless theory. They're all bloody doctors these Huns, have you noticed that, Douglas? . . . Studied at Tübingen. Only came into the police service one year ago, straight from lecturing at Munich.'

'Wireless mechanics don't study at Tübingen and lecture at Munich,' persisted Douglas.

'All right, all right, all right,' said Harry. 'I haven't got your command of the German language but I can find my way through a record card.' Harry gave Douglas a sly smile and, like a stage conjurer producing a rabbit from a hat, he pulled a record card from his inside pocket. 'There you are, old lad, read it for yourself.'

Douglas took it, and read it in silence.

'Come on, Super, give us a smile. You're wrong and you know it.'

'The Major,' said Douglas, speaking slowly so that he could think about it himself, 'is a physicist, an expert on radio-active substances. He was a lecturer on nuclear physics.'

'You've lost me,' said Harry, rubbing his nose.

'Those burns on the dead man's arm,' said Douglas. 'Sir John didn't mention those last night. Perhaps the little Major went there to examine them.'

'From a sun-lamp?'

'Not from a sun-lamp, Harry. Those burns were bad ones, the sort of skin damage a man would suffer if he was exposed to the rays that come from radium, or something like that.'

There was another knock at the door. The SS guard commander came to say that SS Signals wished to report that four new telephone lines were connected and tested. No sooner had he said so than Huth's direct line rang. Douglas picked up the phone on his desk and said, 'Standartenführer Huth's office, Detective Superintendent Archer speaking.'

'Archer – oh, splendid. General Kellerman here. Is the Standartenführer with you?' Douglas looked at his watch. That Kellerman should be telephoning here at this time was amazing. He was not noted for his long working hours.

'He's in number three conference room, General,' said Douglas.

'Yes, so I understand.' There was a long pause. 'Unfortunately he's left orders that no calls should be put through to him there. That doesn't apply to me of course but I don't wish to make the operator's life too difficult, and there seems to be something wrong with the phone in the conference room.'

Douglas realized that Huth had given the phone operator the 'direct orders of the Reichsführer' stuff, and then left the phone off the hook, but he had every reason to help the General save face. 'The phone is probably out of use because the Signals staff have been changing the phone lines.'

'What?' shouted Kellerman in shrill alarm. 'At this time of night? What are you talking about?' He changed to German and became more authoritative. 'Look here. What is this about changing phones in my office? Explain what's been happening. Explain immediately!'

'Purely routine changes, General,' said Douglas. 'The Standartenführer preferred that Sergeant Woods and myself were accommodated in the clerk's office next to his. This meant putting in extra lines for us and bringing our outside line up here – it's usual to keep an outside number unchanged during the process of an inquiry . . . informants and so on.'

From somewhere near the General's elbow there came the petulant murmur of complaint. It was youthful and feminine, and Douglas found no resemblance to the voice of the General's wife, who had flown from Croydon to Breslau to see her mother the previous week.

'Oh, routine, you say,' said Kellerman hurriedly. 'Then that is in order.' He paused with the phone capped at his end. Then he said, 'Have you been with the Standarten-führer this evening?'

'I have, sir,' said Douglas.

'What exactly is the problem, Superintendent? He never arrived at the Savoy, you know.'

'The Standartenführer has a great deal of urgent work outstanding, General,' said Douglas.

At that moment Huth entered the room. He looked at Harry Woods who was resting against the desk with his eyes closed. Then Huth looked at Douglas and raised his eyebrows quizzically.

At the other end of the phone, General Kellerman said,

'Do you think I should come over there, Superintendent Archer? I can rely upon a loyal and conscientious officer like you to assess the situation.'

Huth had walked over to his desk and now stood with head bent towards the earpiece of the phone.

'I'm sure that the General . . .' Huth tried to grab the phone but Douglas held on to it long enough to say, 'The Standartenführer has just come in, sir.'

Huth took the phone, cleared his throat and said, 'Huth here, General Kellerman. What is it you want?'

'I'm so pleased to locate you at last, my dear Huth. I want to tell you – '

Huth interrupted Kellerman's greeting. 'You're in a nice warm house, General, in a nice warm bed, with a nice warm woman. You stay there and let me continue my work without interruption.'

'It's simply that my switchboard couldn't seem – ' the phone clicked as Huth dropped the earpiece back on to its rest.

Huth looked at Douglas. 'Who gave you permission to discuss the workings of this office with an outsider?'

'But it was General Kellerman . . .'

'How do you know who it was? It was just a voice on the phone. I'm reliably informed that your drunken friend here . . .' he jabbed a thumb at where Harry Woods was blinking at him, '. . . can manage a fairly convincing imitation of General Kellerman's English.'

No one spoke. Any of Harry Woods's previously stated intentions to tell Huth straight about the decorum of having the little Major along to the mortuary had been put aside for another time.

Huth tossed his peaked cap on to the hook behind the door and sat down. 'I've told you once, and now I'll tell you for the last time. You'll discuss the work of this office with no one at all. In theory you can speak freely with the Reichsführer-SS, Heinrich Himmler.' Huth leaned forward with his stick and jabbed Harry Woods playfully. 'You know who that is, Sergeant? Heinrich Himmler?'

'Yes,' growled Harry.

'But that's only in theory. In practice you won't even tell him anything, unless I'm present. Or if I'm dead, and providing you've satisfied yourselves personally that my life is extinct. Right?'

'Right,' said Douglas quickly, fearing that Harry Woods was working himself up to a physical assault upon Huth who was now waving his stick in the air.

'Any breach of this instruction,' said Huth, 'is not only a capital offence under section 134 of the Military Orders of the Commander-in-Chief Great Britain, for which the penalty is a firing squad, but also a capital offence under section 11 of your own Emergency Powers (German Occupation) Act 1941, for which they hang offenders at Wandsworth Prison.'

'Would the shooting or the hanging come first?' said Douglas.

'We must always leave something for the jury to decide,' said Huth.

Chapter Eight

Long ago Seven Dials had been a district noted for vice, crime and violence. Now it was no more than a shabby backwater of London's theatre-land. Douglas Archer got to know this region, and its inhabitants, during his time as a uniformed police Inspector, but he little thought that one day he would live here.

When Archer's suburban house – situated between two prongs of the German panzer thrust at London – had been demolished, Mrs Sheenan had offered him and his child bed and board. Her husband, a peacetime policeman, was an army reservist. Captured at Calais the previous year he was now in a POW camp near Bremen, with no promised date of release.

The table was laid for breakfast when Douglas Archer got back to Monmouth Street and the little house over the oil-shop. Mrs Sheenan's son, Bob, and young Douggie were being dressed in front of a blazing fire, in a room garlanded with damp laundry. Douglas recognized the striped towel that cloaked his son. It was one of the few items he'd managed to salvage from the wreckage of his house in Cheam. It brought back happy memories that he would have preferred to forget.

'Hello, Dad! Did you work all night? Is it a murder?'

'It's a murder in an antique shop, isn't it, Mr Archer?'

'That's right.'

'There told you so, Douggie,' said young Sheenan. 'It said so in the newspapers.'

'Hold still,' said Mrs Sheenan as she finished buttoning

her son's cardigan. Douglas helped her dress young Douggie. That finished, she reached for a pan on the hob. 'You like them soft-boiled, don't you, Mr Archer?' She kept their relationship at that formal stage.

'I've had my eggs this week, Mrs Sheenan,' said Douglas. 'Two of them fried on Sunday morning – remember?'

The woman scooped the boiled eggs with a bent spoon and put them into the egg cups. 'My neighbour got these from her relatives in the country. She let me have six because I gave her your old grey sweater to unravel for the wool. All the eggs should be yours really.'

Douglas suspected that this was just a way of letting him have an unfair share of her own rations but he started to eat the egg. There was a plateful of bread on the table too, with a small cube of margarine, the printed wrapper of which declared it to be a token of friendship from German workers. What about a gesture of friendship from German farmers, said the wags who preferred butter.

'Suppose there was a murder in a French aeroplane flying over Germany, and the murderer was Italian and the man murdered was . . .' Bob thought for a moment '. . . Brazilian.'

'Don't speak with your mouth full,' said his mother. On the radio the announcer played a Strauss waltz, requested by a German soldier stationed in Cardiff. Mrs Sheenan switched the music down.

'Or Chinese!' said Bob.

'Don't pester the Superintendent. You can see he's trying to eat his breakfast in peace.'

'That would be for the lawyers to decide,' he told Bob. 'I'm only a policeman. I just have to find out who did it.'

'Mrs Sheenan is going to take us to the Science Museum on Saturday,' said Douggie.

'That's very nice of her,' said Douglas. 'Be a good boy and do as she tells you.'

'He always does,' said the woman. 'They both do; they're both good boys.' She looked at Douglas. 'You look tired,' she said.

'I'm just getting my second wind.'

'You're not going back there again, without a rest?'

'It's a murder inquiry,' said Douglas. 'I must.'

'Told you so, told you so, told you so!' shouted Bob. 'It's a murder! Told you so!'

'Quiet, boys,' said Mrs Sheenan.

'I have a car here,' said Douglas, 'I'll pass the school – in about half an hour – will that be all right?'

'A car. Have you been promoted?'

'I have a new boss,' said Douglas. 'He says he likes his men to have the best of everything. His own car has a wireless in it. He can send messages straight to Scotland Yard while he's driving along.'

'Listen to that!' said Bob. He pretended to use the phone. 'Calling Scotland Yard. This is Bob Sheenan calling Scotland Yard. Like that, Superintendent? Does it work like that?'

'It's morse code,' explained Douglas. 'The wireless operator has to be able to use a morse key but he can receive speech messages.'

'What will they think of next?' said Mrs Sheenan.

'Can we see your car?' said Bob. 'Is it a Flying Standard?'

'The police have all sorts of cars, don't they, Dad?'

'All sorts.'

'Can we go to the window and look at it?'

'Finish your bread and then you can.'

67

With whoops of joy the two children went into the front room and raised the window to look down into the street at the car.

'The bath water is still warm,' said Mrs Sheenan. 'Only the boys have used it.' She looked away, embarrassed. Like so many people, she found the social degradation of the new sort of poverty more difficult to bear than its deprivations.

'That would make a new man of me,' said Douglas, although in fact the new changing rooms at the Yard had baths, and hot water in abundance.

'There's a bolt on the scullery door,' she said. 'Are you sure you won't get into trouble taking us to the school?'

'It will be all right.'

'The regulations about the misuse of fuel are horrifying. That manager in the coal office in Neal Street was sentenced to death. I read that in the *Evening News* last night.'

'It will be all right,' said Douglas.

She smiled contentedly. 'It's more than a year since I was in a motor-car. My Uncle Tom's funeral. That was before the war – seems like a hundred years ago, doesn't it?'

Mrs Sheenan came and sat near the fire, and looked at it as it burned. 'The wood is almost finished,' she said, 'but the oil-shop man will lend me a few more logs until the new ration period starts next week.'

Her voice made Douglas start, for the food, the hot tea and the warmth of the fire had caused him to close his eyes and nod off.

'There's something I have to bother you with, Mr Archer,' she said.

Douglas reached into his pocket.

'Not money,' she said. 'I can manage on what you give

me, and the supplementary ration card you get makes a wonderful difference.' She put out a hand and mechanically felt the heat of the tea-pot under its knitted cosy. 'The two boys have an extra hour's music lesson on Tuesdays and Thursdays. It's only a shilling a week and they seem to like it.'

Douglas knew that she'd originally started to say something different but he didn't press her. Instead he closed his eyes again.

'More tea?'

'No thanks.'

'It's the German ersatz. They say it's made for them to have with lemon. It's not very nice with milk is it?'

She disappeared behind the hanging gardens of damp garments, touching each of them to see how they were drying. She turned some of the garments round. 'The woman down the street saw an ambulance train going through Clapham Junction last Monday. Carriages crowded with wounded soldiers – dirty looking and with torn uniforms – and two red cross coaches on the back, the sort they have for stretcher cases.' She put the pegs in her mouth while she rehung a child's pyjama top. 'Is there still fighting?'

'I'd be careful whom you tell that to, Mrs Sheenan.'

'She wouldn't make up stories – she's a sensible woman.'

'I know,' said Douglas.

'I wouldn't tell strangers, Mr Archer – but I always feel I can say anything to you.'

'In the towns it's just bombs and murdering German soldiers. In the country districts there are bigger groups, who ambush German motorized patrols. But I doubt if they will survive the winter.'

'Because of the cold?'

'You can't light fires, because of the smoke. The leaves come off the trees, and so there's no concealment, no cover. And in winter the spotting planes can see a man's tracks better on the ground – and if it snows . . .' Douglas raised his hands.

'Those poor boys,' said Mrs Sheenan. 'They say it's terrible in the unoccupied zone now, with the winter not even started. Shortages of everything.' She hovered over Douglas and he knew she had something to tell him. Like any good policeman he let her take her time about it.

'This music master who does the lessons – he's very young, wounded in the war and everything, so I wouldn't like to complain about him,' she paused, 'but he was asking the boys a lot of questions, and I knew you wouldn't like it.'

Douglas was suddenly wide awake. 'Questions? What sort of questions?'

'Yesterday afternoon at the music lesson. They have a proper gramophone and loudspeakers, and everything to play the music – it's music appreciation really – and he has someone to work it, that's why it costs the extra shilling.'

Douglas nodded. 'What's his name?'

'I don't know, Mr Archer. Your Doug told me afterwards that the teacher was asking about you – what time you got home and so on. I didn't want to question Douggie too much about it. You know how sensitive he is, and what with losing his mother . . . sometimes I could cry for the little love.' She smiled suddenly and shook her head. 'I'm probably being a silly old woman. I should never have worried you about it.'

'You did right,' said Douglas. 'Questions, you say?'

'Oh, nothing like that – rest your mind. He's not that sort of man at all. I can spot those sort of men a mile off.'

'What then?'

'I think he wanted to know if you liked the Germans.'
She stood up and straightened her hair, looking in the
mirror. 'I don't want to get either of them into trouble.
And I know you wouldn't either. But if something happened to you or your Douggie, how would I be able to
live with myself if I'd not told you?'

'You're a sensible woman, Mrs Sheenan. I wish I had a
few more police officers as sensible as you are. Now tell
me more about these two teachers.'

'Only one's a teacher, the other just helps with the
music. They're from the war – officers I should think,
both wounded; one has lost his arm.'

'Which arm?'

'The right one. And he used to play the piano before
the war. Isn't it a terrible thing, and he can't be more
than twenty-five, if that.'

'I'll have that bath now, Mrs Sheenan. You get the
boys ready and I'll take you to the school in about fifteen
minutes' time.'

She got the children's raincoats from the cupboard.
One of them was threadbare. 'Bob's raincoat was stolen
from the cloakroom last week. He's back to wearing this
old one again. I've told the boys to take their coats into
the classroom in future. There are some terrible people
about, Mr Archer, but there, you must know that better
than any of us.'

'This fellow had a false arm, you say?'

'No, his arm is missing, poor boy.'

71

Chapter Nine

When Douglas returned to Scotland Yard, having dropped the others at the school, he sought out a young police officer named Jimmy Dunn, and got permission to use him on plain-clothes duty. PC Dunn was keen to get into CID. He'd proved a good detective for Archer on previous cases.

'Find out what you can about this music teacher,' Douglas said. 'Political? Sexual? Someone with a grudge against coppers? I don't want to do it myself because it sounds like he'd recognize me.'

'Leave it to me, sir,' said Dunn who could hardly wait to get started.

'Might be just a crank,' said Douglas. 'Might be nothing at all.'

Happily, Jimmy Dunn began tidying up his desk. He only tolerated his job with Assistant Commissioner Administration because his office on the mezzanine was so close to the Murder Squad and Flying Squad teams.

'Oh, and Jimmy . . .' said Douglas as he was turning to leave. 'There's a million to one chance that this one-armed fellow might be connected with the Peter Thomas murder. I think you'd better draw a pistol from our friends downstairs. I'll give you a chit.'

'A pistol?'

Douglas had to smile. 'Take something small, Jimmy, something you can tuck away out of sight. And keep it out of sight, unless you have to defend yourself. We can't be too careful nowadays. There are too many guns in this

72

town at present, and there's the devil of a row if someone loses one.'

In the new office on the other side of the building Douglas found Harry Woods valiantly telling lies to all-comers to cover Douglas's absence. General Kellerman's office had been asking for Douglas since nine o'clock that morning.

From Whitehall came the constant sound of workmen hammering. Berlin had announced that, to celebrate the friendship between Nazi Germany and the Union of Soviet Socialist Republics, a week of Kameradschaft would be celebrated in all parts of the two vast empires. It was to begin the following Sunday, when in London, units of the Red Army and Navy, complete with band and choir, were to combine with the Wehrmacht for a march through town.

The whole route was being decorated, but Whitehall and Parliament Square was coming in for special treat-ment. As well as hundreds of flags, there were heraldic shields bearing entwined hammer, sickle and swastika surmounting a small Cross of St George which had now replaced the Union Flag for all official purposes in the occupied zone.

Hitler had provided the Red Fleet with anchorages at Rosyth and Scapa Flow as well as Invergordon. Goeb-bels's Propaganda Ministry said that this was a natural outcome of the bonds of friendship that drew these two great peoples together. Cynics said it was Hitler's way of putting some Russians between him and the Americans.

In spite of all the extra work that the German/Soviet Friendship Week would give Scotland Yard, General Kellerman remained his usual genial unhurried self. Even when he returned from a conference at the Feld Komman-dantur with a brief-case loaded with FK-Befehle he was able to laugh about the way these reams of printed orders about the Friendship Week required the full-time attention of a roomful of clerks.

The proliferating orders coming from the Military Commander GB (and the Military Administration Chief GB who supervised the British puppet government and the German officials) were a sign of growing fear that the Friendship Week might become the occasion for violent demonstration. And yet the intense rivalry – not to say hatred – that the German army Generals felt for Himmler's SS organization, and police affiliates, determined the army to ask from General Kellerman no more than the normal police requirements.

'What do you think?' General Kellerman asked Douglas. 'You can be quite frank with me, Superintendent, you know that.'

Kellerman spread out on his desk that morning's newspapers. They all headlined the Friendship Week announcement from Berlin. There was a certain irony in the way that the official Nazi newspaper in London, *Die Englische Zeitung*, did little more than print the official announcement verbatim, within a decorative box on the front page. The *Daily Worker*, on the other hand, devoted four pages to it – 'Britain's Workers Say Forward' with photos of the Russian and British officials who would be present at the saluting base. Stalin had already penned a suitable message. Those who remembered the congratulations Stalin sent to Hitler after the fall of France found his latest missive no less fulsome.

'Will there be trouble?' asked Kellerman.

'From whom?' said Douglas.

Kellerman chuckled. 'The regime has enemies, Superintendent.' He scratched his head as if trying to remember who they were. 'And not all of them are on the General

Staff.' Kellerman smiled, enjoying his joke. Douglas was not sure whether he was expected to participate in this gross defamation of the German high command. He nodded as if not quite understanding.

'There will be a lot of extra work for us,' said Kellerman. 'Berlin insists that the army line the entire route with soldiers. I should think there will be precious few left to march in the procession.' He chuckled again. There seemed to be nothing to compare with the German army in trouble to put General Kellerman in a light-hearted mood. 'And they plan to have Gendarmerie units every three hundred metres. How will they manage?'

'And the Metropolitan Force?'

'Normal police duties except for the issuing of movement passes.'

'How will that work, sir?'

'London Outer-Ring residents will be permitted to come into Central London each day for that week only. Local police stations will be issuing the passes, I'm afraid. Daily passes.'

Douglas nodded. It was easy to imagine the chaos that was going to descend upon suburban police stations. Half London had close relatives they could not visit because of the travel restrictions. 'It would cut the work by half if the police stations could issue some passes for the whole week.' Kellerman looked up and stared at him. Douglas added, 'They would only be issued in the case of proved compassionate necessity.'

Kellerman looked at him for a long time before his face relaxed into a slight, inscrutable smile. 'Of course, Superintendent. Only in the case of . . . what was it – proved compassionate necessity.' Kellerman picked up the FK-Befehle and found the paragraphs referring to the issuing of passes. 'I see no reason why I couldn't introduce that provision into the orders.' He smiled at Douglas. They both knew that this would provide a loophole, by means of which the local police stations would cut their work-load drastically.

'And the passes would make such splendid souvenirs,' said Kellerman. 'I'll have a designer from the Propaganda Department work on it. Lots of decorations, with only the barest minimum of printing on the counterfoil.'

'Yes, sir,' said Douglas. That would be a way of preventing the Wehrmacht doing any proper analysis of the counterfoils.

'None of this should affect you personally, of course, but I always value your views on these matters.'

'Thank you, sir,' said Douglas.

'I know that your work with the Standartenführer is of special interest to the Reichsführer-SS. I've therefore taken it upon myself to excuse you all other duties.'

'That's very considerate, General.'

'You look tired, Superintendent. I suppose you got to bed rather late?'

'I haven't been to bed at all, sir.'

'Well, that's dreadful! I can't allow that. Not even a brilliant young officer such as Standartenführer Huth can be permitted to totally exhaust my officers. Especially one of the most able officers I have in my entire command.'

'The General is most gracious and generous.'

Kellerman walked over to the tiny turret appendage of his room. 'Have you seen that?' Douglas followed him. They looked at Westminster Bridge; gangs of painters were colouring it gold. Red flags and swastikas were being fixed along a scaffolding some three metres tall. Douglas guessed that this was a means of concealing bridge, river and roadway; probably because it would be used to concentrate mobile Gendarmerie units on both road and river, ready to move to any trouble spot.

'Do you like it?' said Kellerman. Douglas recalled a quotation from the Classics about building for your enemies a golden bridge but decided against mentioning this to Kellerman.

'I'm a Londoner,' said Douglas. 'I like things to stay the way they always have been.'

'I like an officer who speaks his mind,' said Kellerman. 'I want you to remember, Superintendent Archer, that you are an important man here at Scotland Yard. Any suggestion, any complaint would carry a lot of weight with the people at the top.' Kellerman got his humidor and opened it. This time he didn't go through the ritual of lighting a cigar for him. Douglas had the idea that Kellerman was treating him differently from the way he'd been treated at all their previous meetings.

Kellerman waited while Douglas selected, cut and lit his own cigar. Then, when it was well alight, he said, 'More influence than perhaps you realize, Superintendent Archer. Berlin congratulated us on the crime figures. You played a major part in those, you know.'

'Only the homicide,' said Douglas.

'And who do you think reads beyond the murders? Police forces, and their commanders . . .' he grinned and scratched his pink cheek, 'are judged according to the proportions of murders solved. No one worries about the really important crime – fraud, sabotage, arson, robbery, blackmail and so on. No, they concern themselves with murder, the only crime seldom committed by criminals. So you chaps in the Murder Squad are damned important, and that's why cunning old foxes, like me, make sure that the best detectives are assigned to homicide cases.'

'I see, sir,' said Douglas doubtfully.

'The point I'm making, Superintendent, is that I will back you through thick and thin. Remember that. If you are happy working with this new fellow Huth – fine. But if any difficulties arise, come and see me and I'll give him another officer.'

'Thank you, General. I've no complaints.'

'You're not the sort who complains, Superintendent. I know that well enough. But my door is always open . . . Open to you, that is.'

'Thank you, sir.'

Douglas reeled out of Kellerman's office, light-headed from the loss of sleep, sweet cigar smoke and the rich diet of flattery.

Harry Woods was snowed under by paperwork when Douglas returned to the office. The Gendarmerie had had no idea that the Peter Thomas murder might come into Wehrmacht jurisdiction until Harry Woods had arrived with a handful of Luftwaffe petrol coupons, and a written statement mentioning the Feldwebel and his black-market activities.

The military police and their civil counterparts were usually able to come to terms with this sort of crime, and in the usual course of events this matter would have probably been handled by the police unit best able to investigate the most serious part of the crime. In this case the Metropolitan CID would have been asked to investigate the murder.

But then came the top priority teleprinter message from Oberkommando der Wehrmacht, Berlin, instructing, with lots of Streng Geheim, Chef Sache and so on, that all files, documents and memoranda should be passed to SS-Standartenführer Huth at Scotland Yard.

Everyone informed of this new development knew that to deny that they had any files, documents or even

78

memoranda would be interpreted at best as an indication of sloth and incompetence, at worst as a wilful refusal to obey this order from the most exalted levels of command.

In the circumstances it was unreasonable of Harry Woods to curse the men who were transferring to him virtually empty files, blank filing cards and meaningless dockets, every one of which was registered as very secret and so required faultless paperwork that the sender could produce, should the subject be raised again.

Douglas helped Harry Woods sort out some of the most difficult ones. Many of the forms, printed in German, were new to both men. Douglas had one of the porters bring them tea and sandwiches, and they worked through the lunchtime. They always got on well together when they were working, and Harry Woods was, for a time, his old self. There was no sign of Huth. A message said he was in conference, but Harry said he was probably in bed and asleep.

It was two-thirty that afternoon when the phone call came from PC Jimmy Dunn. 'I've seen the man, sir,' Dunn told Douglas. 'I didn't speak with him of course but he met his friend the music-teacher for lunch today at the school. He's due to be at the music class there this afternoon, the headmaster said. John Spode his name is.'

'Good work, Jimmy,' said Douglas.

'He's not a teacher, he just got himself a termporary job there on a day-to-day basis. I got his address from the school. I said I was from the Education Authority but I'm not sure they believed me. Then I went to look at his rooms. It's a broken-down old place in Mafeking Street, Marylebone, not far from the school. No proper locks on the doors, and the caretaker was out, so I walked in and looked round.'

'And?'

79

'Two rooms, and share a bathroom. Not bad really, considering the way things are. It's a bit grubby but there is a lovely little inlaid desk and some pictures on the wall that look as though they are worth a bit of money. I mean, art and antiques are not in my line, sir, but these things are old-looking but in very good condition. And I think that's usually a sign things are worth something.'

'But he's clean?'

'Well I haven't turned him over, sir. But he's clean I'd say: clean but not kosher.'

This had become the English policeman's way of describing offences to which he would turn a blind eye.

'Stay there, Jimmy,' said Douglas. 'I'll come over and have a look round myself.'

Chapter Ten

The top storey of the house had been burned out by incendiary bombs, and Douglas could see through empty spaces that had once been windows, to charred rafters criss-crossing the sky. The ground floor windows were boarded up, the high price of glass made that a common sight in this neighbourhood. The suspect's rooms were on the second floor. Jimmy Dunn led the way.

He'd rightly described the furniture as valuable. There was enough in this room to keep a man for a decade, a choicer selection by far than the items for sale in the Shepherd Market antique shop.

'Still no sign of the caretaker?' said Douglas.

'There's a bottle of milk outside his door. Looks like he's been out all night – missed curfew and stayed overnight perhaps.'

Douglas nodded. Breaching German regulations – which required special permission for anyone, except the registered occupiers, to stay in a house overnight – was common enough.

'Is there something funny about this place, Jimmy? Or am I just getting too old.'

'In what way, sir?'

'Valuable antiques in this room, and a cracked soap-holder in the bath; priceless carpet on the floor and dirty sheets on the bed.'

'Perhaps he's a miser, sir.'

'Misers don't buy soap at all,' said Douglas. It was a silly answer but he knew this wasn't the squalor of the niggard. 'Smell the moth-balls?' Douglas got down on his hands and knees, and sniffed the carpet, but that had not been wrapped with moth-balls. 'It's been in a store room,' said Douglas, getting to his feet and brushing his hands to remove the dust. 'That would be my guess.' Douglas began going through the small chest of drawers, turning over a few shirts and underclothes, most of them British army issue. 'There *must* be something more personal here,' said Douglas as he rummaged, '. . . ration books, discharge papers, pension book or something.'

'A lot of people carry all those sort of things with them,' said Dunn. 'There's so much house-breaking. And it takes so long to get papers replaced.'

'And yet he leaves all these valuables, without even a decent lock on the door?' Douglas opened the next drawer, and went through it carefully. 'Ah! Now what's this?' Under the newspaper that lined the drawer, his fingers found an envelope. Inside it he found half-a-dozen photos; Spode's parents standing in a suburban garden somewhere, with two young children. A child on a tricycle. 'A man finds it difficult to throw these kind of souvenirs away, Jimmy,' he told the Constable. 'Even when his life is at stake, it's difficult to throw away your family.' The next photo depicted a bride and groom. It was a snapshot, slightly out of focus.

Douglas looked through all the pictures. The largest one was an old press-photo; sharp, contrasty, and well printed on glossy paper. It was of a group of laboratory workers, in white coats, standing round an elderly man. He turned the photo over to read the caption. Rubber stamps gave the date reference number and warned that the photo was the copyright of a picture agency. The tattered typewritten caption-paper said, 'Today Professor Frick celebrated his seventieth birthday. With him at his laboratory were the team who worked with him when, last year, his experiments brought him world-wide acclaim. By bombarding uranium with neutrons to form barium and krypton gas, he proved previous theories about the disintegration of the uranium nucleus.'

It was hardly the stuff of which newspaper headlines are made. The names of the scientists were also listed. They were meaningless except for the names 'Dr John Spode and Dr William Spode'. Douglas turned the photo over to study the faces of the men squinting into the sun on that peaceful day so long ago. 'Is that our man?' he asked Dunn.

'Yes, sir,' said Dunn. 'That's him all right.'

'Christ! This one next to him is the dead man in that Shepherd Market murder!'

'Shall I ask the photo agency if they have a record of anyone buying an extra print of this photo?' said Dunn. 'It's been sent here to this address.'

'It's worth a go,' said Douglas. He made another circuit of the room; walls, cupboard, floorboards, all without marks of recent disturbance. Nothing hidden in the cistern of the WC, only accumulated filth on the cupboard tops, and dust under the carpet.

Douglas looked at the big kitchen table that had been pushed into a corner to make more room. He felt underneath to be sure that nothing was hidden there by means of sticky-tape. Then he knelt down and looked under it too. 'Look at that, Jimmy,' he said.

Like most kitchen tables it had a cutlery drawer, and this one was concealed by the way the table was pushed against the wall. Together they heaved the heavy table aside until there was enough room to open the drawer.

It was a big drawer. In it there were a few spoons and forks, and a broken egg beater, but occupying most of the space there was an arm. It was a right arm made of lightweight unpainted alloy that had come to pieces after a nut and bolt had loosened. Douglas knew exactly the part it needed, and, with the stagecraft of an amateur conjurer, he took it from his pocket and held it in place.

Dunn gave the low appreciative whistle that was obviously expected of him.

'That's enough for me,' said Douglas. 'That came from the scene of the murder. I wonder if it was loosened in a struggle?'

'The Peter Thomas shooting?'

'We can start calling it the William Spode shooting from now on, Jimmy.' He put the piece back into his pocket and replaced the false arm in the drawer. There was a paper bag there too. He looked inside it and found a well worn, but well cared for, Leica camera. There were some accessories too; extension rings, filters, lens hoods and a set of four legs, tied together with string to which was also tied a large ringlike holder for them. 'Worth a few pennies, that lot,' said Douglas. They replaced the things and moved the table back against the wall.

'Leica cameras have become a second currency,' said Dunn. 'I know a man who's invested his life savings in a couple of dozen of them.'

'Sounds like a dangerous investment,' said Douglas.

'But so is paper money,' said Dunn. 'So you think the dead man was mis-identified?'

'We'll never prove it was deliberate,' said Douglas. 'They'll all insist that they did it in good faith. But I'd bet my month's tobacco ration that they were lying.'

'Why, sir?'

'Too many witnesses telling me the same thing, Jimmy.'

'Perhaps because it was the truth, sir.'

'The truth is never exactly the same thing,' said Douglas. 'You say this fellow Spode is at the school this afternoon?'

'Should be,' agreed Dunn. 'Are we going round there?'

'I'll phone Central first,' said Douglas. 'I think my new boss will want to get into the act.'

Douglas Archer's prediction proved correct. Standartenführer Huth, in the words of Harry Woods, provided 'a typical example of SS bullshit'.

Chapter Eleven

Beech Road School was the same sort of grim Victorian fortress in which so many London children spent their days. On one side there was a semi-derelict church, a paved part of its graveyard provided the recreation yard for the school. What a place to consign a child to waste away a precious youth, thought Douglas. Poor little Douggie.

A tea-shop faced the school. In other times it had been a cosy little den, smelling of Woodbine cigarettes, buttered toast and condensed milk. Douglas remembered it from when he was a young detective, its counter buried under slabs of bread pudding; heavy as lead and dark as thunder. Now the tea-urn, its plating worn brassy, provided only ersatz tea, and there wasn't enough warmth in the place to glaze its window with condensation.

'We have four platoons of infantry in reserve,' Huth told Douglas. 'I'm keeping them out of sight. The rest of the men have the block surrounded.' Douglas went to the door of the café and looked out. The men were in full combat order, from battle-smocks to stick grenades in the belt. There were lorries in Lisson Grove, and standing alongside them were the mass-arrest teams, complete with folding tables, portable typewriters and boxes of handcuffs.

Douglas knew that it was official German policy to make 'the enforcement of law and order a demonstration of the resources available to the occupying power' but he didn't expect this.

'You should have let me do this alone,' Douglas told Huth.

'I want to show these people that we mean business,' he replied. 'Let's go and get him, shall we?'

The men walked across the road. A soldier laughed. Douglas looked back to where the assault teams were standing together in those relaxed postures that soldiers assume the moment they're given the chance. He wondered if the SS soldiers would obey an order to open fire on the school. If he knew anything of children, they'd be pressing their noses against the windows by now – or fretting for permission to do so. Anxiously he looked for his son's face but didn't see him.

As they stepped into the entrance hall, a fussy porter came to greet them. There was a false calm in the air, as if the school had been ordered to ignore the military activity in the street outside.

'What can I do for you, gentlemen?' said the porter.

'Get out of my way!' said Huth. 'Where's the head-master – hiding under his desk?'

Douglas said to Huth, 'Standartenführer, this man is the subject of my inquiries. I must insist that his civil rights are not infringed. I will be the one to take him into custody.'

Huth smiled. 'We're not going to shoot him "while he tries to escape" if that's what your little speech is about.' He stepped forward, opened the swing doors through which the porter had disappeared, and shouted, 'Hurry yourself, headmaster, damn you!' into the dim corridors. Then he turned back to Douglas Archer and said, 'Too many questions remain unanswered for him to be endangered at this stage of the game.'

The headmaster arrived in a fast walk that would not have disgraced an athlete. 'Now what is the meaning of this interruption?' he asked in the sort of voice Douglas had not heard since he was at school.

Huth turned to look at the headmaster. Then he took his silver-topped stick and reached forward until it touched the man's chest. 'Don't,' said Huth, pausing for a long time during which the silence was broken only by the headmaster's heavy breathing, '. . . talk to me . . .' Huth spoke very slowly, prodding him to emphasize the most important words, '. . . or to my police officers like that. It provides a poor example for your pupils.'

The headmaster's eyes popped open very wide, and the measured speech, and dignified tone, gave way to a gabble. 'Is this about the Spode fellow? Wish I'd never given him a job. He's been nothing but trouble, and I'm not sure he's been loyal to me . . .'

'Where is he?' said Huth, still speaking as if to a small child.

'Spode?'

'Who else could I mean? Do you think I'd pop in and consult you about the whereabouts of Reichsmarschall Göring?' – a long pause – '. . . or about the whereabouts of the King of England, the Queen and the two Princesses?'

'No, indeed. Very amusing, Herr Colonel. The King . . . well, ha, ha! I know the King is at Windsor with the Royal Family and they are all in very good health. I read the bulletin about that, and I make sure that all my staff know I won't tolerate the disgraceful rumours about His Majesty being confined in the Tower of London.'

'Where's Spode?' said Huth, easing his hat back a fraction on his head, as though the head-band was constricting him.

'Spode?' A nervous smile. 'Spode? Well you know where he is. He's at the police station.' Another smile that, as he watched Huth, became a frown. 'Isn't he? An official came this morning and asked for Spode's home address.' Huth raised an eyebrow at Douglas who nodded affirmation. The headmaster watched the exchange anxiously, and then continued, 'Naturally I helped in every possible way, and don't imagine that I pry into your way of doing things. I don't. Before the war I had holidays in Germany. I admired the system – still do, of course, especially in Germany . . . or rather that's not to say I don't admire the system in England . . .'

Douglas moved across the hall to where PC Dunn was waiting. 'Better pop back there and get that false arm, Jimmy, and the photos and stuff.'

'Control yourself, you wretch,' said Huth. 'Where is this man Spode?'

'I've told you, Herr Oberst. The police station phoned and wanted him. Of course I gave him permission to leave his class.'

'Who took the phone call, headmaster?'

'My secretary. I sent for Spode immediately and let the police talk to him. There is only the one phone, you see.'

'How long ago?'

The headmaster looked at his watch, tapped it and put it to his ear. 'About an hour ago.'

Huth went to the main doors, stepped outside and blew two short blasts on his whistle. Infantry doubled across the recreation yard with a loud clatter of tipped boots. They formed up before Huth as if on parade, their officer in front of them with his hand raised in what the English were learning to call the German Salute.

'Take this fool into special custody and hold him apart from the rest.'

'You mean the phone call was from one of his accomplices . . . Oh my God!' said the headmaster. He grabbed Douglas Archer's arm, and held on to him. 'This man Spode tricked me,' he told Douglas. 'Tell them. You're English, I know you are . . . Tell them I'm innocent.'

Douglas went rigid in shame. A soldier prised the headmaster's fingers away. 'Then at least let me phone my wife,' implored the headmaster. But already the soldiers were hustling him away through the entrance. 'Take all the teachers,' Huth told the SS officer, 'and take the older children too. We can't be sure the children aren't involved. We've had fifteen-year-olds killing our soldiers in the past few months.'

'I'll try and get some sort of lead as to where Spode went,' said Douglas.

'He's well away by now,' said Huth. 'These people are damned efficient.'

'Who's "they"?' said Douglas.

'Terror fighters,' said Huth using the official German term for the Resistance, armed or otherwise. 'No. Go and see your son – he's here today, isn't he? Take him home. Explain to him.'

'Explain to him!' said Douglas. He knew no way of explaining the insanity of the world to his child.

'Children are flexible creatures,' said Huth. 'Don't try to shoulder all the guilt for your son being motherless.'

Douglas didn't answer. They both watched the soldiers herding a group of teachers into the school yard. Lorries were being backed through the narrow gates.

'We don't need all this,' said Douglas. 'These teachers are innocent; they know nothing.'

'Too late to stop it now,' said Huth, 'even if I agreed with you.'

There was a crash as a tail-board dropped. Then the first of the teachers climbed into the lorry. He was an old man, and needed the helping hand of a soldier. One of his colleagues gave a soft cheer and the old man smiled sheepishly. It was always like this with the mass arrests, thought Douglas. The prisoners were reassured to be together with people they knew. They felt that nothing too bad could come of it, and were always comforted by the thought that they had committed no crime. The arrest procedure became an outing, a picnic, a break from the monotony of everyday life. The soldiers knew this, and they encouraged the levity, knowing that their task would be easier, and less harrowing, if the prisoners smiled all the way to the detention centre.

'Have you heard anything more from the girl?' said Huth.

Douglas was disconcerted and didn't answer.

'I know about the Trafalgar Square business, you idiot,' said Huth. 'Has she contacted you again?'

'You have me followed – but you don't have her followed?'

Huth feigned a look of pain. 'You touch a nerve, my friend. She was quick and clever – more clever than the man assigned to her.'

'One man?'

'The voice of the professional! Yes, my people have a lot to learn. They didn't realize they were dealing with a very experienced agent.'

'Sylvia?'

'You didn't realize that, eh? Yes, an important little girl. We should have put her in the bag while we had the chance – her sort can smell trouble coming.'

'She smelled trouble coming?'

'Or someone told her. There's always someone to tell people. Someone phoned Spode and told him to lace up his walking shoes, didn't he?' He sniffed. 'No matter, they'll try again, because they desperately want to make contact with you, Superintendent.'

'Do they?'

'I think so – look at the risks they take . . . probably won't be the girl next time. Could be anyone. Say yes to whatever they want. Get their proposition.'

'Proposition?'

'They are probably going to try another rescue attempt on the King.'

'At the Tower of London?'

'It's not impossible. They tried early last month, from the river, and nearly got away with it.'

'Good God!' That explained a number of things to Douglas. The custody of the King was General Kellerman's most important responsibility. Now Douglas remembered last month's great upheaval amongst the SS security units, and General Kellerman's subsequent shake-out of senior personnel.

'They'd do better by negotiation than by terrorist attacks,' said Huth.

'You think so?'

'It's not an opinion,' said Huth. 'It's the message I want you to deliver.'

'I see my son,' said Douglas.

'Take my Mercedes. The boy will love the super-charger.'

'It's not far,' said Douglas, 'and walking will give me a breath of fresh air.' But Douglas didn't go. He stayed on, worrying that the children might be manhandled or that the whole thing might degenerate into violence.

He was still standing there when young PC Dunn came hurrying across the yard, red in the face and perspiring heavily. 'It's gone, sir. The arm is gone. And the paper bag with the camera stuff in it.'

'Are you sure?'

'He hadn't even bothered to push the table back after getting it. He must have gone home while we were phoning the Yard.'

'Quite a coincidence,' said Douglas bitterly.

PC Dunn looked at him for a moment without understanding. Then he said, 'You don't think someone at the Yard phoned him?'

'I'd dearly like to know,' said Douglas. 'Well at least he's still got a part missing,' said Douglas, putting a finger in his waistcoat pocket to make sure he still had it. 'That limb was the standard sort that the Ministry issue to war casualties, wasn't it?'

'It looked like it.'

'A man would have to give his real name to get one of those, Dunn. The Ministry would check it against their records and he'd probably have to provide evidence of army service – name, rank and number – or produce his "panel" card if he's a civilian. Get on to the Ministry, and see what you can find out. If he applies to them for that missing piece, I want to be told about it before they answer.'

'He might think that's too dangerous,' said Dunn.

'It *is* too dangerous,' said Douglas, 'and so is cutting back to your lodgings when there's a police Superintendent on your tail. No, this fellow needs his arm, and I think he'll go to a lot of trouble to get it working again.' Then Douglas spotted his son and went over to him.

By now the mass-arrest teams had set up their folding tables and chairs and they were typing out the sheets and having them countersigned by the officer in charge. Not only were people being documented but the same diligence was given to the paperwork, books and files that the search-parties were bringing out of the building.

There was boredom written on the faces of the soldiers, for they knew that this operation, and dozens more like it which took place every day, was unlikely to discover anything of importance. They were staged simply to emphasize the fact that any sort of opposition to the Nazi invaders brought inconvenience to the innocent and guilty alike.

The schoolteachers crowded into the lorries were more solemn now. Some were trying to see if friends or relatives were anywhere in sight but the soldiers were dealing roughly with any sight-seers. One of the older children, in the nearest lorry, had tears in his eyes. A teacher was talking to him trying to comfort him. A grey-haired man with bent spectacles smiled at the boy and in a thin piping voice began to sing:

'If you're happy and you know it, clap your hands.'

He clapped his hands. The wavering tuneless voice could be heard in the parade-ground silence of the school yard. So could the lonely sound of the man's hands clapping. A second voice joined in the old Boy Scout song,

'If you're happy and you know it, clap your hands,'

and there was the sound of a dozen or more hand claps, and now the child joined in, still crying. The Germans looked round for orders to stop the singing but when no such order came, did nothing.

'If you're happy and you know it, then here's the way to show it.
If you're happy and you know it, clap your hands.'

And now all the prisoners clapped their hands.

'Move out!' yelled Huth. The lorries started their engines, and the first one began to move forward. By now the whole convoy of prisoners was singing. Theirs were not hearty voices, it was the unmusical chorus of frightened men, but there was no mistaking the note of defiance in these discordant voices, and it gave heart to every Englishman who heard them.

'If you're happy and you know it, stamp your feet.
If you're happy and you know it, stamp your feet.
If you're happy and you know it, then here's the way to show it.
'If you're happy and you know it, stamp your feet.'

Douglas could still hear the men's feet hammering on the floorboards of the lorries, as the convoy roared off towards Edgware Road. Douglas took his son's hand, and held it as if it was the only thing in the world he had. Until now he'd found it possible to work with the Germans. After all, he'd been hunting murderers and he'd not had to search his conscience about that. But increasingly he found himself being drawn down into a deep, dark vortex, moving at a snail's pace, as things always happen in a nightmare. And yet he saw no way of escape. Under the new regulations policemen were not permitted to resign from the Force, and men who tried to do so found themselves devoid of ration books and work cards and became little better than beggars. Douglas gripped Douggie's hand tight. 'That hurts,' said the little boy.

'Sorry,' said his father. He wondered if his son was judging him with that merciless impartiality to which all men subject their father.

In Marylebone they passed a man selling fried turnip pieces. Young Douggie went to the stall to look at the fryer and his father followed him. The crisply fried vegetable chunks were filling, warming and unrationed, and cost only two pence for a small bagful. The old man selling them put in an extra piece for Douggie.

'Say thank you, Douggie,' said Douglas automatically.

'That's all right, Mr Archer. It's good to see the boy looking so well.'

Douglas looked puzzled. 'It's Mr Samuels, Dad,' said the child. 'You remember.'

Douglas was shocked to realize that this was the proprietor of Samuels' Restaurant and Tea Rooms, a well known West-End meeting-place, famous for its fine bread and cream cakes before the war. Douglas had noticed that the restaurant had lately been converted into a Soldatenheim, a recreation centre for the German soldiers. Now he saw that the dispossessed Samuels had become an old man, his skin leathery and his eyes sunk deep into their sockets.

'I'm getting so absent-minded,' said Douglas in an attempt to explain why he'd not recognized Samuels. Before the war, he'd regularly taken his wife and young Douggie there to eat cream cakes. 'Can I have a packet too? They look delicious.'

Mr Samuels shovelled the warm pieces of vegetable into newspaper and screwed the top closed. Douglas gave him a pound note. 'I've no change of that, Mr Archer. I'm sorry.'

'Give me the change next time I see you.'

'No,' said Samuels but he changed his mind and put the note into his pocket gratefully. As Samuels rummaged through the old sweaters that he wore under his overcoat, Douglas noticed the star of yellow cloth that he wore.

'Your boy always says hello,' said Samuels, as if not many others did.

'It will all work out, Mr Samuels,' said Douglas. 'I promise you it will.'

Mr Samuels smiled but did not answer.

Douglas hurried on to catch up with his son, who had his nose pressed against the window of Benson the tailor. The cost of cloth had driven many tailors out of business but Benson – with a daughter who spoke a little German – was thriving, his window filled with German uniforms, buttons and badges. Young Douggie took his father's hand and they continued together along the High Street. 'Do you work for the Gestapo, Dad?' said his son without any preamble.

'No. I work at Scotland Yard. I'm a detective with the Metropolitan Police, just as I've always been – you know that, Douggie.'

'The Gestapo are at Scotland Yard,' said Douggie.

'They are in the next-door building – Norman Shaw North – and they are nearly all Germans.'

'But you work *with* the Gestapo . . .' his son coaxed him.

'Well, I . . .'

'Sometimes you do, don't you?'

'Is that what you've heard?'

'The boys at school said so.' He tugged at his father's hand. 'Dad, me and some of the boys were wondering . . .'

The boy's voice trailed away.

'Well, come on, Douggie, out with it. We're friends aren't we?'

'Could you get a Gestapo badge?'

'The Gestapo don't have badges; they have only special identity tags.'

'Well, could you get one of those SS armbands . . . or one of the silver-wire SD badges?'

'I don't think so, Douggie.'

'Oh, Dad,' the child was desolated. 'I bet you could, Dad. I bet if you asked some of the people at Scotland Yard, someone would give you one.'

'What for, Douggie?' said Douglas. 'What would you do with it?'

'Oh, I don't know,' said the child. 'All the boys collect them but no one's got any SS badges yet. They asked me to ask you.'

By the time they got back to Mrs Sheenan's home, the sky had darkened and the first few drops of rain had fallen. Douglas sneezed. He feared he was getting influenza. He sat near to the fire, now burning very low, hunched into his overcoat, with his hands in his pockets. Douggie sat at the kitchen table doing his homework. Occasionally he asked Douglas for help. But eventually the child heard the sound of deep breathing and knew that his father had gone to sleep in his chair. He didn't disturb him. They had a small piece of boiled fish for the evening meal and after putting young Douggie to bed, Douglas turned in himself. He'd been guarding a tiny portion of Scotch whisky and now he poured a measure for Mrs Sheenan and took his glass to bed with an Agatha Christie book. But before he'd read more than four pages the detective was sound asleep.

Chapter Twelve

Douglas Archer started early next morning and worked hard. He tried most of his best informants but it soon became clear to him that his usual underworld grapevine could tell him nothing that would help his murder investigation. He realized too that there was an intensive drive for information, and some of the better-known informants had been taken into custody. By the end of the morning Douglas knew that the people involved in this murder case had kept themselves away from London's vast army of informants.

That afternoon, Douglas Archer was one of the few British nationals present at Caxton Hall. A senior official of the Reichsleitung der NSDAP – the Nazi Party Supreme Directorate – was in London on the usual spree of shopping, eating, drinking and sight-seeing. He paid for his supper with a three-hour speech to the senior officers of the London police and SS headquarters.

Even the wily Huth found no way of avoiding it, and Douglas watched him yawning and nodding and providing perfunctory applause with his gloved hands. It was interesting to compare this with Kellerman who was also on the platform. He was an old hand at such occasions, leaning forward and nodding at each over-simplification and half-truth, and uttering loud cries of excited enlightenment as all the old slogans were trotted out. And Kellerman was able to convert his yawns into smiles, and, by pinching the bridge of his nose while bowing his head, he could make his dozing look like the deep concentrated thought that requires closed eyes. And, at the end of the Party official's long speech, while Huth was groping under his chair for his cap and stick and looking to see which was the nearest exit, Kellerman was at the podium, clapping his hands energetically and smiling at the guest. And it was Kellerman who, disregarding the programme, stepped up to the microphone and improvised a brief word of thanks 'for a speech permeated with true National Socialist feeling and clarity of thought and purpose which admits no compromise' – a verdict he'd pronounced upon dozens of equally dreary interruptions to the working day.

And as the assembly began to disperse it was Kellerman who, while still smiling at everyone in the room, muttered to Douglas, 'Now perhaps you'll know better than to put your name down as a speaker of the German language, Superintendent, eh?'

By the time Douglas got back to Scotland Yard, Harry Woods was eating tea and toast. 'Detective Constable Dunn phoned,' said Harry with unusual formality. He was irritated that there was a third officer working on the investigation.

'That's good.'

'The picture agency says someone wrote to them for a copy of that photo. But that's all they know about it. Paid for by postal order. No way to trace identity.'

'Too bad,' said Douglas.

'You shouldn't go to these Nazi speeches if it puts you in a bad mood,' said Harry. 'Dunn wants to check up on all the people in the photo – just as a long shot.'

'Is there any tea about?'

'I didn't know about that photo you found at the schoolteacher's place.'

'Well, you know now.'

'I told Dunn to let me have it tomorrow. I'll see what I can do. No, there's no tea left. It was horrible anyway.'

'Then you can untell him. If he phones back, you tell him to carry on with the jobs I gave him.'

'Dunn's only a kid. This could be dangerous, you know that. And I'm not sure that Dunn has the experience to handle a complicated case like this one.'

Douglas walked over to a table in the corner. Here were the results of what must have been unimaginably long hours of painstaking work. The ashes of the papers burned in the grate, at the Shepherd Market flat, had been separated flake by flake, pieced together and sandwiched between sheets of glass.

'Just do as I tell you, Harry. Right?' Douglas looked closely at one of the black jig-saws of burned paper. He could see nothing there.

'Yes, sir!' said Harry with a mocking subservience.

'I'm packing up for today. Where's Huth?'

'Talking to some SD people from Norway. Something about a heavy water plant. Does that sound right to you?'

Douglas grunted an affirmative.

Harry Woods said, 'And what do I say if he wants to know where you are?'

'Say you don't know,' suggested Douglas with a blank smile, and left.

Chapter Thirteen

Bertha's was a private drinking club in Old Compton Street, Soho. It was no more than a cramped little bar on the second floor, between film-cutting rooms and old Charlie Rossi's tailor's shop. Daylight was eclipsed by a jungle of potted plants that seemed to thrive on squashed cigarette ends, and alcohol poured on their roots by wary girls and resolute policemen.

Bertha presided over barman and clients from her stool behind the ornate cash register. Her sharp tongue and coarse vocabulary earned deference from even the roughest villains. The Germans used it as a listening post and often there was some polite young tourist sitting in the corner behind the piano, saying very little and hearing everything.

There were half-a-dozen regulars there when Douglas arrived. All of them had been at the race meeting at Epsom, one of the few race-courses in southern England to survive the fighting. Now they were explaining their losses and arguing about their winnings. On the bar there was a bottle of French champagne, another was in the ice bucket in the sink. The men greeted Superintendent Archer warmly, although he'd put two of them away for three-year sentences, and brought trouble to the other four. 'Straight' Roger was there, melancholy looking, an Australian gambler who made a steady income from dice games, in spite of always using honest dice. 'Straight' Roger's wins were due to the dice used by the mug; they were loaded to roll low scores.

'Awful' Jimmy Secker's gambling was even more honest. Usually Jimmy and his cronies lost heavily to the mugs. Unfortunately, Jimmy's illegal games were always raided by the police who confiscated all the cards, dice and money as evidence. His victims were usually relieved to hear no more about it.

'Bertha, a glass for my old pal, Superintendent Archer of the Yard.'

The words were spoken by a man who was clearly the leader of the group. He was smartly dressed in a suit of expensive Donegal tweed, flecked with brown and black twists of yarn. In his top pocket, arranged too obviously, there was a silk handkerchief of dark gold colour. Only his face jarred with this carefully chosen outfit; his complexion was yellow and waxy, his eyes small and furtive. Neither did his moustache fit with his country gentleman's wardrobe; it was thin and carefully trimmed, the sort of thing an actor might have chosen when playing the role of a gigolo.

'Cut it out, Arthur,' said Douglas. He was about to say how much he detested being called Archer of the Yard but decided not to reveal this fact.

'No offence, old cock,' said Arthur, grabbing the champagne from the barman and adding another measure to the amount already there. 'Pour that over your tonsils, Superintendent, it's the real thing.' He twisted the dripping wet bottle, to show Douglas the label.

'I believe you, Arthur,' said Douglas. Arthur – the snout-king – traded in stolen wine and cigarettes and these were good times for such men.

'We heard you are leaving the Yard, and going on some special job for the Herberts.'

'I'm sorry to disappoint you,' said Douglas, 'but as far

103

as I know, I'll be around for a little while yet.' Douglas sipped some of the drink. 'Very nice, Arthur.'

'Well drink up,' said Arthur. 'It's a short life.'

'You seem to be in high spirits,' said Douglas.

'No,' said Arthur. 'I'm in tobacco. Scotch-Johnny is in spirits.' The villains all laughed and Bertha cackled. Even Douglas smiled.

'I can't believe you made that up, Arthur,' said Douglas.

'Now don't be a bloody misery, Superintendent. We've all had a nice day – and strictly legit, too.'

'Good health,' said Douglas and drank.

'Now that's more like the Superintendent Archer I used to know,' said Arthur. They all drank. Behind the cash register Bertha lifted her glass too, holding it to her lips, and tasting only the edge of it, the way people do when they live amid alcohol.

'How much did you win, Arthur? I never thought of you as a man interested in the horses.'

'And you were right, Superintendent. We went out there today to see some old pals, and have a flutter on the geegees, but what I won didn't even pay for the taxi.' Arthur drank in that agitated way that indicated that he'd not yet finished talking. 'My old Mum – God bless her, and keep her – always says horse sense is the thing that prevents horses betting on people – get it?'

'Your old Mum sounds like a bit of a comic,' said Douglas affably.

'You met her,' said Arthur. 'You met her, Superintendent. Here at Bertha's; Christmas Eve 1938. She thinks the world of you. You bought her a port and lemon, and told her that I was an honest hard-working lad, who'd got mixed up with the wrong sort of people.' Arthur laughed strenuously enough to spill champagne on Douglas's

104

sleeve. He mopped it up, still laughing. 'Here, my sincere apologies, Superintendent. Have a little more. It's the real thing – from France.'

'As opposed to all that French champagne you make in that basement you rent in Fulham.'

'Now, now, now, Superintendent – fair do's all round, eh? Every man to his trade. I don't tell you how to nick villains.'

'If you didn't win money on the horses, what are you celebrating? Where did the money come from?'

Arthur noticed more spots of champagne on Douglas's sleeve. He took the silk handkerchief from his top pocket, and dabbed at it. 'Legit, Superintendent,' said Arthur. 'Strictly legitimate. You know Sydney Garin?'

'Everyone knows him,' said Douglas. 'The little Armenian art dealer.'

'Little *German* art dealer now,' Arthur corrected him. 'Graf von Garin, the famous expert on Aryan art.' They laughed. As if in response, Arthur poured more champagne for them all. 'Well, Garin has gone into partnership with Peter Shetland, who became the Duke of something when his father died last year. You know him, Superintendent; Peter Shetland: tall, skinny kid, used to drink here at Bertha's from time to time.'

'I know him,' said Douglas.

'Peter Shetland – with a monocle now . . .' Arthur pulled a face, '. . . is very well in with the Herberts. Those squareheads like a bit of class! With Sydney Garin as the brains, and Peter as the frontman, they are doing nicely.'

'At what?'

'They sell paintings and art treasures to the Germans and they sell *for* them too. When one of the top Nazis pinches some altarpiece from a cathedral in Poland, it's

Garin who goes to Switzerland or New York, and acts as agent to put it on to the market without too many questions about where it came from. They're in the money, those two. I mean, some of these paintings sell for a hundred thousand pounds – and they take a nice agency fee, you can imagine.'

'I can,' said Douglas.

'They keep the stuff in Peter Shetland's mansion house out in the country – near Newmarket. It's a bloody great place, Elizabeth slept there, and all that kind of cobblers. They take the Herberts down there for a weekend of hunting, shooting and fishing, and sell them stuff by the cart-load.'

'I still don't understand how you come into it,' said Douglas. 'And how I come to be enjoying this splendid champagne?'

'You've got a touch of class, governor, have I told you that before?'

'Not as far as I recall, Arthur,' Douglas said. 'I can remember you shouting that you were going to do me, from the dock, when you went down for that three-stretch for grievous bodily harm against the bookmaker.'

'Natural exuberance,' said Arthur modestly. 'I was just a young lad in those days, Superintendent. No, as I say, you've got class. If I had you fronting for me – and keeping me out of trouble with the law – I could really make my business go.'

Douglas ignored this invitation to be corrupted. 'And you've sold champagne to Sydney Garin?'

'Have I sold them champagne! No less than fifty cases of it. Tonight they are having the biggest damned celebration this town has seen all summer. You go along to Portman Square tonight, Superintendent, and you'll clear up half the unsolved crime in London.'

106

'I might do that,' said Douglas. 'Will you be there?'

'Give over!' said Arthur. 'I'm what they call "trade". They wouldn't let me in the front door, not even to collect the money they owed me for the champers.'

Impulsively Douglas said, 'And is that where Peter Thomas got the antiques for his shop?'

Arthur went over to the bar, got a packet of cigarettes, then came back to resume the conversation. 'You're joking, Superintendent. There's no Peter Thomas, surely you know that? And our Sydney doesn't deal in that kind of stuff. Garin and Shetland are fine-art dealers, they buy and sell museum pieces.'

'And Peter Thomas?'

'Peter Thomas never did exist. Peter Thomas is just a front for the Resistance. They used that shop as a way of handling money, and paying people, and so on. Sometimes well-wishers gave them antiques to sell for the cause.' He turned and caught the eye of a stern-faced Bertha. 'It's all done with now, Bertha, can't be no harm in telling about something that's finished and done with.'

'So who was the dead man?' said Douglas. 'You seem to know all about it.'

'I know only what I hear,' admitted Arthur. He belched softly; he'd had too much to drink. 'He was the elder of the Spode brothers; a scientist. Before the war he was involved with all this splitting-the-atom rigmarole. Quite a brainy bloke, I'm told.'

'And he worked in the antique shop?'

'Naw!' said Arthur. 'All those scientists were collared by the Herberts, five minutes after they got here; you know that, Superintendent. Some of them were taken off to work in Germany, some of them – like Spode – are working on secret weapons for the Herberts, here in England.'

'Spode?'

'Some big secret German army depot in Devon. They're trying to make some new sort of poison gas, I heard.'

'Bringle Sands?'

'Could be,' said Arthur. 'Here, drink up.'

Douglas continued his conversation with Arthur but it soon became clear that he knew nothing more, and what he did know was little more than gossip.

It was from the phone box at Bertha's that Douglas phoned Sydney Garin at his big house in Portman Square. 'Superintendent Archer,' said Sydney Garin, as smooth as silk and twice as slippery. 'What a truly amazing coincidence this is. Right there, on the table in front of me, as I talk, there is a one-pound packet of Ceylon tea that I was about to send to you. I know how much you enjoy a cup of the real thing, and it would be no use giving this to people who might put milk and sugar into it.' His speech was careful and slightly accented.

'Very kind of you to remember me, Mr Garin,' said Douglas, 'but you know how I feel about that sort of gift.'

'Please don't get the wrong idea, Superintendent,' said Sydney Garin without faltering. 'This is a personal present from the leader of this Indian trade delegation newly arrived in London. He's given me a few packets to pass on to people who have the palate to appreciate it.'

'Perhaps we could drink a cup together, Mr Garin.'

'A pleasure doubled, Superintendent.'

'I hear you are throwing a party tonight.'

'A modest affair by pre-war standards,' said Garin, 'but I've been fortunate enough to stumble over some rather scarce food and drink.'

'I've just been talking to one of the stumbling blocks,' said Douglas. 'Arthur the snout-king.'

'Ah! Yes, very amusing, Superintendent. Arthur, yes, what a splendid fellow. He's been doing one or two errands for me.' While they were talking Douglas could hear a voice in the background. He recognized it as the carefully modulated tone of Peter Shetland, who, having finally read the name Archer scrawled on the desk blotter by Sydney Garin, said, 'What the hell does he want?'

But Sydney Garin had survived too many life and death situations not to know when to bow to the inevitable. 'Look here, Douglas,' he said, having successfully searched his memory for the policeman's first name, 'why not come over here this evening and see for yourself? You'll meet some delightful people and some of your superiors from Scotland Yard.'

'Well that sounds like a very mixed collection,' said Douglas.

'You will have your little joke, Douglas,' Sydney Garin laughed. 'Ha, ha. But will you be able to come?'

'I hate to disappoint you, Mr Garin,' said Douglas, 'but yes I will. It sounds as if you'll need someone to keep an eye on the diamond tiaras.'

'You can't work twenty-four hours a day, Superintendent.'

'I wish you'd explain that to my boss,' said Douglas.

'And who's that?' said Sydney Garin, all ready for another joke.

'SS-Standartenführer Dr Oskar Huth,' said Douglas.

'People will start arriving about eight-thirty,' said Garin, all amusement gone from his voice. 'Black tie of course.'

'Or uniform?'

'Or uniform, Superintendent, yes, that's a good joke. But I must go now; *à tout à l'heure.*'

'*Arrivederci,* Mr Garin,' said Douglas.

Chapter Fourteen

While the *Tatler* and *Queen* and other high-society gra-
vure magazines were showing how Britain's nobility and
country gentry were celebrating their weddings and
twenty-first birthdays with toasted cheese snacks and home-
made beer, a new class of men had emerged from the
wreckage of defeat. Shetland, the hard-eyed aristocrat, and
Sydney Garin, one-time Armenian, typified the emergent
super-rich. And so did their guest list.

'Good evening, Mr Garin. Good evening, Mrs Garin.'

Garin's wife – a mousy little woman with a bodice full
of diamonds and pearls, and tight wavy hair – smiled as if
pleased to be noticed. Their son was there too smiling
dutifully at each new arrival.

It was to be expected that the Germans would be here;
Generals and Admirals and men from the tiny civil
administration which – under the command of the military
Commander-in-Chief – controlled occupied Britain. And
there were Englishmen: Members of Parliament and
members of the puppet government who had learned to
play their role in the new Nazi super-state that covered
most of Europe. The Prime Minister sent his regrets; he
was addressing a gathering of German schoolteachers.

Here too were the men of Whitehall; top-ranking
bureaucrats whose departments continued to run as
smoothly under the German flag as they had under
conservative and socialist governments. There were
nobility too, placed in the guest list with that seemingly
artless skill that a gardener uses with a few blooms that

110

flower in the heart of winter; nobility from Poland, France and Italy as well as the homegrown variety. And always there were businessmen; individuals who could get you a thousand pairs of rubber boots, or a hundred kilometres of electrified fencing; three crosses and nine long nails.

It was like half-awakening from some terrible nightmare, thought Douglas. The long dresses of fine silks and hand embroidery, the carefully tailored evening suits of the men, and the impeccable clothes of the waiters, came as a shock after the cruel and cynical mood of defeat that prevailed beyond those wrought-iron gates and well-kept gravel drive, and the neat lawn that was shiny and pink in the last evening light.

And the voices were different too; quick-witted responses and relaxed movements in these large, warm and comfortable rooms were quite unlike the hushed voices and furtive movements that had become a standard part of British life. But more than anything else Douglas was surprised by the light; there was so much of it and every room was the same. Rich golden light picked out the superb mouldings, the marble mantelpieces and Adam furniture, glittered in the cut-glass chandeliers, and shone through the bubbles in the endless champagne.

It was a magnificent house, comparable with Portman House round the corner, containing enough beautiful things to be a museum. And like a museum it was crowded with such objects, so that they were too close together, as if in some monstrous competition of the absolute.

At the far end of the ballroom, through two smaller reception rooms, and beyond the folding doors with sixteenth-century flower paintings on the panels, there were spotlights. There, mounted on a specially constructed platform – discreetly clothed in red velvet – was a small fifteenth-century Flemish diptych that Sydney Garin had purchased in Geneva. For this one evening only it was on display for the private pleasure of Garin's invited guests. Tomorrow it was to be crated for delivery to Reichsmarschall Göring's art gallery at Karinhall. In exchange, Garin and Shetland had accepted eight 'decadent' surrealist paintings that Göring had confiscated from non-Aryan owners.

Around the ballroom there were little groups of middle-ranking German officers, self-conscious in their uniforms and awkward in their lack of English language. Here and there some self-appointed spokesman fronted each group, behaving like some travel courier guarding a bunch of elderly tourists. There were high-ranking officers, elderly self-assured men with closely cut grey hair and sometimes monocles, wearing the gold insignia of Admirals on their white mess jackets, or the wide red trouser-stripe that denotes the General. Some were accompanied by personal interpreters in the special Sonderführer uniform.

There were girls there too. Plump girls with too much expensive make-up, and dresses that were cut tight across the bottom and deeply at the neckline. Elsewhere in London at this time such girls might have gone unremarked but in this temperate assembly they were conspicuous in a way that perhaps they intended to be. Already such girls had learned how to sandwich together a few German phrases – pronunciation perfect – and when their knowledge of German ran dry, a smile or a laugh would usually do. There were lots of smiles and laughter, and the couples who could not converse together danced instead.

Gathered in a defensive circle, under a magnificent Cranach Crucifixion, Douglas recognized a representative collection of London's new socialites. Upon them fortune had smiled since the night when a German news agency message reported Churchill's request for a cease-fire.

Here was a man whose modest restaurant in Soho had sold more than two thousand bottles of champagne in that first week of celebration. There, glittering with diamonds, was a widow who a year ago had been skimming fat and patching sheets in her failing third-rate Bayswater Hotel. Close to a large, German officers' club, it fast became a favourite rendezvous for officers and girls – no questions asked, short day-time stays a speciality – until she sold it to a consortium of German businessmen for close on a million pounds.

All the famous hotels were promising shareholders high dividends but there were other beneficiaries for whom the Germans had arrived like the Good Fairy in a pantomime. Pottinger – a dark-complexioned man with a beard and moustache calculated to make him look French – had gone deeply into debt with his mail-order English language courses. Now he was embarrassed by a cash-flow so large that he was paying for advice about reinvestment.

The red-faced man in lacy shirt, kilt and sock with jewelled dagger, was the owner of a dilapidated distillery in Argyll. His long-term contract with German EVM procurement officials was enough for him to form a public company and become wealthy overnight. The same German official who benefited from that arrangement had made the Scotsman's brother-in-law a purchasing agent, supplying Irish horses and fodder to the German army's Southern Command (GB). Now this magnificent array of beautifully dressed people chatted happily together at the feet of the tormented Christ.

Douglas stood aside, as an elderly Colonel eased his way to one of the buffet tables. In tow he had a pretty young boy in a very new dinner suit. Some Luftwaffe

113

fighter pilots nearby laughed; the Colonel flushed but did not look up.

'You've got a wonderful little Turner watercolour there, Superintendent.' Douglas turned from the painting to greet the elegant Peter Shetland. 'Not many people realize that Turner could work to that degree of realism. That fly-speck, coming through the Arch, is Napoleon. Yes, you've got a collector's piece there.' From Sydney Garin, Shetland had acquired this curious manner of talking about such things as if they were already sold to the person viewing them.

'I've seen it before,' said Douglas.

'Ah, what a memory you have,' said Shetland. 'It once belonged to the Tate Gallery but they have so little space, and it's a shame to let a masterpiece like that moulder away in the Tate's storage rooms.'

'It's for sale?'

'All the museums have had to get rid of things,' said Shetland with a shrug. 'It's just as well really. Let it find its market, I say.'

Douglas looked at the painting.

Shetland pulled at his long thin bony nose until he acquired a sorrowful look. 'State subsidies are now reduced to almost nothing, and we can't expect the German administration to finance our art museums, can we?'

'Oh, my goodness, no,' said Douglas energetically enough for Shetland to look at him to see if he was being sarcastic. Douglas Archer had a reputation for being sarcastic. 'And you are the agents for the sale?' added Douglas.

'We've found it cleaner, better, and more businesslike to buy from the museums. Then we resell to clients in our own time.'

'And more profitable too, I should imagine,' said Douglas.

'Not always,' said Shetland airily.

'I'm surprised,' said Douglas.

'You've got the mind of the policeman,' said Shetland. He smiled.

'I prefer to think of it as the mind of the accountant,' said Douglas. Across the room he saw Garin introducing his seventeen-year-old son David to a German Colonel from the Legal Department.

Shetland drifted away with a smile on his face.

'Attaboy! It's good to find someone who answers back.'

Douglas turned to see Barbara Barga, in a magnificent long grey silk dress with a lace bodice. 'Hello, Miss Barga. What a nice surprise.'

'You might compliment me on the dress,' she said. 'It's a Schiaparelli from Paris, and cost me three months' salary. A compliment or two is not much to ask.'

'It left me speechless.'

'Nice recovery, Superintendent.' She laughed. She was particularly beautiful when she laughed, Douglas noticed.

They turned to look to the ballroom, where a dozen or more couples were dancing to a skilfully orchestrated version of 'Red River Valley', muted saxophones modulating gently and lifting the melody away from the woodwinds.

'Takes me back to my days in high-school,' she said.

'In America?'

'Wisconsin. My boyfriend was on the football team, and had the keys to his Dad's new Chevvy. I had good grades, and knew no worries other than was I going to be a cheer-leader.'

'Would you care to dance?'

'We could give it a try,' she said.

115

Barbara Barga was not a very good dancer but she was light on her feet and happy, and ready to fall in love. 'Say, you're a good dancer, Superintendent!'

'You mustn't believe all you read about policemen's feet. I used to dance a lot at one time.'

'I heard about your wife, Superintendent. That's a terrible thing. And you have a little boy too.'

'I'm not alone in misfortune,' said Douglas. 'So you've been making inquiries about me?' He was flattered and he showed it.

'That was dumb of me that day. I should have got your name and realized that you were Archer of the Yard. It was only afterwards . . . Do you mind not being recognized by aggressive newspaper women?'

'Not being recognized is a part of the job.'

She smiled and whispered a few words of the lyric.

'What happened to the footballer at the high-school in Wisconsin?' said Douglas.

'I married him,' she said. 'Any progress on that murder case?' Before Douglas could answer she said, 'But what the hell . . . you didn't ask me to dance in order to talk about murder cases, did you?'

'Well, I . . .'

She put a hand to his mouth as they danced. 'Now I'm going to be very offended if you say yes to that one, mister.'

'Are you still married?' said Douglas.

'Now that's more like it,' she said, and snuggled closer so that her head touched his shoulder and he could smell her perfume. 'I love this song, do you know that? No, I'm not married. Not any more I'm not.'

She hummed the melody and crooned a little of the lyric into his ear. 'Never stray from my side if you love

116

me. Do not hasten to bid me adieu. But remember the Red River Valley, and the girl who is waiting for you.'

Barbara Barga was a very attractive woman. That night, her soft young body, quick mind and easy smile awakened in Douglas Archer thoughts that might have been better dormant. Her freshly shampooed hair swung against his face and he held her a little tighter. She turned her head suddenly and gave him a shy smile. 'Douglas,' she said softly, 'don't go home without me, will you?'

'No, I won't,' he replied and they went on dancing but now they talked not at all.

If Douglas thought that he might be able to spend the evening monopolizing one of the most attractive women present, these ideas evaporated soon after the music paused. Some newly arrived New York reporters recognized her from across the room, and Douglas relinquished her to their shop-talk, while he went to find two glasses of champagne.

He elbowed his way through a noisy group of Red Army officers who were suspiciously sniffing at the caviar but downing Scotch whisky by the tumblerful.

'Two glasses of champagne! Now isn't that rather overdoing it, Superintendent?' It was the deep cheerful voice of George Mayhew.

'One is for my mother, sir. She's waiting outside in the street.'

'I believe I saw her. Was she wearing the uniform of an SS-Gruppenführer?'

This cruel joke about the matronly physique of SS General Kellerman was one which Douglas hesitated to recognize, but he allowed himself a trace of a smile.

'It's good to see you, Archer.' George Mayhew was a man who combined the grace of the natural athlete with the bearing of a professional soldier. His dinner-suit was tailored in a style that was conservative, not to say old-fashioned, and he wore a wing-collar rather than the turned-down style he said suited only men who led dance-bands. His hair was still dark and thick, and brushed back close to his head, and he still retained the blunt-ended moustache that he'd first grown in 1914 to make himself look old enough for the responsibilities of a company commander. That was before he wore the ribbons of the DSO, MC and bar.

Between the wars, Colonel George Mayhew had become an important figure in that twilight world in which the briefings of the police commissioner overlap with those of counter-intelligence. Mayhew was often seen in Whitehall: the staff of Scotland Yard, the Home Office, the Foreign Office and the House of Commons knew him as a regular visitor. More than once he'd played for the Metropolitan Police rugby team and even now he seldom missed seeing an important game, while his baritone rendering of 'Old Man River' was regarded as a mandatory feature of police concerts.

'How's Harry Woods these days?' Mayhew asked. It had been Harry's time on the rugby team that had first drawn Douglas Archer and George Mayhew into the same rugby club functions.

'It's difficult for Harry,' said Douglas.

'Difficult for all of us,' said Mayhew, rubbing his hands together as if suddenly feeling cold. Mayhew had always had a special affection for Harry Woods and his out-spoken 'village copper' philosophy. Mayhew eyed Douglas, took in the borrowed evening suit, and tried to calculate in what role this police Superintendent attended such a grand function. It was not simply a chance to have some caviar and champagne, no one who knew Douglas

Archer, not even his criminal adversaries, would believe that.

'Age is an important part of it,' said Douglas. 'At Harry's age it's not easy to go suddenly from being at the heart of Empire to being an outpost of an occupied colony.'

'Poor old Harry,' said Mayhew. 'He'll retire soon, I suppose?'

'It's not easy to live on a Sergeant's pension.'

'Things will get better,' said Mayhew as if he had some special reason for saying so. He sipped some champagne. 'But only if we make them better.'

'And how do we do that, sir?'

'Do you really want to know, Archer old lad?'

'Yes, I do.'

'Can we talk . . . later this evening?'

'Of course.'

'There's someone I'd like you to meet.'

Douglas nodded and looked to see what Barbara Barga was doing. Colonel Mayhew noticed this, and said, 'You've made a hit there, old boy. Miss Barga thinks London policemen are wonderful.'

'Do you know her?'

'She's a damned good sort, Archer . . . if I was a few years younger, I'd give you a run for your money.' Douglas looked at him in surprise. Mayhew thought he'd offended the Superintendent and hurriedly added, 'I meant nothing personal, Archer.'

'I'll look forward to seeing you later this evening, sir.'

For Douglas, the evening passed more quickly than any others he cared to remember. He danced with Barbara and they ate lobster and agreed that Manet was better than Rubens, champagne bubbles got up the nose and that London wasn't what it had once been.

It was Bernard Staines who came to tell Douglas that Colonel Mayhew was looking for him. Bernard had been cox in the university boat when Douglas got his blue. Bernard Staines had the same birdlike physique that he'd had then, except that his more serious demeanour, hunched shoulders and spectacles had transformed the wagtail into a barn owl.

'I never see you at the Oxford and Cambridge, Douglas.' Bernard, unlike so many of Douglas's Oxford friends, never called him Archer.

'I feel out of place there, to tell you the truth. In these days, people want to be able to go to their club, and let their hair down, without worrying that there might be a policeman listening to them.'

'Anyone who thinks there's anywhere in this town he can relax without a policeman listening to him, is a fool,' said Bernard in the same soft diffident voice that had betrayed so many into contradicting him, both in college and board room.

'You're right, Bernard,' said Douglas. 'And just make sure you never forget it.' Bernard was pleased to have his friend's approval. Like so many men who'd had his sort of success, Bernard continued to regret that he'd not used his learning in some more scientific way. Detective Superintendent Douglas Archer personified these vague unfulfilled ambitions, and although Douglas did not suspect it Bernard envied and admired his friend.

Like most of these grand eighteenth-century houses, hidden doors and narrow staircases provided a way for servants to move, silent and unseen, through the house. A liveried servant stood aside while another opened an unmarked door, cut into the panelling of the wall. Bernard led the way upstairs. There was another servant on

120

the second floor, a tall man with the physique and bent nose that many associate with the professional fighter.

'I understand there is a card game,' said Bernard.

The man looked at Bernard and then at Douglas too before replying. 'Yes, sir. The other gentleman is there already.' He stood back to reveal George Mayhew.

'That's all right, Jefferson,' Mayhew told the servant. 'These are my people.'

The three men walked down the shady corridor, past a large empty billiard room and other rooms in which dustcovers hid the furniture. Douglas had no doubt that these rooms had for decades been used for the sort of unlawful high-stake gambling that was exceedingly difficult to locate or take action against. The room at the end of the corridor was lighted. Mayhew led the way into it.

There was only one light, an elegant brass angle-light with a green glass shade. It put a pool of yellow light on a card table, while making the rest of the room a mysterious jungle of verdant gloom out of which huge decapitated herbivores peered. Seated at the antique card table, his face awash with reflected light, was the unmistakable figure of Sir Robert Benson. Douglas knew him only by reputation; a powerful man in the corridors of Whitehall, shunning any sort of publicity, and winning every argument without raising his voice above a whisper. Recently Douglas had heard many people ask how the august Sir Robert could stomach his new position, where he was little more than a rubber stamp for the German Commissioner-General for Administration and Justice, which had absorbed the most vital departments of the Home Office. Perhaps, thought Douglas, this evening would provide an answer.

'Bridge?' said Colonel Mayhew, picking up the pack of cards. 'Penny a point?'

'Never thought I'd see the day when I'd have to start an evening like this with a pack of used cards,' said Sir Robert. Then he laughed and said, 'Archer. There's no man I'd rather have with us this evening.' He shook Douglas's hand with a firm but brief grip.

'Thank you, Sir Robert,' said Douglas. 'I'm pleased to be here.'

There was a cautiousness in the reply that the others did not miss. To Colonel Mayhew, Douglas said, 'I think my bridge playing might try beyond endurance even Sir Robert's renowned diplomatic skills. Particularly if he had me as a partner.' Sir Robert – sitting opposite him – smiled grimly.

'Whist then,' said Mayhew as if this was an important decision.

'Wonderful,' said Sir Robert without enthusiasm. 'I haven't played whist since I was in the trenches.'

Bernard Staines shuffled the cards, let Douglas cut them, and then began to deal them. He explained to Douglas, 'We usually play for money. It makes it more . . .' He shrugged and smiled.

'More exciting,' said Mayhew, from where he was standing.

'And also . . .' said Sir Robert.

'The Superintendent understands,' said Mayhew.

'Of course he does,' said Sir Robert. Douglas nodded. He understood that if you formed some Resistance cell, and held regular meetings round a card table with money piled in front of you, you could possibly fool someone that your only secret was illegal gambling.

Mayhew turned to the sideboard where, faintly discernible in the half-light, there was a tray with four glasses and a decanter of wine. The butler had left the empty wine bottle alongside the tray. Mayhew picked it up and read the label before replacing it. 'Sydney has provided a couple of bottles of his Château Lafite 1918.' Mayhew took the decanter and poured the wine respectfully.

'That's remarkably civil of him,' said Bernard. 'I'd be grateful for a glass of claret. Champagne gives me indigestion, I'm afraid.'

'Champagne is for youngsters,' pronounced Sir Robert. 'Claret is the only drink for a man of my age.'

Mayhew turned to face the light, so that he could see through the wine. As he poured he said, 'Sydney Garin is a good fellow.' Douglas knew the remark was addressed only to him but he did not respond, neither did Mayhew raise his eyes. Mayhew was typical of all the professional army officers Douglas had met. There was something about the way such men stood; necks stretched and their hands fidgeting. Even if Mayhew was fighting-drunk, Douglas suspected, he'd still have his chin tucked in and his thumbs trying to get in line with the seam of his trousers. Such men never relaxed.

Only Bernard looked out of place in this quartet; he was soft and inclined to plumpness, with white hands and a hesitant manner. He took off his horn-rimmed spectacles and polished them on the silk handkerchief from his top pocket. Mayhew set a glass of wine before him. Bernard blinked and nodded his thanks.

Sir Robert tasted his wine. 'Rather good,' he said guardedly. It was not a vintage of which he expected very much, but he prided himself upon keeping an open mind on all things. He smiled. It was the sort of smile that men give when they have had very little experience of smiling. His face was hard and granite-like, except for the tiny veins in his cheeks and nose. His hair was grey, and long enough to curl at the ears and neck. His forehead was shallow; his bushy eyebrows near to his hair-line. And beneath the curly eyebrows his eye sockets were deep and dark-rimmed so that his eyes sometimes disappeared into dark shadow.

Sir Robert Benson was sixty but his stamina was that of a much younger man. He could go without sleep with no apparent loss of efficiency for days on end, or so they said. But it was only his small blue eyes that revealed the quick brain, for his physical movements were slow and deliberate, like those of an invalid. He spoke with a voice that was gruff to the point of hoarseness.

'George was at Harrow with my youngest brother,' said Sir Robert, indicating Colonel Mayhew. 'They were a couple of scallywags, from what I hear . . . organized a betting club, so I give you fair notice of what to expect.'

'And Sir Robert's other brother was there with Winston,' said Mayhew.

'Is it true, Sir Robert,' said Bernard, 'this rumour that Winston Churchill has been executed?'

Sir Robert nodded gravely. 'Tried by secret military tribunal at the Luftwaffe's 1st Air Fleet HQ in Berlin. We all told Winston not to wear that damned RAF uniform, but he wouldn't listen.' Sir Robert sighed. 'That gave the Germans a legal pretext for the court-martial.' He picked up the cards on the table in front of him and sorted through them without seeing them. 'Certain high-ranking British politicians have been told, but the execution will not be officially announced for some time.' He slapped the cards down on the table.

'You mean Churchill is dead?' said Bernard.

Sir Robert scratched his head and picked up Bernard's cards and looked at those too. The other three men saw what he'd done but no one wished to tell him. 'Shot! By a Luftwaffe firing squad, at the Guards' barracks at Berlin-Lichterfelde. Death by military execution was a special dispensation of the Führer,' added Sir Robert dryly. 'They say that Winston refused the blindfold, and held up his fingers in a V sign. I like to think that's true.' He sorted Bernard's cards into suits. 'Well, come along, what's holding up play?' He looked at the other three men and then at the cards on the table before he realized that he'd picked up the wrong cards. 'Oh! What a fool I am!'

Colonel Mayhew reached out and gathered all the cards together, talking hurriedly to cover Sir Robert's embarrassment. 'And young Bernard here is married to my wife's cousin. Lucky dog – she's a beautiful girl.'

'We grew up together,' said Bernard. 'Every summer my family went to Scotland; her people had a farm nearby.'

'All gone now, alas,' said Mayhew. 'The farmhouses are derelict and the fields gone to rack and ruin.'

Bernard said, 'And when Sir Robert took his Company into the front line, before the Battle of Amiens in 1918, my father was the Company Commander he was relieving.'

Army, family, school; tightly interwoven threads that bind upper-class Englishmen more tightly than do money or business. The totalitarians of right and left have constantly to describe the faith they have in common. But for these men, and thousands like them, the means was the end; playing in the team was more important than the game, provided that they played together with men like themselves.

'And I was with Douglas at Oxford,' said Bernard bringing his friend into the circle. 'And how I envied you doing Greats, while I pegged away at my Civil Law.'

Sir Robert looked at Douglas for enough time to make

125

the Superintendent feel slightly uncomfortable. Then he said, 'I knew your father, Archer.'

'You did, sir?' His father had died when Douglas was still a child. 'When?'

'We were close friends, from 1916 until the time he was killed. Your father was twenty-eight years old when I first met him; and that's too old to be an infantry subaltern. I know, because I was also an infantry subaltern, and I was ten years older than him.' Sir Robert gave a dry laugh. 'We were the battalion's two old fogies; the younger chaps were always having to come back and help disentangle us from the barbed wire and encourage us to sit down and rest when we should have been drilling. Your father was a civil engineer, wasn't he?'

Douglas nodded.

Sir Robert said, 'He should have been with the Engineers, but he felt he would be letting the battalion down. Deserved the Victoria Cross a dozen times over, your father, did you know that? All his men knew it, and his Company Sergeant Major worshipped him.'

'My mother had a letter from the Sergeant,' said Douglas. 'She still keeps it.'

'I should have told you all this long ago,' said Sir Robert, 'but it seemed rather a cheek to be so personal. And I wasn't sure if you'd want to talk about your father.'

'I'm grateful,' said Douglas.

'He would have been proud of you,' said Sir Robert. 'Archer of the Yard they call you, don't they?'

'I'm afraid they do, sir, yes.'

'Well, that's all part of the job nowadays. Solving a murder or two never did a police force any harm. Might as well let a few people read about it in the newspapers.'

'I'm sure you're right, sir,' said Douglas.

Mayhew rippled the cards. 'You want to play, Archer?

126

You're sure?' There was more hanging on the reply than just a game of cards.

'I'll take a hand,' said Douglas.

'Cut for partner,' said Mayhew putting the cards down in front of Douglas. He cut and found the deuce of spades. Sir Robert also cut a deuce, the other two court cards.

For a moment no one spoke, then Sir Robert said, 'We're partners,' in the same tone he'd used to announce the death of Winston Churchill.

Mayhew led with the four of hearts, Douglas played the seven, Bernard the King and Sir Robert took the trick with the Ace.

'I wish I'd studied law,' said Sir Robert. 'An honours degree in history is not much help when I'm trying to untangle all these German regulations. Do you know, one of my chaps was telling me today that all the Gestapo are immune from arrest. That can't be true can it?' No one answered. 'You must know all this kind of thing, Archer. What do you say?'

'No, Sir Robert. No one is immune from arrest under the German system. He was probably referring to the fact that members of the SS can be tried only by their own courts. But the Gestapo is not a part of the SS.'

'Ha,' said Sir Robert. Clubs were trumps, and he began to lead them, raising his eyebrows when Douglas's Queen dropped on his Ace. With trumps cleared, he made four tricks in his long suit, diamonds. They won the hand ten-three. 'Sorry about your Queen,' he said. 'Had to clear them out. Got to be ruthless.'

Mayhew continued talking while he dealt. 'Really? The Gestapo is *not* a part of the SS?'

'By no means,' said Douglas. 'The Gestapo is part of the police service. Some Gestapo men are members of the SS, and some of them are members of the Nazi Party, some are neither.'

'Let me get this straight,' said Mayhew craning forward. 'The SS is not a part of the Nazi Party either?'

'Technically they are a part of it,' said Douglas. 'Every SS identity card is headed Schutzstaffel der NSDAP but there is no real connection. And the SA – the brownshirts – consider themselves even more distanced from the Party.'

'That explains a lot,' said Mayhew reflectively. 'And the SD – that your chap Huth belongs to?'

'They are the secret intelligence service of the Nazis. They're a super-élite, the only people allowed to pry into everyone,' said Douglas. 'They do what they like.'

'Except for the Wehrmacht,' said Bernard.

'Yes, the German armed forces have their own legal system. No one from the Gestapo, or even from the SD, can take direct action against a soldier.' Douglas led a low trump.

'Come along,' Sir Robert said. 'We're playing cards.' And he took the trick. 'I'm glad that you confirm that. Some of the army chaps have been most helpful to us. With the Gestapo on their tail they might have to be more circumspect.'

Douglas nodded. He dearly wanted to know in what capacity Sir Robert had been helped by the German army but he didn't ask.

'And what about these fellows with honorary SS ranks, or SS officers employed by the civil administration?' said Sir Robert. 'We have several working with us. Are they too subject only to the SS legal system?' He pushed his cigar case towards Douglas who took one and nodded his thanks.

'Himmler is at the top of the police system, as well as

128

the head of the SS,' said Douglas. 'In such cases it's his decision. In any case, part-time SS men are subject to the ordinary civil law.' He lit the cigar and puffed at it before adding, 'But Himmler uses those honorary SS ranks as a way of muzzling and bribing his opponents. Some of these men are Himmler's most bitter enemies.'

'My God, I've made a trick,' Mayhew said. He continued without a pause. 'What do you think of this fellow Rear-Admiral Conolly?' His question was not directed at anyone in particular but Douglas knew that this must be something the others had discussed many times.

Douglas said, 'A cool customer, from what I hear. Although I've not heard much. To walk off an aircraft carrier in Halifax, Nova Scotia, and declare yourself the leader of "Free Britain" shows a breath-taking audacity.' Douglas paused. Everyone else seemed to be absorbed with their cards. Douglas added, 'Especially when – as the German propaganda service said – Conolly is no more than a Commander in the Navy List.'

Sir Robert drew the last trump. 'The rest are ours, I think.' He put down his hand.

Douglas said, 'I wonder if anyone remembers that French army officer – de Gaulle – who escaped here to England when France fell? Did more or less the same thing, as I remember; promoted himself to General, and declared that he was the voice of France. It never came to anything. As far as I know the Germans never bothered to include him on the Primary Arrest List.'

'You're wrong, you know,' said Sir Robert gently. 'Conolly was acting on the instructions of the War Cabinet. It was Winston's idea, when he himself refused to go on one of the flying boats that left for Iceland, at the very end. And Conolly's promotion to Rear-Admiral was signed by the King's own hand. I saw it myself. And although Goebbels's press release said that Conolly addressed Congress and claimed to be the leader of "Free Britain", the Congressional Record reports him as saying that he spoke as a representative of the British nation, and as Minister of Defence, appointed by the Cabinet and confirmed by the King. And at the end of his address he repeated that he was a loyal subject of King George and any legal successors.'

'But how many people on this side of the Atlantic know what he said?' asked Douglas. 'And what chance is there to tell them?'

'We're not immediately concerned with that,' said Sir Robert. 'Our primary task is to ensure that Rear-Admiral Conolly's position in Washington cannot be attacked through either the legal process, or through the Protocol Office. Last week he had to fight off attempts to take physical possession of the Embassy building. And the Germans are using some of the best lawyers in America.'

Bernard said, 'Even now, the case is not settled. If the Germans take over that building it will be a bad blow to Conolly's prestige in Washington.'

'Then you are in touch with Conolly?' said Douglas. He was unable to keep a note of surprise out of his voice.

No one answered. Having declined Sir Robert's Upmann cigars, Mayhew took his time lighting one of his own Romeo y Julietas. Bernard! thought Douglas. He must be the courier.

They continued to play, offering each other considerate words, as men might do when their card game occupied their thoughts to the exclusion of all else. Sir Robert alone played with the intensity of a man who hates to lose. 'Not many people using the Tower of London nowadays,' said Mayhew casually, as if discussing attendances at the Test Match against Australia.

So that was it, thought Douglas. Huth was right. These men were contemplating an attempt to get the King released from the Tower. 'The SS Special Security Battalion is quartered there,' said Douglas.

Sir Robert's eyes opened a fraction wider. Mayhew permitted himself a flicker of a smile. If that wasn't Superintendent Archer's way of saying he wanted no part of any attempt to tackle those SS infantrymen, it sounded an urgent caution.

'If the King was free and able to confirm publicly Conolly's rank and position, it would transform Britain's position in the world,' said Bernard.

Would it, wondered Douglas. He was cynical enough to suspect that it might only change the position of Conolly and his associates. He looked at the other three, resenting the well-bred superiority of their manner. 'You're not seriously suggesting a physical assault against the Tower of London, are you?' he asked.

The three men moved uneasily. Then Mayhew said, 'With respect, Sir Robert, and in spite of our previous conversation, we'll have to put Superintendent Archer in the picture.'

'I was thinking that myself,' said Sir Robert.

Bernard said nothing. He had no need to remind them that this was exactly what he'd told them to do.

'The German army will help us in every way they can, short of getting into a fight,' said Mayhew.

'Why?' said Douglas.

'They feel that it is incompatible with the honour of the German army that the King of England should be in custody and guarded by SS units.'

Sir Robert added, 'And the escape of the King from SS custody would disgrace the SS and consolidate the army Commander-in-Chief in his position of power here.'

'Not only here,' said Mayhew. 'The repercussions would be felt in Berlin. We have the support of the General Staff for this business.'

Douglas nodded. As preposterous as it would be in British terms, it fitted in to his knowledge and experience of the Germans. 'I think I might be able to provide for you an even more valuable ally,' he said. 'I believe SS-Standartenführer Dr Oskar Huth might wish your expedition well.'

'Huth?' said Mayhew. 'Why?'

'Kellerman is the senior SS officer in Britain, as well as being police chief. Any failure to keep the King in custody would inevitably result in his being fired. I believe Huth covets Kellerman's job, but the two men hate each other with such venom that ambition would be only of secondary importance.'

'Well, I'll be damned,' said Sir Robert.

'It makes sense to me,' said Mayhew. 'With a fellow like that prepared to turn a blind eye to it, things would be much easier.'

'What's the next step?' said Sir Robert. 'Can you sound out your man Huth?'

'Not without mentioning names,' said Douglas. 'You'd better nominate someone who'd be prepared to act as go-between.'

'It could be dangerous,' said Mayhew. 'It could be a trap.'

'That's a monumental understatement,' said Douglas. 'It might well be a trap.'

'I'll be the go-between. I think it's worth the risk,' said Bernard. 'What do I have to do?'

'Nothing,' said Douglas. 'I simply have to have some-one I can name as a spokesman for you all. But think about it overnight, Bernard. Sir Robert and Colonel

132

Mayhew might decide you're too valuable to be risked in a gambit like this.'

'I think so,' said Sir Robert. 'I'm sorry, Bernard, but I couldn't allow it.' There was a long silence in the room; the discussion was at an end.

'Well, let me know,' said Douglas. 'I'll protect him as far as I can, of course.'

Mayhew put the pack of cards together decisively. 'I think that's enough.'

Douglas looked at his watch. 'I should be going.'

'Just a moment,' Sir Robert said. 'These gentlemen owe us money.'

A handful of pennies were exchanged. Douglas said goodnight to Sir Robert and Bernard and Mayhew walked with him along the dark corridor. They stood at the top of the staircase. 'I'll say goodnight, Archer,' he said but he stood as if there was something else.

'You haven't asked me to let up on the Shepherd Market murder investigation,' said Douglas.

Mayhew flinched. 'It would be a good thing for all concerned,' said Mayhew.

'Including me?'

'In the long run, yes.' He smiled. 'You knew what I was going to say?'

'Half the population of London seem to be concerned lest I solve that murder. Why should you be an exception?'

Mayhew's smile was fixed on his face like a cheap papier mâché mask. 'Well, think about it, Archer,' he said.

'I already have,' said Douglas. 'Goodnight.' He did not offer to shake hands.

133

Chapter Fifteen

Douglas was in the car with Barbara Barga before they had exchanged more than a brief greeting and a circumspect hug. She was not drunk, or even under the influence as the English courts define it, but she was relaxed, and cat-like, inclined to smile at jokes that she did not reveal. 'Wasn't that a swell party?'

'Parties like that are an acquired taste.'

'Then I've acquired it,' she said. 'Even as we were leaving, the waiters were bringing Moët by the case, and those one-pound size tins of beluga caviar. Some style those guys have.'

'You could as well say Al Capone had style.'

'But honey, I did say that. I did a two-part feature story for *Saturday Evening Post* a year or more back. I located two old-time beer-barons in Gary, Indiana – that's just across the stateline from Chicago, one-time haven for the hoodlums . . . and these guys gave me a great story. And I said that Al Capone had style – I actually said that.' She tugged at Douglas's sleeve with that earnest determination to be understood and believed, that so often comes with an extra few drinks.

Douglas looked out of the window of the car. He resented the way in which Garin and Shetland had provided a car-service for the guests, and resented the influence that had provided for the cars the 'Essential Service' windscreen stickers that enabled them to break curfew. He resented the way that he'd had to revise his

opinion about Garin and Shetland – shameless collabor-
ators and crooks – and come to terms with the fact that
they were respected and admired by Mayhew and Sir
Robert, and his old friend Bernard. Only slowly could he
bring himself to modify that resentment. Hearing Barbara
Barga praising the party did nothing to help.

'Don't be sore,' she said, reaching out a hand from
where she was slumped in the corner of the soft leather
seat. 'Don't let Al Capone come between us.'

'I'm sorry,' said Douglas. He turned just as she leaned
forward. They collided.

'Ouch!' she said and rubbed her nose. The sudden and
unexpected physical contact reawakened in Douglas a
mixture of urgency, awkwardness, ardency and despair
that he had not known since the calf-love of his
schooldays.

The car was heading towards Belgravia. 'This is not the
way to the Dorchester,' said Douglas.

'Do you have to be a cop twenty-four hours every day?
I've rented a little town house near Belgrave Square. It
belongs to friends who've returned to Missouri for three
months, and didn't want to leave it empty. Do you know
they've had fourteen robberies in that tiny mews in the
last three months.'

'Well don't hold me personally responsible for all the
crime in London,' said Douglas clumsily. It had always
been like this when he was young; the girls he wanted
most were the ones he offended and with whom he made
a fool of himself.

'I'd ask you in for a drink,' she said, 'but they asked us
all to send the cars back as soon as possible for the other
guests.'

Douglas reached across her and opened the door before
the driver could do so. 'No problem about that – stay

135

where you are, driver! – I can phone for a car from the Yard.' He got out with her.

'My researcher says that having access to a car in this town is a sign of favour – you must be an important man at Scotland Yard.' She got the keys from her handbag.

'Everyone keeps telling me I am,' said Douglas. He looked at the tiny mews house; cobbled forecourt and ivy on the walls. A few years ago they were considered only just good enough for coachmen or chauffeurs; now, with the coach-houses converted to sitting-rooms, such places were becoming chic.

Once inside she switched on the lights one by one. Douglas admired the paintwork and panelling, all done with a craftsmanship that was fast disappearing – and the furnishings too. It wasn't to his taste – huge Chinese vases converted into table lamps, white moquette on the floor and a Persian carpet on the wall – but it was undeniably comfortable. 'What does your friend from Missouri do for a living?' said Douglas. 'Run an opium den?'

'You're a cruel bastard,' she said affably.

'Well it's all very luxurious.' He took off his overcoat.

She had not removed her coat and now she turned up the fur collar.

'Do you know the origin of the word Mews?' she asked, and hurried on before he could spoil the obvious pleasure she got from telling him. 'It means a cage for hawks. In the olden days a Mews was where the royal hunting birds were kept.'

'I didn't know that,' he said.

She smiled. Just for one moment he saw the little girl she once was; smiling proudly at some word of praise. He loved that little girl and the clever, and beautiful, young woman she'd become and for the first time, he dared to think she might feel the same way about him.

He didn't dwell upon the thought. He turned away and studied the books on the shelf, forcing himself to read the titles and exclude all else from his mind. *Encyclopaedia Britannica*, 14th edition, four guide-books to London, one of them with a cracked spine, a large Sears Roebuck Catalog with more than a dozen page-markers visible, a Manhattan telephone directory, a small atlas and a pocket-size English dictionary with a companion volume German one. He felt her watching him, but he did not turn round. He looked at the typewriter on a small table by the fire. Alongside it, a half-used packet of lightweight paper, held down by a Rolleiflex camera, a pot of face-cream and a dozen hairpins. The waste basket was half-filled with screwed-up sheets of typing paper.

'Matches?' He went to help her.

'You Brits don't feel the cold, do you?' They were very close now, crouching together at the fireplace. He could almost feel the warmth of her body. She was looking at him, perhaps trying to see why he didn't feel the cold. She got to her feet, and stepped back from him. 'There's no heat here,' she said.

He knew she meant central heating. He smiled. He turned the tap and lit the gas. There was a loud noise as it ignited. He stood up.

'In my country,' she added quickly, 'even a blue-collar worker wants something better than a cold-water walk-up, with fixed-point heating.' She stepped back again and stood very still. For a moment he was about to put his arms round her but she shivered and turned away, and went through the swing doors into the adjoining kitchen.

'Gee, there were some terrible people there tonight,' she said from the kitchen.

137

Douglas followed her. 'That's the trouble with wars,' he said.

'You can say that again. I was in Catalonia and in Madrid. That's the way it goes, believe me. Blackshirts, redshirts, brownshirts; the same lousy crooks are trying to take over the world. I've seen those same sort of greedy-eyed politicians from the Chaco to Addis Ababa.'

'That sounds like a lot of wars.'

'I was eighteen when my paper sent me down to Paraguay, to cover the fighting in Chaco. Since then I've sent stories from China, Ethiopia, Spain, and last year I was in Abbeville when the German Panzer Divisions arrived.'

'It's a strange job for a woman,' said Douglas.

'Don't be an English stuffed shirt.' She turned on the water-tap. The pipes squealed and the metal drummed as she filled the percolator. She got a tin of coffee from the cupboard. 'I've got real coffee. What would you say to that, Superintendent?'

'You went to a war when you were only eighteen?' said Douglas. 'What did your father say?'

'He owned the newspaper.'

She looked up at him and smiled. He looked back at her and stared calmly into her eyes. Until then, the prospect had been nothing more than a flirtation, or at the most a brief affair. It would not be the first time she'd exploited some influential official in some war-torn land for the sake of her job. But now she found the tables turned; she was beginning to like this gentlemanly English cop in ways over which she had no control.

She tried all the tactics that had worked so well before. She remembered all the other lousy selfish foreign lovers she'd had. She concentrated upon the latter part of her failed marriage, the misery of the break-up, and the

138

bitterness of the divorce. But it was no good; this man was different. 'Do you take sugar, Superintendent?' Or was it just that she was more vulnerable, lonelier in this god-forsaken miserable city than she'd ever been before?

'Douglas,' he said. 'People are calling me Douglas now. It's all part of the new mood of informality that the newspapers say the war brought.' He opened the new can of coffee, and their fingers touched as he handed it to her. She shivered. 'Douglas, eh? Well, I think I like that better than Superintendent.' She tipped the coffee into the percolator top, closed the lid and set it on the heat. She didn't look round, but she felt his eyes upon her. She spoke again hurriedly. 'Now you're not going to give me the third degree about what kind of black-market deal did I have to do to get coffee, are you?'

'I heard that the US Embassy has arranged a ration for Americans living here.'

'I'm just kidding,' she said. 'Yes, I got it from the Embassy.' She busied herself in the kitchen. She set up a tray with her best cups and saucers, and the silver spoons and sugar bowl. Then she opened a tin of milk, and put it into the cream jug. 'Bring that bottle of brandy and glasses,' she said as she picked up the tray. 'Winter in this town is going to kill me if I don't find some way of keeping warm.'

'There I might be able to help.'

She walked into the lounge with the tray. This room was once a stable for the grand house that backed on to it. Wood blocks had been laid upon the original stonework but even with the white carpets in place, it was not enough insulation against the cold. She put the tray down as near the fireplace as possible. Then she pulled some cushions from the sofa, and dropped them beside it. They both sat close to the fire. Douglas poured some brandy

139

for them. He sipped his but Barbara Barga gulped her measure.

'Don't get me wrong,' she explained, 'but I'm freezing.' She held a cold hand against his face to prove it. Douglas reached behind him and switched out the table lamp. 'Now, that's really cosy,' she said, but with what degree of sarcasm it was difficult to know. Perhaps she didn't know herself. Now the room was lit only by the red light of the gas fire, and the only sound was its hiss, and the popping noises made by air in the gas pipes. Douglas put his arm round her. 'The coffee will boil over,' said Douglas.

'And I was giving you the last of my coffee ration,' she said, but the words were lost in the kiss and urgent embrace that followed. For a long time they remained still and silent. 'Was I so obvious?' she said finally. Somewhere, deep inside her mind, a little man was still waving a danger flag.

'Say nothing,' said Douglas.

'A cop's good advice,' she said. 'I throw myself on the mercy of the court.' As they kissed again, they sank back on to the cushions. The hard red light of the fire made her skin look like molten metal. Her hair was ruffled and her eyes closed. Douglas began undoing the tiny buttons of her bodice. 'Don't tear anything,' she said. 'I may never get another Paris gown as long as I live.'

From the kitchen there came the sound of coffee boiling over, but if they heard it they gave no sign.

Chapter Sixteen

The low, growling siren of a German armoured car patrol, going down Knightsbridge at high speed, awakened Douglas. He looked at his watch; it was a quarter to four in the morning. Barbara was asleep beside him, their clothes were nowhere in sight. A gas fire filled the bedroom with a red glare. His movements wakened her. 'You're not leaving?' she said drowsily.

'I must.'

'To go home?'

'I'm not going to the office, if that's what you mean.'

'Don't be irritable,' she said running her fingernail down his bare skin. 'I'm just trying to discover if there is someone else.' She wanted to hug him and keep him there but she didn't try it.

'Another woman? Absolutely not!'

'That kind of certainty only comes when a love affair has just ended.'

'That's right.'

'Kiss me.'

Douglas kissed her tenderly. Then he gently broke from her embrace, stood up and went into the next room. He fetched his clothes, and dressed by the light of the fire. She watched him and said, 'I wish you'd stay a little longer, so that I could fix breakfast for you. Shall I make you some coffee now? It's probably freezing cold in the streets at this time of night.'

'Stay where you are; go to sleep.'

'Do you need a razor and stuff?'

'A proper razor?'

'Don't look at me that way. It belongs to the people who live here. It's in the bathroom cupboard – top shelf.'

Douglas leaned over and kissed her again. 'I'm sorry,' he said. 'Will we see each other again?'

She had dreaded the thought that he might not ask. 'Can I meet your little boy? Does he like the zoo? – I'm crazy about the zoo.'

'He likes it,' said Douglas. 'Give me a day or two to work things out. It's a long time since anything like this happened to me.'

He thought she might laugh but she didn't; she nodded.

'Douglas,' she said. 'Those people you spoke with tonight – Sir Robert Benson and Colonel Mayhew and Staines . . .'

'Yes . . . what?'

'Don't tell them no. Tell them yes, tell them next week, or tell them maybe, but don't tell them no.'

'Why?' He moved back a pace into the bedroom so that he could see her. She had turned her head away and was very still. 'Why?' The sheet rumpled at her neck like an Elizabethan ruff, and long strands of her hair made lines across her skin, like the graining of rose-coloured marble. 'Who are they? Are you involved with them?'

'They told me to go along to the Peter Thomas antique shop that day. They told me to ask you if you'd found a roll of film.'

'And you did what they wanted?'

'No. They also wanted me to identify the body as Peter Thomas.'

'That would have been a serious offence,' said Douglas.

'And I could see that you were going to be a tough proposition, so I backed off. I owed them nothing.'

'What else?'

'Nothing else, except that a friend of mine – reporter who covers the White House for the *Daily News* – says that Bernard Staines met the President three times last month. One of the meetings was on the Presidential yacht, and it lasted nearly two hours!'

'President Roosevelt?'

'I don't mean the President of Macy's department store. These guys are into something big, Douglas. I'm telling you, don't go back there and say "no deal".'

Douglas grunted.

'They'll kill you.'

Douglas found it difficult to believe. But these were mad times, and it was unwise to rule out even the wildest ideas. 'You don't mean that?'

She turned over in bed, so that she could see him. 'I'm a war reporter, Douglas. I've seen a thousand guys like this all over the world. If it came to choosing between your life, and a chance to get US government recognition of the Conolly set-up, do you think they'd hesitate for one moment?'

'Is the Queen in the Tower too?' Douglas asked this woman who seemed to know everything.

'The Queen and the two Princesses are in New Zealand, living there in their private capacity. They have no political importance.'

Not as long as the King remains alive, thought Douglas, but he didn't say this.

'Can I use your phone to get a car?' he said.

'Help yourself, darling.' She snuggled into the pillow.

'Barbara . . .'

She looked up again. He wanted to say, I love you, but memories of saying it to Sylvia intervened. It would keep for another day. 'Little Douggie and I – we both like the zoo,' he said.

Douglas dialled Whitehall 1212 and asked for the CID duty officer. After he'd given his name there was a multiplicity of clicks and a long wait. Eventually came the voice of Huth. 'You're phoning for transport – where are you?'

Damn! Now he must bring the girl into it, or risk a deliberate lie. 'I'm at the far end of Belgrave Square,' said Douglas giving an address just round the corner.

'You fool!' said Huth without anger. 'Why do you think we authorize a car service for these big parties?'

Of course, the drivers would be reporting which guests went home, which flouted curfew and perhaps even the remarks of tongues loosened by alcohol. 'You're with the girl, are you?' said Huth.

'Yes, sir.' He expected Huth to make some remark about that but he didn't comment. 'Stay there. I'm sending someone to collect you and bring you to me.'

'To the Yard?'

Huth replaced the phone without replying.

Douglas had a hasty shave without wakening Barbara. Even when it was time for him to go downstairs she was still asleep, the sign of an easy conscience.

It was a big BMW motor-cycle, with an airship-shaped side-car, and an axle that connected the two rear wheels. With a machine like that, he could climb a mountain. It had SS registration plates and a London SS HQ recognition device. Douglas climbed into the side-car and gave the rider a nod. Then he had to hang on tight to the machine-gun mounting, as they roared down Grosvenor Place with noise enough to wake half London.

In the air there was the green, sooty fog typical of those that London suffered, but the rider did not slacken speed. A Gendarmerie foot patrol was marching through the Victoria railway station forecourt but they ignored the SS motor-cycle. The fog was worse as they neared the river, and Douglas caught the ugly smell of it. After Vauxhall Bridge, the motor-cyclist turned right, into a street of squat little houses and high brick walls, and advertisement hoardings, upon which appeals for volunteers to work in German factories, announcements about rationing and a freshly pasted German-Soviet Friendship Week poster shone rain-wet through the fog.

Once on the south side of the river the motor-cyclist parked in a hastily constructed official compound – no more than a section of the street surrounded by coils of barbed wire and sentries – outside an ugly little building marked 'Brunswick House, Southern Railway'. The fog was much thicker on this open land that extended down to the warehouses and granary on the river-front. From the Pool, they could hear the noises of ships preparing for the high tide that would come in half an hour.

Outside the house, rigid as statues and oblivious of the swirling fog, were two SS sentries, complete with the white gloves and white belts of a ceremonial guard. The rider went with Douglas as far as the door of the house. To the corporal of the guard he said, 'This is Superintendent Archer, for Standartenführer Huth.'

An elderly SS officer examined Douglas's pass and then spoke in excellent English. 'You have to go to the far end of the marshalling yards. Better if you keep your transport. One of my people will go with you to make sure you get through.'

Not many vehicles could have done the short journey: the wheels thumped against the train lines, and were hammered by half-buried wooden sleepers. Douglas had never been here before – Nine Elms, one of the largest freight yards in Europe. It was a desolate place, the ground strewn with debris that leapt out of the headlight

145

beam; rusty train wheels, smashed crates, and, worst of all, the switch gear that lunged at them like spearsmen as the rider twisted between the long lines of goods wagons that clanked and groaned all round them in the dark green fog.

Ahead they saw floodlights and SS infantry wrapped in the huge ankle-length sheepskin coats that were usually reserved for more northerly climates. A railway checker's hut had been converted into a guard post. At the barrier Douglas's pass was again scrutinized before they phoned to announce his arrival. He was permitted to traverse the final 200 metres with armed escort. They went across the rails and ducked under the couplings of a goods train. Only then did Douglas see his destination. A line of rectangular yellow lights stretched away until swallowed by the fog. It was a train.

They passed another passenger coach drawn up alongside, and heard the hum of air-conditioning and Franz Lehar. The music came from a wind-up gramophone in the compartments assigned to the sentries. From there came also the smell of fried onions.

Now Douglas could see the train to which he was going. It was very long, with flat-cars where helmeted men at full readiness manned heavy machine-guns. 'What train is this?' Douglas asked the SS man.

'Nearly there now. No smoking,' said the man.

They climbed up the steps into a coach, but this was no ordinary train. The fittings were exquisitely designed and finished in chrome steel and leather. Chairs and writing tables were made to fold away so that when the train was moving this coach could be changed into an observation car. Douglas sat down in one of the soft leather armchairs.

He had waited two or three minutes when a door opened at the far end of the coach. Huth looked in. He saw Douglas and nodded before disappearing. But before the door was completely closed Douglas saw behind him a man in shirtsleeves. His head was turned away and the hair cut so short that the white of his scalp showed through it. Just as the door was closing the man turned to say something to Huth. Douglas found himself looking straight at the round face, stubble moustache and pince-nez of the Reichsführer-SS, Heinrich Himmler.

It was another five minutes until Huth emerged from the conference. Douglas was astounded by his appearance. The tall Italianate prince with his fine uniform was now bowed by fatigue, his eyes dark-ringed and red with exhaustion. His uniform was rumpled and stained, and the leather overcoat, slung across his arm, was ripped and muddy like his boots.

Huth was not alone. With him there was a man Douglas recognized as Professor Springer, in SS-Gruppenführer's uniform, complete with the silver-faced overcoat lapels, that was reserved for the very top ranks of the SS. In Himmler's entourage – a collection of street-fighters, ambitious bureaucrats, unscrupulous lawyers and ex-cops – Professor Maximilian Springer was the only true aca-demic. And yet, like so many Germans, Springer effort-lessly assumed the demeanour of a Prussian General. He was tall and thin, with a leathery face and ramrod back. Once out of the Reichsführer's conference, Springer snatched the spectacles off his face and tucked them away in his pocket. It was not soldierlike to wear spectacles.

'Who is this?' said Springer.

'My assistant,' said Huth. 'You can talk in front of him.'

Springer unrolled the papers he was carrying. It was the same chart that Douglas had found in Huth's brief-case. Here were the magical symbols of water and fire,

147

and the magical sword that symbolized 'the omnipotence of the adept'.

'Have you ever heard of an atomic bomb?' Springer asked Douglas.

'Before the war . . . there were newspaper articles but no one took them seriously.'

Springer nodded and turned away. Only by dressing up the complexities in a mumbo-jumbo of Black Magic was he able to get much of a response from the Reichsführer-SS. Even now very few people would believe his estimates of the damage an atomic explosion could cause, and even fewer could follow the reasoning that led him to that conclusion. Douglas stood back while Springer talked with Huth.

Soon it was obvious that Huth's knowledge was no more than a hasty reading of relevant theories, skilfully applied to the fact of everyday problems. But even this was beyond the vocabulary of Douglas's excellent and fluent German, and the ideas were beyond his grasp of science. But now he understood the way in which the two men had got the support of Himmler's personal astrologer. With the aid of the Black Magic chart they had persuaded the Reichsführer-SS that the atomic explosion was part of a pre-ordained destiny, a means by which Himmler and his Führer would lead the German people to world conquest. But Springer and Huth had no illusions about Black Magic. They were concerned with more practical aspects of their future. 'Do we know how far the army have got with their programme?' Springer asked Huth.

'The pile must have been running,' said Huth. 'It probably got too hot, and the reaction got out of control. That's the only way to explain the burns on Spode's body.'

'The army have kept their secrets well,' said Springer. 'They must have captured the British work more or less intact.'

'I'm hoping that we'll be able to discover whether Spode's burns were from uranium or plutonium,' said Huth.

'Not plutonium,' said Springer. 'If they've got as far as that, we'll never get control of the programme.'

'This officer is working on the Spode murder,' said Huth.

Springer turned to look at Douglas, as if noticing him for the first time. 'Do you know what radio-activity is?'

'No, sir,' said Douglas rather than hazard a guess for this forbidding man.

'It's the emission of radiation from unstable atomic nuclei – alpha particles, nucleons, gamma rays, electrons and so on. For the human body it can be fatal; we call it radiation sickness,' said Springer.

'Would it burn the skin?' Douglas asked. 'Like sunburn?'

'Yes,' said Huth, anticipating the next question, 'Dr Spode was dying of it.'

'Is it infectious or contagious?'

'No,' said Huth.

'We don't know,' said Springer, looking sternly at Huth. 'But, if unshielded, any radio-active substance can kill an unlimited number of people.'

'Should we search the house in Shepherd Market?' asked Douglas anxiously.

'We've done that already,' said Huth. 'There is nothing there. I have a special unit, with detection apparatus, on standby day and night.'

Springer nodded. 'I must go back to the Reichsführer now,' he said. He rolled up the diagram. 'I'm thankful that he has realized that this could mean the end of us all.'

Douglas wondered whether Springer was referring to the demise of the whole of mankind or only to the political career of his master and immediate circle. Springer gave a click of the heels and a jerk of the head before returning to the map room.

'There's a standing instruction,' Huth told Douglas angrily. 'All senior police officers provide a contact address, or phone number, day and night.'

'Yes,' said Douglas.

'Day and night,' said Huth again as if he was trying to provoke a quarrel. Then the anger went out of him. He slapped Douglas on the arm. 'Let's get out of here. I'm going to give you a lesson you'll never forget.' He opened the door of the coach and climbed down the steps. From somewhere on the far side of the yards a steam engine gave a grunt and a gasp, then there came a long trickle of metallic sounds, as a goods train settled its couplings and moved a few inches forward.

When they reached the motor-cycle, Huth pushed the rider aside. He threw a booted leg over the saddle, and stood tall to kick the engine into life. If he was aware of the dangers to a uniformed German riding the dark streets, he gave no sign of it.

They began a hair-raising journey through the fog, as Huth craned forward over the handlebars like a witch riding a broomstick. He had pulled the silver cords of his peaked cap under his chin, and found goggles in the pocket of his leather overcoat. The dirt on his face corresponded to the shape of the goggles and his beak-like nose. He seemed oblivious of Douglas in the side-car beside him. Within him there was an anger, a motive force that gave him the strength to continue long after his physical power had ebbed away.

Douglas never did forget that journey at reckless speeds through the evil-smelling London fog that swayed in front of the headlight, sometimes blinding them with a wall of reflected green light, and sometimes moving aside to reveal long ghostly corridors that ended in miserable grey streets. And all the time there was the deafening roar of the engine. Exposed and unsilenced, the four cylinders bellowed and screamed at the narrow streets of south London, voicing Huth's contempt and fury.

Douglas feared for Huth's sanity that night. Like a man deranged, he crouched over the handlebars, looking neither to right nor left but shouting at the world: 'I'll show you!' 'Just wait!' and 'You'll see what your friends are like!' Although the wind snatched away his voice and mangled it, Douglas recognized the words, for Huth repeated them time and time again in a litany of wrath.

The journey took them through the depressing urban sprawl south of the river, a wilderness silent and empty except for the tread and challenges of foot patrols. After Clapham they encountered more and more signs of battle damage unrepaired from the street fighting of the previous winter. Shell craters, and heaped rubble, were marked only by yellow tapes, soiled and drooping between roughly made stakes.

Half-way up Wimbledon High Street – at the corner that makes such a perfect spot for an ambush – there was the blackened shell of a Panzer IV, a monument to some unknown youth who – with a Worthington beer bottle, filled from the service station at the top of the hill, and a box of Swan Vesta matches – passed into legend, and into songs that were sometimes crooned softly where no German ears listened.

Wimbledon Common still bore the skull and crossbones 'Achtung Minen!' signs that a company of Royal Engineers had made overnight and planted along the grassland, when, with no more than a dozen anti-tank mines remaining, they tried to prevent the spearhead of 2. Pz. Div. outflanking the defences that were being organized at the top of Putney Hill. The churned earth of the common showed how the bluff failed.

They were at Motspur Park before Douglas realized that they must be headed to Cheam Village where he had once lived so happily. It was a small place, set amid parks, golf courses, sports fields and mental homes. For most people it is remembered as nothing more than the place they turn the corner, on their way to Sutton. Such transients knew Cheam only as the ugly modern houses that followed the main road, but behind that it was a pretty little place. The street where Douglas had lived then consisted of clapboard-covered frame-cottages, built long before the fire regulations prohibited such designs. That's why they had suffered so badly from what the official diarist of 29. Infanterie Division (mot.) recorded as only Plänkelei, or skirmishing. In Sycamore Road, skirmishing infantry used flares and smoke grenades, and the resulting fires destroyed more houses than five previous Stuka attacks.

The machine-gun mounting on the side-car clouted Douglas on the side of the head, as Huth swung the heavy bike at full speed up on to the grass and through the remains of a neighbour's house. Now Douglas saw it, the ruins of his home, ripped open to expose its charred interior. As he climbed out of the side-car Douglas felt under his feet the crunch of ashes that even the months of rain had not washed away, the buried broken pieces of his life. And he smelled the unique and unmistakable odour of war; it is a curious mixture of organic smells, carbon, ancient brickdust, sewage-impregnated soil. This persists long after the stink of putrid tissue is gone. Douglas smelled this odour now and was grateful, for it alienated this place, so that his memories of it were subdued, as is a dream in fitful sleep.

'Is it Jill?'

Huth wiped his dirty face with the edge of his hand. 'What?'

'My wife. Is it something to do with my wife?'

'No,' said Huth. Douglas followed Huth's gaze to where a German army lorry, an ambulance and a couple of cars were parked in what was once his neighbour's garden. Now there was no sure way of knowing where one property ended and another began. From here, he could see the place where the next row of houses had been ploughed into the earth by counter-battery gunfire that destroyed two German 8.8cm guns. Their twisted barrels could still be seen.

Here, on the edge of Surrey, the fog had cleared but low clouds raced across the moon, so that its hazy blur changed shape constantly and sometimes disappeared to darken the whole wasted landscape.

Huth turned away to yell at a couple of engineers who were rigging an electricity cable. 'Ladder! Give me a ladder, here! Right away!' It was the peremptory voice of the parade-ground bully, and the SS soldiers responded to it with redoubled efforts. Two more men came running across the uneven ground, holding a reel by means of a metal spike. Behind them the cable paid out to where more men were struggling with the starting motor of a mobile generator.

'Come with me,' commanded Huth and without waiting for the ladder he began scrambling up the heaped rubbish.

Douglas kept close behind him as they clambered over loose timbers, and scattered ash and plaster-dust into the air. Huth coughed, and then cursed as the belt-buckle of his unbuttoned overcoat caught in a tangle of rusty wire, and tore off. Huth kicked toe-holds in the plaster and teddy-bear wallpaper of what was once the bedroom of Douglas's son, and heaved himself up to the almost intact balustrade of the upstairs landing.

Huth was breathing heavily and made no attempt to help Douglas as he ascended behind him but he moved aside to make room on the precarious perch. As Huth put his weight against the wooden rail, Douglas heard the creak of breaking wood and grabbed Huth's arm as a section of the flooring gave way. The two men hunched together, and heard the clatter of the broken timber falling upon the rubble below them.

If Douglas was expecting thanks for saving the Standartenführer from a broken limb, or broken skull, his expectations were in vain. All he got was one of Huth's cold humourless smiles that lasted only as long as it took him to get out his handkerchief and sneeze into it noisily.

'Are you all right, Standartenführer?' came a voice from the darkness below.

'No more than a head cold,' Huth called in reply, and blew his nose. Below them someone laughed softly. 'Edge along to this side,' said Huth.

Douglas followed him as he disappeared through what had once been the upstairs linen cupboard. Its hot-water boiler, crushed almost beyond recognition, dangled into the room below. On this side of the house, the upstairs front, enough of the floor's supporting beams survived to hold the weight of the huge brass bedstead that had been their wedding present from Jill's parents.

'Throw the cable!' shouted Huth. Immediately a length

of cord was tossed to him. With an easy expertise, he looped the cord and drew a hand-lamp up to where he could use it. 'Give me light, damn you!' he shouted when he found that he could not switch it on.

'Immediately, Standartenführer, immediately!' called some anonymous voice desperately seeking the extra few moments that a placatory reply provided.

By now Douglas's eyes had become accustomed to the shadowy remains of the bedroom. He saw the bed, its brass disfigured, the frame warped beyond repair and the springs a tangle of rusty wire. And yet, thought Douglas, some looter must have coveted it, for the great bed had been tilted on its end, and propped up where once the window of their bedroom looked out over the tiny front gardens of Sycamore Road. The fast-moving scud thinned enough to provide an extra glimmer of moonlight. And now Douglas saw something else. Someone was here with them. Uncaring of their voices the figure remained spreadeagled across the bed, in a pose that seemed to defy equilibrium.

'Light!' yelled Huth again. 'Light, damn you!' a style of order which Douglas had come to recognize. There was a brief babble of German, a couple of attempts to start the generator, and a cry and curses as it backfired.

Bewildered, Douglas moved forward a fraction. Below him he saw the flashlights of the soldiers. The frame of the house creaked, and there was enough wind to hum in the telephone wires that were draped across the charred room beams. Then, with a cough, a stutter and a roar, the generator started, but the lights did not come on; neither the one in Huth's hand nor the floodlights the engineers had erected in the garden below.

'Did anyone ever tell you that the Germans are an efficient race?' Huth inquired of Douglas.

155

'It's all a question of priorities,' said Douglas. As he said it, the arc lights spluttered into life, their beams cutting through the night like steel scalpels as they sought a meeting place. Douglas closed his eyes and turned away from the glare before he was able to focus his eyes on the bed and its occupant.

He was dressed only in tattered bloodstained under-clothes, hands wired to the bed-frame, head bowed, face bloody; like a Christ, as the men who'd tortured him intended he should be.

'Jimmy Dunn!' said Douglas.

'You've seen a dead man before, Superintendent,' said Huth.

'Poor Jimmy!'

'On an errand for you?'

'Investigating the murder,' said Douglas.

Huth reached forward and, using a stick, he prodded at the large piece of cardboard that was wired across the dead man's chest. 'I was an English hunting dog, working for the German huntsmen,' said the crudely written sign.

'Poor little Jimmy.' So Harry Woods had proved right. It *was* too dangerous for an inexperienced young police-man and now Douglas tormented himself with responsibility for his death.

'The gallant British patriots!' said Huth. 'Are you proud of them?' Douglas turned away. 'Oh, no you don't!' said Huth, trying to turn him back to face the floodlit body with the cuts and burns that marked the young policeman's last tormented hours. The two men struggled there atop the rubbish heap, until Douglas punched hard enough to produce a grunt of pain. Then Douglas broke free and began to pick his way down through the wreckage.

Behind him came Huth. He said, 'So at last, a flicker of emotion! I thought I'd never see it.'

'Jimmy was a good copper,' said Douglas.

'And that's the ultimate accolade in your book, is it?'

'I sent him.'

'And your friends of the Resistance murdered him.' Huth stumbled but found his balance again. 'But you punch *me*,' he said.

'My wife is somewhere under this lot,' said Douglas by way of explanation but there was no note of apology in his voice.

'I know, I know,' said Huth.

'When did it happen?'

Huth jumped down from the last of the rubble. 'An army foot patrol found it up there at 22.47 hours. There are two hours between each patrol . . . regular patrols! These army idiots will never learn how to deal with partisans.'

The two men walked towards the vehicles. 'This is an announcement that they intend to kill you,' Huth said softly. 'You realize that, don't you?'

'Perhaps.'

As they reached the cars, Huth turned to a young SS officer who was hovering nearby, with stiffened body and robotic face, anxious only for a word of command. 'Let the photographer go up there,' said Huth. 'I want this grotesque tableau dismantled, and out of sight before daybreak.' To Douglas he said, 'You'd better go home and get out of those ridiculous clothes.' Douglas looked down to see the dinner suit revealed by his flapping raincoat.

'Take a car,' added Huth. His face was drawn and deeply lined and his chin unshaven. He rubbed his face and paused as if waiting to sneeze, but no sneeze came.

157

'I'm about all in,' he said, in one of his rare admissions of human weakness.

'You're getting Jimmy down now?'

'Go home,' said Huth. 'That's not "Jimmy"; that's a carcass.' Huth followed Douglas's gaze and added, 'We've cleared all the houses as far as the railway station. None of your one-time neighbours will have seen anything.'

Huth had some perverted talent for discovering the workings of Douglas's mind. And he made Douglas despise himself because of them. What should Douglas care if those neighbours saw the things these people had done to Jimmy, and why should Douglas feel guilty about it? And yet he did.

'No feelers yet?' asked Huth. 'Nobody asked you subtle questions about how you like working for the Huns?'

'No!' said Douglas. To say yes would be enough to have Huth screening every guest at the Garin party, and threatening and pushing until the clandestine meeting was uncovered. 'No,' said Douglas again with less emphasis.

'Curious.' He sniffed, and wiped his nose with a coloured handkerchief. 'Very curious,' he told the handkerchief. 'I expected some whining and sniffing round you by this time.'

'I'll get back home,' said Douglas. 'Perhaps there will be a carrier-pigeon waiting for me.'

'Save the humorous asides for Harry Woods,' said Huth. 'Sergeants *have* to laugh at their superior's jokes.' He blew his nose. 'These are dangerous people, my friend. Don't try to play both ends against the middle.'

Douglas opened the door of the Volkswagen car.

'Do you know any remedy that will help my sinus?' said Huth.

Surprised, Douglas said, 'An inhaler to put in your nose?'

Huth smiled. 'I've got too much up my nose already. Take this officer home,' he told the driver.

Wind chased away the cloud and revealed a dark blue night. And as they reached central London, dawn ruled red lines across the eastern sky. Douglas let the latch close softly, so as not to wake the house but Mrs Sheenan heard the car.

'Is that you, Mr Archer?'

He tiptoed upstairs. From the oil-shop came the smells of freshly chopped firewood, and paraffin. By now he'd grown used to it and it was like a welcome home.

'Sorry to wake you, Mrs Sheenan.'

'I'm having tea. Would you like some?' Since taking in her two lodgers, she had slept in the front room above the shop. Now Douglas found her sitting up in bed, a thick knitted cardigan wrapped tightly round her, sipping tea.

'Get a cup and saucer from that cupboard, would you?' With two young children in the house, Mrs Sheenan had gathered into this tiny room all the fragile memories of her married life. Here were china dogs that barked Margate and Southsea, a young sepia bride, a chipped Staffordshire teapot, the pocket-watch engraved with her father's name and best wishes from his employer after 25 years' service, two tinted photos of her husband and all four of his POW-camp postcards.

She poured tea for Douglas. 'Is it raining?'

'No. And the fog is all gone.' He sipped the tea. 'This is good.'

'There's one spoonful of real tea added to the ersatz. I always wake up about four, and I never really go back to sleep again.'

159

'You don't look very well, Mrs Sheenan; there's a lot of influenza about.'

She noticed the dinner suit he was wearing under his raincoat but she did not comment on it. 'Do you think I'll ever see Tom again, Mr Archer?' She stirred her tea with unnecessary care and attention. 'The boy keeps asking me, you see, and I just don't know what to tell the child.'

She looked up, and Douglas realized that she'd been crying. He knew she had no living relatives and the responsibility for her son weighed heavily on her. 'Tom will come back, Mrs Sheenan.'

'We only hear every two or three months. Even then he's only permitted to send a printed card that says he's well.'

'Better than a long letter to say he's ill,' said Douglas.

With some effort, she smiled. 'Of course, you're right.'

'The armistice gives no date, but the Germans have promised to return the prisoners of war as soon as possible.'

'What do the Germans care?' she said bitterly. 'German mothers and wives got their men back months ago. What do they care about our lads? – They're using them as cheap labour. What can our government offer in exchange?'

Douglas could find no arguments to counter her reasoning. At present the Germans promised that one British POW would come home in exchange for every ten workers who volunteered for German factories. It would be a long wait for Tom. 'Don't let your son see that you are unhappy, Mrs Sheenan. It could affect him more than having his father away from home.'

'At school they have a new teacher who told them that Churchill – and all the British soldiers – were criminals. My boy came home and asked me why.'

160

'I'll speak to him,' said Douglas, 'and tell him that his father is a fine man.'

'They are told to report parents who go against the propaganda.'

'These Germans have brought evil ideas with them.'

'My son thinks the world of you, Mr Archer.'

Douglas finished his tea, and stood up.

'I don't know what we'd do without you, Mr Archer. And I don't mean just the ration card and the money.'

Douglas looked embarrassed.

'Oh, I forgot to tell you about the parcel,' Mrs Sheenan went on quickly.

'What parcel?' said Douglas.

'The printed label says it's from Scotland Yard. I thought perhaps Sergeant Woods had sent it. I know he loves your Douggie like a father.'

'A parcel for you?' said Douglas.

'No, for your Douggie. To Douglas Archer Junior, like they say in those American films, you know.' She saw the fear on his face. 'I put it in your room. I didn't do wrong, did I?'

'No, no, no,' said Douglas. 'I'll look at it.' But she heard him going up the stairs very hurriedly.

Douglas studied the parcel very carefully. The HSSPf label and the Scotland Yard rubber stamp looked authentic, and the typewriting had all the characteristics of the new Adler machines that the Germans had installed in their offices. The postage had been paid, not with ordinary postage stamps but with the special Dienstmarken adhesives that prepaid all official German mail.

Douglas picked up the parcel and decided that it wasn't heavy enough for a bomb. He was in fact too tired to take all the usual precautions, and he cut the string and wrappings off with his penknife. Inside there was a model motor car from the Schuco toy factory in Nuremberg. It was beautifully made, and complete with gear lever, miniature steering, differential and a front that opened to reveal a detailed engine. A compliments slip accompanied the gift and, in General Kellerman's fine penmanship, bore the message, 'To Douglas Archer, a brave boy – for his birthday. With fondest love, Fritz Kellerman.'

Douglas knew that his son would adore it, and treasure it all the more for the signed note. Yet it made him uneasy.

Douglas put the elaborate toy back into the box and refolded the wrappings. His son's birthday was not for another three weeks. By then the whole world could have changed.

Chapter Seventeen

Douglas scarcely slept before thoughts of Jimmy Dunn intruded upon his sleep enough to make him awaken. What had happened to the photo in the brown envelope that had formed the basis of Dunn's inquiries?

Douglas sat up in bed, now fully awake. Where would I conceal an addressed envelope, he asked himself. There was one excellent place to hide it – the nearest post-box. It was a long shot, but Douglas knew he would not rest until he checked it. He looked at his bedside clock. It was already too late to intercept it at the sorting office. By now it would be on its way for delivery.

There was something forbidding about Mafeking Road, where the younger Spode brother had lived. The military success that, at the beginning of the century, added to British dictionaries a new word for joyous celebration, had no echo here; but the name dated the grimy little brick houses.

There was no gate. It had been taken during one of the scrap metal collections that had grown more demanding month by month. In the ruins of the bombed house next door cabbages had been planted, but now, as the crop ended, weeds were strangling the decaying brown plants.

Douglas could not find a doorbell, so he rapped loudly on the boarding that was nailed across the front-room window. It took nearly five minutes to get a response, but eventually a fat, unshaven man in soiled undervest, and corduroy trousers opened the door. He yawned, hoisted the straps of his braces and said, 'Yeah? What?'

'I was here before,' said Douglas. 'The schoolteacher upstairs – Spode.'

'What now?'

'I'll have to come inside,' said Douglas.

'You'd better tell me what it's about,' insisted the fat man without yielding an inch.

Douglas put a hand on the man's belly and pushed. His hand had almost disappeared in the soft flesh before the man moved. 'Don't worry your pretty little head what it's all about, sleepy head,' said Douglas. 'Just curl up and go back to sleep.'

'I've been up for hours,' said the fat man. Douglas pushed past him, went along the corridor and opened the door of the warm well-lit little sanctum from which the fat man had come. It smelled of unwashed bodies and old cabbage. Douglas looked round the room. The big dresser housed a mixed collection of plates, cups and saucers, unpaid bills, a half-used strip of aspirin tablets, a glass tumbler containing the pieces of a broken pocket-watch, a tin-opener and a legion of dead flies. Propped on the top shelf there was a fly-specked calendar, folded to reveal a coloured view of Mount Snowdon, and the month of October 1937.

In the corner of the room there was an unmade bed, without sheets, and with a coloured cushion to replace the pillow. On it there was a copy of *Dandy* comic. On a chair, within reach of the bed, a tray showed the remains of a hearty breakfast; smears of egg and half a dozen bacon rinds. Only a small table was clean and tidy; with pens and pencils arranged alongside a sheet of blue blotting paper. Behind the telephone there was a box file labelled 'Contributions Mafeking Street 1941'. And yet, dominating this chaotic room there was the blazing coal fire. Such a conflagration was seldom seen in these hard times.

'Bloody cold out there this morning, eh, Sergeant?' said the fat man.

'Superintendent,' said Douglas. 'Detective Superintendent Archer from Scotland Yard.' From the wireless set with its fretsawed rising sun loudspeaker there came the sounds of a repeat 'In Town Tonight' interview. Douglas switched it off.

The fat man belched, and summoned up enough energy to rub his bare arms briskly before he tested the door again, to be quite sure that it was tightly shut against draughts from the corridor. 'Superintendent . . . yes, that's what I meant; Superintendent.'

'Anyone been to look at the room upstairs?' said Douglas while he looked to see if there was any sign of the morning's mail. For this man was one of the 'block-wardens'. The Germans had used the Air Raid Precautions organization to provide themselves with a network of Nazi Party officials along the lines of the ones they had in Germany. Through such men as these the Nazis distributed supplementary food coupons, mail from POW camps, winter relief and soup vouchers for the very needy. In return for the power and influence such 'wardens' were granted, they were expected to co-operate against 'anti-social elements'. A scrutiny of their neighbours' mail would be an essential part of that co-operation.

'Certainly not. That room is closed, just as the police ordered.'

'Don't give me the old-soldier stuff,' said Douglas flipping open the Mafeking Road contribution file. 'This is a murder investigation.'

'Well, don't think I'd protect the little bastard,' said the fat man indignantly. Douglas looked at him. He couldn't imagine the fat man protecting anyone. 'Bloody aristocrat!' said the fat man. 'Throwing his weight about, with his fancy accent, and lah-di-dah bloody orders about emptying the rubbish.' The fat man followed Douglas round the room. 'No time for bloody aristocrats – not now, not under this regime, eh?'

Douglas said, 'Belching and farting and eating two or three eggs and half-a-dozen rashers for breakfast, in a room hot enough to stay in your underwear! . . . A lot of aristocrats would like to know where to find such luxury!'

'Ah. Well now. In a badly bombed house like this, you've got to try to keep the damp out.'

'Postman been yet?'

The fat man opened a drawer and consulted a tin alarm clock. 'Any time now, Superintendent,' he said with a trace of sarcasm.

Douglas went to the dresser and looked through the picture-postcards and undelivered letters. They were addressed to other people. 'I collect stamps,' explained the fat man. 'My neighbours give them to me.' He went to the cupboard under the dresser. 'Would you fancy a little something to keep the cold out, Superintendent?'

'What is it, a mink coat?'

He chuckled. 'You're a caution, you are.' He found a rum bottle, uncorked it noisily and poured a measure into the tea he was drinking from a cup marked 'Savoy Hotel'. Having decided that Douglas's reply was in the negative, he replaced the rum and sat down with a loud sigh.

A few minutes later there came the rattle of the letter-box. The man started to get to his feet but Douglas pushed him back into the soft armchair with a heavy hand on the shoulder. 'You've done enough hard manual work for one day, warden,' he said. 'I'll get your mail for you.' As he went out of the room Douglas helped himself to the key to Spode's apartment, that was hanging on the key-board.

Douglas's long shot paid off. Jimmy Dunn's last act before being kidnapped was to throw into the mail the large manila envelope marked 'Photos do not bend'. He picked it up and took it upstairs. In the room where Douglas and Jimmy Dunn had found the false arm in the kitchen table drawer, Douglas stood for a moment before opening the envelope.

Inside the envelope there was the photo of Professor Frick and his fellow scientists. There was also a letter from Jimmy Dunn. It was written in pencil, on the back of a large buff-coloured form about supplementary soap rations for workers in vital industries. Most post offices had bundles and bundles of them, for some administrator's error had provided half London with paper for notes, wrapping and toilets.

To Sergeant Woods,
Since you will be taking this job over tomorrow, I thought I would list all the libraries and archives that I have phoned or visited concerning the present whereabouts of the scientists who once worked with the late Professor Frick. As you see from the attached sheet I have kept busy. But some person or persons have been working even harder to remove from these places all references to the Professor and his work. In my travels and inquiries I have not been able to locate one copy of anything the Professor has ever written. Furthermore all documents referring to the Professor have also been taken away.

Because I thought this might have been done on official orders, I cross-checked with Scotland Yard Registry, with Gestapo records and also with SS Central Archives, but they all tell me that the works of Professor Frick have not been censored, banned or confiscated and there is no outstanding official order concerning him or his family. I would be very grateful if you would tell me any mistake or omission that you see in what I've done. And I hope you will be able to tell me the answer to what I think is about the biggest puzzle I've come across in my brief experience in police-work.

Incidentally please tell Det. Supt. Archer that I traced the elbow pivot for the artificial limb. A man calling himself Spode has made an appointment for it to be fitted at Little Wittenham Depot (General Detention Camp) Berkshire at 3.30 P.M. on 17 November.

> Yours truly,
> James Dunn

Was it, Douglas wondered afterwards, a sense of fore-boding, idle curiosity, or no more than a need for more daylight that made him go to the window to read the note again. As he looked away from it he saw a horse and cart across the road. A man waiting on the street corner with a salvaged armchair lifted it into the cart and then climbed in after it. The cart's canvas top hid him from Douglas's view. Fifty yards along the street, two cyclists had stopped and were talking together. It began to rain – dark spots appeared on the road. The men buttoned their collars.

Douglas opened his brief-case and put the note and the photo inside it. Then he removed them again. Douglas Archer read the note for the third time. In his career respect for the preservation of evidence was well known to all his colleagues, but now he was learning new rules. With a pang of conscience he tore the note into small pieces, and flushed them down the toilet. Then he did the same with the list of libraries Dunn had contacted.

He went back to the window. There was no driver with the horse and cart; its reins had been looped to the lamp-post. The horse stood patiently in the drizzle of rain. Douglas locked his brief-case and started down the stairs.

The floor below was empty, except for some broken pieces of furniture that had been bundled together for firewood.

He tried the light-switch for the dark hall below, but the light did not work. He waited a moment to let his eyes become accustomed to the darkness. The only light came from the crack under the door of the warden's room, and from there also came the music of the radio – Harry Roy's dance band was playing, 'Somebody loves me, I wonder who'. As if in response to the sound of footsteps on the stairs, the volume of the radio was increased.

'Keep coming, Officer!' Now Douglas could see him, standing on the welcome mat, a shadowy figure with his shoulders flat against the inside of the door, and keeping very, very still.

'Who the hell are you?' said Douglas.

'I'm a Colt forty-five staring at your belly-button, Officer! So keep coming.' It was a West Country accent, Devon perhaps. And the only people to address policemen as 'Officer' were those who wanted to appear to be respectable members of the middle classes. Douglas stepped down another step, very slowly. The man moved forward to meet him. There were three stairs to go when Douglas heaved the brief-case at him, and jumped the last three steps.

There was a sharp intake of breath – it was a heavy brief-case – and then came the soft plop of a silenced gun, followed by the crash of glass as a bullet went out through a pane of the back door's fanlight. And then Douglas was on him. Douglas Archer was not in first class physical shape but, like so many men who neglected the need for exercise, he was heavy. The force of his jump knocked the man backwards, and he hit the door

169

with a crash that almost took it off its hinges. There was a low pitched 'Ahhhhhhhhh!' of pain as his breath was expelled past Douglas's ear. Douglas jabbed him in the belly, just in case he should try inhaling and stepped back as he jack-knifed forward, one hand clutching his middle and the other holding the gun as he gasped desperately for air.

Douglas kicked the pistol with enough force to scuff his shoe and then stooped down to retrieve it. He levelled it at the man. This Colt .45, with a huge home-made silencer fixed to the barrel, was as big as a blunderbuss and twice as badly balanced. With a smaller gun the man might have brought it round fast enough to shoot.

'Get up!' said Douglas. 'Let's see what you look like in the light.' Douglas stepped back to give him more room. Had the man on the floor been less dazed, he might have provided Douglas with a warning, but he had both hands on the floor, his head was bowed and he was trying to vomit.

Douglas was suddenly pinned by someone with arms like steel cables. He tried to twist away but he couldn't move a muscle or even turn his head. The dirty wallpaper was bathed in light as a door opened behind him, and the music of Harry Roy became very loud.

'Who started bloody shooting?' It was the fat man's voice.

'Get back in your cage, you gorilla,' said a voice very close to Douglas's ear. 'This won't take a minute.'

Douglas smelled a sweet sticky smell, and then there was a wet cloth across his face that made his eyes tingle. He gasped for breath but could only inhale the smell. He tried to twist his head away but the hand gripped roughly at his face. The lights dimmed and Douglas sank into a bottomless hole that was turning very slowly.

It was Harry Woods who was holding Douglas as he came conscious. A voice from someone out of sight said, 'We won't need the ambulance – he's coming round now.'

Harry Woods's face came very close. 'How are you feeling?'

'I'm feeling stupid,' said Douglas and closed his eyes again.

'I've got a car. Think you could manage, if I help you?'

'My brief-case.'

Harry Woods shook his head. 'I looked already; I guessed you'd have it . . . they must have taken it with them.'

'The warden?'

'Scarpered!'

'Let's get out of here,' said Douglas. He looked at Harry Woods and wondered whether he had really failed to find the brief-case and, more important, the photo of Professor Frick that was inside it. Douglas stared at his Sergeant, silently accusing him of complicity in everything that had gone wrong with this inquiry but Harry Woods stared back guiltlessly.

'You're burning the candle at both ends,' said Harry Woods. 'Everybody gets careless when they're exhausted. Take my tip; stay in bed and sleep the clock round.'

'I'm going to the office,' said Douglas.

'Please, Douglas,' said Harry Woods. Only rarely did he address his superior by his first name. 'I wouldn't tell you wrong – you need rest.'

No matter how much his reasoning warned him that Harry Woods was deeply involved with one or other of the Resistance groups, Douglas found it impossible to disregard the devotion and loyalty that his Sergeant had always shown for him, first as a child and later as a police Superintendent. Harry Woods had been like a father to

Douglas. No matter how much the rift, now between them, widened, that relationship remained. 'I must go back to the Yard, Harry. But I'll get away soon and have an early night.'

'You'd better,' said Harry with mock severity.

Chapter Eighteen

It was the middle of the afternoon when General Keller-man asked if Douglas felt well enough for 'a chat'. Douglas arrived upstairs in the famous office to find his General in that state of post-prandial euphoria that Harry Woods euphemistically termed 'over-refreshed'.

Kellerman's wardrobe of British native costume was still being expanded. Today he was wearing a smooth herringbone, single-breasted suit, complete with waistcoat and a cream-coloured Sea-Island cotton shirt with foulard bow-tie and brogue shoes. It was the sort of outfit that a foreigner would expect to see on a typical Oxford University lecturer, a consideration not entirely absent from Fritz Kellerman's motives in choosing it.

On the side table Kellerman had a silver tray with a big pot of real coffee that perfumed the whole room. There were two Limoges cups and saucers, and an assortment of extras. Kellerman took his time in preparing coffee topped with a large dollop of cream and dusted with a little powdered chocolate. 'Ah, Vienna,' said Kellerman, remembering that Douglas drank his coffee without any such additives. 'So out of date, so passé, so decadent . . . and yet still the most enchanting city in the world. Spiritually I am Viennese.'

'Really?' said Douglas politely, and sipped his black coffee appreciatively. All the Austrians he'd met in London seemed anxious to describe themselves as German. Perhaps only men who wore the neat little gold badge – that distinguished the first one hundred thousand members of the Nazi Party – that Kellerman now wore, and whose accent was unmistakably that of Munich, amused themselves by claiming to be Viennese.

'Yes, indeed. Vienna is a city with a soul.' Even in English, Kellerman was able to introduce into his speech that slight nasal braying that could make an Austrian joke so much funnier. 'You'll have a bruise,' Kellerman said suddenly. 'It's changing colour already. Damned gangsters! Are you sure you wouldn't like to go over to St George's Hospital at Hyde Park Corner?' Out of deference to the feelings of his English subordinate, he did not call the SS General Hospital by its proper name.

'Cannon Row police station gave me some aspirins from their first-aid box,' said Douglas. He drank some more coffee. 'And thank you for the present for my son. I'll give it to him on his birthday, and then he'll write to you.'

'All boys like cars,' said Kellerman, 'and I decided that you would prefer him not to have a military toy.'

'It was most thoughtful, General.'

'Are you an angler, Superintendent?'

'No, sir.'

'Pity. Best pastime a police officer can have, in my opinion. Fishing teaches a man patience; and teaches him a lot about men.' He stepped across the room to tap a glass case. Inside it there was a large trout, stuffed at the moment of pulling a face. 'I caught that fellow, Superintendent.'

'Really, sir,' said Douglas, although Kellerman had drawn his Superintendent's attention to that fact a dozen or more times, and the circumstances of the unfortunate creature's demise were recorded in gold lettering on the case.

'Standartenführer Huth, on the other hand,' said Kellerman, walking back to his desk but not sitting down, 'is a ski champion.' Kellerman picked up the coffee pot and smiled at Douglas.

Douglas, deciding that some reaction was expected, said, 'I didn't know that, sir.'

'He went to Garmisch for the 1936 Olympics,' said Kellerman – unable, in spite of his animosity, to keep a note of pride out of his voice. 'He was a competitor in the men's combined downhill and slalom event. He won no medals but it is a distinction to compete, eh?'

'Indeed it is,' said Douglas. By now his head was beginning to ache; it was the after-effect of the ether with which he had been drugged.

'The sport a man chooses tells you a lot about his personality.' Kellerman smiled. 'Standartenführer Huth is always in a hurry; I am never in a hurry. Do you understand what I mean, Superintendent?'

'I do indeed, sir.'

'Have a little more coffee,' said Kellerman, pouring it for him. As he came close, Douglas smelled the mint cachou that Kellerman used to sweeten his breath.

Outside, in Whitehall, the combined bands of Army Group L (London District) HQ were beginning a rehearsal for the German-Soviet Friendship Week ceremonies. Douglas recognized the 'Petersburg March', which at one time only the 2 Garde-Infanterie Brigade were permitted to march to, and which the Berliners sang to well-known ribald lyrics.

'Are you sure you won't have cream?'

Douglas shook his head. Kellerman tightened the window-fastening but it didn't reduce the sound of the band. 'The Reichsführer-SS was asking me about developments on this murder you're working on – the one in Shepherd

175

Market. I told him I knew very little . . . I felt rather a fool, to tell you the truth.' Kellerman played with the coloured sugar in the bowl.

'There's nothing much to report,' said Douglas.

'I don't understand why you went back to the house this morning?'

Douglas drank some coffee, and took his time. Huth had told him to keep the investigation secret, but without written instructions from someone superior to both of them, Douglas regarded General Kellerman as his senior officer. 'One of my officers – Constable Dunn, working in plain clothes . . .'

'The one who was murdered last night?'

'Yes, sir. Dunn helped me. We found a photograph at the suspect's home. It is a photo showing the men who worked with Professor Frick before the war. I sent him to investigate those men. I believe that Dunn realized he was being followed and slipped the envelope – it was already addressed to the Mafeking Street house – into the post, knowing that in such an inquiry the mail would eventually be forwarded to me here at the Yard.'

'But you went to the house to get it?'

'Yes, sir.'

'Does it seem odd to you that these Resistance men – and such groups always have ways of stealing mail in transit – not only had to go to the address to get it, but actually arrived too late to intercept the postman?'

'The warden at the house must have phoned them,' said Douglas. 'He disappeared along with the people who attacked me.'

'And you lost the photo of Professor Frick and his co-workers?'

'Yes, sir.'

'You needn't look surprised at how much I know,

176

Superintendent. Your police Constable phoned inquiries concerning Professor Frick to Registry, SS Central Archives and the Gestapo too. Naturally, inquiries such as that are reported back to this office.'

'Of course, sir.' Outside the German bands halted. After a brief pause they began to play 'Tannenbaum, O Tannenbaum'. Or could it be 'The Red Flag' thought Douglas? How convenient that the music was the same.

'Professor Frick is dead. He died in the fighting last year. His staff are engaged on special work for the Reich.'

'Special work?' said Douglas.

'Oh, that doesn't mean that you will be asked to slacken the pace of your investigation. It simply means that you must leave Professor Frick's scientists out of it.' Kellerman used the spoon to scoop up a tiny fraction of the whipped cream and put it in his mouth. 'And that order is on the authority of the Führer. Not even the Reichsführer-SS himself has the power to go against it. Have I made the position clear, Superintendent Archer?'

'Crystal clear, sir.'

'Good fellow!' said Kellerman, pushing aside the cream jug as if he no longer needed it. He looked up, beamed and tossed his head to replace a lank of white hair that had fallen across his face. 'I knew that with you, a nod would be as good as a wink.'

'That's for a blind horse, sir,' said Douglas.

'You will have your little joke, Superintendent,' said General Kellerman.

The dusty yellow sunlight that colours London in autumn, had followed the showers of morning rain. Douglas paused in the Embankment corridor and looked out of the window to see the combined bands marching along the street. They looked magnificent in their dress uniforms, with dozens of brass instruments shining in the sun, and the jingling Schellenbaum complete with horsetails that marked its origin as the instrument of the Janissaries. They had an imperious splendour. Artfully the Germans used their military music to awe and pacify the conquered people of Europe. By the time Douglas got back to his office they were playing 'Greensleeves'.

The communicating door to Huth's room was open, and Douglas could see Harry Woods going through the official papers that were piled up on the Standartenführer's desk. 'What are you doing, Harry?' Douglas sat down at his desk and began to sort through the backlog of paperwork.

'Perfect timing, sir.'

'I'm beginning to realize that you only call me "sir" when you are up to some damned mischief.'

Harry grinned. In spite of generous applications of Brilliantine his short-cut hair would not stay in place. It gave him a somewhat comic aspect. 'Have a look at this,' he said, waving a pink carbon copy of a typewritten report sheet. 'I can't read all the German, but I get the gist of it.' Douglas went into Huth's office but did not accept the offered form. 'Read it,' said Harry. 'You'll be tickled to death. Go on! Machiavelli won't be back for five minutes or so; I've timed his bodily functions.'

Douglas took the report sheet.

PERSONAL FILE

CONFIDENTIAL REPORT. Security Classification
Det. Supt. Douglas ARCHER.

1. At a time when few Metropolitan Police officers have University education or professional qualifications, the above officer has demonstrated how valuable such preparation can be, in spite of opposition to direct entry (to Inspector rank) by the majority of the police service.

2. The difficulty that any graduate from the Hendon Police College encounters when requesting transfer to CID work is proved a short-sighted policy by Det. Supt. D. Archer's outstanding aptitude in detective work.

3. Douglas Archer is the son of a moderately successful but undistinguished civil engineer who was killed on the Western Front. His mother is the daughter of a well known racing-car driver. Archer attended one of the minor public schools as a day-scholar, and then studied law at Oxford University before going to the Hendon Police College. His strict upbringing and education has resulted in a conservative, humourless personality dedicated to the slow, inefficient, and out of date methods still current in British police procedure.

4. Although he is credited with considerable powers of intuition in his work, a more rational explanation of his remarkable career as a police detective is that he has closely studied the scientific methods of the forensic theorists including our own great pioneer Dr Hans Gross. His careful methods, and long hours of work, are those of a neurotic personality obsessed with a determination to apprehend the wrongdoer. For this reason, and others, this officer's security classification is hereby raised from Ba to Aa.

5. It must be added that this officer is one of the most popular and respected of men serving with the Metropolitan Force and that, in contradiction to the findings of this report, his English colleagues believe him to be a wit and raconteur of considerable skill.

> Signed, Fritz Kellerman, Gruppenführer
> (Höherer SS und Polizeiführer).

'What do you say about that?' said Harry. 'Sounds like you're being short-listed for a staff job at Hendon.' It was more of a stricture for Hendon than an accolade for his partner.

'Am I really a humourless, conservative personality?'

'You were all right until these bastards arrived,' said Harry. 'With these Huns breathing down your neck, we're all losing our sense of humour.' He took the report

179

and pushed it back into the file. 'And look at this one,' he said.

'I don't want to look at any more,' said Douglas. Outside the band was playing 'D'ye ken John Peel'.

'These German bastards love to rub it in, don't they,' said Harry. Douglas frowned, but Harry grinned back and said, 'I mean our German visitors love to rub it in.'

'They probably think that playing old English folk melodies is sensitive and endearing.'

Harry Woods made rude noise.

'A lot of people feel as you feel,' said Douglas. 'But they keep it to themselves.'

'Then I wish they wouldn't,' said Harry bitterly. He leaned closer to Douglas. 'Would you like to meet some of my friends? . . . they'd interest you, I know they would.'

Douglas wanted to confide in Harry, and tell him about the meeting with Mayhew, tell him he was already in contact with anti-Nazi groups. Douglas had always confided in Harry, ever since he was a child. He had asked Harry's advice about every decision he'd made in his police career, and told Harry about his decision to get married even before he told his own mother. When Jill found she was pregnant, they called in to tell Harry the good news on the way to Jill's parents.

But he did not confide in his old friend. 'You've always been a joiner, Harry. Back in the old days it was the Rugby Club and the Boxing. Then you became secretary for the Stamp Collecting Club . . .'

'Philatelic Society,' said Harry primly.

'You've always enjoyed meeting and talking and – '

'Boozing, that's what you were going to say, isn't it?'

Douglas held up his hands in a gesture of deference. 'It's what makes you a good copper, Harry. And it's what

180

makes us a good team. You've always done the footwork, buttonholing the snouts, chatting up the villains and filing it all away in that memory of yours. I'm not like that – I'm just the legal man.'

'Talk to my friends, Doug. Talk to them, *please*.'

'Harry, you're not making it easy for me. I came in here just now determined to persuade you to break free from these people. And here you are, trying to involve me too.'

'Please, Doug.' It was no more than a whisper but it was from the heart, and only with difficulty was Douglas able to do what he knew was logical and sensible. He shook his head.

From the corridor they heard the sound of boots on the mosaic flooring and the armed sentry coming to attention and murmuring, 'Heil Hitler!' The door opened and Huth entered. He was wearing a Luftwaffe black leather zipper jacket, and a pair of army trousers. Only his shirt and tie were part of his normal uniform.

'Either of you two know a tailor? I need a new uniform.' He did not seem to notice that his two subordinates were leaning over his desk.

'There's a man in Lambeth Road,' said Harry, who always had an answer for such a question. 'He does German uniforms. A lot of the Savile Row people sub-contract jackets to him. Very good quality.'

'I'm not competing in a beauty contest,' said Huth. 'Is he quick? I must have it by tomorrow night.'

'I'll phone him, boss.' Huth did not react to being called boss, and Douglas guessed that this had become a regular form of address. Harry had not mastered the complexities of the SS rank system.

'Harry,' said Huth affably. 'Would you send this up to

the photo department and ask for three dozen copies and the negative. I need it within the hour. I'm preparing "wanted" posters.' He passed to Harry the same picture of Professor Frick that had been stolen from Douglas. 'And list everyone appearing on that photo on a Primary Arrest Sheet and bring it to me for signature.'

'General Kellerman is the only person here authorized to sign the PA sheets,' said Harry.

'Not any longer,' said Huth. Douglas looked at Harry, who raised an eyebrow.

When Harry Woods had departed to the photo department, and Douglas was working at his desk, Huth came and propped himself on the window-ledge alongside. 'Sergeant Woods is a hard worker,' said Huth.

'He's the best damned copper in the building.'

'But that wouldn't be any good at all, unless you were here to give him covering fire,' said Huth.

'What's that mean?' said Douglas without breaking off his work.

'Sergeant Harry Woods is a liability to you – a dangerous liability. That's what it means. How long do you imagine you are going to be able to protect him from the inevitable?'

'How long do you think?' said Douglas with a calm he did not feel.

'Not long.' Douglas looked up in time to catch one of Huth's razor blade smiles edge-on. 'Not long.'

'This one needs your signature,' said Douglas. He twisted the form round on the desk, so that Huth could read it. But Huth tugged a gold pencil from his shirt pocket and signed the form with no more than the merest glance.

'Don't you want to read it?'

'It's a memo from Kellerman,' said Huth. 'It tells me

that one or the other of his administration conferences will be held on Tuesday in future – instead of some other time in the week. A lot of decisions will be taken on Tuesday in future. You see if I'm not right, Superintendent Archer.'

Huth took a packet of Players cigarettes from his pocket and lit one with all the casual skill of a movie cowboy. He inhaled and breathed down his nostrils. 'Because I can't be here on Tuesdays,' he explained. 'The General is frightened of what my remarks might put into the printed minutes of his cosy little conferences.' Huth put away his cigarettes without offering one to Douglas. 'General Kellerman is concerned that someone might take over this nice job he has in London. Flattering to think that he sees me as the most likely candidate, don't you think?'

'Very flattering, sir.'

'You're a fool, aren't you, Archer?'

'A lot of people have expressed that opinion recently, sir.'

Huth got to his feet and turned to look out of the window. Douglas's telephone rang. It was his direct line. 'Detective Superintendent Archer? This is Colonel Mayhew.'

Anxiously Douglas glanced at Huth but he was taking no interest in the phone call. 'Yes?' said Douglas guardedly.

'I understand you will be visiting Miss Barga this evening.'

'Yes,' said Douglas quietly. He wondered if the switchboard man was monitoring the call.

'I'll see you there . . . about nine?'

'Very well.' Douglas replaced the phone without saying

183

goodbye. He looked up at Huth, but the Standartenführer was still staring out of the window.

'Am I to understand that you are ordering the arrest of everyone in this photograph?'

'Correct,' said Huth, without turning round.

'For the murder of Dr Spode?'

'For questioning in connection with the murder.'

'There is good reason to believe his young brother murdered him. He was certainly at the flat that day.'

'I'm keeping an open mind,' said Huth. 'I want all of them arrested.'

'But if I find any of Professor Frick's staff, you want me to arrest them, and ask them about it?' Douglas was exasperated by Huth's reticence.

'You won't find Professor Frick, and I doubt if you'll find any of his staff.'

'Why not?' said Douglas.

Huth turned round slowly and looked at Douglas. 'Because Professor Frick's co-workers are under the protection of the German army.'

'But the "wanted" notices, that you just ordered Harry to prepare . . .?'

'Just a device, to force those army idiots to tell me where they are . . . even to let us see them.'

'I see,' said Douglas who did not see at all. Had Huth not seen the railway ticket to Bringle Sands that had been in the dead man's pocket? Harry Woods must have destroyed the ticket. Now Douglas had no doubt that Professor Frick's team were working for the German army somewhere near to Bringle Sands, where the dead man had come from.

Huth said, 'You find where the army have hidden Professor Frick's scientific staff and I'll give Harry Woods the sort of protection that no one dare challenge.' He inhaled on his cigarette, still staring at Douglas. 'Back in Berlin I had a drunken homosexual working for me. Some of his treasonable remarks would have made even you turn pale.'

'I turn pale very easily,' said Douglas.

Huth wasn't listening. He had those steely grey eyes drilling into Douglas's head. 'Do you know what I did?' Without pausing he added, 'I wrote instructions for him to act as an agent provocateur.' Huth laughed briefly. 'A perfect defence. From then onwards he had no one to fear.'

'And whom has Harry Woods to fear?'

'Well certainly not that white-haired fatherly old Fritz Kellerman. He's a Prussian gentleman of the old school.' Huth laughed, got up, put on his overcoat and picked up the piece of paper on which Harry Woods had written the name and address of the tailor in Lambeth. When he got to the door, he turned and said, 'Are you going to find young Spode for me?'

'I think so.'

'Time is running out,' said Huth, and left.

Chapter Nineteen

Douglas found it difficult not to feel smug when he first noticed the man. He was exactly the type Huth would be bound to choose. He was twentyish, perhaps younger, a thick-set man with the reddish complexion that still suffered the skin eruptions of adolescence. He wore a belted coat, and a tweed hat of the sort favoured by anglers and college professors. He carried a carelessly rolled umbrella, and a street-map, which he consulted each time Douglas halted.

In the Haymarket Douglas jumped aboard a passing bus. Its platform was already crowded but the others made room for him. He looked back to see the young man frantically elbowing his way through the home-bound office workers, and craning his neck to keep Douglas in sight. By Piccadilly Circus Douglas had lost sight of his pursuer. Half-way up Regent Street, he got off the bus and went east into Soho.

It was too early for Bertha's bar. Douglas walked up to the floor above and returned the dinner suit to Charlie Rossi. He grumbled about the marks on it in a good-natured way that a couple of cigarettes smoothed over. There, ready for him, was his own suit, folded more carefully than it had ever been folded before. Douglas remembered the time when Rossi's hire service had been distinguished by the use of black and white layers of tissue paper, and dozens of pins, and beautiful boxes with Rossi's name in scrollwork. Now the old man had wrapped his suit in newspaper, and could spare not more than two layers of that.

Douglas insisted on paying for the hire of the suit and Rossi responded by bringing from under the counter a bottle of Marsala and two glasses. Compared with his fellow tradesmen, Charlie Rossi was a lucky man. As an Italian, he enjoyed the special status of being allied to the Germans. But as the old man said – straight-faced but with twinkling eyes – the British had not interned him at the beginning of the war, and that had been his downfall. In fact, they both knew that Charlie had been famous for his anti-Mussolini jokes for more than a decade.

It was twilight as Douglas emerged into the crowded streets of Soho. In spite of the restrictions on the use of electricity, there were still many illuminated signs, and Germans of all shapes and sizes in every imaginable kind of uniform were spending their money on the delights everywhere offered. At the end of Old Compton Street, the Feldgendarmerie unit attached to West End Central Police station manned the regular check-point. The NCO recognized Douglas and let him through the barrier ahead of two black-uniformed tank officers and their girlfriends. They objected to this but the Gendarmerie Feldwebel told them that Douglas was a SIPO officer and this silenced the officers immediately.

Douglas hurried on self-consciously. He turned south past the ruins of the Palace Theatre, now a 'garden' of weeds and wild flowers that were said to thrive on the cordite traces. In the lower part of Charing Cross Road, Douglas stopped to look at an outdoor rack of second-hand books. Then he saw him again. Of course Huth would have assigned an experienced man to this task. Douglas wondered if it was something to do with the phone call from Colonel Mayhew, although at the time Huth appeared not to notice it. Douglas stopped to give a penny to an old man at the handle of a street-piano and turned to look round. The man stopped and looked at his map.

Irritably, Douglas decided to give this man the slip once and for all. He moved through the crowds quickly, keeping close to the buildings so that as he reached the Leicester Square entrance to the Underground he was able to move smoothly down the stairs, dodging in and out of the people coming up. Once at the lower level, he ran across the concourse, past the ticket offices, machines and kiosks. Holding up his police pass he went through the barrier with a nod from the ticket inspector. Then he hurried down the long moving staircase that went to the Piccadilly Line trains.

The platform was crowded, and Douglas imagined the young man still fumbling with his change at the ticket office, or arguing with the ticket inspector. But Douglas did not depend on that. He forced his way through the people, and on to the first train that arrived. A porter had to help crush the last few passengers in. The automatic doors slammed shut and the train lurched away.

At the next stop – Piccadilly Circus – Douglas waited until the doors were about to close before stepping out on to the platform. Then he crossed to the Northbound side and waited until a train disgorged its passengers, before melting into the crowd, to go with them along the exit tunnels.

Douglas was at the foot of the moving staircases when he saw the man again. By now he had abandoned the idea of disguising his intentions, and, this time, when Douglas stopped to look back, the man did not consult his street-map. Douglas stepped on to the moving stairs, and stood still to let them carry him upwards. Both men needed a moment to catch their breath. The two of them – seemingly oblivious of each other – stared at the advertisements that floated past, and took deep breaths of warm, stale air.

By now the contest had become a trial of strength. Each persuaded himself that nothing was more important. In his state of stress and tiredness, Douglas began to believe that he would become the laughing stock of the entire Metropolitan Police Force if he failed to shake off this limpet. Douglas turned to assess the man. The Piccadilly line trains are deeper than any others in the London Underground, and here they are at the lowest part of the railway system. The escalator joining them to street level is of dizzying length. Douglas watched him carefully. The man was toying with the handle of his umbrella and did not look up. Perhaps this was a good thing. If he thought Douglas had given up hope of shaking him off, one last ruse might do the trick.

As, at last, Douglas reached the very top, he waved his pass at the ticket collector but instead of exiting he turned round to descend on the escalator alongside. Soon the two men were abreast of each other, each moving in different directions. The man's face contorted with anger. He pushed his umbrella into the belt of his coat and began to climb from one moving staircase to the other. He gripped the electric light stanchion with one hand and rolled his body over until he got one foot on to the moving handrail of Douglas's staircase. For a moment it seemed he must fall. With the agility, and the handgrip, of an athlete, he threw his weight into a kick that moved him far enough to grab the handrail with his free hand. The floppy umbrella slipped loose and came clattering on to the steps, the man followed it. A woman screamed.

He had landed heavily, knees bent and body crouched forward, as if about to faint or vomit. As he straightened, he was holding the umbrella in two hands. The hands parted and Douglas saw the shiny length of steel blade that had been concealed within the bamboo stick. And suddenly the man was leaping forward.

He lunged with all the desperate anger of the assassin. His arms stretched wide, uncaring for his own safety, the blade high in a tightly clenched fist. It swung down, beginning a curve that would have ended in Douglas Archer's heart, had sheer terror not made the intended victim totter on the edge of the step. The sharpened blade sliced the shoulder strap from Douglas's raincoat, and blood gushed from his ear.

A woman screamed and kept on screaming and another voice was shouting for the police. Already the man was swinging his blade for the second cut. His face was so close that Douglas felt warm breath, and saw the dilated eyes fixed upon the chest, as he calculated the jab to his heart. Experience and training told him to stay calm, and use only that minimum of force that the law decrees permissible in a case of self-defence. But instinct said fight.

Douglas struck out. He heard the man yell with pain, and felt his fist connect with his attacker's face. But the blow did nothing to stop the man's descent. The whole weight of him collapsed against Douglas and for a moment it seemed as if they both must topple. Then Douglas grabbed the moving handrail, to pull himself out of the way. Forced back against the handrail, Douglas kicked viciously. His shoe hit the man's knee, and this time produced a louder howl of pain.

The attacker kept going. His knees folded, and with arms stretched he dived face-first down the stairs. He struck the steps with a terrible sound. He bounced, arms and legs flailing the air desperately. But now nothing could stop him. Like a bundle of rags in a pulping chute, he tumbled down the seemingly endless staircase. When he hit the bottom level, he seemed to disintegrate, as shoes, hat, umbrella and map flew in different directions and his coat busted its belts and buttons, and wrapped itself round his head.

There was a small crowd there by the time Douglas reached the bottom, and the railway police arrived soon after. The man was dead, his skull cracked and his face brutally crushed. Douglas went through the dead man's clothes. Inside his jacket, a specially-made pocket contained a thin bundle of Resistance leaflets, reduced now to a bloody pulp. His wallet contained over two hundred pounds in fivers and a forged curfew pass that would not have fooled even the most myopic of patrol commanders.

Douglas waited until the body was collected, and talked with the Scotland Yard duty officer to make sure that a full report would go to Standartenführer Huth's desk for immediate attention. Douglas declined the suggestion that he should go for a medical check-up and a dressing for the cuts on his neck and ear. Already he was late for his appointment with Barbara Barga.

Chapter Twenty

'When I was a young Sub-Divisional Inspector I often found myself in a brawl with drunks on a Saturday night. But this was different. I never dreamed what it might be like to have a strong, determined kid, with a knife in his hand, trying to murder me.' Douglas sat back in the best armchair, and sipped the hot soup.

Barbara Barga said, 'And you don't think he could have had any connection with Standartenführer Huth?'

'To murder me! Huth doesn't have to go to all that trouble. Now that he's empowered to sign the Primary Arrest Sheets he could pop me into a concentration camp, and I'd never be seen again.'

She shuddered. 'But could he have sent this man just to frighten you?'

'Huth frightens me enough already,' said Douglas. 'He doesn't need anyone waving daggers.' Barbara came round the back of the chair, and leaned over to kiss him.

'Poor darling,' she said. 'Have another bowl of soup.'

'No thanks; I'm fine.'

'I still think you need a Scotch.' She took a slice of bread and a toasting fork. 'You're in shock.'

Douglas took the bread and toasting fork from her and leaned forward to hold it near the hissing flames of the gas fire. His hand trembled.

'In England, it's a man's job to make toast,' said Douglas. It was his way of saying he didn't want to be treated like an invalid.

'Or every Englishman's sneaky way to hog the fire,' was her way of saying she understood.

'Is that your experience of Englishmen?'

'Of some of them . . . people are depressed and nervous, aren't they, Douglas? This lack of self-confidence makes them devious and unreliable.' She paused, uncertain of whether she'd offended him.

'We've always been like that,' said Douglas, and made light of her criticisms. 'But if that's the way you feel, why are you risking your neck with . . .?' Douglas didn't say the names of Mayhew, Benson and Staines.

'Oh, my, you are discreet,' she said. 'A lady's honourable name has nothing to fear at your hands, Doug.'

The toast smoked. Douglas turned it over, and held the other side to the fire. 'You still haven't told me.'

'Let's just say I can't resist a titled Englishman.'

Douglas knew there were other reasons but he did not press it. The radio was broadcasting dance music, direct from the Savoy Hotel ballroom. Carrol Gibbons was playing his famous white piano. For a few minutes they listened to the vocalist singing 'Anything goes'.

She had butter for the toast – pale and spotty, it was home-made and delicious. 'I'm not really a part of it, Doug,' she said suddenly. 'But with my syndicated column I can be valuable to Mayhew and the others . . . and, from my point of view, it's a story no good reporter could pass up.'

'But how did you contact them? And why should they trust you?'

'My ex-husband works for the State Department in Washington.'

Ah, so *that's* it, thought Douglas, an ex-husband!

'He's been helping Rear-Admiral Conolly's people find their way round town.'

'What are Conolly's chances?'

'He's . . .' she was about to make some flippant remark but she saw that Douglas depended upon her answer. 'Not good, Douglas. Congress distrusts military rulers. They've seen too many of them in South America. If it was Churchill there in Washington, or even Lord Halifax, or just some name they'd heard before . . .' She waited to see how Douglas would take this pessimistic assessment. He nodded. She said, 'Colonel Mayhew believes that it would be worth almost any kind of risk to get the King out of German custody.'

'So he told me,' said Douglas. 'But you're the one who warned me about Mayhew and the rest of them.'

'And I still warn you,' she reached out and pressed his hand affectionately. 'When Mayhew says he will risk anything, he means he'd risk any number of guys like you.'

'You don't like Mayhew?'

'He's too much like my ex-husband,' she said, and Douglas was pleased with both judgments.

Colonel Mayhew arrived at nine-fifteen. He came into the cramped little living-room, shaking the rain off his Melton overcoat. 'Good evening, Archer.' He took his coat off. 'Now that the curfew has forced Boodles and Whites to close early a man like me has no place to spend his evenings.'

Barbara and Douglas smiled politely. They both knew that Mayhew had never been the sort of man who spent his evenings in gentlemen's clubs. 'What happened to your neck?'

'A kid tried to knife me tonight,' said Douglas.

'My God,' said Mayhew. 'And came damned close to killing you, by the look of it. Who?'

'One of your boys I think,' said Douglas.

'I have no *boys*,' said Mayhew coldly. 'Have you got a corkscrew for this?' He held up the bottle of wine that he'd had in his overcoat pocket.

Barbara had a corkscrew ready in her hand.

'Ah, the ever-practical American,' said Mayhew. With all the skill of a wine-waiter, he removed the foil, wiped the top of the cork, and withdrew it without shaking the bottle. 'I have no boys,' he said again, holding the bottle to the light to be sure that the sediment was undisturbed. 'And I don't have killers either.'

'He had a pocket full of these,' said Douglas. He passed him a leaflet.

Mayhew took it by the corner and held it with obvious distaste. 'What are these stains?' He gave it back to Douglas.

'Blood,' said Douglas, 'he's very dead.'

Mayhew had handled the leaflet with the same kind of delicacy that he'd given the bottle of claret, from which he now poured.

.'People want to do something,' said Barbara. 'Even if it's only passing round leaflets, with slogans like this. People want to show how much they hate the Germans.'

'You see,' said Mayhew. 'These Americans! Impetuous, impatient, and so full of energy.' He handed wine to her, and another glass to Douglas.

'Good health,' said Douglas. They drank Mayhew's wine.

Douglas said, 'My job is solving crimes. The British public have a right to be protected against murder, robbery and violence. Do I have to tell the victims of such crimes that I don't like working under the Germans?' He touched his neck. It was tender and beginning to throb.

195

'Hold your horses, my dear chap. No one is criticizing the police, just as no sane person would say the fire-service is disloyal because it extinguishes fires under the German regime.'

'I wish someone had explained all that to the kid who came at me tonight.'

'You're a special case.' Mayhew put down his glass, raised his hands to warm them at the fire and rubbed them together vigorously. 'All that "Archer of the Yard" publicity . . . of course, you've not encouraged it.' He smiled briefly, as a film star smiles for a photographer. 'But it's always the prominent people who are singled out for attack. None of the chorus, the dancers or the musicians who do those special Wehrmacht shows at the Palladium, get threatening letters – but Maurice Chevalier does get them, and so do the other top-name stars.'

Barbara held her empty glass for more wine. Mayhew poured it. She said, 'But all this is academic, Colonel. The most urgent thing is that you do something to prevent any other Resistance man trying to kill Douglas.'

'What would you have me do, dear lady? Shall I tell the world that Douglas Archer is now a fully paid up member of the Resistance?'

'Jesus Christ, Colonel,' said Barbara. 'You're going to leave him, like an Aunt Sally, a target for any crank or crackpot who comes along?'

'I'll do anything that you, and the Superintendent, wish. But I believe a few moments' reflection will tell you that it is far more dangerous to be known as a member of the Resistance, than . . .' He left the rest unsaid.

'Colonel Mayhew is right, Barbara. I'll just have to be careful.'

'It's probably going to be the best thing that ever happened to us,' said Mayhew. 'From what you tell me, no one could believe that this was a put-up job.' He drank some wine. 'From now onwards the Germans will regard you as one of the most reliable men they have.'

'And if the next attempt on my life *succeeds*,' said Douglas, 'the Germans will put up a statue to me. You make it sound very attractive, Colonel.'

Mayhew smiled. It was an engaging smile and in spite of his feelings, Douglas smiled too. 'That's better,' said Mayhew. 'When the King is freed and makes a statement about the true status of Rear-Admiral Conolly, everything else will begin to fall into place.'

'Where will the King go?' asked Barbara.

'A lot of people will have to be disappointed. The Canadians will expect him to go to Ottawa, I expect. But politically he'll be more effective in Washington DC. On the other hand, His Majesty might prefer to join his brother in the Bahamas, or even go to Bermuda.'

'I'll drink a toast to that day,' said Barbara.

'And a scoop for Barbara Barga,' said Mayhew, careful never to overlook the vested interest of each party in every discussion.

'Not much chance of that,' said Barbara. She drank. 'Is it really a possibility?'

'We've been having talks with a man named Georg von Ruff, a Generalmajor on the staff of Admiral Canaris, the head of the Abwehr – military intelligence – he's a General mark you, but one of a group of convinced anti-Nazis. He hinted that there is even a plan afoot to assassinate Hitler.'

'And you believe him?' said Douglas.

'Yes, I do,' said Mayhew. 'These are men of fine German families, professional soldiers of the old school. They have no time for the Nazi Party and the SS ruffians.'

197

'There are bitter feelings between the German occupation army, and the SS,' agreed Douglas.

'And we must exploit this division,' said Mayhew. 'But I thank Providence that I'm having to find common ground with these Prussians, rather than those SS cutthroats.'

'But will they really do something?' said Barbara. 'Or is it just talk?'

'There's an element of self-interest,' said Mayhew. 'The army strongly oppose this new idea that Great Britain should soon be ruled by a Reichskommissar rather than by the army C-in-C. They want to stay in control here, and I believe it's in our interest that the army do remain in control. Anything that strikes at the prestige of Kellerman, and his SS, automatically benefits the army.'

'Setting the King free would certainly make the SS look foolish,' said Douglas. 'Kellerman would probably be sacked.'

'And you say that that would suit your man Huth – right?' said Mayhew.

'It would,' said Douglas. 'But to what extent he'd actually assist, remains to be seen.'

Barbara said, 'If Huth is let into the secret, he could betray you.'

'That's where Superintendent Archer has agreed to help,' said Mayhew. 'He can leak rumours of the idea to Huth, and tell us the Standartenführer's reaction.'

'Yes, I can do that,' said Douglas.

'Be careful, Doug,' said Barbara. He reached for her hand and pressed it in reassurance.

Mayhew got to his feet. 'Well that's the next step, Archer. I leave it to you how you go about it.' He looked at himself in the ornately framed mirror over the fireplace. 'Don't over-play your hand, it's too risky. Just a hint will be enough.' Mayhew frowned at his reflection and tugged at the ends of his spotted bow-tie to tighten the knot. 'Simpsons of Piccadilly have a small stock of long combination underwear; wool, pre-war quality. I bought some yesterday. It's going to be a damned cold winter.'

'It won't be cold in the chair I'm using,' said Douglas.

Mayhew smiled. 'Well, goodnight. Get in touch when you think you have an answer. I don't have to tell you what will happen if we get this one wrong.'

'No, you don't,' said Douglas.

'Well, be a good chap, and stay out of the glossy magazines for a week or so.' Douglas nodded. He knew that Colonel Mayhew liked to have the last word.

Chapter Twenty-one

The clouds that had been hugging to the earth the last traces of the summer's warmth had gone. The air was cold. Douglas had breakfast with the boys and Mrs Sheenan before setting out for Little Wittenham (General Detention Camp) Berkshire.

Douglas managed to get one of the Flying Squad's cars for his journey along the Thames Valley to Wallingford and the camp. It was a Railton Special and, on the main road, Douglas put his foot down and got over ninety out of it. He was there well before noon.

It was an ideal place for a prison camp. This piece of farmland was locked inside a loop of the river Thames, its circumference completed by the road between the two waterside Wittenham villages. To the west, fast-moving clouds promised more rain, while, brooding on the eastern skyline, the Sinodun Hills, and their prehistoric fortifications, shone bright and hard in the cold sunlight.

It was a miserable spot. Perhaps even a measure of squalor would have improved it. It was a characterless square mile or more of pre-fabricated War Department timber huts, of the sort that every British soldier knew. But now they were surrounded with high wire fences that separated the prison camp from the area where the artificial limbs were made, and the huts near Day's Lock where the amputees came to collect them.

The Kommandant's office was in the high security detention area – a fine old house in Long Wittenham village. Douglas was met with courteous punctilio but he was not welcome there, and no one worked hard to conceal it. The Kommandant gave him no more than a nod and passed him over to an escorting officer.

The artillery Captain was a young man. Tall and thin, he had that sort of pigmentless complexion that kept his face pale in any sort of climate. His hair was fair and wispy, so that his eyebrows were almost invisible but his eyes were deepset and darklined and his lips pale and bloodless. And yet his appearance was not that of a man who has lived a dissolute life; rather he had that frail and sensitive aspect fashionable amongst Pre-Raphaelite painters.

'After you,' said the Captain, opening the door for Douglas with exaggerated politeness.

The young Captain talked in the same nervous way that ambitious hostesses entertain important visitors. He was from Cologne, and his sophisticated chatter, and accent too, was in contrast to the majority of his Füsilier-Regiment, and indeed of the whole 35. Infanterie Division, raised as it was from the Black Forest region, and based at Karlsruhe. And not only was the captain a social misfit, he was a very experienced professional soldier, who had worked in the War Ministry in Berlin, and served some time on a Divisional Staff. He was one of the few artillery officers with combat experience of the entirely new tracked and self-propelled guns. It was galling indeed to find himself employed as no better than assistant adjutant in a prison camp. And he made sure Douglas knew it.

It was a monotonous place with its white-painted stones lining every path, and the ropes that marked the forecourt of the guardroom and the polished fire extinguishers, all arranged with the obsessional orderliness which armies inflict upon both men and nature. As they passed into the next compound, Douglas saw the signs that directed visitors to the guard commander's office, and noticed that this was not a General Detention Camp, but the Generals' Detention Camp, where the Germans confined British and Allied officers of the rank of Brigadier and upwards.

'It provides work for them,' explained the young artillery Captain. 'They are marched across here each day, to make and repair artificial limbs for the war casualties.'

'Do officer POWs work too?'

'The Geneva Convention, you mean?' He adjusted his grey silk scarf and flipped up the collar of his heavy uniform overcoat. 'That was a problem at first, but the Legal Department soon came up with the answer. We discharged these Generals from the British Army. Technically speaking, they're now civilians held under detention.'

'Then they should be in the custody of the civil police,' said Douglas.

'Well there's the cunning bit of it, you see. They are held pending inquiries into what they did while in the army. This justifies holding them here in this military detention camp.'

'Very clever,' said Douglas.

'And they are deprived of trial by court-martial too,' explained the Captain. 'Under international law a POW has the same rights of trial as a soldier of equal rank in the army that captures him. And in the German army that means the right to be tried by men of equal rank. Can you imagine that? To try one of these fellows would have required a tribunal made up of German army Generals.' He chuckled at the thought of it.

They walked briskly. The wind was plucking at their coats, and lashing the trees into a demented dance. They reached the barrier and the barbed wire. The sentries saluted and the Captain walked as far as the first shed, and ushered Douglas inside. 'It's easy work,' said the Captain. 'And they have their food and a bed. They are better off than many civilians.'

'Is that what *you* think, Captain?' said Douglas.

The shed was unheated. The elderly prisoners worked at benches, using simple machines – hand presses, drills and hammers – to construct the false limbs. The interior echoed with the noise of their efforts. None of them looked up at the visitors.

'Do you want to see what they are doing?' said the Captain raising his voice above the noise.

Douglas shook his head. But then he saw a face he recognized from the newspapers and newsreels of those final days of fighting. 'I would like to speak to that man,' said Douglas.

The Captain grabbed the man Douglas had indicated. 'You!' he said. 'Name, ex-rank and camp number!'

The old man came to rigid attention, fingers extended straight and chin pressed in, as recruits learn at Prussian cadet schools. 'Yes, sir,' he said loudly without raising his eyes. 'Wentworth, Major-General, prisoner number 4583.'

'You commanded Force W?' Douglas asked.

'Yes, I'm that Wentworth,' said the old man. It was at the very end, with Wentworth's makeshift, mobile-brigade spread thin along the river Colne. The German armour tried to outflank Colchester, and roll up the defences from the seaward flank. By that time the result was no longer in doubt, but Wentworth's determined stand had given a destroyer flotilla of the Home Fleet enough time to steam out of Harwich. At the time, the rumours said that Churchill and the King were aboard the warships. Some people still believed it.

'You fought well, General,' said Douglas.

'I did what I was paid to do,' said the General.

'More,' said Douglas. 'You made history.'

Something within the old man flickered into life. His eyes brightened, and he stared at Douglas, trying to see whether he meant that Churchill and the King had escaped. Then he nodded, and turned his face away as if suddenly interested in the metal he was polishing. And Douglas was pleased that the old man was moved. Now the hammering had almost ceased and the shed quiet. Perhaps the conversation would have ended there but the men did not move.

'I was there,' said the Captain. 'I commanded a battery of self-propelled artillery – StuG III with assault guns – the only SP guns there.'

'You came up the London road, about five o'clock in the afternoon,' said Wentworth. He nodded. 'My CRA came on the blower and said counter-battery fire would be no good – you were moving all the time.'

'I was supporting our Panzer-pionier battalion,' said the Captain. 'We were sent to attack the defence line of Colchester and hold you there. Our casualties didn't matter, they told us that.'

'By the time you arrived it was more or less all over,' said the General. 'I was surprised that my boys stuck it out as long as they did. They were good troops, you know.' A gust of wind hammered the window panes and doors with enough noise to make the old man look up anxiously. 'At seven o'clock that evening, I told the gunners to destroy the breech-blocks. I told my unit commanders to decide their own course of action. Already the infantry trapped on Mersea Island were putting out white sheets from the houses there. And the

204

navy reported that your big guns were ranging on to the harbour at Harwich.'

'Can I take a message for anyone outside?' Douglas asked the old man. He looked at the Captain, half-expecting him to object. But he moved away and showed no more interest in the old General.

'My wife,' said the General. 'Tell her you've seen me, and that I'm well and cheerful.' Laboriously he unfastened the button on his army shirt and found a slip of paper with his wife's address and phone number. It was as if he'd been carrying this mangled piece of paper about for months, hoping that someone would make such an offer.

Douglas took the paper and followed the young Captain who was already moving towards the far door. He looked back at Wentworth and found himself meeting the gaze of the rows of old men, their faces registering various amounts of wonder, contempt, hatred and jealousy.

'Why him?' said the Captain. 'Why Wentworth?'

Douglas reached into his top pocket and found the SD pass that bore the unmistakable signature of the Reichsführer-SS. It was a curious zig-zag handwriting that bore an uncanny resemblance to the SS runes. Douglas held up the pass until it was level with the Captain's eyes. The Captain gave a weak smile and nodded. There were no more questions about Wentworth.

'You still want to go to the issuing department?'

'That's it,' said Douglas.

They stepped out into the cold again. They walked past lines of huts each identical except for the painted numbers. The Sinodun Hills were being swallowed by mist, and dark clouds were racing across the sky as fast as coal-fired locomotives, and twice as dirty. By the time they reached the four linked huts that were used as the issuing department they felt rain in the air.

The longest shed was divided by a counter along its length. Behind this counter, rows of shelving, holding documents, tools and spare parts, were attended by a dozen elderly men in brown warehouse coats. In front of the counter were the amputees, attending by appointment.

'Who gets limbs here?'

'British ex-servicemen, of all ranks, who live in the southeastern control zone,' said the Captain. His voice was curt and formal. The enthusiasm with which he described his part in the Colchester fighting was now gone.

'Or who lived there when the application was made?'

'Yes,' said the Captain.

'What documentation do they need to get through that door?'

'No one gets even past the outer gate without a pay-book, proving discharge from the British army without labour service obligation, and endorsement to prove they are not listed for the War Crimes Tribunal. They also need a current identity card, to show that their place of residence is registered with the local police. And then, of course, they must produce the card that is mailed to them to confirm their appointment here.'

'Sounds all right,' said Douglas.

'It *is* all right,' said the Captain. He smoothed his collar at the place where a Knight's Cross would have hung, had he been awarded that coveted decoration.

'You've just told me the theory,' said Douglas. 'When was the last time you sent someone to try and gain entrance without all that paper?'

The Captain grimaced and nodded. 'Do you want me to alert the sentries?'

'That's the last thing I want,' said Douglas. 'I want my man to get through.' Douglas turned and looked along the counter. 'Now show me where you keep the elbow joints and pivots.'

'Is that a joke?' said the Captain.

'When I make jokes I waggle my ears.'

'Replacements are done at the far end of that counter. Through that door there is a work-room, where they fit new parts and do small repairs.' They both turned to watch a young man with a shiny-new artificial leg. It was obviously the first time he'd worn it. Perhaps he'd hoped to strap it on and run home. Tragic disappointment was written all over his face. An old man, in a brown warehouse coat, supported him, an arm wrapped tightly round the young man's thin body, and taking most of his weight. 'It's always difficult at first,' said the old man gently. The boy's forehead glistened with sweat and pain.

'Let me go!' said the boy softly but urgently. 'Let me go!'

'No one ever did it first time,' said the old man. His voice was rich and mellow; an authoritative voice. It was all he could do to support the weight of the boy, and the old man's lips were pursed with the exertion.

'I'll be all right,' insisted the boy, his voice as thin as the body from which it came.

'You'll fall, lad!'

They were only a short distance from the horizontal bars, and the boy's hand reached out towards them. But the old man didn't release him.

'Let me go!' The boy's voice was louder now, and pitched higher. He struggled to get free. 'You're not a bloody General any more. Let me go, you silly old bastard!'

The old man stiffened, halted and let go, but his hand stayed in the air as if holding an invisible string. The boy tottered forward, biting his lip in determination and clawing at the air. At first it seemed that he would get there but before he could grasp the bar, his metal leg twisted under him, and he collapsed with a terrible crash that knocked the breath from his lungs. For a moment he was still and lifeless but then his body trembled and began to shake as he sobbed in silent and inconsolable despair.

The old man waited. He watched the boy carefully, seemingly oblivious of everyone else in the room. Then, kneeling down with the carefulness of the aged, he whispered, 'Just one more try, eh?'

The boy did not answer. His face was buried in his arms but the back of his head moved in an almost imperceptible nod. The old man ruffled the boy's hair with his fingers, in a gesture that was both admonitory and affectionate.

'Arm parts are here,' said the Captain.

There were racks of them, stretched up to the ceiling, the larger items in shallow trays, and the small ones stored in tin boxes, with a sample of each wired to the end for identification.

Douglas saw the tin he wanted. He moved the stepladder and climbed to the high shelf for it. Inside the tin he found a part like the one he'd picked up from the floor of the Shepherd Market flat. It was not a component in much demand, and the tin held only one such piece. It bore a tie-on label 'Robert John Spode – urgent'. Douglas looked at it. It was not exactly the same as the piece he'd found in the flat. The tube that had made the other one so strong and heavy was not a part of this simplified lighter-weight component. He put it into his pocket. He looked down at the artillery Captain but his face was blank. 'Are you nearly finished?' said the Captain. 'If we are not sitting down for lunch by one o'clock sharp, we'll have to eat with the duty officers in the transit mess, and that will be a meal you won't forget for a long time.'

'I won't be having lunch,' said Douglas. 'I'm hoping to make an arrest.' He came down the steps.

'Not here,' said the Captain sharply.

'What do you mean?'

'You said you wanted to talk to a civilian, and there is no objection to that. But this is an army establishment; it's nothing to do with the civil police or the SS either. Even the authority of Heinrich Himmler cuts no ice here. Our orders come from the OKH in Berlin, via the Commander-in-Chief of the occupation army, and the Kommandantur. You'll not arrest anyone here.'

'I'm investigating a murder,' said Douglas. 'The British army always let the civil police . . .'

'I'm not interested in ancient history,' said the Captain. 'If there is a man to arrest, the German army will arrest him. But you'll have to provide me with all the paper-work, and show competent authority to take custody of the prisoner.'

'Then I'll stand outside the gate and arrest him *off* army property.'

'Excellent,' said the Captain. His face was calm but his voice was acid. 'But if you are armed and there is shooting, I will instruct my sentries to take any necessary steps to protect themselves, and the installation, and the staff, and the detainees. And that might mean more shooting. It would be your responsibility and furthermore, I would regard an arrest made close to our perimeter

209

fence as an act of provocation. And my report about you would say that.'

'I've been a police officer since you were at school,' said Douglas. 'I haven't needed a gun yet to arrest a man, and I won't need one today.'

The Captain nodded and looked at his watch again, as if checking how close it was to lunch-time. 'Why don't you make yourself comfortable in the guard hut?' he said in a more conciliatory way. 'Spot your fellow coming up the road from Clifton Hampden – they have to come that way to the gate this side – and grab him long before he gets here?'

'Very well,' said Douglas. The Captain opened the door and they stepped out into the cold and walked in the direction of the guard hut.

'You won't mind if I go to the mess for lunch?' said the Captain. 'I missed breakfast this morning.'

'You didn't sleep late?' said Douglas with a trace of sarcasm.

'I went to church,' said the Captain haughtily. 'I will send a tray to the check-point hut for you. Anything you don't like?'

'There used to be,' said Douglas, 'but now I've forgotten what they are.'

'The pork chops are always reliable,' said the Captain.

'You're most kind,' said Douglas.

The young Captain touched the peak of his cap in a salute that carried more than a hint of mockery. His eyes were hard and unfriendly. 'Always pleased to help the gentlemen of the Sicherheitspolizei,' he said. He opened the door of the guard hut and waved Douglas inside. It was a wooden construction, with windows on all sides – like a railway signals box – and it occupied the centre of this narrow country lane. On one side of the hut there was a small counter, and a sliding window, through which visitors presented their credentials.

The hut was very warm, its air perfumed by the heat of the paraffin stove and the last traces of hastily extinguished cigarettes. There were three men inside the hut. One sat at the sliding window and stared down the lane to where a road led eventually to the delights of Oxford. The other two sat at a table, trying to repair the damaged wing of a huge model aeroplane. The soldiers came to attention. 'This is Superintendent Archer of Scotland Yard,' said the Captain. 'He'll be using the hut for an hour or so, but he won't want to do anything that will interfere with the Standing Orders, will you, Superintendent?'

'No, I won't,' said Douglas.

When the Captain had gone, the men relaxed and gave Douglas a chair near the stove. He turned so that he could see as far down the lane as possible. After a decent interval the soldier at the counter lit a cigarette and the other two went back to work with balsa wood, and the pungent-smelling glue.

The surveillance was a boring task, and Douglas was pleased when a white-coated mess servant brought him a tray of food; bouillon in a vacuum jug, pork chop and cabbage, green salad, Liederkranz cheese and black bread.

He was still eating the last of the cheese when, at three-fifteen, the Captain returned. 'Still no luck, eh?' He let the soldiers stand at attention, while he positioned a chair facing Douglas. 'How long are you keeping up this vigil?'

'He'll come,' said Douglas. The Captain dropped into the chair.

By now dark clouds had closed across the sky, and a

drizzle of rain had begun. The Captain loosened his wet overcoat, stretched out his booted feet, and gave the sort of sigh that comes after a heavy meal. 'I remember the time when I was in charge of 800 prisoners, taking them on the Harwich ferry en route to Germany. It was night . . . only natural that they would want to escape, they all had wives and families in Britain. Some of them could almost see their homes; they were from a regiment recruited in that part of the country. I knew I had to be vigilant. On the previous transport, the officer in charge had been court-martialled for losing two POWs . . .' The Captain seemed not to notice the three soldiers and he let them remain rigidly at attention. 'And there was good evidence to show that the missing men had drowned, but the officer lost his commission just the same – damned bad luck.'

'Damned bad luck,' said Douglas, but the sarcasm went unremarked.

'Your Highlanders were the toughest – hard men, and we had two companies of them on that ship. They didn't take kindly to the idea of going into a prison camp . . .'

Douglas detected something unusual in the Captain's tone and manner. He saw him glance sideways. Douglas got to his feet, to see through the window behind him. About thirty yards away, there was a man dressed in the brown coat that many of the prisoners wore. He was carrying a large cardboard box, holding it on his shoulder in such a way as to conceal his head from the men in the guard hut.

Douglas walked to the door of the hut. The Captain watched him. 'Wait!' he called. But Douglas had it open and was through it.

The box the man was carrying prevented him from seeing Douglas as he hurried across the grass, squelching in the soft ground that the endless rain had made. Douglas reached into his back pocket. 'Don't shoot or I'll fire,' shouted the Captain, thinking Douglas was bringing out a pistol.

By that time Douglas had the man's forearm. The hand in his pocket emerged with handcuffs, and swung them over Spode's wrist before he'd even loosened his hold on the cardboard box. The right arm of his cotton coat flapped in the cold wind. 'OK,' said Spode, 'OK,' and the cardboard box fell to the ground with a thump.

Douglas looked back to where the Captain was standing outside the guard hut, holding a rifle he'd grabbed from the rack. Whether it was to shoot Spode, to shoot Douglas or defend the sacred soil of the German army's Detention Camp, Little Wittenham, Douglas could not tell. He smiled at the Captain and locked the second half of the handcuffs on to his own wrist. 'You're under arrest, Spode,' he said.

'For what?'

'Murder. I'm from Scotland Yard and I warn you that anything you say may be taken down and used in evidence against you.'

'Oh, for murder,' said Spode sadly.

Douglas kicked the cardboard box. It tipped over, and inside it he saw the separated pieces of the false arm. Douglas picked it up, bending awkwardly with the prisoner fastened to his wrist. The Captain walked over to them. 'What were you saying about arresting people on army property, Captain?'

The Captain looked at cuffs and prisoner and back at Douglas again. 'What do you want now, Superintendent?' he said. 'A round of applause?'

Douglas had outwitted the Captain and all his regulations. The only way he could prevent the police officer

213

taking his prisoner back to London was by holding Douglas too. He had no way to be sure that he was carrying the key to the self-locking cuffs, and to search his person would mean assault or arrest, and even the Captain baulked at that.

'I need a room suitable for interrogation,' said Douglas.

'Yes, and I was wondering how you'd be able to drive your car,' said the Captain. He smiled. 'We'll compromise,' he suggested. 'I'll be present at the initial interrogation. If you convince me that you have a prima facie case for your charge, I'll provide you with a driver and armed escort back to London.'

'Very well,' said Douglas. The prisoner gave no sign of understanding the German they spoke but as they moved away he seemed to know where they were headed. The three men went through the distributing hut, and through the narrow passages of the stock shelves. Douglas noticed that the tin box of pivots was still there on the counter, open and empty the way he'd left it. But someone had unwired the sample from the outside of the tin, and taken it. Doubtless it was all ready for Spode's appointment, thought Douglas. There were times when he sincerely admired the resource of his fellow countrymen.

The Captain led the way over to one of the creosoted timber huts. There was little change from when it had been used by the RAF; the same thirty metal bedframes, fifteen dented lockers, two plain wooden tables, four hard chairs, one stove and a metal box for its coke. Except that no RAF occupants, in those times before the armistice, had polished the cracked lino to reflect like mirror, burnished the metal stove like chrome, scraped the wooden table until the air smelled of sap, or folded blankets with such precision.

Above each bedspace, a small wooden frame held a

carefully lettered rectangle of paper; and each one named a British General. The Captain went to the rooms at the end of the hut, which in former times had housed the NCO in charge. Douglas noticed that faintly, under the paintwork, the name of some long-forgotten RAF corporal could almost be discerned. Now, fixed over that place, a brass frame held an engraved calling card. In Gothic lettering it read, 'Dieter Scheck, Unterfelderwebel 34. Füsilier-Rgt.'

'Scheck is one of my people,' explained the Captain. 'An ex-artilleryman. He's home on leave. We can use this room.' He opened the door for them.

It was a tiny room but this German had done his best to make it comfortable. On the wall there was a small antique crucifix, the taut and angular Christ unmistakably German in its stylized agony. Hung above the metal bed there was a coloured postcard of a Giotto Madonna and Child. Douglas glanced at the bookshelf; a biography of Wagner, Wordsworth in translation, a Bible, some German detective stories and books about chess. On the bedside table there was a box of chessmen, a folded board, some Feldpost letter-forms and a bill from a cloth merchant in Oxford.

'Will it do?'

It was too small but Douglas said it was good enough. 'Are you staying?' he asked the Captain, hoping that he might have changed his mind.

'Yes,' said the Captain. Douglas turned the key in the lock and put it into his pocket.

'Are you armed, Captain?'

'No. Why?'

Douglas simply wanted to know if there was a gun in the room but he just shrugged without replying. He hated explaining things. He never had to explain anything to

215

Harry. Douglas unlocked Spode's handcuff. 'Don't do anything silly, lad,' he said.

Spode smiled. He was baby-faced, the sort of man who can still pass himself off as sixteen when he's thirty, except that such people do not enjoy the visage of youth that red cheeks and curly hair endows. He was not handsome in the way that actors are handsome, he had no presence, no deep voice and no distinguished features. And yet he had the innocent manner and calm of a child and it was difficult to disregard this quality.

'Is your name Spode, and are you the brother of . . .'

'You needn't bother with all that,' he said. He smiled. 'Do you mind if I . . .' he pulled the coat off his shoulders. It was an awkward action without the use of one arm but he managed it all right. He put the cotton coat, damp from the fine rain, over the back of his chair. Under it his clothes were old but of good quality and Douglas noticed that his hand was white and soft, like the hand of a young child. 'Tell me how you got on to me?' he said. There was no whining, no bitterness, no recriminations. There were few arrested men at peace with themselves as this man was at peace.

'The pivot of your false arm. I found it in the flat at Shepherd Market. It had rolled under the chair.'

'I knew it was risky to come here today but it's damned difficult to manage without it.'

'It was bad luck,' said Douglas sympathetically.

'It was, wasn't it?' He seemed comforted by the remark. 'I knew there was a chance it had fallen off in the flat but it was a million to one chance.'

'A million to one,' said Douglas. 'You're employed in the camp here, are you?'

'My discharge is all in order! And I'm not liable for compulsory labour service in Germany; that's only for *fit*

216

men between the ages of 18 and 40. You were expecting me to come down the road, eh? I nearly got past you, didn't I?'

'Very nearly.'

'And I gave you the slip at Beech Road School?'

'I was careless,' said Douglas.

'I only wanted a chance to talk to you. He's a nice boy, your son. I asked him when you were at home, so I could come round and talk to you.'

'To give yourself up?'

'They say you are a decent sort. You always catch your man, that's what they say in the papers, don't they? Looks as if the papers are right.' Spode smiled.

'Did you kill your brother?'

'Yes, I did,' he said but now he was no longer smiling.

'Why?'

'Has anybody got a cigarette?'

'Yes,' said Douglas but already the artillery Captain had produced a heavy cigarette case of the sort that mothers hope will protect the heart against bullets.

'Why don't you both try mine?' said the Captain. 'What do you prefer, Superintendent? I have French, I have Turkish and I have American.'

Douglas looked at him for a moment without replying. Then he said, 'It's a long time since I tasted a French cigarette.' The Captain passed one to him and lit it for him before saying, 'And you permit the prisoner to smoke?'

'Very well,' said Douglas.

Spode was sitting on a small upright chair, with its back close to the door of the room. The Captain held the case open for him. 'Turkish on the left . . . here are the French, always the tobacco falls out . . . American on the right.'

217

'Thank you,' said Spode. The Captain lit the young man's cigarette too. After he'd exhaled a cloud of sweet-smelling blue smoke, Spode said, 'I loved my brother . . . more than anyone else in the world.' He looked out of the window to where the red afternoon sun was dropping into a furious boil-up of rain clouds. 'My brother wanted me to be a musician.' He stopped as if that was sufficient to make Douglas understand why he loved his brother.

'My father had no faith in me. He loved me but he had no faith, not in me, not in God, and not in anything else.' He was looking at his cigarette now as if his thoughts were far, far away. 'I feel sorrow for my father – may God bless him.' Still preoccupied, he raised his cigarette to his mouth delicately, and drew deeply upon it.

'So why did you kill your brother?' Douglas intended it brutally and so it sounded.

Spode was not so easily provoked. He smoked and smiled. 'I did it. Isn't that enough? Would you like a signed confession too?'

'Yes,' said Douglas.

Spode used the only writing paper available, a Feldpost letter-form from the table. He took a pencil from his pocket and scrawled across the paper that seemed to evade the clumsy white fingers of the one-armed man. 'I killed my brother,' he wrote, and signed it. He passed the paper to the German Captain. 'Witness that, Captain, would you?'

The Captain scribbled his name, rank, number and the date under the pencilled confession, and passed it to Douglas. 'Thank you,' said Douglas, 'but I still want to know why?'

'You're really like someone out of an old detective story,' said Spode. 'A detective has to look for the means, the motive and the opportunity. Isn't that what they tell detectives at their training schools?'

'No,' said Douglas. 'It's only what they tell them in whodunnits.'

'This is the best cigarette I've tasted in an age,' said Spode. 'Is yours good too, Superintendent? They have no cigarettes in prison I suppose.' There was no provocation in his words. He was like a simple boy, never devious or scheming. Douglas found it easy to understand why so many people were ready to protect him from the law.

'Were you in the army?' Douglas asked him.

'My brother and I worked in a laboratory together. But when the German tanks came I tried to set light to one with a bottle of petrol. Molotov Cocktails they called them in the Home Guard. The instructor made it all sound easy but the one I used failed to ignite. Were you in the fighting too?'

'No,' said Douglas. 'The first Germans I saw were a military band marching down Oxford Street, and I was told that London had been declared an open city sometime during the night.' Douglas hadn't intended to sound apologetic but the task of arresting someone who'd lost an arm fighting a tank single-handed made it difficult to be otherwise.

'You didn't miss anything,' said Spode. 'It was all over before it began. Only a bloody fool tries to jam the sprocket wheel of a Mark IV with a tyre lever. He went past me without even noticing – and took my arm with him.' He sighed and smiled. 'You being there wouldn't have made much difference, Superintendent, believe me.'

'But still . . .' said Douglas.

'Is it a confession you want – or absolution?' He smiled. The Captain took off his uniform cap and wiped the leather band. He was prematurely balding, and the thin lank blond hair did little to conceal the pale skin of his scalp. The removal of his hat seemed to age him by twenty years, for his eyes were not those of a young man. This was not the place for a proper interrogation, thought Douglas. Spode did not seem to be taking his arrest seriously.

'Your brother had been burned by radiation,' said Douglas. 'Do you know what that is?'

'I'm a physicist,' said Spode. 'Of course I know.'

'You worked with him?'

'We were in Professor Frick's team.'

'Where?'

'In a laboratory.'

'Don't be a fool, lad,' said Douglas. 'You'll have to tell me sooner or later.'

'What is radiation?' said the Captain.

'It's some kind of emission from unstable atomic nuclei,' said Douglas. 'It can be fatal.'

'It was the first time we'd ever argued,' said Spode. 'My brother always looked after me. He helped me with my homework, saved me from the bullies, took punishments himself, rather than let me take the blame for things. I admired him and I loved him . . . we'd never quarrelled until we began working on this damned atomic bomb experiment. I never wanted to work on the bomb. I told him it would be the death of us, and it was.'

'A bullet was the death of him,' said Douglas.

Spode reflected on this for a moment, then he nodded agreement. 'Have you got the elbow pivot with you?' he asked.

Douglas reached into his pocket and found it. He showed it to Spode who examined it as though he'd never seen one before. 'You found it at the flat?'

'That's right,' said Douglas. Spode treated the alloy component as if it was a thing of great wonder. This didn't surprise Douglas, he'd known other men just as fascinated by the evidence that finally betrayed them into forfeiting their life. It was only after putting the piece back in his pocket that he felt the hard shape in his other pocket. Douglas realized that he'd shown him the lighter-weight model without a strengthening tube, and not the one he'd have to produce in evidence. But Douglas saw no reason to tell him of this. At the time it seemed of no importance.

'I got there early,' said Spode. 'I knew he always left the doorkey under the mat. I let myself in, and waited for him to come home.'

'With a gun?'

'He had the gun, Superintendent. He bought it in a pub near Euston railway station. Three pounds he gave for it.' The little room grew darker and there was a sudden patter of rain on the window. The dull light from the narrow window shone on the table-top and picked out the shape of the crucifix.

'Why?'

'He was in great pain. And he had a medical qualification as well as his physics. He knew it was all up with him.'

'Are you saying it was suicide?' Douglas asked.

'It's difficult to explain,' said Spode. 'We both knew the risks. Once you start on a thing like that, the neutron flux starts to rise and before you know what's happening you've got a chain reaction.'

'But you'd quarrelled?' said Douglas.

'He had no shield but I did have one.' Spode crossed himself. 'We quarrelled because I was worried for him, for him and for his soul.'

221

The Captain put his cap on. 'Is that murder, Superintendent?'

'Murder is killing with malice aforethought – express or implied.'

'So it's not murder?'

'That's for the court to decide,' said Douglas. 'Come along, lad. Get your coat on again.' Douglas stood up. He looked out of the window. It was still raining.

'Eleazar,' said Spode. 'He delivered himself to death to save his people.'

'Who is Eleazar?' said Douglas. As he turned back to Spode, he saw that he was kneeling in prayer. He waited awkwardly, embarrassed, as so many are in the presence of intense devotion. Spode's soft prayer was almost inaudible through the hand that he held close to his face. Then he toppled gently forward against Douglas's knees. He rolled on to one side, and crashed face-down to the floor with a crunch.

Douglas leaned down and grabbed Spode by the collar, his fingers probing into the slackened mouth. He smelled the acrid and unmistakable odour of bitter almonds. 'Cyanide,' said Douglas. 'He's taken poison!' He rolled the body over, and looked around for water to wash out Spode's mouth. 'Phone your medical section,' he told the Captain. 'Get cardiac stimulants. We might save him.'

The Captain picked up the phone. 'He's done for,' he said calmly. 'I saw the effect of those cyanide capsules when the arrest teams were picking up War Criminals for the first few days of the Armistice.' He clicked the telephone rest. 'Come on, come on,' he said to the unanswered phone.

Spode's limp body did not respond to Douglas's attempt to make him vomit. The eyes were glazed over and there was no pulse.

The Captain replaced the still unanswered telephone. 'Bloody telephone operators,' he said. 'The army is going to the dogs, now that the war is over. All they can think about is how quickly they can become civilians again.'

'Poor kid,' said Douglas. He closed Spode's eyes.

'You're not a Catholic are you?'

'No,' said Douglas. 'I'm not anything.'

'You wouldn't understand,' said the Captain.

'Try me.'

The Captain studied Douglas thoughtfully and then looked at Spode's body. 'Thomas Aquinas argued that suicide is a sin because it is an offence against society. By taking one's own life a man deprives society of something that rightfully belongs to it. And modern technology has extended compassion to men who give their lives for the greater good . . . physicians who deliberately risk their lives during epidemics, men of the Church who risk the persecution of a Godless state. And there are holy virgins, who killed themselves rather than be violated. These are now venerated as martyrs.'

'Eleazar, I heard him say Eleazar.'

'Who exposed himself to death in order to deliver his people. Yes, for the suicide all is not lost. The essence and beauty of the sacrament is, and must always remain, reconciliation. And if we have charity enough to believe that we saw repentance before death, he could even be granted ecclesiastical burial.'

'But?'

'He killed his brother. A Catholic would not wish to live long with such a thing on his conscience.'

'I should have searched him.'

'What do you care?' said the Captain. 'You've got your confession, and your written scrap of paper. You can close the file now, can't you?'

223

Chapter Twenty-two

'I should have you shot for this,' Huth told him as soon as he'd pressed the scrambler button.

Douglas didn't reply.

'You go off on your own, without leaving a contact number, or telling me or Sergeant Woods what you are up to. Then you force your way into an army establishment . . .' Huth stopped, as if at a loss for words. 'Those army bastards are always trying to find something wrong with us, and you've given them a perfect chance to complain. Do you realize that I've spent the last ten minutes apologizing to some bloody little army Colonel . . . I hate your stupid face, Archer. Why the hell don't you say something? Have you been struck dumb?'

'I've got the signed confession,' said Douglas.

'You stupid pig. I've got a thousand men working on this business. I've got inquiries in progress from the heavy water plant in Norway to the Curie Laboratory in Paris. Do you think I'm interested in one scribbled confession about one damned murder! When the murderer is already dead!'

'You told me to find the murderer,' said Douglas. 'I found him. And the other nine hundred and ninety-nine men you keep telling me about, did not find him. Furthermore I even got a written confession. What the hell more do you want?'

There was a short silence. Then Huth said, 'Oh! That's better. I didn't know you had it in you. I hadn't heard you raise your voice before.'

'Well, now I know you like it, I'll shout all the time.'

'You listen to me, Archer. You've made a mess of this investigation. I didn't want Spode's corpse. I wanted to find out more about him; what he knew, what he did, whom he spoke with on the phone. And I would have intercepted his mail to get a lead on the rest of this band of outlaws.' Before Douglas could answer, Huth said, 'Did he get it out of his pocket, or was it clipped in his mouth . . . the cyanide capsule, where did he have it?'

'What difference does it make?'

'I'll tell you what difference it makes,' said Huth with renewed anger. 'If he got it from his pocket I need more efficient arresting officers. If these people have got the technique of plugging the cyanide capsules into teeth, we'll have to revise all the arrest techniques. And I'd want it on the teleprinters before morning.'

'From his pocket. He crossed himself and said a prayer. He could have put it in his mouth then.'

'And you just stood there and watched him, you dummy?'

'Yes.'

'And this half-witted artillery Captain watched too?'

'Yes,' said Douglas.

'And neither of you saw him do it?'

'No.'

'Any chance that this army officer passed him the capsule?'

'No, sir. Of course not.'

'Don't give me that no-sir-of-course-not stuff. I've heard it all before. I've had the Gestapo files in Berlin checked while we've been on the phone. Someone's just put the teleprinter reply on my desk. This Captain Hesse is a Catholic. Did you know that?'

'We didn't discuss theology.'

'Then I wish you had done,' said Huth. 'This Spode is a Catholic too. Did you know that?'

'There are now reasons to think so,' said Douglas.

'Don't be sarcastic to me, Archer, I don't like it. I'm asking you a simple question, and I want an honest answer. From the moment you arrested Spode, was there even the briefest opportunity for this damned army Captain to pass him anything at all?'

'No chance at all, sir.'

Douglas heard the rustle of paper, as Huth leafed through the reports on his desk. Finally Huth said, 'Don't prepare any written report or even notes, for the time being. We'll go over this together. If we get this one wrong, Superintendent Archer, you'll find yourself in Dachau. Do you know what Dachau is?'

'I've heard rumours.'

'They are all true, believe me.' Douglas could recognize a note of anxiety in his voice. 'The Reichsführer-SS might want a personal report from me about it. I'll want to make sure it's exactly right. I'll draft something myself tonight.'

'Very good, sir.'

There was another long pause. 'Good detective work, Archer. I'll admit that.'

'Thank you, sir,' said Douglas, but Huth had already hung up. For a long time Douglas sat in the office that the Captain had provided for him. It was that of the Transport Officer. The German army was almost entirely horse-drawn still, and from the office window Douglas could see lines of pre-fabricated stables, and smell the dung piled high in the yard. It was almost dark now but Douglas did not put the light on. He looked out of the window. The lamps over the doors of the barrack-huts were reflected in the dark puddles that shimmered in the cold wind. It was deathly quiet. Douglas found it hard to believe that several hundred prisoners – or detainees as the Germans called them – and most of the survivors of 34. Füsilier-Regiment, now assigned to guard duties – were housed in this great compound.

Douglas switched on the desk light and idly looked at the newspapers and magazines that were piled on the blotter. There were postally-wrapped copies of home-town newspapers from Stuttgart and a new copy of *Signal*.

The cover of *Signal* magazine was entirely devoted to a full-length photo of General Fritz Kellerman. He was pictured standing under a 'Scotland Yard' street sign. The caption said, 'In the steps of Sherlock Holmes. A German police General is in command at Scotland Yard, London.'

Douglas turned to the inside. The story was splashed across three double pages of pictures. Douglas himself was prominent in the largest lead picture. He was por-trayed studying the *Angler's Times* with Kellerman, except that a retoucher had lightly air-brushed the cover of it to remove the title. 'General Kellerman gives orders to the famous Archer of the Yard, Britain's young master detective, who has been described as "the Sherlock Holmes of the nineteen-forties". Like most of London's policemen he welcomes the modern and scientific crime-fighting methods introduced by his new German com-mander. Superintendent Archer – and his colleagues – speak warmly of their General, and secretly refer to him as "Father".'

There was plenty more in the same silky journalistic vein. Douglas went cold at the thought that his friends might believe this rubbish. Only now did he understand Mayhew's strange remark about staying out of the glossy magazines. Of course! And this article was probably what prompted the attempt on his life at Piccadilly Underground station. He closed the magazine and held it flat under his open hands, as if trying to suppress its contents. Damn Kellerman. It was all part of his fight with Huth and the SD. Perhaps it was one more valuable step towards the job of Reichskommissar, if that's what Kellerman was after. But it put Douglas into a power struggle that he wanted no part of, and it jeopardized his life.

Damn them all, thought Douglas. Damn Scotland Yard and Harry Woods, and Mayhew and all the rest of them. They were all self-seeking. Even Harry seemed to be pursuing some adolescent desire to be a hero. And damn this artillery Captain, who had called Douglas 'the Gestapo'. Perhaps he shouldn't have shielded the Captain from Huth's suspicious questions about passing the poison capsule. Then the young man would have found out what a Gestapo interrogation was really like.

It was only then that Douglas realized what perhaps he'd subconsciously known all along – the Captain *had* passed the capsule to Spode. It must have been in the cigarette. He'd selected one cigarette for Douglas and passed it with his fingers and then he offered Spode his case. Douglas remembered the remark about the loose tobacco. Was that because he prodded at the end of the cigarette to reveal the capsule that was concealed within that loose tobacco? And the Captain was in a position to get his hands on such sophisticated devices. He's even admitted that he'd come across them when arresting people in the days after the fighting stopped. An officer commanding an arrest team must have found unused cyanide capsules.

It all fitted together. That nervous complaining about his job, was an anxiety about having a SIPO officer arrive unexpectedly. The Captain had offered to escort him, and then had tried to prevent the arrest by forbidding him to do it on army property. Perhaps it was the officer himself who had got Spode – a fellow conspirator – the pass that allowed him into the depot by the staff entrance.

And it was the Captain who had unwired the pivot from the tin box, to give it to Spode privately. And the Captain who had put Douglas in that seat in the guard hut, and faced him the wrong way while Spode arrived for his appointment, not from the public highway but from the camp side. The long lunch and tipsy behaviour was all a pretence; he'd probably spent the lunch-time scouring the whole place to find Spode. Failing to do so, he'd come back to the guard hut and started talking earnestly to Douglas to get his whole attention away from the place where Spode would appear. Even the way he'd left the soldiers at the position of attention was no accident; he'd done it to minimize their efficiency. And when the arrest was made, the Captain grabbed an infantry rifle. Had he intended to shoot his fellow conspirator before he talked?

His cynical remarks about the Geneva Convention, and his harsh handling of Wentworth, had been no more than an act to divert suspicion. But the talk about his faith had not been an act. He'd deliberately taken Spode to the room of a Catholic Unterfeldwebel, so that the sight of the crucifix might provide some solace for the final moments of the boy's life. And the Captain's concern for the theological niceties of suicide vis-à-vis murder was not solely on behalf of Spode. Now Douglas understood why the Captain's voice had held an undertone of agony – for now the Captain had such a sin to live with.

Douglas walked over to the window. It was a flimsy building and he could feel the vibrations caused by the

229

restless horses in the stables below. The yard was wet but the rain had stopped. Between the racing clouds he could glimpse a few stars. Now he could understand the men's religious anguish because, for the first time in his life, he began to doubt his faith as a policeman.

Douglas heard the engine of a heavy vehicle passing through the motor transport yard on the far side of the stables. It was out of sight but Douglas looked at his watch and decided that it was about time that the ambulance arrived from London.

He found two men on duty in the motor transport office. One was an anaemic-looking clerk, with pimples and an easy smile. The other was a mechanic, a muscular sixty-year-old, with curly moustache and metal-framed spectacles. No ambulance, they reported. Douglas sat down with them and asked them how they liked England, and they asked him where he learned to speak such beautiful German.

'And you brought that Railton in,' said the big Ober-feldwebel. 'Now, that's what I call a real car. Not like some of the rubbish we have to service here.' He flicked a nicotine-stained finger towards the lines of old Opel Blitz lorries, commandeered Austins, and brand-new military model VWs, all painted with the fish device that was the Divisional sign. Most of the men of the Division had been recruited from the Schwarzwald and this man's accent had that sort of sing-song lilt that was so often heard in those villages.

Douglas looked around the office. On the wall there was the usual row of clipboards, and above them an order signed by the commanding officer. It listed those officers on the camp staff who were assigned cars for personal transport. 'I know your face from somewhere,' the older man suddenly said to Douglas.

'It's not likely,' said Douglas. He read the list of cars.

'I never forget a face,' he said. 'Do I, Walter? No, I never forget a face.'

'He's well known for it,' said the clerk obsequiously. 'He never forgets a face.'

'You're a policeman . . . here!' He gave a huge smile of pleasure. 'You're from Scotland Yard. I remember seeing on the sheet when we refilled your car for you. Wait a minute . . . no, don't tell me, I'll get it in a minute . . .'

The clerk smiled at Douglas, as a salesman might smile while demonstrating an especially ingenious mechanical toy.

'Archer of the Yard. You're Archer of the Yard. Where the devil was I reading about you just recently . . .?'

Douglas did not help him remember.

The Oberfeldwebel shook his head, his excitement bordering on disbelief. 'You're the detective who solved the Bethnal Green poisonings, and caught "the Rottingdean Ripper" back before the war.'

That Douglas did not acknowledge the truth of it made no difference to the old man. It did not even slow his narrative. 'Archer of the Yard! Well, I'm damned. I follow murder mysteries. Fiction as well as true life. In my apartment in Forbach I have a whole room filled with books, magazines and press cuttings.' He took off his oily cloth cap and scratched his head. 'I was reading about you . . . very recently . . . I knew about you before of course: you're famous . . . but I read about you. Where was I reading about him, Walter?'

'In *Signal*, Oberfeldwebel,' said the clerk.

'Of course,' said the old man, smacking one huge fist into his open hand. 'First time I heard of you was that

231

case in Camden Town. The husband killed his wife with bad seafood – crab wasn't it – and nearly got away with it. Good detective work, that was. That must have been about 1938.'

'December 1937,' said Douglas. 'Not Camden Town – Great Yarmouth.'

'Great Yarmouth, yes, and you found out, from the wife's sister, that she had this allergy for seafood.' He stood back, so that he could see Douglas full length. He looked him up and down and shook his head again. 'Whoever would have believed that I'd be here, talking to Archer of the Yard like this. Coffee?'

'Yes, please,' said Douglas.

The old man took off his spectacles and slipped them into a leather case before putting them into his black overalls. 'Get three coffees, Walter. Tell the Feldwebel it's for me, and I want real coffee, not ersatz muck. And a jug of cream if he's going to want that damned motorcycle overhauled again.'

'The ambulance should be here by now,' said Douglas.

'They'll stop for coffee on the way,' said the old man. 'SS are they? Those people know how to look after themselves, and our Feldgendarmerie don't dare to pick them up.' He looked at his pocket watch. 'Coming to take a body away, I hear. Of course, I should have put two and two together, when I heard you were with Captain Hesse.'

'Put two and two together?' said Douglas.

'To make four,' he said. 'You arriving from Scotland Yard, and then spending the day with an officer of the Abwehr.'

'Captain Hesse is from the Abwehr?'

He chuckled again. 'You don't have to keep up that pretence with me,' he said. 'I won't tell a soul. And

232

anyway, dozens of people here know about Captain Hesse.'

Douglas looked at the man trying to see what he meant. The Abwehr was that branch of the army's Intelligence Service concerned with the foreign intelligence services. 'What does an officer of the Abwehr do here?'

'You know that better than I do,' he said. 'The Captain – he's only a Leutnant really, but the Abwehr use any uniform they like – comes and goes whenever he wishes. We have that nice Horch motor-car over there – no unit markings or tactical signs, you notice – for his exclusive use.' At that moment Walter reappeared with a tin tray and two jugs. 'Just talking about our Captain Hesse, Walter. I'm telling Superintendent Archer what a nice fellow he is.'

Walter smiled and registered the Oberfeldwebel's claim to be on intimate terms with the policeman. He poured three cups of coffee and they drank it in silence.

'My wife and my son will never believe this, when I write to them,' said the Oberfeldwebel. 'They both follow all the big murder cases. Next trip to London I was going to photograph that place in Pimlico, where they found the remains of the girl – the breadknife murders, you remember.' He flipped open the lid of the jug and inhaled the aroma of the coffee. 'Oh, and that reminds me, Walter: Captain Hesse phoned me just before our visitor arrived. He'll be taking his car tonight, about midnight. Make sure the tank is full and his card is ready for signature. You know how he hates to be kept waiting about.' He put on his spectacles again to study the list of vehicles on the clipboard marked with the next day's date. 'So you're waiting here until the ambulance arrives, Superintendent?' He twisted the end of his curly moustache.

233

'No,' said Douglas on a sudden impulse. 'The arrangements to move the body are all made. I'll take my car now. I'll try and get an early night for a change.'

The Oberfeldwebel walked with him across the yard to where the Railton was parked. The conversation now turned to what mileage and speed the detective's car did. As Douglas got inside the man gave the paintwork a loving caress. 'They knew how to make a car in those days,' he said.

Softly on the cold night air there came the distant sound of music. The old man saw Douglas cock his head to listen. 'The choir,' said the old man. 'Divisional HQ choir. Kids! Called up since the fighting stopped. They don't know what a war is. Look at that pimply kid Walter in the office there – they're tourists, not soldiers.'

'And they sing in the choir?' The singing could be heard more clearly now, 'Silent Night, Holy Night', two dozen lusty young male voices but it was musical enough.

'There's to be a big party for the local English children at Christmas,' he said. 'I'm surprised at how much money they've collected. It's weeks to go before Christmas.' He smoothed his hand on the paintwork. 'More and more young recruits will come. We old-timers will go home. Soon the fighting will be forgotten.'

'Perhaps,' said Douglas.

'Not forgotten by those of us who did it, but we'll not be around to talk about it, will we?'

Douglas revved up the engine. 'Damned good coffee,' said Douglas.

The old man leaned closer. 'Any time you want your car overhauled, you come and see me, Superintendent.' He tapped his nose, to show that such a service would remain confidential.

'Thanks and good night,' said Douglas. He drove as far

as the barrier that closed off the entrance to the motor transport yard. As he halted there, waiting for the gate to lift, the young clerk came out of the office brandishing what, in the poor light, looked like a huge gun. He poked its 'barrel' through the window of the car so that it was pointing at Douglas's head. Seeing the sudden movement, a sentry in a guard tower turned the light so it blinded him.

'What?' said Douglas nervously.

'Will you autograph it for me?' said the clerk. The gun barrel was now identifiable as a tightly rolled copy of *Signal* magazine. With shaking hand, Douglas scrawled his signature across the corner of the magazine cover.

'Thanks, and happy hunting,' said the clerk in a salutation that he'd obviously prepared carefully.

'Good night,' said Douglas as the barrier was raised.

Douglas drove down past the 'Barley Mow' and over the narrow bridge that leads to Clifton Hampden. It was the only permitted route after dark, when the camp's other gates closed. There was a German army checkpoint at the bridge. Once through it, Douglas found a disused side entrance in the village, and drove the Railton off the road. He switched off the lights and settled down to wait for Captain Hesse and his unmarked Horch four-door convertible.

It was not long in coming. It turned right at the T junction over the bridge, and then on to the road that led through Shillingford, Wallingford and eastwards to London.

The moon was on the wane, and it was too cloudy to permit more than fitful snatches of moonlight. Douglas was no expert at such jobs but it was not difficult staying behind the Horch. There was only official traffic at that time of night; a long convoy of horse-drawn army wagons, a short convoy of Luftwaffe lorries, a few motor-cycle despatch riders, a civilian bus taking shift workers to and from home. All these made it possible for Douglas to keep out of sight.

There were half-a-dozen check-points but neither car got more than a perfunctory glance at the windscreen stickers. Captain Hesse appeared to know London well. At Shepherd's Bush he turned off down Holland Road, and followed a maze of side roads. Douglas fell back, lest his quarry noticed him on these dark empty streets. But Hesse showed no sign of suspicion. His destination was the Vauxhall Bridge Road and the clutter of seedy hotels and sleazy boarding houses on the Westminster side of Victoria railway station. It had never, in Douglas's memory, been a salubrious district, but the arrival of the Germans had helped it to become one of the most notorious districts in the whole of Europe. But it wasn't only the women that attracted the soldiers here – the official Wehrmacht brothels were cleaner, cheaper and more attractive to all but the most perverse – it was the trading. Here you could buy anything: men, women and children, heroin by the kilo, a factory-fresh P38 automatic pistol still in packing grease, false papers, real papers even. In spite of the regular patrols and severe penalties soldiers still came here. It was as if, in the absence of a battlefield, they needed some alternative hazard.

Hesse parked his car in the ruins of what was once the Victoria Palace Music Hall. Douglas's parents had taken him there when he was a child. Now tall weeds and flowers grew from the orchestra pit, and a row of seats tilted drunkenly from the last remaining section of the Royal Circle. He waited until Hesse reappeared from the shadows of the remains of the auditorium arch. He crossed the road, first to the forecourt of Victoria station, where gigantic portraits of Hitler and Stalin, together with flags and bunting, rippled and roared in the cold wind. Douglas stayed where he was while a Feldgendarmerie patrol marched along Victoria Street. The commander ignored the long figure of Hesse. His long civilian overcoat with its fur collar, the soft felt hat worn at a sober angle, black leather gloves and unhesitating stride marked him as a German officer.

Douglas let the Captain get well ahead, as he walked down Vauxhall Bridge Road illuminated by garish signs of lodging houses and hotels and the lights from an all-night coffee-shop. A man in a tweed overcoat came from a doorway, lurched towards the Captain but, deciding that he was not the type for pornographic photos, stuffed the envelope he was holding back into his pocket. Hesse quickened his pace and turned up the fur collar as if to hide his face.

He'd been here before. Douglas didn't doubt that, for the Captain looked neither to right nor left, nor raised his eyes up to where an amateurly painted sign said 'Hotel Lübeck' over a narrow entrance. A few slivers of broken glass – dark green and curved from a bottle – lodged in the cracks of the dirty linoleum. The floorboards creaked as Douglas followed him inside. The Captain did not look back as he ascended the stairs. His hand reached out for the light switch and, unerring, found it in the dark. Another low-wattage bulb came alight on the first floor landing above them.

'All right, sport, what can we do for you?' A pale-faced man, belted tightly into a raincoat, stepped out of the gloom and barred Douglas's way.

'I'm going upstairs,' said Douglas softly, so that he would not attract attention.

'All private here,' said the man. 'Private hotel – all the

rooms taken – just guests and staff allowed in here.' He put a flattened hand on Douglas's chest. In spite of his reputation for being a policeman of tact and patience, Douglas felt a strong inclination to hit this man. But he did not do so.

'A German officer just went upstairs,' said Douglas.

'I'm quite aware of that, my friend,' said the raincoated man in the pedantic syntax favoured by bureaucrats and bullies. 'But you, I regret, must remain outside.'

'I'm the Captain's driver,' said Douglas. 'He forgot to tell me what time he wants to be collected.'

The raincoated man's shifty eyes flickered over Douglas's clothes and then came back to his anxious face. 'You're his driver?'

'Yes,' said Douglas. There is a natural bond between these pimping strong-arm men and the drivers and doormen who send them their clients.

'Be quick,' he said grudgingly. Douglas went past him, and up to the first floor, in time to hear the Captain's footsteps still ascending past the second floor. Again a landing light came on.

As the Captain almost reached the third floor landing, a door opened suddenly, and a soldier emerged. He was a huge man, his face was flushed from drink and his soft hat askew. He was fastening his fly buttons and singing 'Ich hatt' einen Kameraden'. As he caught sight of Captain Hesse coming up the stairs, the soldier straightened, and began fumbling with the buttons of his tunic. Hesse tried to get past him. But the soldier put an arm out to bar his way, and leaned across to him. He had that condescension that comes naturally to men of such large stature, coupled to the jovial familiarity provided by the drink. 'You look a good sort, Captain.' He could see Hesse's uniform tunic and the rank badges on his collar. The soldier steadied himself on the stair rail. 'Going upstairs, are you?' Hesse tried to get past him but could not. 'That's good. Officers' girls on the top floor, eh? I wondered why they wouldn't let us poor bloody Feldgrauen go up there.'

'Please let me pass,' said Hesse.

'I was wounded at Dover, Captain,' said the soldier proudly. 'Came ashore with the first wave. See that!' He patted the England Combat Shield on his left breast pocket. 'You won't see many of those about. Only the men of the first wave were awarded the one in gold. And there are not many of us left, Captain.'

'Let me pass,' said Hesse. His voice was more impatient now.

'It's no good threatening to call the bloody Feldgendarmerie,' said the drunk, pronouncing the word with exaggerated care. He tapped Hesse's chest. 'Because we are all sinners here. Am I right, Captain, am I right?'

Hesse pushed the man gently and wriggled his way past him.

The soldier turned to watch him mount the next flight of stairs. He raised his voice. 'All sinners here, Captain. Am I right, I say?' Getting no answer he gripped the rail and began to pick his way carefully down the steep staircase. He belched loudly, and then suddenly bellowed his song very loudly. 'Ich hatt' einen Kameraden . . .'

Douglas cowered back into the shadows as the man came level with him. There was the soft plop of a time switch and the landing was plunged into complete darkness. The man's song ended abruptly. 'Not many of the first wave left, Captain,' he said quietly and sadly, as he continued on his way, suddenly sobered by the memory of it.

Douglas hurried up the stairs in time to hear Captain

Hesse ring a doorbell somewhere on the top floor. Two shorts and two long. The door buzzer sounded deep inside this grimy labyrinth. After a long pause, the well-oiled door bolts could be heard sliding open. The Captain was admitted without a word of greeting. Douglas saw the shaft of yellow light reach out on to the landing and heard boots being wiped on a doormat. Then the door closed.

Douglas climbed the stairs, until his eyes were level with the floor of the top landing. The door through which Hesse had passed was old, and its blue paint was darkened and cracked with age. A brass number – 4a – had been carelessly splashed by the ancient paint.

The last of the light switches plopped and the whole staircase was dark. Douglas went to the door and listened. He could hear music. Judy Garland sang 'When you wish upon a star' but it seemed to be coming from some other floor. Douglas put his hand to the bell-push and repeated the signal that Hesse had given. He had the feeling that he was being scrutinized by someone unseen.

The bolts slid back and when the door opened slowly, Douglas stepped back, not knowing what to expect. The light was behind the man who came to the door. He was wearing a German officer's grey leather coat, and his right hand was in the pocket of it.

Douglas squinted into the light from the bare bulb that hung in the hall. 'I want to talk to Captain Hesse,' said Douglas. He said it quickly as a way of gaining time.

'Superintendent Archer. You'd better come in.' It was Colonel Mayhew. He bit his lip in a rare gesture of anxiety. 'How the devil did you find this place?'

It was a squalid little flat: three rooms and a kitchen. The usual whorehouse configuration, three girls working, and

240

some old woman who opened the door for the clients, cleaned up after them and made endless cups of tea, as well as providing an ever-present witness in case some mad fool took his flagellation too seriously.

At least that's the way it had been until recently. Now the beds were dismantled and leaning against the walls, and the chipped enamel bidet was tucked away behind the filing cabinet. Box files were stacked upon the tiny sinks. Only the curtains remained of the original furnishings; whorehouses always have respectable curtains.

Captain Hesse was standing near the electric fire. He still wore his heavy overcoat with the fur collar, and his regulation gloves. He moved his head a fraction in order to see Douglas but he didn't turn round to face him. Instead he shivered and drew nearer to the fire.

'It's all right, Hans,' Mayhew told him. 'This is one of my people.' Hesse nodded as if that only postponed his fate.

'What brought you here?' said Mayhew, keeping his voice quite neutral in tone.

'Captain Hesse did,' said Douglas. 'I followed him from his camp at Wittenham.'

'He phoned me,' said Mayhew. 'I know all about it.'

'And?'

'Sooner or later you would have been told about this,' said Mayhew.

The door to the next room opened. A man dressed in the uniform of a Feldgendarmerie Major said, 'Hesse. Come in now.'

Hesse went rigid, clicked his heels and followed the Major, who closed the door behind them.

Left alone with Colonel Mayhew, Douglas went over to the fire and warmed his hands in a gesture that permitted Mayhew time enough to decide what to say.

'These are all Abwehr people,' said Mayhew finally. 'We have been negotiating with them for a couple of months.'

'Negotiating?'

'They will help us liberate the King,' said Mayhew. 'The German army feel that their honour is impugned by the present situation. They have always felt that the King should be guarded by units of the German army, not by the SS.'

'It seems trivial to me,' said Douglas doubtfully.

'Well it's not trivial for *them*,' said Mayhew. 'The high command in Berlin have secretly authorized the Abwehr to assist in the escape. They will stage the whole operation, providing we help to cover up afterwards.'

Douglas stared at Mayhew, trying to see inside this devious and complex man. 'You're not telling me the whole truth, Colonel,' he said.

Mayhew pursed his lips, as though tasting an especially sour lemon. 'The Germans have taken over the Bringle Sands Research Establishment in Devon. They are hoping to produce an atomic explosive. It was there that Dr Spode suffered radiation burns. Spode stole some of the most vital work, years and years of mathematical calculations.'

'The papers that were burned at the Shepherd Market flat?'

'Yes. His young brother John persuaded him that he must prevent the Germans getting such a weapon.' Mayhew reached out and searched for the heat of the fire.

'Huth is trying to piece together the charred remains but there is nothing there.'

'Some of the Germans think the whole project is a complete waste of money. Others, including Huth and Springer, understand that if this fantastic experiment bore fruit it could mean military domination of the whole world. And the men, and the organization, in charge of such a project would become similarly important within the system.' Mayhew rubbed his hands briskly. It was a nervous mannerism and he smiled at Douglas, as if admitting to some secret anxiety that he could not speak of.

'But if the papers are destroyed, will the army go through with the plan to help the King escape?'

Mayhew grabbed Douglas's arm and held it in a painful grip.

'We can be quite certain that there is a duplicate set of those papers, Superintendent Archer. Dr William Spode was far too careful to commit a life's work to his brief-case, without taking some sort of precaution.'

'You believe that?'

Mayhew looked over his shoulder, at the door through which Hesse had gone. 'We both believe it, Archer,' he said conspiratorially. 'Just make sure you tell them so. If they give up hope of retrieving those papers, there's little chance that we'll ever see the King alive again.'

Hardly had Mayhew said it when the door opened again. The Major said, 'The General will see you both now.'

The inner room had been rigorously scrubbed and cleaned, but the stained old floral wallpaper, warped floorboards and bare bulbs provided an atmosphere of stark poverty. In the centre of the room half-a-dozen hard chairs were arranged round a polished table. On its scarred top there were four scribbling pads, a jam-jar containing sharpened pencils and some rolled maps.

The Major who had brought them in resumed his seat at the table. With him there were two men in the uniform of infantry Captain, and a tall, elderly, white-haired man

243

in a grey, striped civilian suit. His gold-rimmed spectacles and neat moustache went well with the stiff wing collar and gold tie-pin. Douglas recognized him as General-major Georg von Ruff whose Front Line Intelligence Detachment had secured Portsmouth's cranes and storage tanks before the Royal Navy's demolition teams could destroy them. For this he had received the immediate award of the Knight's Cross. He smoked a cigarette in an ivory holder and toyed with a cigarette case on the table in front of him.

Captain Hesse, still wearing his overcoat, was seated away from the others. 'So the younger Spode is dead too?' said the Feldgendarmerie Major. He was a middle-aged man, with horn-rimmed spectacles, and a habit of tapping the table top with the end of his pencil.

'So I understand,' said Mayhew. He stood erect as if in the dock of a law court. Everyone in the room seemed in awe of von Ruff. Everyone, that is, except Douglas Archer.

'And your police officer followed Captain Hesse here?'

'Yes, I followed him here,' said Douglas, resenting the way in which his presence was being ignored.

'I will come to you later,' said the Feldgendarmerie Major.

Douglas stepped forward, picking up a chair by the backrest and swung it into position, to sit down on it uninvited. 'Now you listen to me, Major,' said Douglas quietly. 'And you tell your General to listen too, since he is perhaps unable to speak for himself. I don't intend to sit here while you discuss me. If you want my co-operation you'll have to woo me, because I'm very difficult to please.'

The General turned his head stiffly and looked at

Douglas without changing his blank expression. Then he lit a new cigarette from the stub of the previous one.

The Major tapped his pencil to get attention and said, calmly, 'You have the impertinent manner of the revolutionary. It will get you nowhere. Let me remind you of your position . . .'

Douglas reached across the table, far enough to touch the Major's hand with his fingertip. The Major flinched. 'No,' said Douglas. 'Let me remind *you* of *your* position. I am a policeman investigating a murder. I have reason to believe that Captain Hesse is implicated, and I followed him here to question him.' He looked at the Germans one by one. 'And I find him in circumstances that I can only describe as most unusual. If there is any explaining to be done – then you'll do it.'

'You're playing a dangerous game, Superintendent,' said the Major.

'Not nearly so dangerous as the one you're playing,' said Douglas. He felt frightened and he realized that his voice sounded higher in pitch and was strangled by the nervous tightening of his vocal cords. 'Do you really imagine that you'll get any support from the German C-in-C Great Britain, or from Berlin, if I submit a report about young Spode's death this afternoon?'

'You're not out of here yet,' said the Major. The General narrowed his eyes, as if pained by the crude threat.

'My car is equipped with radio telegraph,' said Douglas. 'I would not come into a notorious district like this, late at night, without taking precautions.'

'What have you said?'

'Nothing that cannot be unsaid,' replied Douglas. There was a long silence. Douglas clenched his fists, and felt the sweat on his palms. Mayhew had remained silent throughout the exchange, ready to jump either way.

General von Ruff leaned forward, as if to share a confidence. When he spoke his voice was blurred by the bronchial wheeze of the heavy smoker. 'Can you help us recover Dr Spode's calculations, Superintendent?'

'I believe I can, General.'

'We'll need assurances,' said the Major, tapping the pencil on the table before writing on the pad.

'Of course,' said Douglas.

'Captain Hesse must not be included in your report to your authorities.'

'He'll go on record as a witness to Spode's death. I can't change that.'

The General raised his eyes slowly to where Mayhew stood, one hand in pocket and a fixed smile on his face. It was an artificial posture for such a man, and Douglas guessed that Colonel Mayhew was as frightened as he was.

'I'll need to know how you will dispose of His Majesty,' said the General. His voice revealed a measure of veneration for the imprisoned monarch. 'Our honour requires that his safety is assured.'

'We'll fly him out of one of the old disused airfields, sir,' said Mayhew. 'One of your officers is advising us on which one to choose.'

'You'll go too?'

'I've had no orders so far, sir.'

It was the sort of answer that the General understood and thoroughly approved. He looked at Douglas in the hope that he might see some of the same willingness to take orders there but he did not see it. Douglas brought out a handkerchief and wiped his nose. The General looked away and blew a smoke ring. 'There is nothing more,' said the General. He dismissed all those present with a nod and got to his feet. The German officers jumped to attention, and stood rigid while their master said good night. Then one of the Captains helped him into his overcoat. Douglas remained seated and the General did not glance in his direction as he left without speaking. Only when the Abwehr chief had gone did his staff unbend a little. The Major unclipped his collar and heaved a sigh of relief. He took no further interest in Douglas.

It wasn't until Mayhew was in the car with Douglas that the great head of steam that had built up inside him was released. 'You're a mad bastard, Archer. All these years I've known you, and I never suspected that you could take leave of your senses as you did up there tonight.' There was nothing in Mayhew's voice to suggest even a grudging admiration.

'Really.' He didn't care about Mayhew's opinion. Douglas Archer was a changed man, and he was enjoying this new persona.

'General von Ruff is the senior Abwehr officer in Great Britain. Do you realize what that means?'

'I don't care what it means. I've had enough of being kicked around by these Germans.'

'Very impressive,' said Mayhew in a tone that suggested more reproach than respect. 'And how am I supposed to clear up the mess?'

'Mess?'

'You've convinced these Huns that you really have the atomic physics paperwork. But it will grant us no more than a breathing space. Soon they'll want a few pages, as a sample. What the devil do I do then?'

'You still live in Upper Brook Street?' said Douglas, turning the corner.

'Yes,' said Mayhew.

'An aeroplane,' said Douglas. 'Flying out of a disused airfield. Was that just for the Huns, or do you really consider that's the best way to get the King out of the country?'

'Do you have a better way?'

'If what you tell me about Franklin Roosevelt is true, you have only to get him as far as the US Embassy. They could crate him out as diplomatic mail. I've seen even railway containers with diplomatic seals on them.'

'Top marks for ingenuity,' said Mayhew in a patronizing tone. 'But Mr Joseph Kennedy is the US Ambassador to the Court of St James. Do I have to remind you what he told that convention of German manufacturers last week? No friend of Britain there, and certainly no monarchist either.'

Douglas grunted.

'You're a political innocent, Archer. Can you imagine what would happen to Roosevelt politically, if it became known that he'd helped the King escape from Britain?'

'Forged documents then. Ones that would convince the Germans that it was a diplomatic consignment,' suggested Douglas.

'Worse,' said Mayhew. 'The Escape of the Royal Family is going to be in every history book ever written. Do you want it recorded that we could only get our King out of the country by forging the signature of a foreigner?' He shook his head to dismiss the idea. 'And for the same reason we can't have His Majesty doing anything ridiculous, such as dressing up as a chambermaid, or pretending to be a German lavatory attendant.'

'Better that the history books just say he died bravely?'

'Don't be offensive, Archer,' said Mayhew in a quiet voice that was all the more menacing because of the

248

sincerity of it. 'Just tell me how I'm expected to deal with this fairy story of yours . . . what am I to tell them about the calculations?'

Douglas pressed the accelerator and let the Railton show its paces as they roared up Park Lane northwards, passing the remains of the bombed Dorchester Hotel. They were outside Colonel Mayhew's fashionable London house before Douglas answered. 'There'll be no mess to clear up, Colonel,' he said as Mayhew opened the door of the car. 'I have the calculations; it's just a matter of deciding whether to let your German pals have them.'

Mayhew was on the pavement by this time. Now he craned into the car to see Douglas. 'Where?' he said, unable to conceal the sort of surprise and curiosity that in any other circumstances he would have thought vulgar. 'Where are the calculations?'

Douglas leaned across to lock the car door. Then he jiggled the accelerator to make the engine roar a couple of times. 'In my waistcoat pocket,' he said, smiled, and drove away. In his rearview mirror he saw Mayhew staring after him in astonishment, and this gave Douglas a childish pleasure, so that he laughed aloud.

Chapter Twenty-three

The next morning, the two boys noticed some kind of change in Douglas Archer's mood, although they didn't realize how profound and permanent that change was. Douglas had shed the depression that had weighed so heavily upon him ever since the Germans had come. He had worried himself sick trying to reconcile his job as a policeman with the repressive, death-dealing machinery of the Nazi administration. Now he knew what he would have to do. And he felt happy in a way he'd not been since the death of his wife.

At breakfast the two boys responded happily to Douglas's jokes and teasing, and Mrs Sheenan remembered a silly rhyme about bagpipes. For the pancakes – the usual way to extend the last of the egg ration – she produced a small jar of home-made honey, from her cousin in the country. Already it was a memorable day.

Douglas walked into Soho. His first call was in Moor Street. Peter Piper once had a magnificent carpeted office a few blocks to the west, in a Georgian mansion in Mayfair. In those days 'Pip' was a brilliant young director in the British film industry.

Perhaps the casual observer, or the tourist, would not have seen much difference between these black-brick terraced houses and their Mayfair counterparts but, once inside, the cost-cutting that had made some long-dead speculator rich, was evident on every side. The only plumbing had been inserted into a corner of the narrow staircase, to provide one grimy little hand-basin on each landing. The only sewage connection was to one water-closet in the tiny back-yard.

Now Pip slept on a folding bed in his darkroom at the very top of this narrow building. Across the landing was a second room which served as office, reception room and studio. On the walls there were dozens of glossy film stills. Some had loosened a pin from the corner, and curled up tight, as if in shame.

A voice called from the next room. 'I'm working in the dark-room. Who is it?'

'Doug Archer.' Douglas heard the sound of running water and guessed that Pip was quickly washing his face, after being awakened by the bell on the outer door. Douglas looked at all the back-lit flattering portraits of the stars while he waited for the photographer to emerge. As he did so he fiddled with the elbow-pivot that he'd found in Shepherd Market. And, as he'd found last night, after stopping the car out of sight of Colonel Mayhew, the strengthening tube inside it was a container. Pushing a finger hard against its base, he slid into sight a metal cassette of 35 mm film. According to the printed label it contained film enough for 36 exposures.

'Doug! – Sorry to keep you waiting, old boy.' There were not many shop-keepers in Soho who regularly called Douglas by his first name but these two men had known each other ever since Pip had a silver Rolls-Royce, staged some of the finest dinner parties in London and was able to get for his friends – including Douglas – tickets to lavish film galas.

'Can you put a film through the developer for me, Pip?'

'Your dark-room at the Yard gone on strike, old chap?'

'Something like that,' said Douglas.

Aware that he'd asked an unwelcome question, Pip

hurriedly covered the faux pas. 'Stay for a cup of tea and a toasted bun.' From the rehearsal room next door there was the sudden sound of jazz music. It made the walls vibrate.

'Perhaps when I pick it up, Pip.'

'Lovely. I'll have it ready about four-thirty this afternoon. Any special instructions? Over or under development? Fine grain soup? Cut into strips, five or six frame lengths?'

'The only special instructions are just keeping your mouth shut about it.'

Pip nodded. He was a neat little man, his suit far too tight for him and a shirt that constricted his neck, so he frequently ran a finger round his collar to loosen it. His hair was unnaturally dark, as so often is that of middle-aged men looking for work, and held in place by generous amounts of scented hair oil which almost obscured the smell of photo-fixer on his clothes and his whisky-laden breath.

'Mum's the word, old boy,' said Pip. 'Even if your Harry Woods comes in for a portrait, I wouldn't mention having seen you.' Pip laughed his deep brief laugh. The idea of Harry Woods having his photo taken seemed an excellent joke.

'You've got the idea,' said Douglas.

'I was a Spy,' said Pip.

'What?' said Douglas in alarm.

'That photo you're looking at . . . that's Conrad Veidt in the film "I was a Spy". Lovely production that was. Filmed at the Gaumont-British Studios at Lime Grove . . . or wait, was it the Gainsborough Studios at Islington? I tell you, Doug, my memory is going.'

Next door the rehearsing jazz musicians were shaking the whole building with their version of 'South of the

Border'. Douglas said, 'I wonder how you stay sane with that noise going on all day.'

'Live and let live,' said Pip. He straightened his tie and smoothed his hair. It was the nervous mannerism of a man trying to shed the reputation of being a notorious drunk. 'Want me to do contact prints?'

'No, just the film.'

'Sorry to hear about your wife, Doug.'

'She was not the only one, Pip. And at least the boy was spared.'

'That's the way to look at it,' said Pip. 'Sure you won't have a cup of tea? It won't take a minute, and I've got a bit of extra tea this month.'

Douglas looked at his watch. 'No, I'd better be on my way. I have to be at Highgate by ten-thirty.'

'This German-Soviet Friendship ceremony?'

'I couldn't get out of it,' said Douglas apologetically.

'Well at least we know where we are now,' said Pip. 'Red bastards and Nazi bastards, there's nothing to choose between them.'

'There's no doubt about that,' said Douglas.

'Shipping out the corpse of Karl Marx, are they? Well good riddance to bad rubbish, I say.'

Douglas touched his friend's arm. It was a gesture of friendship, and yet it was also a warning to guard his tongue. At that moment they heard footsteps on the stairs. The door opened and a German soldier entered. In bad English he asked to have his photo taken. 'Just you sit down there,' said Pip. He switched on the bright floodlights and Douglas squinted to see through the glare from them. 'Shoulder a little bit this way,' said Pip. The soldier twisted on the stool so that the brand new chevrons of the Stabsgefreiter were well in evidence for the camera.

It was the smell of the floodlights that triggered something in Douglas's mind. Yes, of course, the bulb removed from the adjustable lamp in the Shepherd Market flat. The younger brother must have put a photo-flood bulb into it when he used the desk top to photograph the mathematical calculations that he later burned in the grate. Now Douglas was certain about it. 'See you later, Pip,' said Douglas.

Pip came out from under the focusing cloth with his hair disarrayed. 'I look forward to it, Doug.' He turned to his customer. 'Look at the photograph of Tallulah Bankhead, Corporal, and lift your chin a little.'

Chapter Twenty-four

Highgate Cemetery is like a film-set. Overgrown by sooty trees and bushes, strangled by weeds, its narrow paths are lined with ancient tombstones leaning at all angles and pocked with mould and moss. Not even the efforts of a platoon of engineers had lessened the feeling that here was a location for a remake of 'Frankenstein'.

And yet they tried. For this was the final gesture of German-Soviet Friendship Week, and today the ceremonies in Moscow and Berlin had to give pride of place to this ritualistic disinterment of the bones of Karl Marx from the wormy sod of dingy north London.

There was just room for the reduced size Army Group L (London District) brass band, if it stood well away behind the trees. Not all of the USSR delegation could be given a view of the grave, another hundred of them had to be content with a place at the saluting base erected on Highgate Hill.

Only the most important men were at the grave. Foreign Minister von Ribbentrop, in magnificent uniform, was talking to Molotov, the Russian Premier, who'd flown from Moscow just for the occasion. Dr Joseph Goebbels, for whom this whole week of internationally publicized events was a personal triumph, spoke briefly to the two men and held a silver trowel for Molotov to inspect. It was to be used when the new marble block, inscribed with intertwined Nazi and Communist symbols, and a lengthy declaration of amity, was lowered down upon the newly empty grave.

255

In Dartmouth Park Hill, the old hospital's top floors provided staff and patients with a grandstand view of the ceremonies in the street below. The specially selected black horses teamed to a German army-gun carriage moved restlessly and clattered their hooves on the cold road. Their groomed flanks shimmered and the fidgeting wheels made the brakes whimper. Postilions on the horses calmed them, and the escorting cavalry reined in tightly as the clock struck eleven. The commander of the honour guard, a Colonel of the prestigious 5 Kavallerie-Regiment, almost lost control of his fine bay when the motor-cyclists wheeled into position, their polished steel helmets gleaming in the wintry sunlight.

The band played solemn music, as the army stewards made way for the last arrivals: Britain's puppet Prime Minister accompanied by the newly appointed German Commissioner for the Bank of England. Behind them, Douglas recognized SS-Gruppenführer Professor Max Springer of the SD. Huth's boss was the senior SS officer at the ceremony and was here as Himmler's personal representative.

Six pall-bearers – representing the army, navy, air-force, SS, Nazi Party and SA stood ready to take the mortal remains of Karl Marx on the first stage of its journey to Red Square. Room had already been made for him in the Lenin Mausoleum, and by 7 November, the anniversary of the Russian revolution, more ceremonies would accompany the opening of the newly occupied tomb to the Moscow crowds.

Douglas did not have a very good view. He was standing near Kellerman, on the hospital side of the grave and downhill from it. The band was playing solemn martial music. Kellerman passed some banal remark. Douglas turned his head to answer as the shock wave of the explosion punched him in the face like a padded glove. Facing up-hill he saw the earth round the grave shudder as it became first a mound, then a hill and finally a great cloud of smoke and dirt. And the earth showered upon him like a tidal wave, knocking him over and choking him with dirt.

As Douglas struggled to his feet, he saw Kellerman half-buried under a large tombstone. His mouth was moving but he made no noise. There was no sound anywhere, not even from the officer who was struggling to extricate himself from the bloody folds of an ornate military standard. He ripped the torn flag from an arm that was no more than a stump. It spurted blood and the man staggered drunkenly until, bloodless, he fell to the ground.

Now the noise was so great that it penetrated even Douglas's blast-deafened skull. There was the concerted wail of agony and fear and the bells and hooters of ambulances trying to get past the frightened horses of the funeral cortège. The cavalry Colonel's arab bay bolted. He stayed in the saddle, taking some gravestones with graceful strides until she went under some trees and low branches snapped her rider's spine.

Near the Retcar Street gate, bandsmen were trying to rescue dead and bleeding comrades from mangled brass and broken drums. There were bodies everywhere and, to complicate the macabre scene further, corpses had broken from their ancient coffins and sprawled across the grassy tombs as if answering the herald horn of judgment day.

General Kellerman got out from the fallen stone with nothing worse than a torn ligament. Douglas helped him to his feet and supported him as far as two uniformed SS orderlies who carried their General to an ambulance.

With remarkable foresight, Kellerman had included in his orders for the day an ambulance and medical team from the SS Hospital. Such teams had standing orders that SS personnel – however slight their needs and whatever their rank – had medical priority over all other casualties. Now Kellerman was to find himself the first casualty the SS team treated.

The week of ceremonies had been organized by the staff of Army Group L (London District) without much reference to the Militärverwaltungschef (Head of Administration), to the British puppet government, or to Kellerman and his SS and police units. Tickets for most of the best viewpoints had gone to high-ranking army officers and political big-wigs from Moscow. And so it was that they took the brunt of the casualties, with the guard of honour, bandsmen, and those members of the Red Army Choir delegated to sing the new lyrics of the 'Horst Wessel Song'.

The fierce upward blast of the explosion dealt its cruellest blow to a Propaganda-Kompanie film crew, positioned on the roof platform of their specially strengthened 'A Type' Steyr. Tracking forward, all four wheels in gear, and its aircooled V-8 engine's high-speed fan humming loudly, they had been getting 'mute' close-ups of the inscription before the ceremony began. The bomb exploded as they moved away, gutting the heavy car and scattering bits of the dismembered film crew into nearby Waterlow Park. Sheltered by the temporary positioning of the PK car, the celebrities, Goebbels, Molotov and von Ribbentrop, suffered collectively no more than two ruptured eardrums, one twisted ankle and some dry-cleaning bills.

Standartenführer Huth had characteristically placed himself as near to an exit as he could get. He was at the

Swains Lane gate when the bomb exploded. According to the officer standing next to him, Huth did not even flinch when the bang came. Harry Woods embellished this story to relate that Huth had calmly put his fingers in his ears some thirty seconds *before* the explosion. The joke went all round the Scotland Yard building. Even Kellerman laughed when he heard it. It was a defamatory joke, a dangerous jest, but both Huth and Kellerman found it difficult to conceal the satisfaction they felt at such a public demonstration of the German army's security failure.

The army were quick to close ranks. Within fifteen minutes of the explosion, the six-ton mobile command-centre – on hand for traffic control during the funeral procession – had been taken over for a high-level conference. The adjutant to the Army Group commander was talking with a Colonel of the Feldgendarmerie, a GFP officer still in civilian clothes and two military security advisers to the Militärverwaltung, one of them slightly wounded. Two Abwehr officers were there already and more were coming. The bus was parked in front of that weird Gothic folly that faces the cemetery gate in Swains Lane. There, with armed sentries round them, the soldiers rehearsed their answers for the military inquiry that was bound to end with some heads rolling – perhaps literally.

Huth looked at the big ten-wheel Krupp Befehlskraft-wagen, and the anxious soldiers inside it, dimly seen through the frosted glass windows. He smiled at Douglas, and brushed from his tunic some of the dirt and dust that had covered everyone and everything. Then he looked down at his dirty hand. 'Let's get out of here,' said Huth with evident distaste. 'I want to wash the mortal remains of Karl Marx out of my hair.'

Around them medical teams were applying tourniquets,

stanching blood, lifting bodies on to stretchers and rip-
ping uniforms to dress wounds. There were groans and
screams. An Admiral who'd been standing near Douglas
at the time of the explosion was receiving last rites from a
German army chaplain.

'The explosion came from the grave itself, wouldn't
you say?' Huth asked Douglas.

'There's no doubt about that.'

'Probably got in here last night. Got poor old Karl out
of his nice new wooden overcoat and stuffed it with
explosive.' Huth sniffed and pulled a face. The disinterred
bodies, and the disturbed earth of the graveyard, were
making the whole place stink. 'You can bet the army had
no guards here.' He started to move towards the gate,
elbowing his way through the throng. He pushed past a
wounded bandsman standing patiently, hand high in the
air while twisting a string round his arm to stop the
bleeding from a torn vein. The man's tunic was covered
in blood that had run down his arm, and Huth shrank
away to avoid getting stains on his own tunic. Then, as if
ashamed of his behaviour, he said, 'Get along and find an
ambulance. You'll lose your arm if you stay here like
that.' .

'I was ordered to stay here,' said the youth.

Huth shrugged. His conscience satisfied, he continued
on his way, as if his aside to the young bandsman had
never happened.

Tucked away behind the gate-lodge was Huth's favourite vehicle; his 'Krad' the BMW motor-cycle combination.
No doubt he'd hidden it here in the hope of being able to
steal away from the ceremonies before they ended. There
was a uniformed SS man guarding the machine. Now he
wiped the dust from the saddle with his sleeve, before
Huth climbed on to it.

Huth's sinus trouble had been aggravated by dirt and vegetation flung up by the explosion. His eyes were watering, and he blew his nose loudly. 'Do you know a man named George Mayhew?' he asked Douglas and wiped his nose again.

'Colonel Mayhew? Every policeman in London knows him. He was the best scrum-half the police rugby team ever had.'

Huth stared at Douglas as if suspecting that this was an evasive reply. 'And has every policeman in London seen him during the past week?'

'It's highly likely. I certainly have.'

'You know him well?' He put a hand to his forehead. 'Ever had sinus, Superintendent?'

'No, fortunately not! . . . I mean, yes, I know Mayhew well but I don't suffer from sinus.'

'Sometimes I'm not sure you know what you mean.' Huth had taken some papers from his pocket, and now he shuffled through them and passed a small photograph to Douglas. 'Do you see Mayhew here?'

It looked like a very bad photograph, but had Douglas realized the problems of using a long telephoto lens and getting enough light into a camera without having the result spoiled by the sort of movement which so easily affects such lenses, and had he known the chance that the photo-technician had taken, when processing the negative for over twice the normal time, he would have recognized it as being a very good photograph indeed.

'It could well be Colonel Mayhew,' admitted Douglas. 'The man looking at the camera is Generalmajor Georg von Ruff, isn't he?'

'He saw the observation car, and my photographer in it,' said Huth. 'He's a damned suspicious old swine. The third man is Professor Frick, of course.'

261

Huth had a sense of timing that any night-club comedian might well envy, if not emulate. 'Professor Frick!' said Douglas with unconcealed surprise. 'I thought he was dead long ago. I thought he died in the fighting last year?'

'Then he has risen from the dead,' said Huth. 'What would you say those three had in common . . . apart from their obvious desire to avoid my cameraman?'

'This atomic explosive?'

'You should have been a detective,' said Huth. 'But you can do better than that, I'm sure.'

'Can I?'

'Generalmajor von Ruff is the senior Abwehr officer in Great Britain. Behind him, lost in the shadows, is a Colonel from the Heereswaffenamt. Obviously both of them talk to old Frick because they hope he's going to make some kind of super bomb for the army. But what is Colonel Mayhew doing here with them?'

'I don't know.'

'He's doing business with them, that's what he's doing,' said Huth.

The two men looked at each other for a long time. Finally Douglas said, 'You think that Mayhew is selling them scientific research?'

'He's selling them carbon copies of those calculations that were burned in the fireplace at Shepherd Market. And I'd bet my life on it.'

'For money?'

'What would Colonel Mayhew want, more than anything in the whole world, Archer? Come on, you're an Englishman, you know the answer to this one.'

'The King, you mean?'

Huth patted Douglas's shoulder in sardonic congratulation. Then he kicked his big motor-cycle engine into life.

'What do you want me to do about it?' shouted Douglas over the din.

'You tell Mayhew that I want those calculations.'

'What about the other business?' shouted Douglas.

'What other business?'

Douglas snatched a glance over his shoulder. Huth throttled the engine back until it was making a noise like muffled drums. 'The King,' said Douglas.

Huth took back the photo from Douglas, and replaced it in the handful of envelopes, papers and memo sheets that he'd got from his pocket. He shuffled them again and found a small buff-coloured form, folded once. Without opening it, Huth creased it again so that it was narrow enough to slide easily into Douglas's top pocket. Huth smiled his humourless smile. 'Look at that, Archer,' he said, standing up on the footrests of the motor-cycle in order to see the chaos and carnage. 'The Ivans will put the blame on us, and you'll see that picture on the front page of tomorrow's *Pravda*.'

Douglas turned to follow his gaze. Most of the dead and injured were at the top of the rise. The visiting Russians' privileged position at the ceremony had exposed them to the fiercest danger. Wives, daughters and mistresses too – documented as secretaries – had accompanied this contingent of élite communists on their journey westwards. Bond Street silks, and Savile Row worsteds, were torn and bloody; and many of the Russians sprawling in the snowstorm of chipped marble would never get to their feet again.

But there would not be photos of it in the morning papers. Not in *Pravda,* or *Völkischer Beobachter, The Times, Tribune* or any other paper or magazine. At the Swains Lane entrance – and in the streets, park and hospital yard adjoining the cemetery – Feldgendarmerie units checked all cameras and searched everyone carrying press passes. At the gate there was a pile of 35mm film, taken from cameras, cassettes and even from unused packets; it shone brown and grey in the wintry sunshine, trembling, slithering and unrolling like a nest of vipers.

An SS officer hurried towards them. 'It's Gruppen-führer Springer, sir,' he said to Huth. 'Would you come quickly.'

Left alone, Douglas took from his pocket the folded buff form. He had recognized it already as one of the new abbreviated arrest warrants. Little more than an abstract from the Primary Arrest Sheet, it simply gave George Mayhew's name and address, and the reason for arrest: Schutzhaft (Protective Custody), a catch-all word whereby men, women and children disappeared and were never seen again. There was an insolent callousness to the way that Huth had legalized it with a scrawling illegible signature in pencil. Douglas tucked the form into his wallet. There was a loud scream. He turned and saw an army engineer unit winching a slab of stone off a man who was dying noisily.

Douglas hurried through Waterlow Park and found a public telephone box on Highgate Hill. Colonel Mayhew's manservant answered the phone. Douglas knew him, a retired police Constable who had taken the heavyweight boxing trophy two years in succession and missed the third by only the narrowest of margins. He got Mayhew to the phone without delay. 'This is Detective Superin-tendent Archer,' said Douglas formally, 'and I am holding a warrant for your arrest.'

'Can you speak?'

'I'm in a call-box. Standartenführer Huth just gave me the form. He's signed it himself. There's no charge; it's a protective custody order.'

'What now?'

'The traffic is terrible . . .'

'I heard the official statement on the news. The Germans must be regretting that they gave the BBC facilities for a live broadcast . . . very well, you won't be able to get here for at least an hour.'

'That's right.'

'Thanks, Archer. I'll see if I can pull a few strings. In any case I'll contact you at the girl's flat.'

Douglas had the feeling that Colonel Mayhew did not understand the danger he was in. Perhaps Mayhew believed all that propaganda about concentration camps being no worse than hard beds, cold showers and physical training. If so, he'd be in for a terrible surprise. 'Colonel,' said Douglas, 'there might be other warrants that I've not seen. There might be orders that would apply to your family.'

Mayhew remained unruffled. 'Yes, I understand. It doesn't come as a complete surprise, Archer. But thank you all the same.'

'Good-bye, Colonel,' said Douglas and hung up the phone.

Douglas's visit to Colonel George Mayhew's fine town house at the Grosvenor Square end of Upper Brook Street, Mayfair, was no more than a formality. Mayhew's manservant had the right answers all prepared, as might be expected of a police Constable who'd served his time. He showed Douglas through all the rooms and even opened the cupboards.

'If Colonel Mayhew returns, you'll phone me immediately,' said Douglas.

'I will indeed, Superintendent,' said the manservant. The two men both smiled and Douglas took his leave.

* * *

265

It was only when Douglas got back to Pip Piper's dark-room, and put the strips of negatives on the lightbox, that his theories were confirmed. Here was frame after frame of closely typed calculations, some of them with scribbled annotation and changes. Pip remained well back from the lightbox as Douglas leaned over it. 'What do you think of them, Pip?'

'About one stop over-exposed, but that's not a bad fault with this copying work. There will be no trouble reading it. Want a magnifying glass?'

Douglas took the glass and studied the negative. The words and figures were in focus and with this powerful glass there was no great difficulty in reading them. 'It doesn't mean a thing to me,' said Douglas.

'Don't look at me,' said Pip. 'I was never much good at sums.'

'Thank God that jazz band has stopped rehearsing,' said Douglas. Why the devil doesn't Huth guess that there are negatives, he thought. He was looking for carbon copies, and that would mean a search for something as large as a brief-case. But then he realized that Huth's men had found nothing that would suggest the use of a camera. The only clue in the Shepherd Market flat was the position of the desk light and the bulb that had been removed from it. Douglas had replaced the bulb and moved the light's position. Young Spode must have taken the special photo-flood bulb and thrown it away. As for Spode's lodgings, the Leica camera and the bag of accessories had all been removed.

The rain had started again. Douglas stared out of the window at the hunchbacked roofs and crippled chimneys. The wind gusted enough to send a cloud of smoke to darken this dormer window. Douglas smelled the soot, and the dirt irritated his eyes.

266

'Are you all right?' said Pip.

'Yes, I'm all right.' Thoughtfully Douglas fingered the elbow pivot in his pocket. It had been modified to provide a secret chamber. The young Spode was obviously some kind of courier. This space was just big enough to take the 35mm film cassette but the alteration deprived the fixture of a quarter of an inch of screw thread. It weakened its hold enough for a little extra exertion – shooting, or more probably turning over sheet after sheet of paper for the photography – to cause it to come loose. Well, people always made some mistake or other. 'Pip,' said Douglas, 'there was a Leica camera, and four thin metal legs . . .'

'A copying stand. Yes, that's the simplest way to do a job like this. The legs screw into a heavy ring, and that clips to the lens mount. In that way the camera is held exactly the right distance away from the subject for the supplementary lens in use . . . focusing is extremely critical at such short distances – '

Douglas reached forward and touched his friend's arm to cut the explanation short. 'If you saw this copying stand and so on, Pip, would you know that it was intended for such work? Or could it be used for other purposes?'

'No, you can't use the copying stand and supplementary lens for any other purpose.'

'I see,' said Douglas. He turned back to the window. The electric kettle boiled. Pip made tea in a tiny red enamel teapot. It was strong tea, the strongest Douglas had tasted for a long time.

'Are you sure you're all right, Douglas?'

'Why?' said Douglas, still staring at rain hitting the wet slates. There was a curious feeling of isolation living up here where the only view was of the sky and other people's roof-tops. Douglas decided he liked it; it gave him a chance to catch his breath. Perhaps old Pip was luckier than he knew.

'Well this is obviously something you want to keep to yourself,' said Pip, 'so it's not a police matter. I know you too well to think that you're on the take from one of the mobs. And that only leaves one thing.'

'And what's that?' Douglas held tight to the cup of tea so that it warmed the palms of his hands. He wished his father was alive. The memory came suddenly and without warning, as it had done at other crisis times in his life. He tried to dismiss the thought but it persisted.

'You're working against the bloody Herberts,' said Pip softly.

'I can smell more fog coming,' said Douglas. 'People are burning so much wood and rubbish to keep warm. That's what does it.'

'Tobacco you mean,' said Pip. 'I remember a time when only men smoked. Now I see kids and old ladies puffing away, even at the fantastic prices you have to pay for cigarettes.'

'Solace,' said Douglas. 'People who are cold and wet and miserable get a lot of comfort from it.' He could remember little else of his father, a huge man with a cheerful laugh, and clothes that always smelled of pipe tobacco.

'But it's the Herberts too. Every damn one of them seems to have a bloody great cigar in his mouth.'

'The soldiers get harsh punishments for drunkenness,' said Douglas. It was the sort of conversation he'd had before many times, and while he spoke his mind was partly occupied with the business of the film.

'You are, aren't you? You are working against the Herberts?' Douglas didn't reply. He craned his neck to see down into the street where a coalman was leaning forward slowly tilting a sack of coal over his shoulder so that the pieces crashed to the ground through the circular hole in the pavement, and into the coal cellar. In spite of the rain, the man and his sack disappeared behind a cloud of coal-dust. Douglas continued to watch.

Pip said, 'You have it *your* way, Douglas. But your secrets are safe with me.'

Douglas shook his head. 'No secret is safe with anyone.' He kept going over and over the same thing in his mind. Huth's ignorance he could understand. If Hesse, and the Abwehr people, had taken possession of young Spode's Leica and the copying stand and the supplementary lens and so on, why didn't they realize that the documents had been copied by photography? Why were they still asking Mayhew about papers? 'It's better you know as little as possible, Pip,' Douglas told him. 'If the worst comes to the worst tell them you developed a film for me. It's easier for me to invent lies and excuses.'

'I'll just say I was drunk,' said Pip.

And then suddenly it came to Douglas. The Abwehr were every bit as cunning and devious as any of the rest of them. They *did* know about the negatives – and that was why they were still talking to Mayhew – but by keeping it a secret they would be able to verify, to some extent, the bona fides of the other side. They'd talk to Mayhew, and anyone else about documents but they were waiting for someone to say the magic words '35mm film negatives'. Douglas drank the hot tea greedily. Then he switched off the lightbox, rolled the dried film back into a cassette and put it in his pocket.

'Here, that's the way to get scratches,' objected his friend.

'I'm not planning to do exhibition prints for the Royal Photographic Society exhibition,' said Douglas, using a

269

favourite remark of Pip's. He drained his tea and put the cup on the window-ledge. 'Thanks for everything, Pip.' In the street below, the coalman had the circular cast-iron cover in his hand as he kicked the last few pieces of coal down into the dark cellar.

Chapter Twenty-five

Londoners called it 'the night of the buses' but in fact the mass arrests and selective round ups, of people classified as IAa all the way to IIIEa, continued for two nights and well into the third day. As well as this, certain categories were ordered to report to the nearest police station. Posters and whole-page newspaper advertisements to this effect resulted in many people going voluntarily into custody.

Wembley Stadium was used as a holding centre for west London, and the Earls Court Exhibition Hall – with the Albert Hall as an overflow – was the place to which people arrested in east London were taken. The tenants of that vast riverside apartment block, Dolphin Square, were turned out into the streets, with only two hours' notice, so that their flats could be used for hundreds of simultaneous interrogations.

To obtain interrogators every unit in Britain was scoured. As well as the professionals from the Geheime Feldpolizei units, SD men, Gestapo and people from the big Abwehr building in Exhibition Road, there were men with no other qualification than a working knowledge of the English language. These included waiters from the Luftwaffe Officers' Club, two chaplains, a flautist from the German army's London District symphony orchestra, seven telephonists and a naval dentist.

'Keep the boys at home today, Mrs Sheenan,' Douglas told her at breakfast, on the morning following the explosion. She put another slice of toast on his plate, and nodded to show that she'd heard him. The bread was stale but covered with meat dripping it became a luxury beyond compare. Douglas waited to be sure there was enough for everyone before biting into it.

Mrs Sheenan poured more tea for all of them. 'Did you hear the lorries last night?' she said. 'They must have been arresting people across the street. The noise they made! I thought they were going to break the door down.'

'It's going to be the biggest series of arrests I've heard of,' said Douglas. 'Perhaps the biggest in modern history.' She raised her eyes to him. Awkwardly he added, 'I'm not admiring it, Mrs Sheenan, I'm simply stating a fact. Thousands of people will be taken into custody. Goodness knows how the Germans will sort them all out.'

'I can't see how it will help them catch the men who planted that bomb at the cemetery.'

Douglas agreed but did not elaborate on it. He said, 'And if you and the boys just happened to be walking along the wrong street at the wrong time, you could easily get caught up in the muddle. And who knows where you might end up.'

'In Germany,' said Mrs Sheenan. 'Eat up your toast, boys, and drink that tea. We mustn't waste anything.'

'Yes, in Germany,' said Douglas. That was where her husband had ended up.

'Are you arresting them?' said Mrs Sheenan's son.

'Don't talk to Mr Archer like that,' said Mrs Sheenan. 'And don't talk with your mouth full, I've told you before about that.' She smacked the boy lightly on the arm. There was no force behind the blow but coming from such a mild-mannered woman the gesture surprised all of them. Her son sat back in the chair and cuddled his knees as tears came into his eyes.

'No, it's nothing to do with the CID, thank goodness,'

said Douglas, glad of the chance to disclaim all connection with it. He drank his tea. 'I could give you something in writing, Mrs Sheenan,' he offered. 'It wouldn't be official of course, but on Scotland Yard notepaper . . . something like that might be useful.'

She shook her head. Douglas guessed she had thought of that idea already. She leaned across to her son and kissed him. 'Drink up your tea, that's a good boy. It's the last of the sugar ration until next week.'

She turned to Douglas and politely said, 'What use would a piece of paper be to me? By the time I needed it, it would be too late . . . and suppose someone found it? They'd probably think I was – ' She stopped. She'd been about to say 'informer' but now she said, '. . . something to do with the Germans.'

'Yes, of course,' said Douglas stiffly.

'Oh, I didn't mean *that*, Mr Archer,' she said. 'You're a policeman. You have to have dealings with them. What would we do if we didn't have our own policemen? I'm always saying that.'

Douglas realized that she was often saying it because she was often trying to explain why she had a lodger who worked for the Huns. Douglas tucked the napkin into its wooden ring, and got up. 'Leave the shopping for as long as you can – the baker's man and the milkman call, don't they? By the week-end the excitement might be dying down a bit. There simply won't be anywhere to put the prisoners.'

She nodded, pleased that he'd not taken offence at the clumsy way she'd expressed herself. From the cupboard drawer she got a newly knitted pullover. It was white cable-stitch, with the colours of the police cricket club at the vee neck. It was wrapped in pre-war tissue paper.

'It's cold,' said Mrs Sheenan. 'Winter has really begun now.'

She held out the pullover for Douglas but he hesitated before accepting it. He knew she'd knitted it for her husband – a noted slow bowler in the cricket team in those days before the war.

'The post office won't accept parcels containing clothes or food,' she explained. 'It's a new regulation, and they always look inside every parcel.' She opened the tissue and held the shining white pullover up. She was proud of the way she'd knitted it. 'We both want you to have it, Mr Archer,' she said, looking at her son. 'You can always give it back when his father comes home.'

'I'll put it on right now,' said Douglas. 'Thank you.'

'I never thought of you as a cricketing type,' said Huth sarcastically as Douglas came into the office. The room was dark, the morning sky as hard and expressionless as gunmetal, and little daylight got through the heavily leaded windows. Huth was in uniform, his grey jacket over his chair-back, and his rumpled brown SS shirt loosened at the collar. He was unshaven and Douglas guessed that he'd been sitting here at his desk half the night. In front of him there was an empty bottle of Scotch whisky, and the air held the smell of dead cigars. 'Shut the bloody door, can't you.'

Douglas closed the door.

'Pour yourself a drink.' It was as if he'd lost track of time.

'No thanks.'

'It's an order.'

'The bottle's empty.'

'Plenty more in the cupboard.'

Douglas had never seen Huth in this sort of mood, or

274

even thought it possible. He got another bottle of whisky from the cardboard box, 'Specially bottled for the Wehrmacht', opened it and poured a measure into the tumbler that Huth produced from a drawer. 'Water?' said Huth and pushed a jug across his desk, carelessly enough to slop water over the muddle of papers there. Huth picked up one of them, a telex message, and let the water drip off the corner of it, giving it that childlike attention with which drunks survey their world. 'Casualty lists,' he explained, 'they keep dying . . .'

'The explosion?'

Huth waved the wet sheet of paper, with its closely printed list of names. 'The explosion – that's right! Dig up old Karl, after half a century in the phosphate-rich soil of north-west London, and don't be surprised if he farts in your eye – right?'

Douglas didn't respond, but by that time he'd been able to read some of the names on the sheet that Huth was waving at him. The teleprinter message had come from the SS Hospital at Hyde Park Corner.

SPRINGER, PROF. MAX. SS-GRUPPENFÜHRER. NR. 4099.
STAB RFSS. DIED OF WOUNDS 02.33.

'Yes, they keep dying,' said Huth.

'And Professor Springer was killed there?'

'We've lost a good friend, Superintendent.' He reached for the bottle and poured himself another drink, adding water to it with exaggerated care, like a stage drunk.

'Have we?'

'He was my friend at the court of King Heinrich,' said Huth. 'The Reichsführer-SS had given him a free hand to find a way in which the SS could take over the nuclear experiments from the army.' Huth's fist clenched hard.

275

'My authority came through Springer.' Huth looked at his fist. 'I gave him a place at the back, near the Naval Staff, but the bloody fool had to move closer to the grave, to see better. A piece of masonry fell on him.'

'Does it mean your investigation might be stopped?' said Douglas. He sipped at the whisky but drank very little of it.

'Not a chance of that, thank goodness,' said Huth. He was still looking at himself. His trousers were muddy and one knee was torn. Douglas guessed that he'd been one of the working party who extricated Springer from under the fallen stonework.

'You've known Professor Springer a long time?'

'I could tell you stories, Archer. Things you'd never believe. I was with Springer that weekend, when we killed the brownshirt leaders. I met him at Tempelhof when he landed on the special flight bringing Karl Ernst from Bremen. Springer had arrested him in his hotel that morning. Karl Ernst was Röhm's second in command, Reichstag Deputy and Counsellor of State, but he submitted to arrest as meek as a lamb.' Huth sipped his whisky. He was more relaxed but frowning slightly as if making an effort to remember the week-end of the 'putsch'.

Huth smiled. 'They didn't know what was happening to them, those SA men. They couldn't imagine that the Führer might have told us to execute them. Ernst was typical. He thought it was an uprising against the Führer. Just before our firing squad let him have it, he squared his shoulders and shouted "Heil Hitler!" and they fired, and killed him.' Huth closed his open hands over his face as Douglas had seen asthma sufferers do, and like them he breathed slowly and carefully. 'Funny, eh?'

'Not very funny,' said Douglas.

'It taught me a lesson,' said Huth bitterly. 'I watched

that fool die and I vowed that I would never listen to any kind of political claptrap ever again.'

'And did you?'

'Do I look like an idealist, Archer?'

Douglas shook his head but didn't answer lest he spoil Huth's mood for talking. He'd known other men like this. He'd heard them confess to terrible crimes, and, like Huth, such men spoke of themselves with a strange impersonal detachment.

'It was easy to see the Nazis would win,' said Huth. 'The Nazis were the only ones with the brains and determination. And the only ones with the organization. I like winners, Archer. My father liked winners too. He was a ruthless bastard, my God how I detest him still. Being at the top of the class was the only way to win my father's affections, so I made sure I was at the top of the class. Nazis are winners, Archer, don't be tempted into working against them.'

Douglas nodded.

'Next week I'll be in Berlin. I'll talk to the Reichsführer-SS and perhaps to the Führer too. They'll have to give me Springer's job because there is no one with all the information,' he tapped his head, 'and eventually I'll get Springer's rank too. Cheer up! Kellerman's days are numbered, Archer. We'll be rid of him before next month's out. I'll have him upstairs, sitting in a chair, answering a lot of difficult questions about his bank account in Switzerland and the bribes he's getting from some of the contractors building the new prisons.'

The surprise showed on Douglas's face.

Huth said, 'I've got a file this thick on Kellerman. Why do you think he's so keen to get a chance of searching through my documentation? He's not interested in taking over the atomic bomb programme, he's just anxious to save his skin.' He drank water. 'Do you want to stay with me, Archer?'

'On your staff?'

'There's not many of Springer's personal staff that I will want to keep. If you stay with me, you can come all the way to the top. I'll make you a German citizen and bring you into the SD immediately – no more rationing, travel restrictions or finance control.' He looked at Douglas.

'I thought you only liked winners,' said Douglas.

He gave a thin smile. 'Not as a personal assistant,' he said.

Perhaps his offer was well-meant. To what extent it was a spontaneous and clumsy Teutonic attempt at flattery, and to what extent a carefully planned proposition, Douglas could not decide.

Huth got up and went to the window. 'You didn't talk to Mayhew yesterday?' he said without turning round.

'I'll find him,' said Douglas.

Huth was silhouetted against the light and Douglas saw the way in which his fingers fluttered nervously at his side, as if he was trying to remove dirt, or glue or memories from the tips of them. 'Mayhew is an educated man,' said Huth as much to himself as to Douglas. 'A cultured, reasonable individual.'

'Yes, of course,' said Douglas.

'He has no personal quarrel with me, does he? What's he looking for? Prestige and the respect of his equals. That's what motivates all normal men. Between us we can come to some kind of arrangement. And the result will reflect credit upon both of us, and elevate us in the way we wish. Can you tell him that from me?'

It was breath-taking cynicism, even by Huth's standard. 'And what guarantees do I have?'

'You have that wonderful excuse that you only obeyed orders. Be grateful for that, my friend.'

'I'll be a contact,' said Douglas, 'but not an informant.' Even as he said it he recognized the rationalization as something he'd heard from countless men he'd used – and despised – in the past.

There was a knock at the door. Huth bellowed 'Come in' and a porter entered with a bucket of coal and began to build a fire in the grate. Huth nodded Douglas's dismissal.

Douglas got to his feet, and thanked the Providence that Huth was not one of those Germans who went through the ritual of saying 'Heil Hitler!' at the end of each such meeting. In front of the old porter it would have been just more than Douglas could have endured.

A mass of paperwork was piled up on Douglas's desk and Harry Woods was late. Douglas cursed him for an inefficient fool. Today of all days he could have used his help. He looked at Harry's desk diary and found an appointment with the Superintendent Crime at 9.30 A.M. Douglas phoned the clerk and invented a story about Harry being ill. The clerk made a joke of it; Harry's inability to be punctual was well known.

Douglas sent a civilian clerk to look for Harry in Joe's Café. It was too early for the 'dive' of the 'Red Lion', or the CID's 'tank' across the road. Douglas phoned the desk Sergeant at Cannon Row police station next door, to see if Harry was in there gossiping.

When all the answers were negative, Douglas phoned Kellerman's chief clerk. He asked him for the address of the arrest team collecting point in the Islington district where Harry Woods lived. It took him fifteen minutes to get the answer: York Way Goods Depot, behind King's Cross Station up until last night at 10.30 P.M. After that,

279

they began using the Caledonian Road Cattle Market as an overspill.

Douglas phoned Huth in his office. 'Standartenführer. I think it's possible that Harry Woods has been picked up by one of the arrest teams.' There was no reply. Douglas added, 'He didn't come in this morning, in spite of an appointment with the Superintendent Crime.' After another long period of silence, Douglas said, 'Are you there, sir?'

'I can't think how Woods stayed free so long,' said Huth. 'Well, you'll have to get yourself another Detective Sergeant. Can you find someone who speaks German?'

'I'm going to look for Harry,' said Douglas.

'Suit yourself,' said Huth. 'But make sure there is someone behind that desk by eight o'clock tomorrow morning. This is no time to work with a depleted manpower.'

'Yes, sir,' said Douglas and hung up the phone.

Chapter Twenty-six

Harry Woods lived in Liverpool Road. At one time they'd had the whole house but now its upper two floors were rented to another family. Harry Woods and his wife Joan ate their meals in the basement kitchen and that's where Douglas sat while Joan made him a cup of tea.

He guessed what had happened as soon as Mrs Woods opened the door. She was still in her dressing-gown, her hair uncombed and her eyes red with crying. She was much younger than Harry. At one time she'd been the prettiest typist in her office typing pool, where Harry Woods met her while investigating a theft at a factory. Now her blonde hair had gone colourless and her face was pinched with the cold. She smiled as she passed the weak unsweetened tea across the table, ran a hand through her dishevelled hair and self-consciously pulled the neck of her dressing-gown together.

They had arrested Harry Woods at three o'clock that morning. The German officer arrived with his team of twelve soldiers. The very young Metropolitan police Constable, from some outlying Division, had never heard of Harry Woods. 'He'd never heard of Scotland Yard either if you ask me,' added Joan Woods bitterly.

'Didn't Harry show them his warrant card, Joan?'

'The German officer glanced at it, thanked Harry very much and put it in his pocket. He was polite enough, the officer . . . he regretted it, he said. But he spoke hardly any English, and you know Harry's just no good at all with this German, Mr Archer. If you'd been here it would have all been different. You know how to speak with them, Harry always says that.'

'You should have phoned the Yard, Joan.'

'The public phones had soldiers guarding them. They would only permit official calls, you see. I saw the woman next door coming home after trying it.'

'Yes, I suppose they need the public phones in order to keep in touch with the arrest teams.'

'I went round to the police station and waited there for hours. Finally I managed to find the station Sergeant – he's an old friend of Harry's and I know his wife – and he told me to go home and get some sleep. He said it was all a mistake and that Harry would probably be back here before me.' She shrugged. 'But he wasn't, was he?'

'The Germans are holding hundreds – perhaps thousands – to question them about the explosion at Highgate. It might be a couple of days before we locate Harry and then it might take another day to complete the paperwork to free him. It's bound to be a muddle, Joan.'

'You've always been good to us, Mr Archer,' she said. In fact Douglas had always found it difficult to get along with Joan Woods. She resented Douglas's accent and his middle-class manners and the way in which his University education had automatically provided him with Sub-Divisional Inspector's rank, while Harry had spent all his life getting to be a Detective Sergeant.

'We're a team, Harry and I,' said Douglas.

'Harry cried when he found that you'd got his brother off that deportation order. We never realized that it was you who wangled it for us. Harry dotes on young Sid. He cried. If I never move from here alive; Harry cried.'

'Thank the Police Surgeon too, Joan. He wrote a long letter about Sid being too ill to work properly.' Douglas got to his feet. 'Anyway I'll chase Harry up now. But don't be worried if he's still not home tonight. It will be a long job.'

'Harry's a good man, Mr Archer.'

'I *know* he is, Joan.'

Outside the basement window there were only the whitewashed stone steps up to the street level, each step with its potted plant withered by the cold. There was a scurry of wind and some litter tumbled down the steps with a sound like running water. 'It's damned cold,' said Joan Woods, blowing on her hands.

Worse, thought Douglas, for all those unfortunates who were being held prisoner in the open. 'Don't let it get you down, Joan,' he said.

She gave him a flicker of a smile. There was no real communication between the two of them. They had nothing in common, except Harry.

Chapter Twenty-seven

Douglas began in the Caledonian Road Market. He knew it from before the war. On Sundays the whole of London came here to buy anything from old clothes to antique silver. Often Douglas had impatiently followed his Uncle Alex as he studied heaps of radio components, broken typewriters and piles of old books.

Douglas had not expected that there would be as many prisoners as this. In places, the inner perimeter wire had been broken and trampled by sheer weight of numbers. Only the metal rails, that were the permanent part of the cattle pens, steadied the crowd to prevent a major disaster.

The endless sea of heads moved constantly, like an ocean lapping at the high outer wire fence and the deserted roadway where the soldiers patrolled. Large numerals on posts marked the various groups of 'detainees' at the time of their arrival but now the overcrowding had caused the groups to merge and mingle. Even while Douglas watched, a young girl tore the yellow cloth star from her coat and climbed across the low pen railing to join another group of prisoners. In Market Road there were five Midland Red buses bearing 'Im Dienst der Deutschen Wehrmacht' stickers. Douglas guessed that a lot of the Jewish families would never get to the interrogation centres. They would be sent directly to the notorious concentration camp at Wenlock Edge.

Douglas's pass took him through the outer ring of guards, and into the hut near the weighbridge, now occupied by a dozen frantic army clerks, swearing, shouting and arguing. There was no use inquiring about a man named Woods, they were arguing about a discrepancy of ninety persons in that morning's arrivals. Douglas waved his pass and moved off into the inner compound.

Perhaps hell is like that; a discordant confusion of anxious souls. Some argued, some slept, some shouted, some wept, some wrote, some sketched and many conspired about their coming interrogation. But mostly they did no more than stare into space, eyes unfocused as they tried to see tomorrow. After nearly two hours of elbowing his way through the crowds, Douglas had become as dazed as they were. No matter how systematic his search, he knew that it would be possible to pass within arm's length of Harry without seeing him. No matter how methodical his movements, the crowd surged round him so that he saw the same individuals again and again. More than once, footsore and hungry, Douglas was ready to abandon his task. And yet he knew that, if the positions were reversed, Harry would never give up looking for Douglas, simply because the idea would not occur to him.

'Lost someone?'

Douglas rested on a railing, pleased with a chance to catch his breath. 'Big man, in his middle fifties, greying hair, dark complexion, dark business suit and white shirt – arrested in Liverpool Road about three A.M.' He'd said it all so many times that it had become the sort of hasty prayer that is mumbled by those without faith.

'Proper bloody muddle, isn't it?' He was a thin, twitchy little fellow with expensive clothes, a Royal Artillery necktie and heavy rimmed spectacles. 'I live in Highbury Crescent,' he said. Douglas realized that the man had hardly heard Harry's description, and didn't care. 'A lot of these people are riff-raff,' he confided, having approved of Douglas's middle-class appearance. 'You look whacked. Have you eaten?'

'No,' said Douglas.

'Well you've probably got a bob or two in your pocket. If you go along the railing there, the sentries can be bribed to slip across the road and bring fried fish and chips. They must be making a fortune at the prices they're charging.' He smiled to show that he bore them no ill will.

'Fish and chips?' said Douglas. It sounded delicious.

'These people think the Germans will bring them food.'

'But you don't think so?'

'Ask yourself,' said the man scornfully. 'I've seen army field kitchens in action during the last lot . . . during the last war,' he added in case Douglas hadn't understood him. 'Can you imagine how they are going to cope with this chaos? What are they going to get? Slice off the roast beef and two veg . . . huh. They'll be lucky to get a mouthful of potato soup. You get along there and get a feed. Some of these kids, and the old ones, will be in a terrible state by morning unless these bloody Huns get themselves moving . . . Where did you say . . . Liverpool Road?'

'About three A.M.'

The little man nodded. It was the chaos that was so distasteful to him; he had no quarrel with men who knew what they were doing. 'Arrest Team Number 187. They knew what they were doing. Polite young officer. He must have given your friend's wife a yellow docket, with a counterfoil number on one side above his signature. What was the last letter?'

'T.'

'Then you should find him near that large T over there.'

'I went there first,' said Douglas wearily. 'I know the system.'

'Yes, well it will have been Arrest Team 187. Jerry officer couldn't speak more than half-a-dozen words of English. They'd come from Liverpool Road . . . and some stupid kid of a copper; he couldn't have been more than nineteen.' He tapped Douglas's chest. 'They're the ones I blame – the bloody coppers – what are they doing, helping the Jerries arrest innocent people in the middle of the night? I'd put the whole lot of them up against the wall and shoot the buggers. I never have liked coppers.'

'My friend must have been in the same bus with you.'

'Big fellow you say? Grey hair. Did he have a Guards tie?'

'Very likely.'

'The big guardsman. Yes, I remember him. He took it badly, sat up at the front of the bus with his hands in his pockets. Big man, broad shoulders. I remember thinking he must be a hotel doorman or a boxer or something.' The man stood on tip-toe to see across the crowd. Failing to do so, he put a foot on one of the cattle pen rails and hoisted himself up. 'Go over to the S sign. I seem to remember seeing him there, when I got the sentry to buy me some fish and chips.'

'Thanks,' said Douglas as he moved on.

'You'll get yourself something to eat, if you take my advice,' the man called after him.

Douglas saw Sylvia before he saw Harry. She was sitting on the cattle railing, chewing a piece of bread. There was no reason to be surprised at the sight of Sylvia. She was a gambler, and just as an obsessional gambler wins, and returns again and again, to gamble until all the

287

winnings are gone, so would Sylvia keep risking her freedom until she lost it forever.

'We don't need you,' she said when she caught sight of Douglas.

'How did you find me, chief?' said Harry.

'Routine inquiries,' said Douglas.

'Thanks very much, chief. I mean it.'

'No more than you'd do for me, Harry,' said Douglas.

'Why don't you two get married?' said Sylvia. She sniffed, popped the last of the piece of bread into her mouth and got down from where she was perched on the railing.

'I think it's going to be all right,' said Harry.

'How?' said Douglas.

'Sylvia's people are going to fix one of the officers.'

To a Metropolitan policeman fix could mean nothing other than a bribe. Sylvia pulled a face, as if angry that Harry was talking about it. 'It's the best way,' said Harry.

'Yes, it might be,' said Douglas cautiously. If Harry went through the interrogation centre, it must result in an entry on his personal file at Scotland Yard. If Douglas arranged for him to be released, it must result in an entry on Douglas's file. A bribed guard was the only way to secure Harry's freedom without any compromising paperwork.

'We don't need you,' said Sylvia again. It was tempting for Douglas to believe that her contempt was a sign of unrequited love; that hellish fury that scorned women are reputed to conjure up. But he could see that it was deeper than that; it was irrational and unbalanced hysteria, and it frightened him. Perhaps she saw that fear on his face. 'Go back to your office, Douglas,' she jeered. 'We'll do this our way.' She used his first name in an attempt to deprive him of any dignity that his family name or his rank could have provided.

'I hope you both know what you are doing,' said Douglas looking at Harry.

Harry rubbed his jaw. 'No, we'll be all right, chief, honestly.'

'One of your friends can contact me if you want anything,' said Douglas. He was tired from his search and depressed by everything he'd seen. Now he retreated before Sylvia's hatred.

'Tell Joan,' said Harry.

'Tell Joan what?' said Douglas.

'Tell her I'll be home soon.'

'I'll tell her,' said Douglas. He was glad of an excuse to get away from there but once outside he reproached himself for being so quick to accept Harry's reassurances.

The smell of fried fish was on the air and Douglas walked along the road to the fried fish shop that the little man had talked about. There were four people bending over the fryers. All of them worked furiously to supply the endless stream of German soldiers, who carried the paper-wrapped fish across the empty road to where lines of hungry prisoners waited behind the barbed wire of the cattle market boundary. Huge white five-pound notes were being tossed across the counter, handled with the same careless haste given to the newspaper wrappings.

Douglas sat down at one of the marble-topped tables in the empty dining area. 'No service there,' shouted one of the men at the fryer.

'Where is there service?' asked Douglas, going to the counter.

'You'll have to find another fish shop, mate,' said the man at the fryer. He mopped his brow with his hand. 'No time for casuals today.'

289

'You bring me fried plaice and chips,' demanded Douglas.

'Or what?' said the man, leaning across the counter top to put his face close to Douglas.

'Or I'll come round the counter there and dip you, and your three pals in the fryer,' said Douglas quietly.

'You . . .' The man aimed a blow at Douglas but he found his wrist gripped and twisted hard enough for his face to be pressed on to the pile of newspapers. 'All right, all right, don't get nasty!' he shouted. The other three men pretended not to notice what was happening.

A German soldier – with a vested interest in the continued functioning of the fried fish shop – grabbed at Douglas's free arm but was greeted with such a roar of parade-ground German that he let go immediately, and even came to a position of attention. 'Now you give me a nice piece of plaice, and four pennyworth of chips,' Douglas continued, still holding the man, 'or I'll put you over the other side of the street, inside the wire. You understand?'

'Yes, I'm sorry, sir.' Douglas let him go. Sullenly the man slammed a piece of fish on to a thick chipped white plate, following with a portion of chips aimed carelessly enough to scatter half-a-dozen of them across the wooden counter top.

Douglas put a half-crown on the counter and got his change and a surly grunt. The man nodded to the German soldier and another portion of fish landed in newspaper. As his practised hands wrapped it, Douglas glimpsed the *Daily Telegraph* front page. The ancient headline said, 'Germans in retreat near Ashford. Canterbury declared open city as German tanks enter.' What have they done to us, thought Douglas? What has it done to me?

He looked out through the fish shop window, the glaze

of condensation was streaked with tears in which herds of prisoners could be glimpsed. Even above the sizzle of the fryer, and the clink of money, he could hear them.

Douglas sprinkled vinegar and salt upon his fish and chips. All of his working life had been spent in this sort of squalor. But until now he'd been fortified by the belief that he was upholding law and order. Now as he looked across the road that belief faltered.

Douglas thought of the father he'd never known and of the happy marriage so cruelly ended. Now he had only his son. There was no place in his life for the sort of complexities that Barbara Barga would bring. And yet, after all the reasoning was done, he'd fallen in love with her. There was no denying it; he wanted her in every way. But as a policeman, he distrusted love; too often had he seen the other side of it, the violence, the suffering and despair it could bring. He told himself that she represented no more than a chance to escape from the madhouse of deceit and suffering. He told himself it was the idea of America that he was in love with, and Barbara no more than a go-between. But whatever the truth of it, he needed her and had to see her.

Chapter Twenty-eight

'You look like hell,' she said with an amused smile. 'And you smell of fried fish. Douglas Archer, where have you been? I've been eating my heart out.' It was just her way of joking, of course, but it was what he wanted to hear.

They embraced tightly and then she put a hand against his cheek while she looked at him. 'Can I have a drink?' he asked.

'My darling, of course.' His wife had never called him darling, and he found it a strange form of address, one confined, or so he'd thought, to movie stars. And the idea of Douglas asking for a drink as soon as he stepped through the door was one that would have surprised most people who knew him.

She went into the kitchen, prised ice cubes from the tray and dropped them into two tumblers. Douglas told her about Harry Woods at the cattle market but he gave no speaking role to Sylvia.

'Only the Nazi press handouts are going out on the wire service,' said Barbara as she passed him his whisky. 'I've got a great story, and lots of photos, but there is a blackout. Hundreds of people have been arrested, you just have to take a cab up-town to see what's happening. Back home a dozen papers would have broken this story by now.'

'You're not back home,' Douglas reminded her. 'And the arrests number thousands, not hundreds.' A sudden ray of sunlight lit up the white walls of the kitchen but it didn't last long.

'Colonel Mayhew phoned. He wants to see you. He's coming here about eight.'

'I have an arrest warrant for him. Huth wants to frighten him into doing a deal.'

'What kind of deal?'

'Mayhew gets the King and takes him to America. Huth gets a lot of atomic physics research. The Germans are trying to make an atomic explosion.'

She showed no surprise. 'So I'd heard. Can I freshen that drink?'

Douglas put his hand over the glass. 'They're both crazy,' he said.

'Why?'

'Because once the King gets to the USA, Mayhew will be left aside and forgotten. And as soon as Huth gets the research material, he will become superfluous. He is a lawyer; he has no scientific training. He had a lot of stuff extracted from German scientific papers and encyclopaedias as background, and two special reports by Professor Springer. I read it all; now I know nearly as much as Huth does.'

'Perhaps Mayhew and Huth are motivated by something other than ambition?'

'You can't be serious, Barbara.' He smiled sadly. 'I've never met two men so alike in their ruthless ambition.' She saw then the great strength within him, not the athletic superiority that men so often used to intimidate others, but a strength that was kind and unassuming.

They went into the lounge and sat down on the ugly little sofa. Its loose cover, decorated with large green leaves, made it look like some carnivorous plant.

'Do you miss your wife?' she said. She touched the ice in her drink with her fingertip, and watched herself doing it.

'Sometimes. We were children together.'

293

'That's really tough.'

'I have the boy.' She sat down with him and he put an arm round her.

Barbara drank a little of her drink. 'And you have me too,' she said.

'Do I?' He looked at her but she had turned away from him. He touched her back. She shivered. 'Do I?' he said again.

'You know you do,' she whispered to the ice cubes.

'I love you, Barbara.'

'I love you too, Doug. I didn't want to, God knows.' The cloud moved across the sun, and the golden light dwindled and died until the room was almost dark. She leaned over and switched on the table lamp. 'I hate this damned sofa,' she said. 'Don't you?'

'It's the ugliest thing I ever saw,' said Douglas. 'Will you marry me?'

'I was going to have it dyed, but the people who rent me the place probably think it's valuable.' She fingered the chintz cover thoughtfully.

Douglas said, 'My year's salary is no more than you earn for a good story.'

'Let's marry soon, very soon.'

'There's my son, remember.'

'I remember.'

'Don't cry, Barbara.'

With mock severity she said, 'Without your son, no deal,' but the words caught in her throat, and she cried as he put both arms round her and kissed her.

Chapter Twenty-nine

Colonel Mayhew arrived at eight o'clock. Douglas and Barbara felt a childish satisfaction in the way that they received him in the lounge, pretending they hadn't watched him arrive from the window of the bedroom upstairs.

Mayhew dropped his tightly-rolled umbrella into the brass rack inside the door, and hung up his coat and hat with the easy familiarity of a regular visitor. Douglas resented it. Mayhew smiled at Douglas but it was the set grimace that marks anxiety rather than pleasure. 'You've heard the news about Harry?'

'Harry Woods?' said Douglas.

'He was arrested . . .'

'Yes,' said Douglas. 'He's all right. I went over there this afternoon and found him . . .'

'Then you *don't* know!' he said. Mayhew looked at Barbara and back to Douglas and rubbed his hands together. 'Harry was in a shooting incident this afternoon. They say he was hit but I've no confirmation of that. The girl with him – Sylvia Manning, who used to be your clerk – is dead.'

'My God,' said Douglas. His stomach knotted with guilt and he felt worse about the death of Sylvia than he would have believed.

'They got through the barbed wire of the perimeter fence at the Caledonian Market detention camp. Trying to escape, the sentry said. It sounds right.'

'I was there until almost four,' said Douglas. 'They had

their release more or less arranged. They'd bribed the officer of the guard, they said.'

Mayhew nodded. 'Didn't want to get you involved, you see.' He sniffed. 'Always a good sort, Harry. Didn't want to get you mixed up in it.'

'But they both said it was fixed,' said Douglas desperately.

'A dozen or more have got away from that compound,' said Mayhew. 'They were unlucky, that's all. Left it too late. Guards got jumpy. Perhaps the Sergeant Major gave them all a talking to, and they became trigger-happy. You know what it's like.'

'The girl's dead, you say?' said Douglas.

'Came back to try and drag Harry to safety. Sort of bravery that gets a chap a Victoria Cross in wartime, or a commission in the field. Got to admire her pluck eh? She was clear away and safe. Young, you see! She could run faster than Harry, and perhaps the sentry hesitated before shooting at a woman the first time. But when she went back . . .' He pulled a face.

'And Harry's hurt?'

'The Gestapo have already asked the army for him. Since he's a serving police officer, they say the army have no right to hold him.'

Barbara touched Douglas's arm and said, 'Will they torture him to get information?'

Mayhew shook his head. 'Harry knows nothing.'

'Harry was working with some Resistance group,' said Douglas.

'Yes, the remnants of the Camden Town battalion of the Home Guard have been putting sugar in the petrol tanks of army vehicles, assaulting drunken German soldiers and writing rude slogans about Hitler on walls.'

Douglas nodded agreement. He'd heard about the Camden Town battalion.

Mayhew's voice was flat and non-committal. 'Harry Woods knows only the girl who was with him and two other men they worked with.'

'Damn fool,' said Douglas, his distress turning to anger against Harry, as a mother might scold a child who has narrowly escaped death in traffic.

'It takes a lot of courage,' said Barbara. 'I'd be proud of any of my countrymen who did such things against an invader.'

'Harry and the girl carried the leaflets: that's dangerous!' said Mayhew. 'A suitcase full of contraband, or even radio parts, and you might stand a chance in a million of talking your way out of trouble. But the people who carry political leaflets are carrying their own death warrant if they are found with them.'

'What a waste,' said Douglas.

'Anyway the two other men in his cell – or platoon as they like to call it in the Home Guard – have been told of Harry's arrest. They will disappear . . . No, Harry knows nothing that the Gestapo will find very important. Still, being taken to Gestapo HQ in Norman Shaw North is not something to be recommended for someone who needs rest and relaxation.'

'I'd better get back there,' said Douglas.

'Now hold on,' said Mayhew in a different and more urgent tone of voice. '*That* would make them take an interest in Harry. You're not in the right state of mind to tackle those gentry. If they suspected that Harry and you had something to hide, they'd sit you down and tear out your fingernails for starters.'

'That's a risk I'll take,' said Douglas.

'Perhaps it is,' said Mayhew, moving between Douglas and the door. 'But it's not a risk that the rest of the organization have to take.'

Mayhew was right, Douglas decided. He wasn't made

of the sort of stuff that Sylvia had proved to be made of. Douglas sat down.

'Now look at this,' said Mayhew. He got a copy of *Die Englische Zeitung* from his pocket and unfolded it so that the front page was exposed. 'This is tomorrow's edition.' In gigantic Gothic type, across the whole front, its headline said, 'Standrecht'.

Barbara said, 'What's that mean?'

'Martial law,' said Douglas. 'The Germans have declared martial law all over Great Britain.'

Mayhew said, 'One of our people in the telephone exchange got wind of it early. But he had only a little pocket dictionary and the word wasn't in it.'

Douglas was still reading the official announcement from the newspaper Mayhew was holding. 'As from midnight tonight, Central European Time,' he said.

'All soldiers are recalled from barracks, and further leave cancelled,' said Mayhew. 'Side-arms to be carried at all times. Waffen-SS units in Great Britain are to be integrated into the army – and that means used as a replacement pool. It's a bitter blow for Heinrich Himmler.'

'What difference will martial law make?' asked Barbara.

'The German army took precautions in case the Highgate explosion was the beginning of large-scale armed uprising throughout the country. Then they started pressing for de jure recognition of a de facto situation. It looks as if they gained it.'

'Spoken like a true bureaucrat, Archer,' said Mayhew. He put his glass down and clapped his hands soundlessly.

'You'd better understand, Colonel Mayhew,' said Douglas tonelessly, 'that the Germans *are* bureaucrats. It's the key to everything they say, and do . . . and to everything they don't say, and don't do.'

'Quite right, quite right,' said Mayhew with a nod, and a smile that he thought would placate Douglas.

Douglas said, 'And don't tell me you haven't been waiting for this very thing to happen. I'll bet your Abwehr friends are drinking champagne tonight.'

'My Abwehr friends are far too puritanical to be doing anything as human as drinking champagne. Their idea of a celebration is fifty press-ups and a cold shower.'

'Is martial law something that the army should celebrate?' asked Barbara.

Douglas said, 'It changes the structure, Barbara.' He wanted to call her darling but he did not dare. 'It puts Kellerman and his policemen, SD and SS units directly under the control of the army. Their chain of command to Himmler becomes no more than a channel through which they can complain about what they are ordered to do . . . after they've done it!'

'The army will take over the arrest lists?' said Barbara.

Mayhew reached into his pocket and found a red, white and blue armband with lettering on the white section: 'Im Dienst der Deutschen Wehrmacht'. It made the lawful wearer technically a 'Wehrmachtmitglied' and gave him a legal status like that of a German soldier. 'Very clever,' said Douglas. With that Mayhew could resist the arrest order issued by Huth.

'The army take over all the arrest lists from the police and SS,' said Mayhew. 'I'm no longer a wanted man.'

Douglas nodded. 'And will the army send sentries to replace the SS men guarding the King in the Tower of London? Or will they simply supervise matters so that some low-ranking SS officer takes the blame when something goes wrong?'

Mayhew smiled. 'How about giving me another shot of that excellent Scotch?'

Mayhew went through the whole ritual of adding water

299

to his drink, smelling it and tasting it, as if temporizing. But probably he was just relishing the melodrama. 'Tomorrow night we have a visitor arriving. We'll need you, Archer. Try and get a bit of shut-eye in the day-time. Wear your long winter underwear, and bring some impressive SS bumph in case we have to talk our way out of trouble.' Mayhew smiled and wiped his mouth with the back of his hand. 'If Washington gives the OK, we'll have the King out of the Tower next week, and out of the country the same day.' He gave Douglas a cigar from his pigskin case.

'I wouldn't rely too much on that Wehrmacht armband of yours,' said Douglas. 'You'll remain on the arrest sheets for at least six more days, and not many patrol commanders and Feldgendarmerie officers are going to have enough spare time to go through the amendments sheets and cross your name off them. Anyone on the sheets is going to be popped into the van first and the questions asked afterwards.'

Mayhew nodded reflectively. 'Anything wrong with that cigar, Archer, old chap?'

Douglas looked up from the cigar that he'd been toying with. 'No, not at all,' he said. 'It's a magnificent one. Romeo y Julieta. I found a half-smoked one in the pocket of Dr Spode. I was thinking about it, that's all.'

'Well, you don't have to be a detective to solve that one, Archer. The Germans import them by the shipload, in exchange for machine tools and German cars exported to Cuba. Anyone who is in the employ of the Germans, and considered a valuable friend, can get his hands on a regular supply of Havanas.'

'Is that how *you* get them?' Barbara asked. It was a part of her skill as a journalist that she was able to say such things without causing offence.

Mayhew gave a short, mirthless guffaw and a strained

smile. 'Next time I see Generalmajor von Ruff I'll ask for some,' he said. 'It might reassure him of my bona fides.' He waved away his cigar smoke. 'So you're no nearer solving the Spode murder?'

'The brother confessed,' said Barbara.

'Is that the way it happened?' said Mayhew. He leaned across the table and gave Douglas his matches.

'The file is still open,' said Douglas. In the silence the striking match sounded unnaturally loud.

'Well, let's hope you find a satisfactory way to close it.' Douglas noted that he didn't say 'to solve it'.

Mayhew got to his feet and reached for his overcoat. 'I'll pick you up from your place tomorrow evening, Archer. Right?'

Ever since Mayhew arrived, Douglas had been agonizing about passing the film to him. Now, spontaneously, he reached out and handed it over. 'This is film of the documents Spode burned at the flat. I doubt if anyone knows they exist but your Abwehr friends might have found the copying stand, and formed their own conclusions.'

Mayhew unscrewed the brown-paper wrapping and looked at the roll of negatives. 'So it was all photocopied.' He looked at Douglas for a long time and then nodded his thanks. 'Tomorrow night then?'

Chapter Thirty

The next morning Douglas gave General Kellerman his briefing. Kellerman nodded his way through the verbal report and put the file away without looking at it.

'Young Douglas is quite well?'

'Yes, thank you, sir.'

'You've heard of this fine new German School in Highgate?' he said.

'I've heard about it.' It was for the children of SS and Wehrmacht officers and for those of the officials of the German administration.

'The curriculum is in German, of course, but it's a wonderful school, and your German is virtually flawless. You could help your son with his homework. That school could give your young Douglas a grand start in life, and I think I could arrange a place there for him.'

'Will there be other British children there?'

'It's my idea that we should have a few,' said Kellerman. 'I'm on the school administration committee. Don't want the German children to lose contact with their host country . . . and English children would be valuable from the language point of view. Think your Douglas could manage enough German?'

'He could manage a little. All the schools have German language classes now.'

'It could be a fine start for him.'

'I'll have to ask Douglas. You know what children are like about leaving their friends.'

'That's right – you ask him. He's a sensible little chap. He'll see the advantages. Take him along there one afternoon this week; show him the laboratories, the engineering equipment, the athletic field and so on.'

Douglas had spent half the night rehearsing how he could tackle Kellerman on the subject of Harry's arrest. But in the event, Kellerman himself brought it up. 'And that fine Detective Sergeant of yours,' said Kellerman. 'What's this I hear about his arrest?'

'Detective Sergeant Woods, sir. He's being held by the Amt IV people, next door.' He had long since discovered that Amt IV was a popular euphemism for Gestapo.

'Amt IV enjoy rather special privileges, you know. My authority with those gentlemen is somewhat limited.'

'Really, sir?' said Douglas.

'They have direct access to the Reichsführer-SS in Berlin.'

'Even under martial law?'

'Now don't try to out-think me, Archer,' said General Kellerman, his face taking on a pained expression. 'I and my men come under the orders of the Military Commander GB only in matters pertaining to law and order. Administration and discipline remain unchanged. Amt IV is still responsible to Berlin, just as your Standartenführer Huth is still responsible to Berlin. And thus Detective Sergeant Woods is too. Now do you see my position?'

'You can't interfere, sir?'

'Never get involved in a family quarrel. Isn't that something that every police force in the world tells its young Constables?'

'I doubt if Sergeant Woods has told the Amt IV interrogators that he is under Berlin's orders in that way. Standartenführer Huth has rigorously emphasized the secrecy of the work we are doing.'

'This scientific business?'

'Yes, sir.'

'And so he should. Standartenführer Doctor Huth is a

fine young officer, and I'm proud to have him on my staff.' Kellerman nodded his head affirmatively. Having clearly established his claim to be Huth's confidant as well as his commander, Kellerman modified his praise a little. 'Zealous perhaps, and at times somewhat inflexible . . . but the task he's been engaged upon is most delicate.'

'Yes, sir.'

'I can see you are worried about Woods. I think I must cancel my week-end in Germany. I'm going to send for Sturmbannführer Strauss and hear all the details of your Sergeant's arrest.' Kellerman swung round in his swivel chair and put one Oxford brogue on the footstool. He wore a reflective frown on his wrinkled face. 'I take it that Woods was submitting the usual type of reports?'

'Yellow flimsies,' said Douglas. 'With Berlin file references.'

'That's what I mean,' said Kellerman. 'Well, I wouldn't wish to pry into your investigation, but I don't see how a few yellow flimsies could affect that, do you?'

'No, sir.' The yellow multiple-copy sheets were no more than the formality whereby Harry Woods proved he was earning his living. They provided no names, dates or places. They were nothing more than a list of filing numbers, meaningless to anyone other than filing clerks in some remote Berlin archive. And yet Douglas could see that the yellow flimsies would be enough to show Strauss of the Gestapo that Woods's reports – like Huth's and Douglas's own – were going directly back to Berlin.

'Then let me have a couple of Woods's yellows before I see Strauss at . . .' he looked at his diary '. . . I could fit him in at eleven o'clock this morning.' Kellerman coughed again and beat his chest lightly with his closed fist. 'It's all part of the continuous attempt to undermine my position,' said Kellerman in a tone of voice that was both confidential and plaintive.

'Really, sir?'

'Inefficient old General Kellerman sheltering enemies of the State in his own police HQ. That's what will be said.'

'I hope not, sir.'

Kellerman sighed, and with a tired smile he got up from his desk. 'The alternative is even worse,' he said. 'Traitorous old General Kellerman, harbouring enemies of the State . . . do you see the delicate path one treads?' He walked over to the fireplace and stared into the blazing coals. 'Forgive an old man for unburdening himself to you, Superintendent, but you are a most sympathetic listener. And I know you are discreet.'

'Thank you, General.'

Douglas got up, recognizing Kellerman's polite dismissal, and went to the door. Kellerman got there before him and opened it for him. He shook Douglas by the hand. It was a curious way to terminate a briefing but perhaps Kellerman had heard that it was the way that English gentlemen behaved.

The connecting door between Huth's office and the one that Douglas and Harry Woods used, was open. Douglas found him reading the small print in *Das Schwarze Korps*, the official SS weekly, but holding it in such a way that Douglas suspected that he'd picked it up to disguise the fact that he'd been waiting for him.

'And what is Kellerman doing about Sergeant Woods's predicament?'

'He'll ask Sturmbannführer Strauss for details,' answered Douglas.

'He'll ask Sturmbannführer Strauss for details!' said Huth with a sharp intake of breath, and mock surprise. 'Perhaps I could give you a few details, without the help of Sturmbannführer Strauss. Do you know that Harry

305

Woods's name was added to the arrest list at the express order of General Kellerman?'

'It's not true!'

'You've been a policeman long enough to know when you are being blackmailed, surely?'

Douglas said nothing.

'What has the old bastard offered you? A house in the country? Promotion? Not women; you're not the type.'

'He promised me nothing.'

'I don't believe you,' said Huth.

Coldly Douglas said, 'As Harry Woods's senior officer, you are the only one here who could get him released, using the authority you have from the Reichsführer-SS.'

Huth nodded solemnly. 'And as soon as I signed the release order, the Gestapo would find a way of holding me in custody to see if I was Woods's accomplice. Then they'd break the locks off the filing cabinets and read through all my confidential material . . . Afterwards I'd be released, with all kinds of humble apologies and explanations about the mistake, but all the material I¦ve collected about Kellerman would have disappeared.'

'Kellerman said that the Gestapo comes directly under the control of Berlin.'

'Tell me,' said Huth, leaning forward on his desk, 'confidentially, do you still hang a stocking under the Christmas Tree?' He ran his hands together, interlocked his fingers and twisted them to make the knuckles crack. 'General Kellerman has arrested your friend Harry Woods, in order to put a little pressure on you to betray me. The sooner you realize that, the sooner we can co-operate to defeat the ugly old swine.'

'Why don't you hand over the Kellerman inquiry to some other officer?'

'Whom can I trust?'

Douglas didn't answer. He realized that this was a vendetta that neither man could abandon.

'Five or six years ago Kellerman was a nobody,' said Huth, trying to explain his hatred: or was it envy? 'He shared a fly-blown office in suburban Leipzig with three typists and a police detective. He was an Obersekretär, the lowest form of animal life in the German Criminal Police Service. Then he joined the Nazi Party and the SS and grinned and grovelled his way to being Senior SS and Police Commander Great Britain. Not bad, eh! And you needn't take any notice of that shit about how he's got no authority over anything, and Berlin doesn't like him. That's just a part of his style.'

'I'm beginning to believe it.'

Huth said, 'You'll find Kellerman at some of the best houses of the British nobility, spreading his message of peace and prosperity, and giving his expert imitation of an absent-minded old buffer who likes warm beer, tweed suits, cocker-spaniel dogs and house-parties. And who can be easily manipulated and outwitted by any able-bodied young Englishman who cares to get to his feet for the opening bars of "Deutschland über Alles".' Huth folded his newspaper into a tightly wadded parcel. 'You thought he was a snob, didn't you? He likes people to think that.' Huth threw the newspaper into his waste-basket with enough violence to tip it over and spill its contents on the carpet. 'Now tell me what he wanted!' shouted Huth.

'The yellow flimsies,' said Douglas quietly.

'Why?'

'To prove to Strauss that Harry Woods was under the direct orders of Berlin.'

'And you thought, it's no more than a list of numbers. What harm can it do? Right?'

'No,' said Douglas.

307

'Don't no me! I can see it written all over your face.'
He waved a hand in the air as Douglas opened his mouth
to explain. 'OK, OK, OK,' said Huth. 'If it was *my* friend
in trouble, I might have thought the same.'

Douglas said, 'Do you think General Kellerman has
someone who would dig the files out of the Berlin
archive?'

'If Kellerman could get a list of file titles, he would
have a description of all the evidence against him.'

'He's cancelled his week-end trip,' said Douglas. 'He
said it's because he's concerned about Harry Woods.'

'I can hear the violins,' said Huth. 'Kellerman was
invited to a shooting party at Schönhof – von Ribbentrop's
hunting-lodge. That's not something he'd give up because
one lousy Detective Sergeant was arrested on his orders
and then tried to escape.'

'Then why is he staying?'

'Things are moving fast, Archer. Surely you sense
that. Martial law has given all the power to our army
colleagues. Kellerman has to decide whether to hinder
and oppose them, or go across to the army Commander
and do his ingratiating subordinate act. He came back
from Highgate with some crackpot idea that the army
had caused the explosion in order to get power, but the
casualty list persuaded him to abandon that line.'

'And how soon will you have evidence against him?'

'I'll make Kellerman wish he'd never left that flea-
bitten little office in Leipzig,' said Huth. 'My people in
Switzerland have cabled me that Kellerman has tucked
away over fifteen million Reichsmarks in numbered
accounts. When I get the copies I'm waiting for, I'll arrest
him on my own authority using SD units to hold him.'

Douglas nodded. Every week the newspapers printed
the names of men executed for black-market offences,

graft or looting. In this respect the Germans applied the law rigorously to Germans and British alike.

Huth sighed, 'Give the old fool the list of file numbers that we got when someone wanted all that material about billeting and discipline of SS units in western England. It will take him a little while to get the titles. Then tell him the files have false titles for security reasons. It will take another month to find out what we've done, and by that time I guarantee, Archer, we'll be rid of that old crook for ever.' He lifted a fist but then modified the gesture to a wave of the finger. 'But give him one real file number from this office, and by God, I'll . . .'

He didn't finish. A gust of wind rattled the windows and large drops of rain made clear places in the sooty glass. The River Thames was the colour of lead and just as solid-looking.

'I won't give him any real ones,' said Douglas.

'And Archer,' said Huth as Douglas got to the door, 'don't count too much on Kellerman helping our friend Harry. Sort out another Detective Sergeant to start work here tomorrow.'

Chapter Thirty-one

Standartenführer Huth's predictions about General Kellerman proved true and false in equal measure. Kellerman
went to lunch that day with Generalmajor Georg von
Ruff, senior Abwehr officer in Great Britain. That these
two exalted worthies, of military intelligence and secret
policing, had not started at the lowest rung of their
profession's ladder, was evidenced by the way they chose
to meet in the top room of Wheeler's fish restaurant in
Old Compton Street, Soho. To them it seemed enough to
wear civilian coats over their uniforms, and to avoid
being seen together in their respective headquarters. But
any young detective on their staff would have told them
that a private room booked for 'Herr Braun and party' in
any Soho restaurant would have attracted attention during
those first days of martial law, even had their aides not
brought large leather brief-cases that had become the
mark of high-ranking German officials. And even had
both Generals not worn high boots.

Kellerman made peace with his new masters, for he
was a man supple enough to bend to the winds of change.
But the prediction that nothing would be done to help
Detective Sergeant Harry Woods proved wrong. At three
o'clock that afternoon Douglas Archer received a phone
call from Kellerman's personal assistant requesting him –
should his work schedule permit it, and providing he was
not inconvenienced in any way – to spend a few moments
upstairs with the General. Almost as an afterthought, the
caller added that Detective Sergeant Harry Woods would
be there too.

By the standards of the Gestapo, Harry Woods was virtually unharmed. But Douglas was shocked by the sight of him. His face was bruised and one eye puffy so that it almost closed. He winced as he moved his weight on the chair, and he kept one leg extended and still, as if to ease some pain in the knee.

'Hello, Harry,' Douglas said after greeting General Kellerman.

'Hello, Superintendent,' said Harry in a whisper.

'Sit down, Superintendent Archer.'

Sturmbannführer Strauss was also in the room. He sat in the corner with his arms folded across a limp paper dossier. He said nothing. Kellerman went over to the window and opened it so that he could look out to the river. 'You've been a fool, Sergeant Woods,' Kellerman said.

'If you say so,' said Harry reluctantly.

'Well, I *do* say so,' said Kellerman. He turned to face back into the room. 'And so does Superintendent Archer – and so does anyone else – if they are being honest with you. Have you been ill-treated?'

Harry Woods didn't answer. Kellerman went across to where Strauss was sitting, took the dossier from his hand, and walked to his desk to pick up his spectacles. He read the arrest report holding the paper under his desk-light. Kellerman was a different man in his immaculate grey uniform, with its 'Reichsführung-SS London' cuffband, Gruppenführer's silver oak leaves on his collar and medals on his tunic. The fine silver-grey material shone in the desk-light's glare, as did the high boots, polished to gleam like metal. And yet there was a certain awkwardness about the General in uniform; he reached for the waist-coat – where he kept gold watch and fountain-pen – and encountered the tightly buttoned tunic. Constantly he patted the buttons of all four pockets to be sure they were fastened in the correct military style. And, in compliance with SS dress regulations for ranks of SS Oberführer and above, Kellerman wore spurs on his high boots. Perhaps in fear of getting them entangled, he kept his feet well apart, and walked with an exaggerated stride.

When Kellerman finished reading the report he closed the dossier with a snap. 'Now, Woods, have you been ill-treated?'

Harry's whispered words came slowly and Kellerman had to lean closer to understand them. 'Cold baths and no sleep.'

Douglas flinched at the thought of Harry, near retirement and in the poor physical shape that comes from working too hard, drinking too heavily, and taking no exercise, being pushed into ice-cold water and systematically kept awake. Few men could withstand such torture.

'Cold baths and not much sleep,' said Kellerman, folding his arms unnecessarily tightly and nodding. 'Well, that's the standard routine in the German army . . . can't grumble too much about that, Sergeant.' He patted his stomach. 'A few weeks in a recruit camp would do us all good, eh?' He turned his head to smile at Douglas but Douglas was sitting feet crossed, studying his shoe.

Kellerman seemed unable to keep still. He marched across to Strauss and flourished the dossier at him. 'But I cannot understand why this police officer should be held in your custody, Strauss?' Strauss jumped to his feet, and clicked his heels.

'Herr Gruppenführer . . .' said Strauss. In other circumstances it might have been comic to see Strauss bowing low and using such an obsequious form of address, but now no one laughed. 'The prisoner was only passed into my custody this morning. The duty officer who . . .'

'We've no time for an official inquiry,' said Kellerman. 'That will come later. The facts of the matter are that this

312

police officer should not have been arrested in his home by the army arrest team. That does not excuse him for the stupid escape attempt, but we should bear it in mind. Secondly . . .' Kellerman was grasping his fingers as if unable to count without doing so, '. . . if he is to be tried for an attempt to escape from an army detention centre, then it is for the army to try him.'

Strauss did not answer. 'Well, Strauss?' said Kellerman, standing erect and giving a little tug to the hem of his tunic.

'The SS Legal Department said that Detective Sergeant Woods comes under the legal protection afforded to members of the SS,' said Strauss. 'The army's Legal Department agreed. So the duty officer took custody of him.'

'You damned bureaucrats,' shouted Kellerman angrily. 'You'd hang us all to get your paperwork in order. Don't you realize, Strauss, that the army have tricked you? You've helped them cover up their wrongful arrest of one of our best detectives . . . don't you see that?'

Strauss made another curious little bow, like a mechanical doll. 'Yes, Herr Gruppenführer.'

'And don't keep calling me *Herr* Gruppenführer.'

'No, Gruppenführer.'

'You send this prisoner back to the Feldgendarmerie. In fact, go with him, Strauss, just in case they don't give him an immediate "release pending inquiries".'

'What if the Feldgendarmerie keep him in custody, Gruppenführer?'

'You stay with him, Strauss.' Kellerman brushed his pockets to be sure they were buttoned.

Kellerman touched Strauss's shoulder and Strauss sat down again. Then he turned to Douglas. 'Before we cross swords with our army friends,' said Kellerman, 'just let's make sure we know what we are doing.' He walked across the room and put a cigarette into Harry's mouth, then he lit it. Harry began to smoke it without even looking up to see where it had come from. Kellerman said, 'Because the Abwehr are our masters for the moment.' He smiled at the absurdity of this situation. 'Sergeant Woods has been indiscreet, headstrong and premature. He has had dealings with criminals, but this does not make him a criminal . . . are you taking a note of this, Strauss?'

'Yes, Gruppenführer.'

'We shall need a statement that he did no more than was necessary in the course of his investigation into criminal terrorist organizations.'

'Do we want to reveal to the army details of an incomplete investigation?' said Douglas, seeing where such a course was likely to lead.

'Oh for goodness' sake,' said Kellerman testily. 'The young lady is dead. Let's have some details of her. That will reveal nothing we need conceal, and you must know something about her . . . she was your clerk for nearly six months.'

'Yes, sir,' said Douglas. It was almost as if General Kellerman was suggesting ways to preserve Harry's Resistance friends but that was impossible to believe. Kellerman came round behind Douglas. It was a disconcerting trick of his, and Douglas never knew whether to turn and face him or not. This time he did not. 'I'm trying to help Sergeant Woods,' said Kellerman. Douglas could smell the brandy that Kellerman had consumed at his lunch.

'Yes, General,' said Douglas.

'Do you hear me, Sergeant Woods? I'm trying to help you.'

Harry nodded without looking up and put the cigarette into his mouth to inhale.

'If your investigation began as a direct result of the girl being employed in this building, say so. I'm not asking you to hide anything. You'll have to describe Woods's responsibilities working under Standartenführer Huth.' Kellerman went to Harry Woods and patted his shoulder in an avuncular gesture.

'Shall I check that with the Standartenführer?' said Douglas.

Kellerman's reply was no more than a whisper. 'I've asked the Standartenführer for a statement that would assist in Woods's release. I'm afraid that, so far, Doctor Huth will not even make himself available for a talk on the phone about it.' Kellerman sighed.

'Shall we take the statement immediately?' said Strauss, who preferred only to ask questions to which he already knew the answer.

'In the German language,' said Kellerman. 'Half the people in this building can't read a word of English, and in Berlin anything in English is pushed aside and forgotten. Superintendent Archer will translate it for his comrade, won't you, Archer?'

'Of course, sir,' said Douglas, although he and Kellerman both knew that by getting Douglas's name and signature on each sheet of the translation it would be absurd for him later to claim ignorance of anything it contained. It was very nearly as effective as having a statement from Douglas himself. It was a telling blow. To free Harry, Douglas was left with little choice but to render Huth vulnerable. While Kellerman could smile at everyone concerned, and continue in his chosen role of soft-hearted old buffoon.

'Shall we take Harry down to an interview room?' said Douglas.

'Use my secretary's office,' said Kellerman. 'That will give me the chance to help you draft the text.'

They worked hard for the next hour and Kellerman made a phone call to the Abwehr office in Piccadilly. The paperwork was considerable, but by six o'clock that afternoon, Harry Woods was free. At the last moment, Kellerman decided that Harry Woods's statement was not needed at this stage of the proceedings. He locked it away in his safe.

It was masterly, thought Douglas, as he reviewed the sequence of events. Kellerman could now blame the Abwehr for the wrongful arrest of Harry Woods, and also for his wrongful release, should he misbehave. And he'd contrived it in such a way – returning Woods to army custody – that he could claim to be helping the army cover up their mistakes. Additionally he'd got from Douglas and Harry Woods a signed and witnessed statement that might – used skilfully – hamper Huth's investigation of Kellerman.

But if Kellerman had so cleverly outwitted the Abwehr – in spite of the wide-ranging powers that martial law provided for the army – then what of Mayhew, and his network of king-makers? How long would it take before Kellerman discovered that the Abwehr itself was in league with the men he had called 'criminal terrorists'? Or was Fritz Kellerman no more than the amiable old do-gooder that he claimed to be? Or was the truth – like so many truths – not any one of the envisaged possibilities?

Chapter Thirty-two

'I've done enough,' said Harry Woods when they were in the car and driving home.

'Too much.'

'Seriously,' said Harry, 'I've done enough.' When Douglas didn't reply Harry added, '"Ohne mich", the Huns say, don't they? – "without me" – well, that's how I feel. The Resistance can manage without me for a little while.'

Douglas nodded. He too had heard the Germans say 'ohne mich' as they dissociated themselves from some arduous, dangerous or expensive demand of the Third Reich's policies. Out of the corner of his eye he could see Harry touching his bruised cheek, moving the fingertips up his face to discover how far it went, and preparing himself for seeing his wife again.

'Last February,' said Harry, 'it seemed like the only thing to do.'

'Last February is a century ago,' said Douglas.

'And after that I could never think of any way to tell the lads I wanted to get out of it.'

Douglas nodded. He was accustomed to hearing men rationalize their misfortune, and their good fortune too. Only a few days previously, Harry had been trying to recruit him into their Resistance cell, but he did not remind him.

'Was it Kellerman who arranged my release?' Harry asked.

'He said he would,' said Douglas. 'Why do you ask?'

Harry was still fingering his bruised face. 'He's not so

317

bad, perhaps,' said Harry. 'I mean . . . well, I was wondering in there, whether we'd be just as bad as they are . . . if we'd won the war and were occupying Germany.'

They arrived at Harry's small house. There was a chink of light between the curtains of the basement room. Harry got out of the car and looked around as if seeing the street for the first time. Then he turned back and bent down to see Douglas at the wheel of the car. 'I wish it could be like in the old days, Doug.' He seemed oblivious of the rain that was soaking him. Douglas had seen men released from prison stand happily in the worst of weather; it was a celebration of freedom.

'The Germans are here, Harry,' said Douglas. He was impatient with his partner but he tried to keep that out of his voice.

'No, no,' said Harry. 'I mean you and me. I wish it could be like the old days between you and me.'

'It will be, Harry,' Douglas promised. 'Now get inside and see your wife. She's been worried about you.'

As Douglas drove away down the bleak rainswept street he could not resist a glance in the mirror. Harry Woods was standing under a street-light and watching the departing car. As he turned the corner Douglas looked again. This time Harry had begun walking, but instead of going to his own front door, Harry stepped off the kerb to cross the street and head elsewhere. To a public phone perhaps. Oh well, thought Douglas, he was not Harry's keeper, only his friend and partner. He tried not to think about it.

Douglas detoured to avoid the closed streets that now provided a 'fire zone' round Pentonville prison, and followed a series of back-streets to avoid both King's Cross and St Pancras railway stations. All such vital places were now ringed with infantry and armoured cars and there were the fliegende Feld- und Standgerichte – flying field tribunals – complete with execution squads. So far there had been no reports of summary executions but the sight of the tribunals was enough to strike fear into the most innocent heart.

Douglas recognized the unit that waved him to a halt in Tottenham Court Road as one such tribunal. There was an Opel 'Admiral' for the patrol commander, six motor-cycles and two canvas-topped Daimler-Benz G-3 troops carriers. The steady rain shone in the yellow headlight beams. Somewhere on the other side of the railway there was the moaning of a Feldgendarmerie siren. The Feldwebel who asked for Douglas's identity papers had that soft-spoken courtesy which so often is the manner of men who cannot be disobeyed. He read the pass with interest, compared Douglas with the photo, wrote the registration number of the vehicle on his clip-board, clicked his heels, saluted in the military style, and waved Douglas on.

It was the same all over Britain; the German army was demonstrating to the civil population that the 'field-greys' were in total control. And yet, if one noted the way in which the army patrols seemed to take a perverse satisfaction in checking the police and SS vehicles and SS personnel, it was almost as if the demonstration was directed at them.

Chapter Thirty-three

On Saturday morning they went to the zoo. Douglas told his son that Barbara was a friend he'd met in connection with his work. But Douglas need not have worried about how that first meeting would go, for the child accepted this friend of his father as children usually do, with an awesome interest for the first ten minutes and then a friendly indifference. But Barbara knew that young Douglas was an examination she must pass if she was to have his father's love and devotion, and she gave all her energies to winning the boy over.

They rode on the elephants and on the camels. They went to the aquarium and to the rhino house. Eventually Barbara allowed the little boy to coax her into visiting the reptile house. By the time they emerged, little Douglas was holding her hand to comfort her, and telling her not to be afraid of the snakes because he wouldn't let them hurt her.

The zoo was almost deserted. Not many Londoners had enough money to pay for admittance to the depleted collection of animals and the bomb-damaged buildings. And martial law had provided other activities for the army of occupation. Douglas and Barbara watched his son on the tiny merry-go-round. There were no other children there and Douggie was able to keep it revolving by running alongside and leaping aboard for brief rides.

'We bring him to the zoo and he ignores the animals in favour of the swings and roundabouts.'

'He likes being with you,' said Barbara. 'He doesn't mind where.'

'Huth hates his father,' said Douglas. 'It's an obsession with him.' They walked past the wooden benches, newly painted yellow, and marked 'for Jews only'. There was always enough money and labour for hatred.

'Why?'

A light plane flew overhead, banking steeply and wheeling so that the flyers could be sure there were no illegal meetings in Regent's Park. The sky had been busy with these highwing Storks since martial law was declared. Not only were they constantly checking the open spaces and the rooftops but also fetching and carrying between the hastily converted airstrips made from straight stretches of roadway at the Mall, Edgeware Road, Western Avenue, Old Kent Road and Clapham Common. 'Huth wants more admiration than his father is prepared to provide.' It was raining now. Douglas and Barbara huddled together in the lee of a kiosk. Its tiny windows were filled with dummy packs of chocolate and cigarettes, dusty and flyblown. On the padlocked shutter a sign said, 'No cigarettes, no chocolate, no change for the telephone'. The sign was torn and stained with months of rain – it was a long time since it became necessary to tell anyone that there were no chocolates or cigarettes.

'You're angry about something.'

'No.'

'Worried?'

'No,' said Douglas but he was troubled. He felt like a man ordered to dig his own grave. 'You told me that Mayhew asked you to go along to Shepherd Market, and try to get the film. But Mayhew had no idea that any film existed until I told him.'

She said nothing. The rain lessened and young Douggie continued to ride on the merry-go-round. Douglas continued, 'I think you were working for your own government. And I think the younger Spode was working for them too.'

'I'm not a spy, Douglas,' she said. 'A man from the Embassy asked me to go along to the Shepherd Market apartment. He said the film would be waiting there for collection. That's all I know, you must believe me, Douglas.' She gripped his arm; he nodded.

He said, 'Young Spode killing his brother, it didn't make sense. Family quarrels aren't about secret documents, they are about unfaithful wives or who inherits what.'

'Who killed Spode then?'

'I couldn't believe that the younger brother did it and calmly stood there sorting through several hundred pages of mathematical calculations photographing, while his brother was sprawled dead at his feet.'

'He didn't do it?'

'I fell into the trap of thinking that the two brothers must have been there together, simply because they were brothers. As soon as one forgets that they were brothers, the truth becomes easier to see. There was a train ticket in the dead man's pocket. No trains from Devon arrive in London stations during the early hours of the morning. Spode wasn't arriving from the station, he'd been to the flat earlier, to deliver the calculations for his brother to photograph.'

'But young Spode admitted killing his brother.'

'Spode said something about his brother having no shield. I thought he meant that his brother lacked the comfort and protection that Catholicism provides.'

'But?'

'He meant the thermic and biological shields. He was referring to the protection provided for the men working on this nuclear experiment. Spode meant that he was responsible for his brother's death from radiation. He meant he'd made some error during the work at Bringle Sands.'

322

For a long time she was silent. Then she said, 'Yes, the younger Spode photographed the documents so that they could be sent to Washington. He made contact with my Embassy and offered the film to them. That's all I know, darling.'

Douglas held her waist. He wanted to tell her that he trusted her, but he could find no way of saying it that was not clumsy and patronizing. Barbara said, 'But why would anyone want to kill the older Spode?'

'Someone let him into the flat, Barbara. That place was used as a meeting place by the Resistance groups. I can't help suspecting that it was done with Mayhew's knowledge.'

'You have not answered my question, sweetheart. What's Mayhew's motive? Why would he want to murder the best damned atomic physicist in Britain when there's a good chance he could get his hands on the work he'd been doing? Do you think Mayhew is working for the Germans?'

'I just don't know,' said Douglas. 'I suspect that Mayhew's been meeting Huth, without either of them saying a word about the meetings to anyone. But I don't see Mayhew in the role of a traitor. Collaborator, well perhaps; but not traitor.'

'But why did that young Abwehr Captain pass young Spode the poison capsule?'

'The Captain thought I was going to take Spode away, and have him grilled by the Sicherheitsdienst. The SD would have discovered every detail of the army's progress in their atomic research programme, and some damned uncomfortable secrets about the way the Abwehr has co-operated with Mayhew and his Resistance people.'

'Poor Spode.'

323

'I liked him,' said Douglas.

The rain stopped and more aircraft passed over very low. They walked on and into the lion house, with young Douglas holding the hands of both of them.

Chapter Thirty-four

Linden Manor gets its name from the avenue of lime trees that makes the approach to this mansion so unforgettable. The house is a rambling complex of Tudor redbrick, restored in the nineteenth century by a wealthy megalomaniac who added the Gothic chapel and the folly, a grotesque tower inspired by tales of King Arthur. And yet the aesthetics of Sydney Garin's and Peter Shetland's antique-crammed mansion house had little consequence for any except those privileged to enter the surrounding 250-acre estate which kept the vulgar sightseer at a respectful distance.

The enormous dining-room was seen that evening by the flickering light from three eighteenth-century polychrome glass chandeliers. The candle flames danced in the solid silver cutlery, and allowed the Dutch marine paintings to be glimpsed in that darkness beyond the candle-light.

'We don't have all this good stuff in evidence when the Huns come down here to see us,' said Sydney Garin. His speech was accented, his voice nasal. He was responding to a compliment by Barbara Barga about the table setting. He chuckled. 'It would make the articles they can afford to buy look shoddy.'

Mayhew gave a slightly pained smile. Sydney's stories about swindling his customers did not amuse Mayhew, even when the customers were the *nouveau riche*. Even *nouveau riche* Huns. And talk about Sydney's antiques did not interest him, combining as it did both art and trade, two subjects taboo in any decent mess or club.

Mayhew picked at his *Perdreau à la normande*. Shooting partridge was one thing; eating it was quite another. And as for cooking them according to French recipes, with apple brandy, that, Mayhew decided, was quite disgusting. He pushed the food around his plate to make it look as if he'd eaten some.

At one end of the table sat Mrs Garin, a quiet little woman who looked uncomfortable in her glittering brocade dress. Next to her sat her son David. He was attentive to his mother, and they seemed scarcely aware of the conversation at the other end of the table.

Douglas was watching Mayhew. The man was an enigma, and Douglas constantly changed his mind about him. The confident manner, his stamina and his jokes gave the impression of a young man. So did his handsome face, muscular body and dark wavy hair. But close to him one also saw the wrinkles and the slightly yellow teeth and the tension that made Mayhew frown too much and fidget with his knife and fork.

A servant poured Douglas more of the Château Léoville. Barbara Barga laughed at something Sydney Garin said. Douglas looked at his host and was reminded of the rude way he'd treated Garin on more than one previous occasion. He looked, too, at Garin's son, David, a handsome boy with curly hair and the same large brown eyes that his father had. But David had been to an English public school, and had learned to keep his face expressionless and his eyes lowered.

'On that day that my country was invaded, Barbara,' said Garin, touching her arm, 'I said to myself, Sydney Garin, you've got to help throw them out.'

Mayhew frowned as he tried to decide which army had invaded Armenia and when. Just as he had decided that Garin was talking of the Bolsheviks, Sydney Garin said, 'We English have always been like that.' He gestured with his fork held high in the air. 'We haven't had an invader since William the Conqueror.' Garin turned to Mayhew, and in an aside added, 'And that was in 1066, George.'

'Was it?' said Mayhew stiffly. 'I was never much good at history.'

'Don't like your partridge, eh?' said Garin, leaning forward to scrutinize Mayhew's plate. 'Oh well, that's all right. Had a Hun Colonel here last week who said my best beluga caviar tasted salty – bloody idiot, begging your pardon, Barbara.' He lifted his finger and said to a uniformed servant, 'Bring Colonel Mayhew a plate of cold roast beef.' To Mayhew, 'More your sort of thing, George.'

Mayhew had the feeling that he was being made a fool of, or, worse, that he was making a fool of himself. 'No, no, no, no,' he said and raised a flattened hand in polite refusal.

'And some English mustard,' Garin told his servant as he patted Mayhew's arm. 'I know the sort of thing you public school men like – rice pudding, cold meat and lots of gravy. Am I right, George? Am I right?' He turned back to Barbara Barga and said, 'Funny people we English, Barbara. My son, David, eats the same sort of stuff.' David blushed. 'And young Peter is just the same; it's our public schools that do it, serving kids all that filthy stodge. Peter would eat suet pudding every day if I let him.'

'You mean your partner, Sir Peter Shetland?' said Barbara.

'Lord Campion,' said Mayhew, correcting Sydney Garin rather than Barbara Barga. Behind them a servant put on a pair of gloves before taking some logs from the hearth and positioning them on the blazing fire.

'Oh, I don't set much store by titles,' said Garin. 'When

327

I was living in Paris, half the people in the soup-kitchen were Dukes and Princes and so on.'

'Real ones?' said Barbara.

'Now you are asking a profound question,' said Garin, glancing round the table to be sure that the servants were keeping the wine glasses filled. He saw that Douglas had almost finished his main course. 'Douglas is enjoying his partridge, aren't you, Douglas?'

'It's delicious.'

'More partridge,' he commanded his servants. 'Eat it while it's freshly cooked, Douglas. It's not worth anything cold.' Garin sipped some water; his wine was scarcely touched. 'Real? You mean if a chap is called a Duke by his friends he's real, but if he calls himself a Duke he's a phoney?' Garin was looking at Barbara, but he couldn't resist a glance at Mayhew to see if he'd rise to the bait.

'What time is this chappie coming?' said Mayhew, looking at his gold pocket watch.

'I wish you'd let me come with you,' said Barbara.

'And I wish it was possible,' said Mayhew. He flicked a lock of hair from his forehead and gave her his most charming smile. 'But if I take you along as a sightseer . . . even if you are the most influential journalist in Britain, the other chaps will feel it's a breach of security.'

'And who is going to believe that you are an important American journalist?' said Garin. 'They will see this radiantly beautiful creature and immediately say it's another of Sydney Garin's harem.' He snorted with merriment at the idea. His wife looked up and smiled politely. He winked at her.

Mayhew stopped smiling and turned to Garin. 'What time did you say he was due?'

The servant put a plate of cold beef on the table but Mayhew hardly glanced at it. From the fireplace there came a series of cracks, a bright moment of flame and a smell of sap as the log caught fire.

Garin reached across and put a calming hand on Mayhew's arm. 'Don't fret, George. My people will light the fires as soon as they hear the engines. And the pilot is sure to circle a couple of times, to be sure he's not dropping his passenger in the wrong place. There'll be plenty of time for you to have your plate of cold beef, and a cigar and brandy, and put your feet up for five minutes.' Mayhew reached for his wine and drank some as if suppressing a desire to argue. 'If you relaxed a little more, George, you wouldn't need to carry those indigestion tablets in that silver box in your waistcoat pocket.'

'This fellow's come a long way,' said Mayhew. 'I want to be there, to make sure that the fires are in the right pattern and well alight. We can't afford any mistakes.'

'My dear George,' said Garin in a voice that was kindly and in no way patronizing, 'I've spent all my life being hunted and persecuted. I'm giving you good advice, my friend, when I tell you to slow your pace, live for each day and learn to enjoy the small pleasures of life . . .' he waved vaguely in the air, '. . . beautiful women, good clarets and fine food. We can't beat the Germans by next week-end, George, it's going to be a long, uphill struggle. Pace yourself, and take the long view.'

'What time does the moon go down?' said Mayhew.

Garin sighed. 'Very well, George, drink your claret and let's get our coats.'

There were other aircraft in the air that night; three Junkers transports flying at five-minute intervals, heading due east towards Holland and then Germany. Garin offered his silver hip-flask of brandy to Mayhew and Douglas but both declined. Garin put it away untouched.

'You're right,' he said, 'we might be out here for a long time yet.'

'Your men, down there at the other end of the big ten-acre field, know that they mustn't light their fires before we do?'

'For goodness' sake, calm down, George. You'll get me jittery too if you pace up and down like that.'

Soon they heard the engine of the aeroplane. Garin's son ignited the petrol-soaked rags, and the firewood blazed into tall yellow flame.

The men at the landing place knew little or nothing about flying. They had complied with every detail of the radio messages about the preparation of the landing field. The A light – or agent's fire – was at the touchdown point and the two up-wind fires had been double-checked to get them in line and on the correct bearing. Now the aeroplane came low over the moonlit field. The pilot throttled back so that the sound of the engine quietened as he confirmed his navigation by visual checks. The passenger saw the curiously shaped lake flash in the bright moonlight and the pilot glimpsed the ugly tower that in the previous century had held an astronomer's telescope.

After one circuit the pilot tried a landing, cutting back his engine and letting the big aeroplane settle and side-slip a little until the three fires were all in line. He was almost down on the ground when the lights disappeared. The pilot slammed the throttle lever and the engine roared as the aircraft clawed at the cold night and climbed, agonizingly slowly. The pilot cursed gently, his words an afterthought to the moment of fear. Abruptly, he tilted a wing so that its tip almost brushed the tree tops, and turned the heavy biplane so lightly that he came back almost on the same line as the approach.

'What's wrong?' said Mayhew.

'He'll not get into that field,' said Douglas.

'The trees!' said Sydney Garin. 'Are the trees too tall?'

'There was nothing in the radio message about the height of the surrounding fields' trees,' said Mayhew. 'Damn the man; he *must* do it!'

Douglas looked at Mayhew. His hands were thrust deep into his overcoat pockets, and his face was tight and drawn. 'He'll be worried about flying out again too,' said Douglas. 'He probably guesses how wet the ground is, after all the rain we've had.' The aeroplane came over them, flying very low.

'I hope he doesn't circle too long,' said Mayhew. 'He'll start attracting attention if he's seen going round and round Linden Manor all night.'

Sydney Garin said nothing. When the aeroplane returned it did not throttle back at all. The pilot was simply confirming what he already knew to be true, as he flew down the length of the lighted fires and took a good look at the height of the trees. The noise of the biplane tilted up again and the men on the ground heard briefly the full force of the engine noise, as the propeller blades took the weight of the aircraft and dragged it upwards in great spirals, like a moth that could not resist the light of the moon.

The biplane was no more than a speck against the gathering clouds as the parachute opened. The moonlight caught the billowing silk. For a moment there were two moons in the night sky, then one grew steadily larger until Garin's farm-hands, dousing the up-wind fires, shouted that the parachute would land on the far side of the ornamental lake.

'Farther than that,' said Garin calmly. 'He'll come down in the lower pasture. I hope there's not too much noise.'

'The Germans?'

'No. I've got a mare in foal over there.' To his son he said, 'Don't let anyone disturb Buttercup.'

'Right you are, Dad.'

'Not you two!' Garin said to Mayhew and Douglas as they were going to follow. 'The lads in the village can keep their mouths shut about things dropped out of aeroplanes . . . but a toff falling into a ditch in evening dress will strain their vows of silence beyond breaking point.'

'One of us had better be there,' said Mayhew.

'My lads can think of a million reasons for scrambling across the countryside after curfew. But they'll never be able to account for chaps like you being with them.' Garin gave another of his snorting laughs. It was an ugly sound but it had an infectious quality that made Mayhew and Douglas laugh too.

Sydney Garin said it would take only half an hour for his 'lads' to bring the parachutist back to Linden Manor. But the wind took the parachute farther than anyone at the landing fires was able to judge. The parachutist twisted his ankle landing in a muddy piece of scrubland near the river. He showed an exaggerated caution in ignoring the calls of the search-party, and was found only because of the behaviour of a little mongrel dog belonging to a stable-lad.

'Its mother was always following the foxhounds,' said the boy proudly as the parachutist was brought back to the Manor.

It was almost two hours later before he arrived in the drawing-room where Mayhew, Garin and Douglas waited impatiently after the news came that the parachutist had been found. This was the same room where they had met before dinner. The silk curtains were closed now, as they had been then, and the fire was not much lower, and yet the interior had changed in the way that all rooms change at night. Every sound came edgy and distinct; in the silence they heard an owl, the trees moving in the wind, the steady tick of the skeleton clock, the movement of the burning coals settling into the grate, and then a servant's footfalls along the corridor. The room was filled with the aromatic smoke from Mayhew's Havana cigars.

'Your visitor, sir,' said the butler as the parachutist entered the drawing-room. He was American, no longer young and yet, like so many of his compatriots, he had all the movements and gestures of youth. He seemed restless but it was not the sort of nervous fidgeting that Douglas had noticed in Mayhew that evening, rather it was the kind of impatience that is evident in athletes just before some testing event. His handsome face was square-shaped and tanned, his eyes narrowed; the face of a man who'd spent most of his life on some sunbaked prairie or desert, or was it from holiday beaches and swimming pools? The American's hair was fair, and cut very short all over his head. Douglas had heard of this strange new hair fashion but this was the first time he'd seen it. In Britain such haircuts were seen only on newly-released prisoners and some of the German occupation army.

As if aware of the effect of his crewcut, the American ran a hand across his head. A man's hands betray all his secrets, and these hands were soft, white, uncalloused and slightly wrinkled, with cared-for nails and visible vein lines. They were the hands of an affluent sedentary man without manual skills; a man nearer forty than thirty and vain enough to have regular manicures.

In the hearth, Garin's huge Irish Wolfhound stirred to see the newcomer, yawned and settled back to sleep as Garin handed his guest an empty glass and inclined the whisky bottle. The American nodded and Garin poured him a large measure. A servant followed carrying a portable radio transmitter. It was part of the parachutist's load, its canvas case designed to make it resemble an accordion. But what chance did this urbane man have of passing himself off as an itinerant musician?

'We thought the wind was going to carry you into the dark interior of Essex,' said Mayhew.

The American sipped his drink. 'I heard the jungle drums,' he said. 'Umm! That's the first drink I've had in nearly three weeks.'

'US warships are dry,' said Mayhew with a nod. 'I was warned about that.'

'The ship was British, a fifteen-thousand-ton merchant-man,' said the American. 'You'd better remember that. We painted over the markings on the plane and your people gave the pilot a commission in the Royal Navy, just in case.'

'Pray God he'll not require it,' said Mayhew.

As the American lifted his glass to drink to that, he winced with pain and rubbed his back. 'We catapulted off the ship using an old catapult from one of your battle-cruisers. For a moment I thought it had wrenched my head off.'

'Your driver was a bit nervous,' said Mayhew.

'Did you see those Junkers transports?'

'The Germans are bringing in another infantry division, by air,' said Mayhew. 'They were the empties, going back for more.'

'There wasn't enough room to get into your field,' said the American. 'And we sure as hell didn't want to leave a wrecked airplane for you to explain away tomorrow morning.'

'That was most considerate,' said Garin. 'Are you hungry?'

'We had a steak dinner before take-off. The Scotch will do me fine, thanks.' He looked down at his shoe. The impact of his parachute landing had split the sole away from its upper. He twisted the shoe against the carpet to see the gap.

'You talked to your people in Washington? What will be the arrangements?'

'I talked,' said the American, 'and how I talked!'

'And?'

'And they say "no!"'

Mayhew stared at him. 'No?'

'I even talked with the President . . . for thirty minutes. He kept the Secretary of Labor waiting while we talked.' The excitement was draining out of him, revealing a tired man. He walked across the room, sank down on the sofa and stretched his head to ease his neck muscles. 'And I talked to several personal friends at the State Department, as well as to the Senate sub-committee set up to deal with your people.'

'And the army and the navy?' said Mayhew.

'And the army and the navy.'

'Surely to God, American Jews understand that Hitler has got to be stopped?' said Garin.

'There aren't too many Jews in the Chief of Staff's office,' said the American dryly. 'Your King would be a liability to America. Do you think Roosevelt wants to go into schoolbooks as the man who invited the King of England back to the US of A? No sir! And what the heck would they do with him? Do they want us to give him a room at the White House, one Admiral said to me, or would we have to build a palace?'

'I'm sure the President didn't say anything like that,' said Mayhew.

'You've got to stop thinking that Roosevelt is some kind of fanatical Anglophile. He's a politician, and back home that means a wily bird.'

Mayhew said, 'Of course it's politically sensitive –'

335

'Correction, buddy; politically it's suicide. Every politician is promising he won't get American boys into a foreign war. You think anyone is going to invite your King there, when he's the focal point of the whole European wrangle?'

'War,' said Mayhew, coldly objecting to the word 'wrangle'. 'We call it war.'

'You call it anything you like, but for most people back home, it's in the past tense. And the Krauts have changed the tense.'

'We were asking a lot of you,' said Mayhew. 'Perhaps Sir Robert Benson should have gone to Washington.'

The American leaned back and closed his eyes. It was difficult to decide whether he was tired, disillusioned or just counting to ten before exploding with anger. 'We went all through that weeks ago,' he said softly. 'You were the one so keen to send me. You said a well-informed American, sympathetic to Britain, would have the best chance.' He put a hand over his glass to decline the whisky that Garin offered him. 'Don't think I pulled my punches. And don't think America is blind to what's happening in the world. Congress has given the army six billion dollars in the last six months, so we can get a fighting army, and buy the Air Corps better airplanes. But we've got our own Hitler; he's got a yellow face and narrow eyes, and he signs his mail Tojo.'

Mayhew rested a hand on the fireplace and stared into the flames. 'The King will have to be told,' he said sadly. 'He'll go to Canada, and that's that.'

The American found some dried mud on his trouser leg, picked it off and threw it into the fire. 'I'm just not getting through to you, am I? Is it my accent or something?'

'I beg your pardon?' said Mayhew sharply. He turned to face the American.

'I mean your King will not be welcome in North America. And that goes for the real estate north of the forty-ninth parallel.'

'Washington dare not forbid Canadians to give refuge to their sovereign!'

'Washington forbids nothing. The Canadians won't take him. I was up in Ottawa talking with them. They have the same political problems we have. Having a King Emperor as a resident will dwarf the authority of their Prime Minister.'

'The King will take no part in Canadian politics,' said Mayhew.

'The Canadians felt the heavy paternal hand of London for too many years, Colonel. Finally they get a degree of independence. Now you want them to have the King living there. No politician wants to risk what the opposition will do to him if he's a party to that step backwards.'

'They have all Britain's gold, valued at six hundred and thirty-seven million, in old pounds sterling. And when HMS *Revenge* took that first consignment, more than a thousand million pounds of securities went there too.'

'No sweat,' said the American. 'The securities are in the Sun-Life insurance building in Ottawa – the gold's in Montreal. No one's going to gyp the King out of his dough.'

'It's not the King's money,' said Mayhew with a flash of anger.

The American made an apologetic gesture with his hand, but Mayhew turned away to flick ash into the fire, and took an exaggerated interest in the clock.

In a posture that was unmistakably American, the other man sat back with one foot resting on his knee, while he massaged his broken shoe as if it were a small animal that needed comforting.

'Your shoes are ruined,' said Douglas. But he knew

that the American would not be conspicuous in a land where half the overcoats were fashioned from army blankets, and women were sewing curtains to make dresses.

'It doesn't matter,' said the American. He stopped rubbing his shoe and opened his hand to look at the cuts he'd suffered as the parachute dragged him through a hedge. The palms were mottled by liberal applications of brightly coloured iodine. 'I'll be back on ship by next week.'

'The ship is waiting out there?' said Douglas.

'Destroyer Squadron 2 – USS *Moffett* and friends – is part of the Atlantic Fleet Fall exercises.'

'This close to British shores?'

'Freedom of the seas, mister. We didn't come into the three-mile limit.'

Douglas looked at the other men. Mayhew was staring into the fire and Garin was using a small ivory-handled folding knife to open a new box of cigars. 'Have you ever heard of an atomic explosion?' Douglas asked the American. There was no reply.

Douglas said, 'The US Navy has sent a destroyer squadron provocatively close to Britain, through water still officially classified as a war zone. And they are staying in the vicinity while you spend a week seeing the sights of London. What for?'

Mayhew straightened up and tugged at his cuffs. The American still did not answer.

'He's going to do a deal with you, Colonel Mayhew,' Douglas told him, while still looking at the American. 'And just to make sure that the bargain will be the best thing America can get, he is starting off with a "no".'

'But whatever for?' said Mayhew, looking from one to the other.

'They want the calculations that Spode burned,

338

Colonel.' The American stared at Douglas without allowing any emotion to register on his face, but Douglas noticed the way that his fingers prised his torn shoe with enough force to make the damage worse.

'An atomic device in the hold of a ship. That's the only kind of weapon that could bring about the conquest of America by a European power.' Douglas stepped nearer to the American and spoke directly to him as if there was no one else present. 'If Hitler gets such a device he'll use it against you, make no mistake.'

'I know,' said the American. He took a huge Colt automatic pistol from his pocket. 'Can I put this somewhere, please? It's already torn a hole in my pocket.' Sydney Garin took it from him and looked at it under the light before placing it in the top drawer of a small antique commode.

The American was tired. Douglas had seen that same quality in the faces of other men. They'd got to a point where they could no longer be bothered to keep to their story. 'You mean that no one in Washington spoke to you about Professor Frick? Or about the atomic physics work that has been done at the Clarendon Laboratory at Oxford, the Liverpool Cyclotron, Chadwick, or by Rutherford at the Cavendish Laboratory? Or of the work the Germans have done since taking over the research at Bringle Sands?'

'No one in Washington was talking about atomic physics,' said the American. He grinned at the idea of it.

But the denial was too laconic to convince Douglas. 'Are you just a messenger boy then?' Douglas asked him. 'Why send warships when they could have posted a letter saying "no"?' Douglas paused and sipped his drink almost without tasting it. 'Suppose I told you that other governments are also interested in the calculations we have?'

'The Russkies?'

339

'The Germans have most to offer.'

'What?'

'They'd rewrite the proposals for the peace treaty,' said Douglas improvising desperately. 'We can have an army, a small coastal force and a proper civil government to replace the toadies of this puppet regime. The Foreign Ministry and Ministry of Defence would be run by us. The occupied zone would be no more than a strip of coast, and we'd control all essential imports, have a merchant fleet and get the value of the pound sterling adjusted against the Reichsmark. Reparations would be slashed almost to nothing.'

'All that for a few pages of calculations?' said the American.

'For many years of hard work, thousands of hours on calculating machines, for the willing co-operation of our top physicists. Do you know that the German army have started to run their pile? They'll get plutonium when it cools. From that it will be only a couple of steps to an explosive device.'

'A Congressional committee has been examining the idea,' admitted the American, relinquishing his pretence. 'They've talked to Einstein. But the estimates are reaching into billions of dollars, and there's no certainty that a bang will ever be possible.'

'Don't underrate the importance of a negative result. A few billion dollars would be a cheap price for discovering that the Nazis can't destroy New York City overnight.'

A slow smile came over the face of the American. 'You're the police Superintendent,' he said. 'I suddenly realized who you are. You're the goddamned Scotland Yard dick I've heard so much about.'

'Never mind who I am,' said Douglas, surprised and annoyed. 'Are you empowered to bargain about the King?'

'I like your style. Do you know that? I like your style. Barb said I would like you, and dammit, I do.' He smiled. 'That's the first time she's got anything right, from the day I married her – or the day before that maybe.'

'You're Danny Barga!'

'Lieutenant Commander Daniel Albert Barga in person.'

'So they commissioned you into the US Navy,' said Mayhew, examining the ash on his cigar.

'The State Department insisted.'

Mayhew nodded. Putting a man into uniform was no different from enrolling striking workers into the army. It was a way of ensuring that he did exactly as he was told.

At that moment a servant hurried into the room and whispered a lengthy message to Sydney Garin who nodded, his face growing more solemn. When the servant had departed, Garin said, 'I'm afraid the Germans have found pieces of our friend's parachute.'

Danny Barga got to his feet. 'They had to cut it; it was tangled into a tree, and they couldn't reach some bits of the cord.'

'Someone must have spotted you coming down. There's a platoon of infantry walking line abreast searching my fields.'

'Will they come here?' asked Mayhew.

'Certainly they will,' said Garin calmly. 'Soldiers are methodical, German soldiers particularly so. They will search every house in the neighbourhood, this one included.' He tried to smile but it was not easy for him.

George Mayhew stubbed out his cigar, as if he didn't want the Germans to catch him smoking it. 'We had better be sure our stories agree.'

Danny Barga stood up. He said, 'I'm on their damned Sonderfahndungsliste.'

'Haven't you got identity papers in some other name?' said Garin.

'Papers are waiting for me in London. Washington forgeries are always weeks out of date.'

'Can you hide him, Garin?' Mayhew asked.

Before Sydney Garin had a chance to answer, there was a rumpus in the corridor that grew louder until the door of the drawing-room opened. A servant rushed in, head lowered like a charging bull. He half-recovered his balance, just stopping himself falling into the fire, and turned to face the man who had propelled him so violently into the room.

'My name is Dr Oskar Huth; Standartenführer.' He looked at the men. 'Ah, Superintendent Archer, I thought I might find you here . . . and Colonel Mayhew, and Mr Sydney Garin. All faces I recognize from my confidential files.'

No one spoke. The servant rubbed his wrist where Huth had twisted his arm up his back. Huth walked across the room behind the men, but none of them turned to watch him. They heard him say, 'A parachute was found nearby, Mr Garin. Did you hear of that?'

Garin did not reply. Huth barked like a parade-ground martinet. 'Did you hear about that parachute?'

'My servants told me,' said Garin softly.

'And you did nothing?'

Garin shrugged. 'What could I do?'

'And you, Colonel Mayhew,' said Huth. 'You contained your curiosity too? How can I not admire this renowned British restraint?' An SS-Scharführer looked in through the door. 'All in order here, Scharf,' said Huth. 'Make sure there are no servants in the out-buildings, then get everyone together down in the servants' sitting-room.' The Staff Sergeant clicked his heels and moved off down the corridor.

342

'And you,' said Huth coming close behind Danny Barga. 'Who are you?'

'I'm an American citizen,' said Barga.

'Sit down, American citizen,' said Huth, applying sudden pressure upon Barga's shoulders. This caught Barga unawares and, weakened by his twisted ankle, he tumbled back into the soft chair.

Huth moved towards the fireplace, and then turned to face the others. 'I don't trust any of you,' he said. 'You act like guilty men.'

'You burst in here – ' said Mayhew.

'Shut up!' said Huth and Mayhew was quietened. 'I'm arresting you all,' said Huth. To Mayhew he said, 'And don't argue with me.'

Huth turned to watch the movement of the skeleton clock's pendulum. Everyone was quite still and now that the wind had dropped, there was no sound but that of the clock.

Douglas stepped over to the commode, quickly opened the top drawer and took out the .45 Colt automatic that the American had brought with him. He pointed it at Huth.

'No, Standartenführer,' said Douglas.

Huth turned to see him. He smiled as if Douglas had committed some inexcusable gaffe. 'Don't be a fool, Superintendent Archer. I have a Sturm of SS infantry with me.'

'Give me the silencer, Mr Garin,' said Douglas. He took it and fitted it to the gun.

'Put the gun down and I will forget about it,' offered Huth.

'If you make a sudden move I will shoot you,' said Douglas.

'You haven't got nerve enough,' said Huth but he did not make a sudden move.

'Get the Standartenführer's pistol, Colonel,' said Douglas, 'and stand well aside from him as you do so.'

'Are you sure you know what you're doing, old boy?' said Mayhew.

'I've never been more sure,' said Douglas, although inside him he could feel his heart pumping blood enough for three men, and his stomach was knotted in anxiety. By the time he had second thoughts Mayhew was undoing the fastener of the leather pistol holster, and reaching for Huth's gun.

'I hate to see you signing your own death warrant,' said Huth.

'How many vehicles?' Douglas spoke to Garin's servant but did not take his eyes off Huth.

'Five lorries and a motor-cycle with side-car,' he replied. Douglas nodded; that seemed about right.

'Phone downstairs, using the house phone,' Douglas ordered Huth. 'Tell your Scharführer to get his men into their transport, and be ready to depart.'

'And what about me?' said Huth.

'Do as I say,' said Douglas, bringing the house phone to where Huth was standing.

'No,' said Mayhew. Douglas paused, gun in one hand, phone in the other. 'Standartenführer Huth and I can probably reach an accord,' said Mayhew. 'Can I speak with you in private, Standartenführer?'

'How can I refuse?' said Huth. Mayhew looked at Douglas. Douglas nodded.

The two men were closeted together for nearly half an hour. When they emerged Huth said, 'Very well.' He looked round the room. 'Very well,' he said again. 'Colonel Mayhew has provided me with an explanation for your presence here this night. For the time being, I'll take no action.' He picked up his pistol from a side table and put it into his holster. 'But I warn you . . .' He turned and stared at Mayhew. 'I warn you that I expect my quid pro quo.' He walked across to the door, rattled the door handle and then turned to face them. 'Colonel Mayhew has persuaded me that no one in this house was in any way connected with the parachute drop. But perhaps you would circulate the information that the Luftwaffe have radio detection equipment that follows the movement of aircraft night and day, and in any sort of weather.'

After they had seen the lorries, and Huth's motor-cycle, depart up the long avenue of lime trees, Mayhew said, 'He'll overlook the business with the pistol, Archer. He's promised, and I believe him.'

'What did *you* promise him?' said Douglas.

Mayhew was evasive. 'The moon and the stars; I promised him anything he wanted, in exchange for a little more time. Now we must get the King out of German custody.' He looked at Danny Barga. 'And we'll show our American friends that a President with an atomic bomb can get re-elected even if he does have the King living there in exile.'

Chapter Thirty-five

The Metropolitan Music Hall, in the Edgware Road, was warm, noisy and smoky with an audience who'd packed in to see Flanagan and Allen, and to hear Vera Lynn sing.

By the summer of 1941 the lyrics of her songs had become a motif of the repression felt by the people of Occupied Great Britain. 'Wishes are the dreams we dream when we're awake,' she sang, and 'We'll meet again, don't know where, don't know when,' was a promise cherished by the thousands of men and women who had their loved ones in some distant German prison camp.

At the end of the first half, she'd come on the stage in a simple white dress, not beyond the purse and ingenuity of any shopgirl, to a roar of applause that forced the orchestra to play the opening bars of 'Wishing' two or three times before she could be heard above the uproar. And when Flanagan and Allen joined her with the full company on the stage to sing 'There'll be blue birds over, the White Cliffs of Dover, tomorrow just you wait and see. There'll be love and laughter, and peace ever after, tomorrow when the world is free,' the audience sat transfixed.

The first half ended with the whole cast throwing paper streamers, wearing funny hats and popping balloons that descended from a great wire basket suspended from the ceiling.

By the time the second half began the audience was overcome with a rare euphoria. Even 'Professor Zingo' did not lessen the contentment, and that says a great deal, for there are few things more exacting than watching the anxious efforts of a magician who has not quite mastered his black art.

Gala evenings were not popular with the cleaning staff, for the festivities left the theatre in a chaos of litter that had to be salvaged for re-use. A cobweb of coloured paper ribbons entangled the big-breasted caryatids, and a few surviving balloons were bobbing around in the aisles. The bar was the only place unaffected by gala nights. It was a long, narrow room at the back of the stalls. Glass windows permitted thirsty patrons to see the stage, but the sound of the music was heard only faintly, except when the door opened. Here in the bar a man could have the best of both worlds; he could watch the legs of the dancing girls while hearing his own voice.

'Suppose he doesn't turn up?' said Harry Woods. He finished his pint of watery ale and signalled the barman for another.

'He'll turn up,' said Douglas. He waved away the offer of another beer. Two pints of that stuff was about as much as his bladder could take and he'd learned not to mix police business with hard drink.

'You get many Herberts in here, Percy?' Harry asked the barman.

The man continued to wipe the counter, mopping up the spilled beer and wringing the cloth into a bucket on the floor behind the bar. 'No,' he said. He opened the damp cloth, shook it and spread it on a beer barrel to dry. 'The Germans have their own shows, with big name stars from Germany. It only costs them sixpence. Here you have to pay that to get into the "gods". Anyway they can't understand the songs and the patter.'

Harry lit a cigarette and offered the barman his packet. He took one gratefully. 'You looking for a German?'

Douglas turned his head to see the act on the stage – Professor Zingo was making endless coloured handkerchiefs appear from a seemingly empty tube – but really he was anxious about how much Harry would reveal about the meeting.

'Meeting one: an officer from the army post office – talking to us about mail-bag robberies.'

'Oh yes,' said the barman.

'It's an important matter,' Harry told him as if trying to engage his interest.

'Yes, of course,' said the barman, beginning to rinse the dirty glasses that were lined up on his sink. Harry had certainly done a good job in diverting the barman's curiosity about the meeting.

Professor Zingo was opening and closing the hinged sections of a large black japanned box, accompanied by the pizzicato of the orchestra's six string players. He looked at the audience and at his pretty girl assistant and then he rapped the metal blade of a circular saw. The Tchaikovsky swelled as the door opened and Captain Hans Hesse entered. Thank God he wasn't wearing that overcoat with the astrakhan collar; he'd be surrounded with autograph hunters in a place like this.

'What are you drinking, Hans?' Harry asked him as if they'd known each other for years.

'Beer,' he said, taking off the broad-brimmed black hat and placing it carefully on the shelf. It was illegal for anyone to buy a drink for a member of the occupying army, and illegal too for the barman to serve them. But the beer arrived immediately. Hesse sipped it, winced, smiled and put the beer down on the counter. 'Tomorrow morning,' he said. 'Can you be ready?'

The girl was in the box by now. Again Professor Zingo opened the gaps to show that her torso was there to be bisected. 'Blue-jacket do you mean?' Harry asked Hesse.

348

It was a fine code-word for King George the Sixth, the sailor king, nautical and classless. It would be right for the history books.

'Blue-jacket, yes. Will you be ready?' Hesse followed Douglas's gaze to the spotlighted magician. The circular saw was whirling now, its vicious teeth sparkling in the pink footlights. The girl's face contorted as she feigned fear. The Captain found the conjurer's act banal. He turned away.

'We'll be ready,' said Douglas without taking his eyes from the stage.

'The girl draws her legs up to her chest,' said the Captain as he took another sip of the warm, watery, English beer. 'The circular blade goes nowhere near her.'

'We'll collect him from the Tower,' said Douglas. He'd been given all the details by Mayhew.

'There will be one of my fellows there; a little man with spectacles, wearing the uniform of a veterinary officer. Do everything he says. Do it immediately and without question. Do you understand?'

'Yes, I understand,' said Douglas. In the shadows at the side of the orchestra pit, the emergency doors opened quietly. Two soldiers came into the theatre. In the pink light from the stage, Douglas saw the shine of the metal gorgets that German military policemen wore across their chest while on duty. The two policemen moved very slowly up the slope of the aisle, systematically studying the faces in each row of the audience before moving on.

'Your people,' said Harry. He cleared his throat and sipped some more beer.

'Feldgendarmerie,' said Captain Hesse. 'Probably no more than a routine check.'

Even through the glass they heard the drum-roll. The spinning saw moved towards the girl in the black lac-quered box at a frightening speed. The two soldiers did

349

not look up at the stage. Their heads moved very slowly from left to right and back again, like spectators at some slowed-down tennis match.

'Jesus!' said Harry Woods. He saw the girl throw back her head, as if in a convulsion of terrible pain.

'She pretends,' explained the German. 'It's a part of the act.' He reached for his hat and put it on, pulling the brim down on that side of his face nearest to the two military policemen.

'We'll be in an ambulance,' said Harry Woods. 'Your people specified that it should be an ambulance.'

'Registration number?' said Hesse.

'No registration,' said Harry Woods. 'They'll have to remove the number plates. Hardly worth putting false ones on; no one is going to stop an ambulance because it's got no plates. And if anything goes wrong the absence of any kind of number might give us an extra few minutes.'

'You are right,' said Hesse. He smiled, and the sudden brightening of the stage-lighting made his face shine in the reflected light. 'Now do you see?' he said. 'The girl is quite all right.'

'Blue-jacket won't be wearing handcuffs or anything, will he?' said Harry.

Hesse smiled. 'We Germans are not barbarians, Mr Woods. Why should he be manacled?' There was a chord from the orchestra and a roar of applause as Professor Zingo took the pretty girl assistant by the hand and helped her from the black box that was once more joined up into one piece.

'We'll have no one with us who could handle locksmith work,' said Harry.

Captain Hesse leaned back against the carved mahogany bar and clapped his hands. He was staring at the

350

stage and squinting as the smoke from his cigarette drifted up into his eyes.

The door of the bar opened and the two 'chained dogs' looked in, the metal gorgets that gave them their nickname glinting in the harsh light. Hesse, Douglas and Harry Woods kept their eyes on the stage as if unaware of the military policemen standing in the doorway. 'Any soldiers in here tonight?' one of them called to the barman in a sing-song way that showed he'd learned the phrase parrot-fashion.

'Nix,' said the barman. He put two glasses on the counter and placed a bottle of whisky alongside. The military policemen stared once again at the three men at the far end of the bar, exchanged a look with each other and then came to the bar and poured themselves a drink. Douglas stole a glance at them and could now see that they were not Feldgendarmerie but ordinary soldiers appointed to police duties wearing the Kommandantur gorget.

The barman moved away from the soldiers, and stood behind the three men at the other end of the bar. 'See that?' said the barman as the magician and the girl came back to take another bow. 'Same thing happened on Monday night, first house. She's limping. See the blood on her foot. If she doesn't get her knees right up to her neck, the saw catches her.'

Now the others could see it too. Her white ballet shoe was torn at the toe and there was a little blood there. 'Goes to show,' said the barman. 'You can rehearse and rehearse, but there's always the chance that it will go wrong.'

The three men sipped their drinks and didn't answer him.

Chapter Thirty-Six

The Tower of London. Douglas could taste the fog; its soot got into his nostrils and dried on his lips. Even at ten o'clock in the morning, visibility was down to a few yards. Here at London's river the ambulance was reduced to a snail's pace. At Tower Hill, the soldiers at the first check-point had marked their position with flares. Six flames tore a yellow tunnel through the green swirling clouds. Beyond them, the Tower was no more than a grey shape painted on the soft fog.

Only when the wind ruffled the river could they see the strings of yellow lights that marked the rigging of the light cruiser *Emden*, anchored on the far side of the bridge.

'They picked a good day for it,' said Harry Woods. 'They must have seen the forecast last night, before Hesse came to meet us.' He lowered the window as they approached the second perimeter of sentries.

An officer came quickly out of the guard hut, and stepped up on the running board. He held a handkerchief to his face and sneezed into it. 'Damned filthy country,' he said. 'It's not fit for human habitation.'

On his shoulder straps his Leutnant's stars were accompanied by the serpents of the veterinary corps. 'Drive straight on,' he said. 'Over the drawbridge and through the towers. I'll talk to anyone who tries to stop us.'

He hung on to the mirror fitting, as Douglas manoeuvred the ambulance between the narrow spaces of the Outer Ward, round the buttress of the Wakefield

Tower, past the Bloody Tower and up to the Inner Ward where, like a vast cliff of Caen stone, the White Tower was beheaded by the fog. He followed the line of street lamps, their gas flames showing brightly. A couple of ravens, startled by their approach, lurched drunkenly across the path and flapped away noisily. The ambulance picked its way round the massive Keep and parked outside the chapel.

'Wait,' said the little German officer. He stepped off the running board and disappeared into the gloom, coughing and sneezing his way across Tower Green, and almost stumbling over the 'Keep off the Grass' sign.

The pea-souper had brought an unnatural quiet. The air activity, almost unceasing since the start of martial law, was suddenly no more, the spotter planes grounded by the fog. The grumble of a heavy lorry, going across the bridge in low gear, faded away and there was complete silence. 'Gives you the creeps, doesn't it?' said Harry.

Douglas looked up at the painted notice. In German it said, 'King's House. Here Anne Boleyn spent the night before execution and Guy Fawkes was interrogated here before his confession and subsequent trial at Westminster Hall.' Douglas nodded but didn't answer.

From the White Tower there was the sudden noise of footsteps. Someone with a broad Silesian accent said it was cold, and another man chuckled as if appreciating a witticism.

'Here they come,' said Harry.

The white ambulance was almost invisible in the fog and the men nearly collided with it. There were five of them. Leading the way were two booted cavalry Leutnants. Behind them, flanked by two smiling acolytes, came a Deputy Gauleiter of the Deutsche Arbeitsfront, the Nazi trade union movement.

His tailor had tried to conceal the pot-belly and heavy

hips under a magnificent overcoat, with coloured facings and gold badges, but he could do nothing for the unmilitary swagger, jovial curses and coarse laughter.

'Bloody hell – an ambulance! Do I sit with the driver, or stretch out in the back?' The Deputy Gauleiter laughed loudly, coughed and then spat. 'Bloody fog gets in your throat, eh?'

The two DAF officials stopped laughing at his joke for long enough to join in his complaint about the fog. 'Your car is over here, sir,' said the cavalry Leutnant coldly.

'You know your history, Leutnant,' said the Deputy Gauleiter, turning to the second of the army officers conducting the party. 'All those stories about Sir Walter Raleigh and Lady Jane Grey . . . Goddamn it, you bring it all to life for me.' He tapped the officer on the chest. 'And Sir Thomas More was always a hero of mine . . .'

'Yes, sir,' said the officer.

Douglas and Harry Woods watched the DAF men driven away in the sort of Rolls-Royce that was used for important visitors. Unaware that they were overheard, one of the army officers hissed his contempt through clenched teeth. 'Agriculture Ministry officials, Health Service Commissioner, Deputy Chief of the Women's League, Chief of Staff to the Reich Sport League . . . and now these pigs from the DAF. This is supposed to be a maximum security prison for the King of England not a *Zirkus*.'

The second officer spoke more quietly and was difficult to hear. 'Patience, Klaus, there is a method to all this, believe me.'

'A method? . . . What motive could there possibly be?'

'I have a bottle of schnapps in my quarters, Klaus. What do you say to breaking the habit of a lifetime, and taking a drink before lunch?'

'What did that Nazi pig mean . . . Sir Thomas More

354

was always a hero of his? Thomas More was a scholar, a man who defied tyranny.'

'Calm down, Klaus. Our orders were to be back in our quarters by ten-thirty A.M. and we've only a few minutes to go.'

'Why back in our quarters?'

'Theirs not to reason why, Theirs but to do or die. Into the valley of Death, Rode the six hundred,' misquoted the officer in an uncertain English accent.

'You know your history, Leutnant,' said his friend, imitating the ponderous Silesian accent of the Deputy Gauleiter. 'Goddamn it, you bring it all to life for me.'

It was ten-forty before the veterinary Leutnant returned to Douglas and Harry Woods. He was wheeling an invalid's wooden chair. In it there sat a still and silent figure, hunched slightly as he looked at his tightly clenched gloved hands. He was dressed in a cheap tartan-patterned dressing gown, under which could be seen a brown, polo-neck sweater, grey flannel trousers and scuffed shoes. On his head there was a khaki-coloured knitted helmet of the sort that had become popular with the British soldiers during that first winter of the phoney war.

Harry Woods opened the two doors at the rear of the ambulance. Douglas stood ready to assist the King up the folding step. 'You'll have to help him,' said the veterinary officer.

When the King looked up at the two men, his head scarcely moved, it was no more than a flicker of the eyes. He said nothing.

'We'll help you, sir,' Douglas told the King.

Then Harry Woods leaned over and lifted the King bodily, as a mother might lift a tiny baby. Holding him in his arms, Harry stepped into the ambulance and laid him full-length upon the stretcher that was locked into position there.

'Strap him in,' said the veterinary Leutnant. 'He's completely exhausted. One of you should stay in the back with him.'

'I'll stay here,' said Harry.

'Are you all right, sir?' Douglas asked nervously. He wondered if he should say 'Your Majesty'.

The King gave an almost imperceptible nod and moved his lips, as if he was about to speak. Douglas waited, but when no words came he nodded to Harry and closed the rear doors.

'I'll ride with you through the outer perimeter,' said the Leutnant. 'After that he's your responsibility.'

'Yes,' said Douglas.

The Leutnant blew his nose noisily.

'Is he drugged?' said Douglas.

'He's sick,' said the Leutnant. 'Damned sick!' He wiped his nose again. As the ambulance was going along Lower Thames Street he stepped off the running board with no more than a grunt of farewell.

They were in Lombard Street, heading towards Cheapside, when the first sign of trouble came. The communication flap behind Douglas's head snapped open, and he heard Harry say, 'You want me to drive, Doug?'

'It's the ignition,' said Douglas. 'The power fades when I press the accelerator.'

The ambulance moved slowly past the Bank of England, its armed sentries just visible through the gloomy fog. The traffic lights had failed and a policeman was directing traffic, his dark shape visible only because of the flare that burned beside him. He beckoned them on, and they got down as far as St Paul's Cathedral before the engine stalled again. It started after a couple of tries.

356

'We've only got to get as far as Barnet,' said Harry hopefully. 'There will be another vehicle there for him.'

'Do you know anything about car engines, Harry?'

'Perhaps we'll see a garage,' said Harry.

In St Paul's Church Yard there were four cars and a lorry abandoned in the fog. A uniformed policeman walked over to the ambulance. 'You can't leave it here, sir,' said the policeman. He had that sort of blunt manner that sometimes afflicts young policemen. 'This is a Schnellstrasse; no parking or waiting permitted under any circumstances.' He looked at the licence disc, sniffed and then stared at Douglas.

'There's something wrong with the ignition,' said Douglas. 'Can you direct me to a garage that will do repairs?' Behind him he heard the King cough.

'You'll get nothing like that done today,' said the Constable. 'Can't you understand that the fog has brought everything to a standstill?' He looked at the ambulance and wiped a gloved finger-tip in the condensation on the windscreen. 'Get on to your people to send a mechanic.'

'Can I leave it while I phone?'

'Don't play silly-buggers with me,' said the policeman. By now he'd decided that ambulance drivers did not merit a deferential approach. 'I've told you once, and if I have to tell you again I'll run you in. Do you understand? Now sling your hook!' Douglas swallowed the rage he felt. He nodded and drove on.

'Nasty little sod, wasn't he?' Harry said quietly as they pulled away.

'I never did like coppers,' said Douglas. 'How's . . .?'

Before Douglas could think of an appropriate form of address, Harry said, 'Still the same. He hasn't said a word. He might have dozed off.'

'Could you get him into a taxi?'

357

'Cab drivers stay at home in this kind of weather,' said Harry. 'It would take half a day to earn one fare.'

Douglas nodded. Harry was right, of course. He'd not seen a taxi anywhere. 'I'll phone Barbara,' said Douglas.

They found a phone box in Fleet Street. Barbara was out. The window cleaner answered the phone and offered to leave a message but Douglas said he'd phone again later.

Douglas phoned the office of the Commissioner General for Administration and Justice, what once had been the Home Office. Sir Robert Benson was at a meeting but his personal assistant seemed ready, even anxious, to help when Douglas identified himself.

Sir Robert wouldn't be back until after lunch, according to his P.A.

Douglas told him it was very urgent, and after some hesitation the man divulged that Sir Robert was lunching at the Reform Club.

'We'll go there,' Douglas told Harry when he got back to the ambulance. 'I think I can get this thing as far as Pall Mall.'

'The fog's getting thicker,' said Harry. 'It could hang on for days.'

'Are you quite sure you haven't got the name of the people at Barnet?'

'I'm sure,' said Harry.

Douglas got in the ambulance and looked at the King. He was sitting up in the stretcher, a thin grey blanket pulled round his shoulders, his face blank. 'Are you all right, Your Majesty?' said Douglas.

The King looked at him but did not answer.

'It must have been that bomb that hit the palace just before the end,' said Harry in a whisper. 'There were rumours that the King had been badly injured, do you remember?'

358

'You think he's been like this all that time?'

'I've seen plenty such cases,' said Harry. 'It's the concussion – the blast effect can kill without leaving a mark on the corpse. Or it can just numb the mind and shake a man's brain loose.' Douglas looked round anxiously but the King had not heard.

'Do you think he'll recover?'

'God knows, Douglas. But can you imagine what effect he'd have in his present state, if he was in Washington?'

'I've been thinking of little else,' said Douglas sadly.

'Can you really get this damned thing as far as Pall Mall?'

'I'll try,' said Douglas, and as if in encouragement the engine fired at the first attempt, and laboriously they trundled on up the Strand. For a few minutes the engine ran smoothly, but before either of the two men voiced the hope that they'd get as far as their original destination in Barnet the engine died once again. They were outside the Adelphi Theatre when the ambulance finally stammered to a stop. Now it did not answer to the starter. In the tool-box on the running board there was only a greasy cloth and a starting handle. Harry took it and turned the engine by hand, not once but many times. There was no response to his exertions and, red-faced and breathless, he threw the starting handle back into the tool box. He cursed as he wiped his hands on a rag.

'What are we going to do?' said Harry, holding a hand to his chest and breathing deeply.

'There's a folding wheelchair in the back,' said Douglas. 'I'd prefer to take him along with us.'

'Christ!'

'No one will recognize him in the street. London is teeming with the sick and crippled.'

Harry had no alternative to offer, or breath to argue.

They got the King into the wheelchair with some difficulty. Some passing pedestrians looked at the three men with interest but then they noticed the stage door of the nearby theatre and gave no more thought to it.

They wheeled him through the fog, cutting through Trafalgar Square and to the huge forbidding edifice of the Reform Club. 'Wait here with him,' Douglas told Harry. The fog was getting into the King's lungs, and now he gave a body-racking cough.

Douglas had been in the Club before. He asked the porter for Sir Robert and then caught sight of him, standing in the middle of the strange indoor courtyard that is a feature of this odd building.

The porter walked over to Sir Robert and announced the visitor. He turned away from his companion. 'Archer. How nice.' His voice was soft and low somewhere between a growl and a whisper.

It was typical of Sir Robert; a greeting from which it was impossible to detect pleasure or lack of it, surprise or polite acceptance of a punctual arrival, intimate friendship or distant acquaintance.

'I'm sorry to trouble you, Sir Robert.'

'Not at all. You know Webster. He's to be the new Under-Secretary.'

'Congratulations,' said Douglas. Webster was a frail-looking man with tired eyes and a wispy smile. Hard to believe that he had the sort of determination that a man must have to cross that hurdle. Under-Secretary was for a civil servant what his first star-billing is to an actor.

'You were at New College, Archer?' said Sir Robert.

'Christ Church,' said Douglas.

'Webster was at New,' said Sir Robert.

They smiled. There was a widely held belief that all the top civil service jobs went to men from New College, Oxford.

'Can I offer you a glass of sherry?' said Webster.

Douglas was burning with impatience – he was anxious about Harry standing outside on the pavement with the King – but with Webster celebrating his promotion, Douglas could see no way of declining. A club servant was ready to take the order. 'Three dry sherries,' said Webster.

'This is rather urgent, Sir Robert.'

'There is always enough time for a glass of sherry,' said Sir Robert. He turned to Webster. 'Archer has helped me with PQs from time to time.' Douglas had only once been asked to draft some material for the answer to a Parliamentary question but it was enough to explain his unexpected arrival.

Politely Webster offered them a chance to talk privately. 'Then let me have a brief word with the Club Secretary while you talk. It would save me time after lunch.'

Sir Robert smiled and seemed indifferent to Douglas's impatience. The sherries arrived and the congratulations were delivered. When Webster had gone, Sir Robert led Douglas to one of the leather-covered benches by the wall.

Douglas looked round carefully to be sure they were not overheard. 'It's the King, Sir Robert,' he whispered.

Sir Robert said nothing; he sipped his sherry. This calmness did nothing to reassure Douglas, rather it gave him a feeling that he was behaving badly, that he was intruding. 'We are taking him from the Tower . . . as arranged,' whispered Douglas apologetically. 'But there's engine trouble. We need another vehicle for him.'

'And now?' said Sir Robert calmly.

'He's here.'

'In the Club?' His hoarse voice rose a fraction above the customary whisper.

'Outside on the pavement.'

Sir Robert knitted his bushy eyebrows and studied his sherry. Douglas noticed the way the liquid trembled in Sir Robert's hand. Douglas turned his head away and looked at a group of men near the entrance. The effect of the light, coming through the glass roof so high above, made the men seem shadowless, as if in a dream.

'He's in a wheelchair,' Douglas added. 'One of my men is with him.'

'How sick is he?' He glanced round.

'He's virtually comatose, Sir Robert.'

They sat very still. From somewhere high above the fog there came the sound of an aeroplane. Its sound faded before he replied. 'That explains a lot. The Germans have gone to a great deal of trouble to keep His Majesty incommunicado.' Nervously the old man reached into the pocket of his black jacket and found his pipe. He toyed with it, reaming the bowl with his finger and tapping it against the back of his hand.

Douglas said, 'I don't know how we'll get him to the house in Barnet. We've had to abandon the vehicle.'

Sir Robert looked at him and nodded, his mind already calculating every possible permutation of this new situation. 'He'll need medical attention,' he said, and blew through the pipe. It made a sharp sound that was almost musical.

'I think a doctor should look at him as soon as possible.'

'A shrewd gambit,' said Sir Robert. 'They've given us what we most want, and yet dealt us a telling blow.' Suddenly he felt in both pockets and found his tobacco pouch. He unclipped the fastening and fingered the contents. Douglas could smell the strong odour of it. With that dexterous precision that comes only with unconscious action, he filled the pipe, cut the tobacco strands with his

362

thumbnail, struck a match, lit up and inhaled. Then he blew smoke. 'Astute fellows, these Germans, eh Archer?'

'It seems so, Sir Robert.' It was cold in the club and Douglas shivered.

'And what do you do with him now, eh?' He took the pipe from his mouth and looked at the burning tobacco, as if seeing it for the first time. Douglas sipped his sherry and waited. He was frightened, damned frightened, but there was no way of hurrying the old man.

'A few weeks after the *boche* arrived I managed at long last to get decent servants,' said Sir Robert, thoughtfully. 'A man and wife – not young – total abstainers, both of them. The wife's able to cook plain English food, and the husband had been a butler for an obscure Liberal peer. Awfully lucky, don't you know, getting such hardworking servants, at the sort of wages I can afford to pay them.' He put the pipe in his mouth and drew on it meditatively, while fixing Douglas with a piercing stare.

Over Sir Robert Benson's shoulder Douglas saw General Georg von Ruff coming into the club. He gave the porter his silk-lined overcoat, and stood polishing his gold-rimmed spectacles, misted by the warm air. Behind him was a uniformed German soldier who looked round before going back to talk to the porter. Douglas looked away. What a damnable coincidence that of only a couple of dozen men in London who might recognize the King, one of them had to come to the Reform Club at this moment. But was there any coincidence? Undoubtedly this was where General von Ruff and Sir Robert Benson had arranged the details of the King's release from the Tower. Douglas looked at Sir Robert's cold blue eyes – he seemed not to have noticed the General's arrival – and wondered whether the King's physical condition was really the surprise that Sir Robert implied that it was.

'I'm not sure I understand,' said Douglas. 'About your

363

servants; I'm not sure I understand.' General von Ruff walked past Sir Robert without a glance and went upstairs. Of course it would be like that; discreet words in a private room.

'No?' said Sir Robert as if he found it difficult to believe, and studied Douglas with renewed interest. 'Informers, of course. Reporting to the Germans everything I say, write or do. But I talked it over with my wife, and we decided that it was well worth the inconvenience . . .' He worked his lips to remove a strand of tobacco from his teeth. 'To tell you the truth, Archer, I am tempted to a few indiscretions from time to time, just to give the poor devil something to tell his masters. Don't know how we'd manage without them now . . . and the wife irons my shirts better than any laundry.'

'You mean we can't take the King to your house,' said Douglas.

Sir Robert Benson took the pipe from his mouth and used a pencil top to press the burning tobacco into the bowl. 'It would be risky,' he said, as if considering the idea for the first time. 'Colonel Mayhew?'

'Is waiting at Barnet, Sir Robert. I've no way of contacting him. And Bernard Staines is somewhere in South America.'

'And His Majesty is outside in the street, sitting in a wheelchair you say?'

'Yes, Sir Robert.'

He used the pipe to stroke the side of his nose. 'It has an element of farce, Archer. Would you say that?'

'No sir, I would not.'

He nodded mournfully. 'Ummm, your position is devilish difficult, I see that.'

Now Douglas understood how Sir Robert Benson had risen to his high position in the civil service. He didn't give orders and instructions; he simply put you in a situation where you had to do what he wanted. Sir Robert Benson wanted Douglas to wheel the King off into the fog, and solve the problem without involving Sir Robert, or any of his close friends and associates. And he was quite prepared to sit here drinking sherry and murmuring arid non sequiturs until Douglas got up and left. Douglas found this man's cold indifference to his plight more frightening than the machinations of Huth and Kellerman. 'Would it be all right if I used the phone?' said Douglas.

'You know where they are?'

'But I wonder if you could let me have some pennies?'

'Of course.' Sir Robert found four pennies and gave them to Douglas. 'By all means take him to my house, if you think it's worth the risk,' said Sir Robert.

Douglas nodded. The pennies were cold in his hand. Sir Robert would always come out smelling of roses. No one would be able to say Sir Robert Benson hadn't offered his all, even at the risk of certain betrayal to the authorities. 'I'll make sure His Majesty learns of your offer, Sir Robert.'

As if reading Douglas's mind, he smiled. 'You know where the phones are,' he said again. Douglas nodded, got to his feet and went to the phone.

'Barbara, it's Douglas.'

'Darling.' Her voice was no more than a whisper.

'I must come and see you.'

'Could you make it tomorrow, my love?'

'I want to come now.'

'Not now, darling. I'm just going out.'

'Can you hear me, Barbara? Your voice is very faint.'

'I've a car waiting and the fog is dreadful. Can you phone again tomorrow?'

Douglas tapped the earpiece of the phone in the hope that her voice would come louder. 'Barbara. I must see you *now*.'

365

'Don't be a bully, darling. Stay where you are until the fog clears.'

'Barbara, I – '

'It's my work,' she said. Her voice was louder now. 'I have my work to attend to, just as everyone else does. Now will you stop being a bore!' The earpiece purred as she slammed down the phone.

Douglas stood for a moment with the phone in his hand. He was totally unprepared for this rejection and he felt desolate.

'Everything all right?' said Sir Robert as Douglas walked past them towards the entrance.

'Yes, indeed, Sir Robert,' said Douglas. He nodded to Webster. When he got to the entrance hall, the porter had his overcoat all ready for him. The porter knew he wouldn't be staying to lunch with Sir Robert. Over the years he'd learned to recognize men whose overcoats should be kept ready for an early departure.

'No chance of a cab, I suppose?' Douglas asked the doorman.

'I haven't seen one all day, sir, and that must be something of a record here like this at the door of the club.'

They stood together for a moment at the top of the steps of the grand entrance. 'Look at those two,' said the doorman nodding to where Harry Woods was standing with the wheelchair. 'Poor devils. To think that I've fought through two world wars and I end up watching British ex-servicemen begging in Pall Mall.'

'Is that what they are doing?'

'Ask yourself,' said the doorman. 'They're discreet, of course, but I've already seen a bobby caution them, and move them on.'

'What took you so long?' said Harry when Douglas returned to them. 'I've had a beat bobby reading me the

366

Riot Act, and some bloody saucy kid shouting "penny for the guy".'

'Sorry, Harry. But no one wants us.'

'What do we do then?'

'I've got a key to Barbara Barga's house. It's not too far and she's just going out. At least it will be somewhere to sit down and collect our wits.'

'Are you all right?' Harry asked the King, crouching beside the wheelchair and speaking into his ear. There was no response. 'George,' said Harry Woods, 'we're taking you somewhere you can warm your hands.' Standing up again, Harry met Douglas's glare of astonishment. 'Well, what have I got to call him?' said Harry defensively. 'Even "sir" sounds bloody conspicuous when you are bending over a shabbily dressed old gentleman in a wheelchair.'

'I'll push him for a bit,' said Douglas, taking the handles of the chair. Harry noticed the King lifting an arm weakly and he bent over to listen to him, his ear close to his mouth. Douglas halted the chair and waited while the King murmured something inaudible and Harry nodded and gripped his arm in reassurance. Douglas realized that the two men had already established some sort of relationship which he did not share. A social cripple, sometimes he felt desperate at the way in which he was unable to get close to anyone, man or woman.

'I think he's trying to tell us that the empty ambulance will be reported to the police.'

'I know it will,' said Douglas.

'What will Kellerman do?' said Harry. They began walking in the direction of Barbara's mews house. They went across Green Park. It was virtually deserted and here under the trees the fog was so thick that they could see no more than ten yards ahead.

'He'll put out a number eighteen to all Divisions.'

'Bring us in for questioning? That would be a bit drastic.'

'He'll say he was worried for our personal safety.'

'Why bother until he's sure we're not just sick?' said Harry.

'Kellerman will guess that something important is happening. He might even guess that the King is no longer in custody. He has his Leibstandarte honour-guard at the Tower, and even if the army confined them to barracks this morning while we made our collection, they will soon discover that something has happened. The Abwehr people are party to the conspiracy but if they have to save themselves, they'll throw Mayhew and us to the dogs, Harry.'

So this is what they were reduced to, thought Douglas. Two policemen and a crippled King, in a land that was no longer their own. They lost their way in the park and turned left until they saw the gas lamps of Constitution Hill. Beyond that were the ruins of Buckingham Palace. Douglas looked down to see whether there was any sign of recognition from the King but there was none. He was a pathetic figure, sitting with his shoulders hunched and head tilted forward over the thin clenched hands. Douglas remembered the last time he'd seen the King. It was a Royal visit to Scotland Yard soon after war began. He remembered the King in the fingerprint department, giving a sample of his fingerprints and leaving the card there as a souvenir of the visit. He was a handsome figure, with an easy smile and informal manner that had endeared him to all. It was difficult to reconcile that scene with their present predicament but Douglas vowed that he would die before relinquishing his King; whatever the logic of it.

'There will be a check-point at the Arch,' said Harry.

Inside Wellington Arch, Hyde Park Corner, there is a

room for the Metropolitan Police. Lately army patrols had used it as a control post. If Kellerman had put out a number eighteen warning, his SS men might be there looking at identity papers.

'We'll detour,' said Douglas. 'We'll take one of the backstreets, and cut up into Curzon Street and across Park Lane into Hyde Park.'

'You'll be all right,' said Harry in the King's ear. 'Douglas knows what he's doing.'

They could hear the phone ringing while Douglas was putting the key into the door of the mews house. Douglas went into the living-room and answered.

'Miss Barga?'

'She's not at home,' said Douglas.

'Who is this?'

Douglas recognized the voice. 'Is that you, Colonel Mayhew?'

'Archer! I've been trying to find you. I *hoped* you'd contact Miss Barga.'

'The ambulance – '

'Enough said. I'll be with you in a few minutes. Are you all together and quite safe?'

'All three of us are here.'

'I'll give three short rings at the doorbell.'

'It was Mayhew,' Douglas told Harry after putting down the phone.

'Thank the Lord for that,' said Harry. He was lighting the gas fire. Douglas helped the King get closer to it. Then he went into the kitchen to make tea. He could not hide the pleasure he got from handling Barbara's possessions, and from being here in her home. Harry saw this and was pleased too. 'There's nothing like a cup of tea.' He went to ask the King, 'Do you take sugar, Your Majesty?' reverting to a more formal relationship now that there was no longer a danger of being overheard.

369

Mayhew had phoned from his house in Upper Brook Street. He had used the Underground railway to get back from Barnet. It was almost unaffected by the fog. It did not take him very long to get to Sloane Yard Mews. The three men went into the kitchen to talk out of the King's hearing.

Mayhew made no comment about Douglas's conversation with Sir Robert Benson. He leaned forward, holding his hands to the heat of the stove, and rubbing them together. He waited until Douglas had completed his story and then he said, 'They must have found the ambulance a few minutes after you abandoned it. The Constable on the beat reported it, and the police station told Scotland Yard. General Kellerman put it on the teleprinters immediately. A stolen ambulance, it said, no explanation of why or where or when. But it meant that the London Feldgendarmerie had it in writing. That in turn meant that the GFP, and finally the Abwehr, had to cover their backsides.'

'Which is what Kellerman wanted,' said Douglas.

'Yes, he must have guessed what was really happening. It was a brilliant piece of deduction.'

'Or a well-placed informant,' said Douglas. Harry poured tea.

'Yes, we can't rule that out,' said Mayhew. 'Is this my tea? Thank you Harry. Is His Majesty still dozing?'

'He's been like that since we collected him,' said Harry. 'I think we should have a doctor look at him.'

Mayhew nodded, drank his tea and pushed the King to the back of his mind. 'Yes, it forced the army's hand. They had no choice but to respond to the Scotland Yard teleprinter messages.'

'What happened?'

'Grossfahndung,' said Mayhew. 'The whole works; the King escaped this morning, the vehicle has been found abandoned in Central London. Confidential to Divisions, for the time being, but they won't be able to keep the lid on this one for very long.'

'Names?'

'No names so far.'

'Grossfahndung,' said Harry. 'What is it?'

'The highest category of search,' said Douglas. 'Alerts to all departments of the armed forces, police, security units, auxiliary police units, docks, airports and railways police, SS, training camps, DAF, RAD, Hitler Youth, Uncle Tom Cobley and all.'

'Grossfahndung,' said Harry.

'Kriegsfahndung for one hour,' said Mayhew. 'It changed status at one-thirty.'

'I was in the Reform Club with Sir Robert.'

'Well, something happened to make them change their mind.' Mayhew finished the hot tea and got to his feet. 'I think we must get you all out of here. Eventually they will check all aliens' addresses, including Miss Barga's. My car is outside.'

'Do you think we could take one of Miss Barga's blankets?' Harry asked Douglas. 'For the King.'

'The spare bedroom is upstairs,' said Douglas. 'Take one.'

'Kellerman is the unpredictable factor,' said Mayhew. 'At present he believes that you and Harry are totally loyal to him: you because the Resistance have tried to kill you, Harry because he's frightened to death of being re-arrested. But how long that confidence will last no one can be sure. Sooner or later your absence will be noted and they will suspect you are not away working for Huth, but away working with us.'

Douglas nodded. From overhead there came the sound of Harry having trouble with the bedroom door. Douglas was about to tell him that door sometimes jammed but decided against revealing how knowledgeable he was about the bedrooms. There was the sound of Harry moving a heavy weight and Douglas wondered if he was taking extra blankets from a suitcase in the cupboard. Then Harry came down the stairs. It was a short flight of stairs and Harry came down them so fast that he almost fell into the sitting-room.

'Easy there, Sergeant,' said Mayhew, holding his arm to steady him.

'What is it, Harry?'

'Miss Barga,' said Harry.

Douglas looked at him for a moment before he realized what he meant. He pushed past Harry to get to the stairs. But Harry was too quick for him. 'Stay here, Doug . . . listen to me a minute.' He clasped Douglas in a bear hug, and try as he did there was no escaping from this huge man. 'Don't . . . bloody . . . go up there, I say.' Harry was panting with the exertion of holding him.

'All right,' said Douglas the breath almost squeezed out of him.

Harry released him. 'She's upstairs, Douglas. She's dead; I'm sorry.'

Douglas felt giddy.

'Sit down a minute, Archer,' said Mayhew.

But Douglas remained standing. For a moment he thought he would faint but he reached for the panelled door and supported himself. 'You're sure?'

'Yes, I'm sure, Doug.'

'How?'

'She's been knocked about. It's better you don't go upstairs. Looks like she disturbed a burglar and he hit her harder than he meant to.'

'Burglar!' said Douglas. He heard his own voice disembodied and far away. He saw the faces of the two men, stretched, tight flesh across their cheek bones, eyes staring at him. 'Badly knocked about? Poor Barbara.'

'We'd better leave right away,' said Mayhew. 'Get the King, Harry.'

'And we were sitting here drinking tea,' said Douglas. 'While she was . . .'

'For God's sake pull yourself together, Archer. It's terrible for you, I know. But there is no time for grief.'

Douglas blew his nose and then poured the last of the warm tea into a cup and drank it down with plenty of sugar. My God, he thought, the number of times he'd fed hot sweet tea to grieving relatives during his time as a policeman. 'You're right,' he said.

'That's more like it,' said Mayhew.

'My son,' said Douglas. 'I'm worried about him.'

'Leave that to me,' said Mayhew. 'Whatever happens, your son will be cared for, that I can promise you.'

'Ready to go,' called Harry from the other room.

'We're a little behind schedule,' said Mayhew. 'But everyone, all along the line, will be waiting for you. They are specially selected men. There will be no slip-ups.'

'How soon will the Germans be forced to make it public?' Harry asked.

'The King's escape?' said Mayhew. He sniffed and stared at the door as he thought about it. 'Midnight tonight at the earliest . . . noon tomorrow at the latest. I can't believe they'll leave it later than that, or rumours will be circulating all over Britain.'

'How will your Abwehr friends explain why it wasn't put on the BBC news as soon as they knew?'

'They'll say they were hoping to recapture him,' he smiled. 'Capture him before the news of his escape became headlines in the newspapers of the neutral countries. But now that Kellerman has let the cat out of the bag, Berlin will be demanding a scapegoat.'

'And the army will be offering Kellerman as the scape-goat?' said Douglas.

'That's the betting in Whitehall, but Kellerman has a reputation for romping home against the odds.'

'How far will we have to take the King?' Harry asked.

'All the way, I'm afraid,' said Mayhew. 'We're running six hours late. My people have no curfew passes, and their travel papers will be out of date at midnight. Your police passes will get you through.'

'Until Kellerman puts our names on the teleprinters,' said Harry.

'Now that doesn't sound like the Harry I used to know,' said Mayhew. 'If Scotland Yard adds your names to the Situation Report I'll hear immediately.'

'Unless they send it straight to the BBC, for the news bulletin,' said Harry.

'That's right,' said Mayhew cheerfully. 'Now let's clean the fingerprints off these cups, and so on, and get going. My car is quite close by. Did you leave any prints upstairs, Harry?'

'I'll see to it,' said Harry.

'It will be bloody cold where we're going, Archer,' Mayhew promised. 'That raincoat's not warm enough. I have a duffel coat in the car.' Mayhew consulted his pocket watch. 'Ready, Harry?' he called.

Douglas said, 'Can you warn the people at the other end that we're running a few hours late?'

Mayhew gave a brief smile. 'You're going to meet some more Americans, Archer. They've come a long way, and they've chosen a night that will give them low tide at twilight, with a forecast of a calm sea and a full moon. By tomorrow's dawn they'll be gone – with or without the King.'

374

Chapter Thirty-Seven

'This is Bringle Sands.' The accent was unmistakably that of Boston, Massachusetts. The US Marine Corps Captain tapped the map, so that the transparent protective covering flashed in the light of the yellow bulbs. 'Your boats will hit the beach at dusk. The tide condition will be low enough to expose fully any underwater obstacles. You Marines will be crossing about three hundred yards of tidal flat . . .' he hurried on with the briefing, lest his audience dwelled too much upon that danger. '. . . But it gives the engineers a chance to clear and mark a lane. And it also means that, at high-water, the boats will be coming in real close to pick you up.'

He looked at the men, packed tightly together on the metal folding chairs so incongruous in the seventeenth-century style gold and white panelling that the French Line had chosen for their passenger ships. He turned and touched the map of the Devon coastline but the men had eyes only for their Captain's face, trying to see there some pre-knowledge or premonition of success or disaster. The mouth of the River Frane, Exeter, Yorkshire, Timbuktu; it made no difference to them, these were just forgotten names out of schoolbooks. Most of these Marines were farm boys from America's mid-west with no ambition to see Europe. The lawyers had insisted upon them all being discharged from the USMC and re-enlisted (as Canadians) in the British service. To support this deception, they wore small Union-Jack badges on the sleeves of their uniform jackets, but a wise decision of the Marine

Corps planners had enabled them to keep their Browning automatic rifles.

An Englishman – Major Albert Dodgson – left the briefing room, nodding to the armed sentry at the door. He'd heard it all before. In fact he'd helped to write that part of it that described the countryside behind Bringle Sands, so near to his parents' home.

Major Dodgson had been attached to the 1st Marine Division, at its base at Quantico, Virginia, ever since it was first alerted for an amphibious attack upon the French island of Martinique (just after that French colony declared itself loyal to the pro-Nazi government of Vichy). By the time President Roosevelt had authorized this armed raid on Bringle Sands, these Marines – with their amphibious assault training and specially designed landing craft – were the only men who could do it.

Dodgson made his way along the dimly-lit passage. One of the turbo-generators had failed for the third time. With only 2,000 kilowatts, the ship was reduced to emergency lighting and one hot meal a day. Thank goodness the ship's heating came from auxiliary boilers and so was not affected. They'd been at sea twelve long, cold, winter days. Even when this liner was launched in 1931, it had taken her seven days to cross the Atlantic. Now the 'tween deck space forward, designed for cars and general cargo, held two large landing craft. Another two LCMs were fitted into what had once been the aft cargo hold and twenty thousand cubic feet of refrigerated space. And inside each of the landing craft there was a curious hybrid vehicle; front-half heavy truck, and rear-half tank. And inside two of these newly invented M.3 half-tracks, there was a piece of machinery designed and built in the Marines' engineering workshops at Quantico. There, a month earlier, a demonstration had proved that the 'iron maiden' could rip the back from even the strongest German filing cabinet in under ten minutes. Without damaging the papers inside.

Major Dodgson was not a Marine. He'd won his DSO with the Royal West Kents in France in 1940. He'd always hated the sea and this voyage had done nothing to lessen that prejudice. He could not adapt himself to the ceaseless movement, to the cramped accommodation that gave him mild feelings of claustrophobia, and to the loud metallic groans and rumbles that came from the bowels of the ship. But most of all he hated the vibration. One of the screws had been slightly damaged in the first day at sea, and the ship had not been still since. Now, as he made his way up to A deck, and what had once been the cabin-class promenade, the great white marble staircase shuddered underfoot.

It took Dodgson several minutes before he could discern, through the heavy rain, the dark shapes of the other ships. They were wallowing along with no more than stationkeeping lights to prick the grey overcast sky that pressed down upon the smoke from their funnels. He found the other American officers exactly where he'd left them, staring through the wet windows. There was a smell of cigar smoke.

'Have they nearly finished the briefing?' asked Captain Waley, who would be in the first landing craft. Like most of them he was a regular officer. He'd been integrated into the Corps from the Reserve, and frequently complained that he'd have been a Major by now, except that his group had been given seniority in alphabetical order. Waley's task was to join a party of British Resistance men, who would take them by a specially prepared route across country to the Research Establishment. Three of the half-tracks would be under his command. His orders were to take the Establishment, and hold it until a man called Ruysdale told him to retire or until his entire force

377

was eliminated. No one who knew Waley doubted that the order would be interpreted quite literally. Significantly, every man in Waley's party had filled out and signed the printed Last Will and Testament forms that had been given to them.

'Can you spare me a cigar, Jakie?' Dodgson asked Hoge, an officer who was reputed never to be without a pocketful of them.

'Sure thing,' said Hoge. Dodgson got along well with the Americans. His experience fighting the Germans had won him respect; his modesty and some calamitous encounters with Virginia's high society, had won him their friendship. 'Seems to me,' said Hoge in the Alabama drawl that, in his cups, Dodgson tried to mimic, 'that these here Krauts have got to be plumb crazy to have this secret laboratory near the sea-shore.'

Hoge and Dodgson would be together in the diversionary attack, calculated to draw the Germans away from the Research Establishment, while the main force attacked it from the other side.

'Unless the sons of bitches have relocated it to somewhere safer,' said Waley, voicing a fear that was an echo of those in Washington.

Then the last of the group spoke. He was much older than the others, a small, awkward, unsoldierly man, with a harsh German accent. 'An atomic reactor, of the sort they will have built, needs water, lots and lots of water.'

'Wouldn't a river do?' asked Dodgson.

'The re-circulated water will contain radio-active material,' said the German. 'It would not be safe to release it into a river.' The others nodded. He was the only one of them who understood the real purpose of their unprovoked aggression. His papers described him as Lieutenant Ruysdale, a Canadian citizen of Dutch descent, but no one knew his real name. The others

378

usually called him 'Professor'. All they'd been told about him was that, after Waley captured the Research Establishment, Ruysdale would be giving him his orders about which filing cabinets got the embrace of the 'iron maiden', and which documents, what material and which people were to be put into the half-tracks and taken back to the ships; with or without consent.

'Professor,' said Waley without turning away from the rain-splashed windows of the promenade, 'they say that Hitler could knock out the USA with this brass-knuckle we are going to snatch out of his glove. Is that the truth, Professor?'

The others did not look at him, but Ruysdale knew it was the question to which every man on the ships needed an answer. 'It's true, my friends,' he said. But even to him, who'd stood alongside the great Otto Hahn at the Kaiser Wilhelm Institute for Chemistry that day just before Christmas 1938 when he realized that he'd split the nucleus of the uranium atom into two, even to him the promised destructive power of an atomic explosion was scarcely conceivable. The man they called Ruysdale wanted to tell them that this was a mission for which it was worth-while sacrificing their lives, but he'd learned that Americans do not welcome such speeches. Instead he accepted one of Hoge's cigars and said, 'What time are they showing that Betty Grable movie?'

'Two-thirty,' said Waley. It would bring them right up to the time when they must prepare for the landing, unless they encountered German naval forces first.

Now all the men looked through the windows and watched the other transport. That too had once been a ship of the French Line, carrying 643 cabin-class passengers between Le Havre and New York in considerable luxury. But she had none of the jumbo derricks that were needed to take the weight of the four big landing craft.

379

She had only the Assault Landing Craft, small enough to be suspended from the regulation 99-person lifeboat davits. But most of these LCAs had been damaged by the mountainous seas of their Atlantic crossing. The new plan used only two of them. After Waley and his main force were landed, the four LCMs would have to return to the second transport to get the second wave of men, who would move up through the beach parties to deliver the diversionary attack.

Ruysdale had the mind of a scientist rather than that of a soldier, and he found it difficult to reconcile himself to the fact that there would be only half as many places on the landing craft as there were men in the assault force.

Chapter Thirty-eight

You can see Bringle Sands, and the mouth of the River Frane, from the very edge of the steep cliffs. The wind off the sea cripples the scrub, stunts the trees and erodes the cliff face, so that the narrow footpath down to the sea-shore is marked with danger signs.

Half a mile inland there is the railway line. It comes through gently rolling farmland from Bringle and Bringle Sands to Frane Halt before joining the main line and continuing eastwards to Exeter and on to London.

But the men in the railway signal box could see nothing beyond the reflections of the shiny levers and the instruments, and the flickering of the coal fire. The King was stretched out on a folding bed, Harry Woods was demonstrating his ability to sleep standing up, and Danny Barga was sitting in the corner, hands clasped round his knees and head slumped forward.

'Tea?' said the signalman quietly to Mayhew and Douglas. He'd already perched a dented tin kettle on the embers of the coal fire. Douglas nodded his thanks and moved aside as the man placed more coal there.

'It falls off the wagons,' said the man, nodding at the bucket of coal. He was a small, narrow-chested man with a pale face and lank brown hair. It was surprising to see the effortless way in which he pulled the huge signal levers almost as tall as he was. Like so many other veterans of the first war, he'd sewn medal ribbons on the front of his black serge railwayman's jacket; 'mutt and jeff' War Medal and Victory Medal. There was a forlorn defiance in wearing them.

'What's the damned time?' said Mayhew sleepily, too tired to unbutton his overcoat and consult his gold pocket-watch. But before anyone answered he twisted round to get a look at the railway clock that was fixed over the big windows.

'You should try and get some sleep, Colonel,' said the signalman. For a moment Douglas thought that the man had recognized Mayhew, but then he realized that this was no more than the way that many ex-servicemen addressed well-spoken strangers.

Mayhew's reply was interrupted by the sudden sound of the bell-signal: two rings, a pause, two rings. The signalman reached across and repeated the signal on the plunger under the block instruments. He grinned at Mayhew. 'Don't be alarmed, governor. It's a light engine coming down the line. That will be old Bob Swanick, he was driving the train I stopped to get you off.' He set the block instrument to the line-clear position, so that this would show in the next signal box along the line.

The kettle on the fire began to sing gently. He warmed an old brown teapot, and opened the door to throw the water into the chill wind that was roaring outside. 'It's bloody cold tonight,' he said.

'I've never been so cold,' said Mayhew, pulling the collar of his trench-coat up round his neck.

'You should have been with me in 1915 then,' said the signalman. 'Plugstreet, that second Christmas of the war. Real brass-monkey weather that was!'

The bell rang twice. The signalman answered with a double ring and set the instrument to 'train on line'. 'He's passed Charlie's box,' he said. 'If he's got any of your people on board he'll stop here by the box.'

Mayhew got to his feet and pressed his face to the windows, but saw no more than the lights of the railway signals.

'Royal Scots Fusiliers,' said the signalman.

'I beg your pardon?' mumbled Mayhew without looking round.

'Sixth battalion Royal Scots Fusiliers. We had Winnie as the battalion commander at one time.'

Mayhew grunted. He had his hands cupped round his face to see the locomotive. Suddenly they heard the noise of it above the screams of the wind. It passed, leaving a shower of sparks and an acrid smell of smoke. Mayhew bit his lip and looked again at the clock. The signalman hit the plunger a couple of rings, on his way to pouring water into the teapot. 'So what mob were you with?' said the signalman.

Mayhew turned to look at him stirring the tea in the brown pot. The signalman stared back at Mayhew. 'You *were* in the war?'

'Oh, yes,' said Mayhew carefully. 'I was in the ninety-ninth Württemberg Regiment, and my friend here was on Kaiser Wilhelm's personal staff.'

Embarrassed by Mayhew's harsh sarcasm, Douglas said, 'It's good of you to spare some of your tea ration.'

'I like a joke,' said the signalman as if in reply to Douglas's unspoken apology. He busied himself with the teapot and then turned to Mayhew. 'We should have polished off all you bloody Württembergers in 1918,' he said, 'and we wouldn't be in the bloody mess we're in today.'

The two men stared at each other, than Mayhew laughed. 'Too right, old son,' he said and put his hand on the signalman's shoulder.

'Sergeant Major's tea,' said the signalman. 'Lots of tinned milk and so much sugar you can stand the spoon up in it.'

'Can I have mine black without sugar?' said Douglas.

'Certainly, chum,' said the signalman with that quiet

friendliness with which Englishmen address foreigners and lunatics. 'If that's the way you like it.' He looked at the heavy coat that Mayhew had loaned to Douglas, and decided that he must have served in the Royal Navy. The warmth of the fire brought a curious odour from the fabric. Perhaps the signalman could smell it too, a pungent spicy perfume. Douglas wondered where the coat could have been to have picked up such a smell.

The brewing of the tea, and its attendant rituals, took five minutes that were otherwise only punctuated by the bells and signals of a goods train passing down the line.

'Fifty different bells there are,' said the signalman proudly. He handed Mayhew the best china mug – King George V Silver Jubilee 1935 – and the pilgrim-pattern spoon. 'More like seventy now that the Huns are here.'

'Twenty more?' said Mayhew politely.

'That's how we keep tabs on what they are, and where they are; military patrols coming down the track, ammunition trains supply the coastal batteries . . .'

'Or coal trains . . .' said Mayhew archly. They were friends now, these two old soldiers, and Douglas was not of their world.

'They get stopped at every section,' said the signalman with a grin, 'while the boys help themselves to a bucket or two.' He handed Douglas his black tea in a chipped enamel mug. 'You should see the sacks of it that Charlie takes down to the village. Of course Charlie's new, he's only a Leading Porter Temporary Signalman.'

Mayhew nodded sagely at the revelation about Charlie being only a Leading Porter. 'Your tea all right, chief?' the signalman asked Douglas.

'Very nice,' said Douglas. Suddenly there was the creak of the steep wooden steps and the cold draught that came with the opening of the door. The coal fire roared as it fed on the cold air. Mayhew and Douglas were visibly

384

startled. The signalman laughed. 'Don't worry. It's only Sid. He knows I make tea about this time.' To the newcomer he said, 'You smell the tea, don't you Sid?'

Sid was a broad-shouldered man with unnaturally black hair and a carefully trimmed moustache. He wore a railway peaked cap and black uniform overcoat that had been neatly patched at the elbow and hem. He looked round at the folding bed where the King slept, the upright Harry, his heavy breathing nasal enough to show that he was asleep, and the slumped form of Danny Barga. 'Quite a crowd in here tonight,' he said. He took the offered cup of tea after placing his peaked cap on the mantelshelf with a genteel care that was probably in deference to the presence of well-dressed visitors. He nodded to Douglas and Mayhew, and warmed his hands round the mug of tea.

To Mayhew the newcomer said, 'In this matter of football, sir. What takes your fancy, Wolverhampton Wanderers?'

Mayhew looked at him for a moment without speaking. The signalman watched both men. Mayhew said, 'Woolworth's versus Wolverhampton Wanderers, you mean? Woolworth's every time, my dear chap. What varlet would vote Wolves when Woollies will walk away with it?'

Sid laughed. It was a common type of challenge. Few Germans could pronounce Wolverhampton Wanderers without one of the 'w' sounds becoming a 'v'. Mayhew's improved tongue-twister removed Sid's caution, although he might have been alarmed to hear how many Germans, in the more sophisticated echelons of the occupation army in London, could have passed his test with flying colours. Sid sat down on a box and took off his rubber boots.

'Well?' said Mayhew impatiently.

'Boats have been coming and going from the beach,

near the river mouth. Special boats . . . landing craft, by the description. No one can get down there without being fired at.' He looked at the two men to make the most of his dramatic news. Harry Woods and Danny Barga were awake and listening. 'One of the porters said he heard machine-gun fire – lots of machine-gun fire – at that German army camp at Bringle Sands.'

Mayhew exchanged a glance with Douglas, and was relieved to know that the raiders had found their objective.

'Lots of machine-gun fire,' said Sid again. 'He tried to come round by the main road, but the Germans turned him back. There's an unexploded bomb there somewhere.'

'No, they're our people,' said Mayhew. 'A chap in policeman's uniform and a couple of men in army uniforms. It's a way of closing the road. The firing is probably automatic-rifle fire; to the civilian it would sound like machine-guns.'

'You won't be able to stop the German reinforcements with a bobby and a couple of fellows dressed as German soldiers,' said Sid, as though irritated at the way the porter had been fooled by the impostors.

'Of course they won't,' said Mayhew. 'There are other plans to deal with reinforcements. But the check-point will be enough to halt them while our bombing teams go in.'

'People have been killed in Bringle; women, children and old people, as well as Germans.' Sid kneaded his cold feet.

'Don't go spreading that sort of story,' said Mayhew. 'You know as well as I do that the curfew keeps everyone indoors. Is this another story from your railway porter?'

'He went down on his bicycle.'

'You'd better make sure he learns to keep his mouth

shut,' said Mayhew. 'Or I'll start thinking he's playing the German game. Now what about Frane Halt?'

'The American soldiers are there,' said Sid. 'Only half a dozen of them. They've got an armoured car . . . a funny-looking thing, a sort of tank with wheels at the front. They must have brought it off the boat. Some of the soldiers are walking down the railway line. They are coming this way. That's what I wanted to tell you.'

'Harry,' said Mayhew, 'you're in charge here. None of these people may leave. Archer and I will go down to meet the Americans.' Danny Barga glared at Mayhew but didn't object. His twisted ankle still troubled him.

Douglas and Mayhew were only a few minutes' walk along the railway when they caught sight of the soldiers. 'Halt!' shouted Mayhew.

'Teddy Bears!' challenged one of the soldiers.

'Picnic,' replied Mayhew.

'I'm Major Dodgson,' said the tallest of the three soldiers. From the direction of Bringle Sands there came three flashes that lit the horizon. No sooner had the third flash appeared than three explosions rumbled across the dark fields.

'Colonel Mayhew,' said Mayhew.

'We're about ready for you now, Colonel. Where is the King?'

'He's in the signal box just a few hundred yards down the line.'

'Then let's get going,' said Dodgson.

Mayhew put his hand on Dodgson's arm. 'There's something you'd better know, Major. The King can't walk.'

'Can't what?' said Dodgson.

'The King is a sick man, Major. You'll have to get a vehicle.'

'No, the plan is to take him down this side of the river.

387

It's a steep footpath. No vehicle could get down there.'
There were more flashes and more explosions.

'Then get two of your heftiest lads to carry him.'

Colonel Mayhew turned back towards the signal box.

'Yes, that will be the only way,' said Dodgson.

Suddenly there was the sound of distant shooting, and
a couple of flares lit the sky over Bringle Sands. 'It will
have to be you,' Major Dodgson told the two soldiers
with him. 'The withdrawal of the main party must have
started earlier than planned. It will be very unhealthy
along this route in another fifteen or twenty minutes. We
must hurry.'

Douglas had never seen a battle before and he was ill-
prepared for the confusion and the disorientation. During
the first exchanges of fire, both sides had been sparing in
the use of ammunition. But now, as the raiders withdrew
to their boats, they fired longer bursts and the black night
was punctuated with explosions as the bombing parties
went into action, destroying vital equipment in the
laboratories.

The two soldiers carrying the King stopped and half
fell into the spongy field as a burst of tracer fire whipped
across their heads. They remained still only long enough
to snatch a few breaths, and then grabbed the King and
began looking for the tapes that marked the precipitous
track down the steep bluff. Douglas was immediately
behind them. He heard the man at the cliff edge yell,
'Hurry it up, you guys. The boats are waiting. This way,
this way.'

Douglas looked for Harry. He was carrying the torch
he'd carefully shielded with red paper and was close
behind. 'Douglas,' he said, 'not so fast, I can't keep up.'

'Too much smoking, Harry,' said Douglas, although he
too was almost out of breath, and pleased at the chance
to stop for a moment.

The flares were exploding continuously, crackling and spitting in the sky as they hung in the black void. Twice Germans on the other side of the river had tried to illuminate the scene with mobile searchlights but each time someone had shot out the arcs, and the personnel too, with a burst of automatic-rifle fire. Now the light flickered on again. Douglas wondered that men could be so brave or so foolhardy.

'Hurry up, you guys,' said the same voice from the darkness.

Now the searchlight was turned this way, a blinding glare that frosted the grass and made delicate haloes on the warped trees and bushes. From somewhere down the track shots were fired, but it wasn't easy to handle the big automatic rifles while balancing on the muddy path that was in places polished away by the rain and wind. Douglas heard a shout and a cry as some unfortunate lost his toe-hold and slid down the rocky slope, bludgeoned by his equipment and strangled by its straps.

'I've twisted my foot,' said Harry. The searchlight left them in darkness as its beam moved down to illuminate the cliff path.

It was at that moment that Douglas realized that the voice calling 'Hurry up, you guys' was a German one. It was the voice of Standartenführer Huth. Before he could call a warning, a fusillade began. The noise of it hurt his ears, and he felt vibration under his feet as the bullets ripped into the earth, slashed the vegetation and shrieked through the wet air.

The soldiers' cries were audible over the sounds of the guns, but the noise grew louder until the bullets were detonating so fast that it seemed to be one long roar of explosive.

'Come back, Douglas.' It was Harry's voice.

Douglas saw the light sweep across the King and the

two men carrying him. They disappeared into a cloud of flying earth clods, as the machine-guns followed the beam of light. Douglas ran forward but he was downed by a flying tackle that knocked all the air out of his lungs. By the time he'd recovered it was all over. Bodies were strewn in every direction. The Germans had timed it to perfection; not more than a half-dozen men of this party of raiders had got down to the sea in safety. The mangled bodies of two dozen or more of their companions marked the pathway. Among the dead were Major Dodgson, Danny Barga and King George the Sixth, Emperor of India.

Chapter Thirty-nine

When daylight came, one of the landing craft was still on the beach, its loading ramp twisted round the armoured car that had been blown up at the very moment of embarkation. Bodies floated gently in the oily sea and others made contorted shapes on the sand. Everywhere there was the debris of war: steel helmets, life-jackets, ropes, a rifle and hundreds of brass cartridge cases gleaming in the early light.

At the German army's Research Establishment at Bringle Sands, the three laboratory buildings were blackened shells, still being hosed down by the army's fire-fighters. Its medical department was crowded to overflowing as the only surgeon there worked without stopping, and the ambulances provided a shuttle service to the German hospital at Exeter.

Swift retribution had come to the civil population of the district. By eight-thirty the following morning, twenty-seven local men had been shot for assisting the enemy, or failing to account for their movements over the previous twenty-four-hour period. Another hundred-and-sixty-two persons had been moved to a compound near Newton Abbot, the first stage of a journey that would take them to forced labour camps in Germany.

The raiding force suffered nearly 30 per cent casualties and half of those were fatal. But the Marines had done their job well. Guided by a Resistance team, who had studied the Bringle Sands Research Establishment for weeks, they took possession of the whole place after only twenty-five minutes of fighting. Under Ruysdale's instructions they demolished the most vital buildings and equipment, and carried away a heavy load of paperwork in their half-track vehicles.

Now a German scientific team were checking the ruins for radio-activity while burial parties were removing the dead. There were no prisoners to interrogate, as even the badly wounded had been taken back to the ships. Waley was dead, killed in the mortar attack that came near the end, just before the Marines withdrew. Major Dodgson was killed in Huth's carefully arranged ambush, but his friend Hoge came through without a scratch and boarded the last landing craft with a lighted cigar in his mouth. The man they called Ruysdale had found himself curiously unmoved by the fighting and unafraid. He did his job calmly, and took his time inspecting the laboratories. He, too, was on the last landing craft to leave. With him was the aged Professor Frick. The two men had met before, at the Institute of Theoretical Physics in Copenhagen.

Douglas Archer spent those early-morning hours in a small uncomfortable cell under a Feldgendarmerie barracks in Bringle Sands. It was very cold and he was grateful for the heavy overcoat Mayhew had loaned him. It was about eight o'clock the next morning when the noise of the bolts being withdrawn awakened him. Into the cell came General Kellerman. He was dressed in SS uniform, complete with double-breasted overcoat and sword. He swept into the tiny cell like a replete bird of prey, greeting Douglas with a cheery 'good morning', scratching his pink, newly-shaven chin, and bringing a strong smell of cologne.

'Of course,' said Kellerman, 'when I heard that you were in custody I almost – please forgive me – I almost laughed. "You *Dummkopf*," I said, "you've arrested one of my finest officers."'

'But they didn't release me,' said Douglas.

'No,' said Kellerman, quite undismayed by Douglas's unappreciative demeanour. 'They needed me to provide them with a positive identification.'

'Can I have something to eat?'

Kellerman stepped outside the door of the cell. 'Coffee and breakfast for this officer,' Kellerman told the young SS man standing at attention in the corridor. He brought a tray of food so fast that Douglas suspected Kellerman had arranged the whole thing beforehand, but one could never be quite certain with Kellerman.

'Your friend Sergeant Woods was not detained,' said Kellerman.

'He sent me a message,' said Douglas.

'You've probably got Sergeant Woods to thank for saving your life,' said Kellerman. He bent over, sniffed at the coffee and pulled a face.

'He knocked me down when the shooting began,' said Douglas. Kellerman looked at him for a long time as if trying to see something in Douglas's eyes, but then he nodded and said, 'Exactly.'

'And Standartenführer Huth has been arrested,' said Douglas.

'You seem to know a great deal,' said Kellerman.

'No,' said Douglas. 'Only what Harry Woods told me when he tried to get me released this morning.'

'I grieve for his parents,' said Kellerman suddenly. 'Professor Huth, the Standartenführer's father, is a most respected scholar.'

'But why?' Douglas drank his coffee.

'Ah, you did not see what was going on, my dear Superintendent. You are a fine and loyal officer, and no blame could ever attach to you – certainly not in any police force that I commanded.' Kellerman smiled. When he was quite certain that the implication of this remark was not lost on Douglas, Kellerman continued, 'The

393

Standartenführer seemed to be carrying on some perverted crusade against the German army. I do believe he resented the powers the army acquired when martial law was declared.' Kellerman said this as if he found it very difficult to understand such resentment.

'Really?' said Douglas who interpreted it to mean that the army and Kellerman had conspired against Huth. 'What form did this perverted crusade take, sir?'

'He openly assisted your friend, Colonel Mayhew, in a conspiracy that released your King from custody in the Tower of London. Also in this terrorist raid, with the tragic consequences that you witnessed. I can understand, and sympathize with, your Colonel Mayhew, who was obviously motivated by feelings of patriotism and loyalty towards his King.' Nervously Kellerman smoothed his tunic. 'Very commendable,' he nodded. 'But I found it difficult to say anything in defence of Standartenführer Huth's part in this disgraceful plot.'

'Can you be certain that he was implicated?'

'When something like this happens . . . something that could bring dishonour to the whole Wehrmacht, it becomes necessary to adopt special measures. Therefore Colonel Mayhew was offered a free pardon in return for complete co-operation with the court.' General Kellerman ran his fingers down the highly polished leather shoulder-strap, and touched the hilt of his sword, to be sure everything was in the right place. 'The tragic death of his sovereign was what decided Colonel Mayhew, of course.'

'Of course,' said Douglas. The two men exchanged smiles; Douglas a tired and melancholy one, Kellerman's relaxed and confident. So Mayhew bought his freedom in exchange for helping Kellerman and the army to get rid of Huth. Or was that just the way they wanted it to look. 'Will Standartenführer Huth be sent for trial?'

'It's all over,' said General Kellerman. He sighed and

patted his sword so that it rattled in the scabbard. 'A flying field tribunal arrived within an hour of the last shots being fired. Colonel Mayhew gave evidence immediately. Standartenführer Huth was sentenced to death. He'll be executed some time this morning.'

Douglas felt sick. He poured hot water into the remains of his coffee and drank it.

'No need for you to worry,' said Kellerman. 'You were tried by the court *absente reo*. Needless to say, you were cleared. It's better settled that way. A man is seldom asked to face the same charge twice.' Douglas noted that he'd not said that such double jeopardy was impossible.

'Thank you, sir,' said Douglas.

'Standartenführer Huth has requested a chance to talk with you, Archer. In spite of my feelings about his conduct, I can't help feeling sorry for the poor wretch. You'll go of course?'

'If you permit it,' said Douglas.

'In the circumstances I think it will do no harm,' said Kellerman.

'I imagine you will want to eavesdrop on what is said?'

'There is no such thing as a free meal, Archer. I'm sure you are familiar with that proverb.' Kellerman smiled but this time he didn't bother to make it warm and friendly.

Chapter Forty

They'd given Standartenführer Huth a suite in the block reserved for high-ranking visitors to the Research Establishment. His last hours were spent in comfort. There was a bottle of brandy on the sideboard and an untouched breakfast tray with silver jugs, fine German porcelain and white sugar.

'So Kellerman let you come?'

'Yes, Standartenführer.'

Through the window, Douglas could see the burned-out laboratory. There was enough wind to bring charred pieces of paper up to the window before sending them whirling back across the churned-up grass and tangling them into the barbed wire.

'The army has decided to close down its atomic research programme,' said Huth. 'Did you know that?'

'It's what you wanted.'

'But not like this. No one in Berlin supports it, and the Reichsführer will not allow the SS to continue the work. The Americans will make the bomb . . . and win the war that will begin the moment they are ready. We Germans are a short-sighted race, Archer. The German army is already beginning to think that last night's raid was a blessing in disguise.'

'Why can they think that?'

Huth pointed to the window and the ruined buildings. 'That raid will enable the army to keep its martial law for at least a year. God knows how many million Reichsmarks will be given to the army, to prepare defences against another raid. Oh, the Abwehr will be delighted, and what's more they have General Kellerman in their pocket.'

Huth walked over to the sideboard and opened a bottle of brandy. 'And Kellerman will be delighted too,' he continued. 'He'll keep his job, get rid of me and be entirely safe from any charges connected with his financial dealings.' Huth smiled. He guessed that the conversation was being recorded. But whether it was on disc or the newer sort of wire record, it would be impossible now for Kellerman to use it in evidence without risk to himself, or tampering with it in some way that would be immediately apparent. 'Kellerman will have me as a scapegoat,' said Huth. 'Any unsolved crimes, swindles or failures will be put down to my account. He was even trying to prove that I had a hand in the Highgate explosion. Have a drink?'

'Thank you, sir.'

'No need of courtesies any more.' Huth passed him a large measure of brandy. 'We were all playing for high stakes. Kellerman won, so did Mayhew. You'll not hear me whining about it.'

'Mayhew?'

'He promised me the earth. It's his style; flattery and promises, eh?' He dropped into an armchair and drank greedily.

'Yes, that's his style.'

'He told me about the attack, helped me plan the ambush even.'

'I can't believe it!' said Douglas.

'Oh yes. He helped me intercept the diversionary attack. I fell for it. But while we were fighting, his main force went cross-country with their half-tracks and knocked out the Research Establishment.'

'The diversionary attack was virtually wiped out,' said Douglas, aghast at the enormity of it.

'Mayhew was determined to get those Americans into combat,' said Huth. 'He had Dr Spode murdered and all his papers destroyed because Dr Spode wanted to take them to the US Embassy. You gave him a film and he burned it. He didn't want the *Amis* to get the research except by fighting us, because that would get them into the idea of fighting a real war. Only in the matter of the King did Mayhew go wrong.' Huth shrugged. 'But we all make a mistake occasionally.' He smiled in grim self-mockery.

'The King was killed.'

'Mayhew should have had more confidence in his own plan. Originally he was going to send the King to meet up with the main force. They had the half-tracks for the documents. The King could have gone in one of those.'

'Yes, of course,' said Douglas, although he was now coming to the terrible conclusion that Mayhew had not planned anything of the kind. Mayhew had deliberately sent the King by the cliff path, knowing that Huth's men were in ambush there. It was Mayhew playing God. It was Mayhew writing the future history books. It was Mayhew making sure that the King died in battle alongside his American allies. Far better that, than an infirm and pathetic exile King in Washington, butt of the cartoonists' cruelty, darling of the hostesses and constant reminder of the infirm and pathetic Britain occupied by the victorious Germans. Yes, now Douglas began to understand the way that a politician's mind worked. No doubt the Queen and the Princesses were already on their way to Washington DC.

'You are lucky, Archer,' said Huth.

'To escape with my life?'

Huth shook his head. 'No. There was never any doubt that you would escape with your life. That was all decided long ago.'

'Decided? Decided when? By whom?'

'When Harry Woods agreed to be Kellerman's inform-ant, telling him every move you made, every meeting that took place, reporting every word to which he could get access.'

'Harry Woods? My Harry?'

'Woods phoned Kellerman about the ambulance as soon as you'd disappeared into the Reform Club. Keller-man tackled the Abwehr, and pretended he knew what they were up to. That's how he got his men here just as the raiders were withdrawing. Not while the fighting was on, you'll notice. Kellerman didn't want the raid repulsed, he wanted it to be a success. After that he moved in quickly with his flying field tribunal, and their execution squad . . . over there eating breakfast in the mess hall. They've had a busy morning, you know. Their shoulders must be bruised by now.'

'When? When did Harry do it?'

Huth sighed. 'When he was under arrest. They came to terms. You're a policeman, you know what a few hours under arrest does to a man.'

'Harry Woods is as brave as a lion.'

'You don't think Kellerman is crude enough to threaten violence, do you?'

'Then what?'

'You,' said Huth.

'Me?'

'You're a fool, Archer. Don't you realize that Harry Woods looks upon you as the son he never had? Don't you know how proud he is of everything you do? Don't you know that even when Harry has a success, he tells everyone that you were the brains behind it?'

'No, I didn't realize that,' said Douglas softly.

'Kellerman was arranging to have your son sent to a boys' home in Bohemia, a Hitler Youth unit. No need to tell you that Kellerman pretended that it was intended as a wonderful act of generosity, but Harry recognized it for the threat it really was.' Huth sniffed and wiped his nose. 'He knew it was the best way to make you desperately unhappy . . .'

'I'm still not sure that I understand.'

'Harry co-operated with Kellerman so that you and the child would be safe. Come along, Archer, it's a common enough device. Have you never given an informant protection in exchange for a really good tip-off? Well, Harry delivered the goods, and Kellerman kept his word. This morning you and Harry stood trial and were cleared, all inside five minutes. Be grateful.'

'Harry did that for me?'

'He's got little to live for,' said Huth brutally. 'Flea-bitten little house, a shrew of a wife. Perhaps if they'd had kids it would have worked out differently.'

'But Harry loves his wife.'

Huth shook his head. 'That was a long time ago . . . He preferred your secretary, this Sylvia something. The one who got herself killed trying to save him. But that was strictly Resistance business.'

'You know everything.'

'That's why they are executing me,' said Huth evenly. 'I can see into people, Archer. A policeman must be able to see into people.'

'I don't want to be that kind of policeman.'

'You'll have to be any kind of policeman Kellerman needs,' said Huth. 'For the time being anyway.' He sipped some of his brandy. 'What time is it, they took away my watch?'

'Nearly ten o'clock.'

'Not much longer.' He lit a cigarette. 'Does your son want to be a policeman?'

'On a motor-cycle, yes.'

400

Huth smiled. 'You're lucky, Archer. Keep him out of this lousy business.'

Douglas didn't answer. Outside the window he could see Kellerman's gleaming Rolls-Royce. The driver was polishing the windscreen, very very carefully.

'I'm sorry about the woman – the Barga woman. I'm sorry about the way that happened.'

'Yes,' said Douglas. He didn't want to talk about it.

'As soon as Kellerman knew you'd abandoned the ambulance he sent a couple of his Gestapo thugs round there.'

'To Barbara's? I phoned, a man said he was the window cleaner.'

'They're not very bright. You know that.'

'I believed him,' admitted Douglas. 'I phoned again. She was there. She was abrupt, rude almost.'

'Trying to warn you off, eh? Well that was foolhardy. She must have loved you very much. It's probably what made them lose their tempers; her warning you off like that. They hit her harder than they meant to. It wasn't part of any plan. The death of an American reporter will take a lot of explaining.'

'Her voice was faint,' said Douglas. 'She'd been whispering so that she was not overheard.'

'Why do these people love you, Archer? Is it simply because you show little or no response to their affection?' He shook his head and did not pursue the conundrum. 'The Gestapo men didn't hear the phone ring. The woman was upstairs putting her coat on. She must have heard the phone click before it rang.'

'And I thought she didn't want to see me.'

'None of us is very clever with the ones we love,' said Huth. 'Could you take a message to my father?'

'I have leave to come and I'm cleared for travel to Germany,' said Douglas, 'but I thought you hated him?'

'Tell my father about the raid, as far as the censorship will permit. Tell him there was shooting and that I got caught in the cross-fire. Tell him I died bravely. Tell him all that crap that fathers want to hear about their sons, and sons want to hear about their fathers.'

A soft knock came at the door and a young SS officer asked that the Standartenführer should be ready in five minutes. He saluted punctiliously.

'Well, I must polish my shoes,' said Huth, 'and part my hair and get ready to play my star role in this Teutonic opera. The official notice will say that I was a casualty of the fighting.'

'I'll take the message,' said Douglas.

'Caught in the cross-fire,' said Huth. 'That would be a good thing to tell him.' He smiled sardonically.

Douglas picked up Mayhew's duffel coat from where he'd left it on a chair. He put it on and closed the wooden toggles. It would be cold outside, and he'd be grateful for this ill-fitting coat with its curious perfume. He recognized it then; the heavy smell of snuff. It would never be enough, of course. The half-smoked Romeo y Julieta and the spilled snuff from the broken tin in Dr Spode's waistcoat pocket: but he knew without any doubt that Mayhew had taken Spode back to the flat in Shepherd Market and murdered him before spending half the night burning all the mathematical papers. He had to prevent the Americans getting their hands on those vital figures and even more important, prevent them talking with Dr Spode. Mayhew was determined to make the Americans fight.

'Caught in the cross-fire,' said Huth. 'We were all caught in the cross-fire.'

'Good-bye, Standartenführer,' said Douglas buttoning up his collar. Through the window he saw General Kellerman's Rolls driving past on the way to the main gate. The pennants were flying.